To Elliott

Signed at the Alamo,

Dean Kirkpatrick

July 19, 2014

The *OTHER ROSE* of Texas

Historical Fiction

by

Dean Kirkpatrick

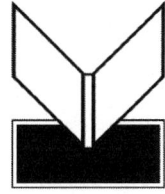

This book is a work of fiction. Names, characters, places and incidents are either imaginary or are used fictitiously. Any resemblance to actual events or locales or persons, living or dead, is purely coincidental.

© Copyright 2013 – 2014 Norval Dean Kirkpatrick
All rights reserved under International and Pan American Copyright Conventions, Published in the United States by K Publications, 15730 Steamboat Lane, Houston, Texas 77079-2575.

www.shop.alamostorytour.com

ISBN: 978-0-578-12924-2
Library of Congress Control Number: 2013915026

Original Cover Art by Wade Dillon
Cover Design by Lyn Belisle

Manufactured in the United States of America
First Edition

Acknowledgements

Stanley Bernstein, Attorney at Law, for Veramendi family research,
Devin Costlow, for Bowie knife research,
Lorin Oberweger, for editing,
My family, for inspiration, and
Jennifer (Jiminy) and John Martin, for reassurance.

Part I - 1812 - 1829

Chapter 1

The heavy White Oak tree limb was normally used for hanging and butchering stock, but, occasionally, it was used for something else.

"Hitch a horse to the flat-bed, James, and pull it up past yonder limb," The Master said, pointing to it.

Located beside a whitewashed horse-barn, the dead tree was topped, and on the trunk above the limb, someone had drawn a scowling face with white paint. Until the limb turned skyward, like a human arm at the elbow, it ran at an almost perfect right angle from the trunk, about fifteen feet above the ground.

"That smart-ass buck ain't gonna make me the fool again," The Master added, rage resurgent in his voice.

The Master, Jim Bowie's father, Rezin, was tall for his time yet thin, and Jim knew from his stories about killing British soldiers during the American revolutionary war, and from the strict discipline he imposed on his slaves and his sons, that his father was a hard man who sometimes seemed to enjoy being cruel.

As Jim aged and became aware, he began to believe that The Master lacked the self-awareness to discern that almost everything he did was motivated by fear, and the only way he knew to manage others was by making them afraid. Though his considerable wealth kept him well fed, Jim joked behind his back that The Master looked malnourished because the devil inside him took his food away.

Now, fearing The Master's retribution, young Jim quickly entered the horse-barn through the only open door. The structure might better be called a mule-barn, since the equine cousins used for plowing out-numbered the horses four to one. Walking inside, Jim breathed the familiar smell, a combination of alfalfa hay and feces, which The Master said was a sign of healthy animals. The early-morning light inside the barn was dim but adequate for the teenager's work.

Minutes later, he walked out of the barn leading a Suffolk mare named Clytemnestra, in harness. Backing her to the front of a nearby wagon, he attached her harness straps through the shaft loops of the wagon singletree, pulled everything tight, and led Clytemnestra to the spot in the bare dirt barnyard.

The simple task completed, exactly as The Master directed, Jim momentarily felt free from pressure. The voice of his father that lived in his mind said, "well done son," words he knew the old man would never speak himself. Then Jim's own voice said, "Ready, Paw!" He had not noticed his father was no longer in the barnyard.

"Paw!"

Concluding that he was alone, he sat on the flat-bed wagon to wait for the others, and gazed out at the barnyard, and the four thousand acres of property used mostly to grow cotton. The Master called his domain a plantation, but it came close to meeting the definition of a farm. Everything it needed to operate was produced on Bowie property, except the fertilizer. The nitrogen, phosphorus, and potassium that cotton required were provided by shrimp shells and seaweed that came up the Mississippi River by barge to Baton Rouge, then overland by wagon. When the breeze blew from the east, the smell from the cotton fields suggested there might still be an ocean nearby.

The smell in the air also signaled when the wind blew in from another direction. From the south, it carried the smell of wood: Cypress for planks, White Oak for posts and rails, or loblolly pine for joists and beams, depending on what the Bowie sawmill cut last.

If the ambient odor was bovine, porcine, and equine manure, a west wind was blowing through the pens, corrals, and other barns adjacent to the horse-barn. If the air was odorless, either there was no breeze, or the season was winter and the wind was from the north, as it was this day.

In a few minutes, Jim saw his father and his brother, John J., walking up the grass-covered hill from the slave shacks to the south with a middle-aged Negro man named Agamemnon, Memnon for short, walking between them. Each Bowie held the loose end of his own thirty-foot rope, tied to iron clevis shackles around Memnon's ankles. When either Bowie pulled his rope, the burrs of the raw metal cut into the black man's flesh.

As he walked, the blood from Memnon's bare feet stained his footprints in the grass. Tears flowed down his face, but he made no sound.

Walking twenty feet behind, Jim saw hundreds more black men, women, and children who comprised the balance of the Bowie plantation slave population. The entire procession reminded him of stories he had read in the bible about the crowds that followed Jesus to Golgotha.

Seeing this, he knew immediately what was about to happen, but he was not prepared for how it would be done. His stomach tightened.

When Memnon had been led to a place under the limb directly behind the wagon, each Bowie threw the unattached end of his rope over the hanging limb and grasped it again. Then The Master yelled in the direction of the slaves. "Four bucks. Come here."

Four older black men scampered from the group of onlookers positioned between the horse-barn and the tree.

"Take these ropes and pull him up."

The black men took the rope ends from their masters, two to a rope, and began pulling. Memnon had the good sense to sit down on the ground, before his feet could be pulled from under him.

The black men, one the slave's own father, and another, his uncle, tried to be as gentle as possible. Soon he hung upside down, his head about three feet from the ground; his face turned away from the Bowies with his shirt-tail hanging down and covering it.

"Higher!"

The men pulled as slowly and gently as they dared, but the rope bumped over the limb, and Jim could tell that Memnon's ascent was painful. However, the negro still made no sound.

"Higher. I want his feet three foot below the limb."

When Memnon hung by his ankles, upside down at the specified height, The Master called to Jim.

"James, back the wagon under him, then come over here."

The Master's tone told Jim he was in what his sons called "command mode" and Jim knew he must move quickly to comply or face his father's wrath.

"John J., go get Rezin P. and Stephen. I want them in on this. Tell your mother and sisters to stay in the house."

After Jim moved the wagon, all four Bowie sons gathered around their father.

"That Memnon used to be my best buck, but he ran. I caught him and whipped him, but he ran again and again. Now he is no count, and I can't turn his head back."

Rezin Bowie looked at each of his sons. Stephen, the youngest at age twelve, was looking at the dangling black-man and laughing.

"Pay attention, boy."

Stephen jerked his eyes back toward his father.

"That buck is worth eight-hundred dollars on the block. Even so, he is not worth a cent if he runs and makes the others think they can too."

Regardless of what his father was saying, Jim knew his motivation in this was not a financial need. In a good year, the plantation produced over one hundred thousand dollars in revenue, and The Master had enjoyed several good years in a row. Fanatical management enabled him to retain almost a quarter of that income in his own New Orleans bank account, despite the extravagant spending of his piously demanding wife, Elve.

As The Master looked each son in the eye again, he continued. "So I'm going to spend that eight-hundred dollars to teach the other ones a lesson, and James is going to help me."

"Yes, Paw?"

"Here's what you are going to do, boy. Listen good."

Jim nodded.

"Climb up on the flat-bed and tear off his shirt. Make sure the darkies all see the welts I put on him with my whip today. Use a double sheet-bend knot to join the two ropes the bucks are holding. Next, tie a rope round his neck, throw it over the limb toward the horse, and thread it through the other two ropes at the joint, take out the slack, and tie it off on the back wagon axle. Then, pull the wagon forward until his head is even with his feet, and do it slow. I want him to stay alive."

Jim tried to visualize how Memnon would look at the end of this process.

"When you finish, he will look like a bird in flight, even when the vultures have picked all the meat off his bones."

Their father's presentation was as nonchalant as a man explaining how to make a rope hackamore and fit it on a horse.

"Now, do you understand?"

Jim dipped his forehead and gritted his teeth, anticipating The Master's next words. "Then tell me."

He had grown to hate the sound of this, his father's way of forcing him to imply approval of an act by articulating it. Yet Jim found it to be an effective technique that he used himself sometimes.

"You want me to tear off his shirt, show his welts, rig a noose over the limb, splice the three ropes, tie them to the axle, and raise him up to look like a bird. Won't that crack his spine, Paw?"

"Probably. May hap the sound when it cracks will help them others remember not to run."

"Can't we just cripple him, so he can't run?"

"Don't sass me, boy. You do what I say, when I say, or I'll use my whip to decorate your own back."

Jim knew he was treading dangerous ground. He had seen others provoke the old man's spiteful temper, and the result was frightening. Nevertheless, he had a personal stake in the welfare of this particular slave, so his mouth gambled with his welfare one more time.

"But he's Sam's paw."

Jim referred to the fifteen-year-old slave boy named Samian that he secretly thought of as his fifth brother. They were both born on April 10, 1796, had both been nursed by Sam's mother, and had never been apart a whole day. They were even similar physically, as each boy had already reached much of the above-average height, he would know as a man, and both were unusually well coordinated. Their only difference seemed to be that black-haired Sam was far more muscular than auburn-haired Jim.

"It don't matter whose paw he is. The other darkies look up to him, and I can't let him challenge me, no more."

With each exchange, Jim felt more helpless. He had lost the hope of sparing Memnon, but thought he still might avoid being the instrument of his torture.

"I can't do it, Paw. Make John J. do it; he's the oldest."

"You'd best mind Paw, James. Don't be such a baby."

With these words, John J. pushed Jim to the ground. The younger brother's temper flared.

"You mean bastards; you just want to kill something because you like doing it."

Jim immediately grasped the impact of his outburst as The Master unhooked a blood-stained whip from his belt. Looking to his closest brother for rescue Jim knew his and Memnon's doom was settled when seventeen-year-old Rezin P. cast his eyes down.

"It's your time, James. You got to learn how to own these darkies," The Master said firmly.

For Jim, the fear was waxing, and the voice of The Master that resided in his head screamed, "You better do it boy, do it now." The old man drew his whip arm back like a coiling snake just as Jim sprang upon the flat bed and began to execute his father's orders. He faced away from his brothers so none would see his tears. That left him facing the crowd of slaves, and his eyes locked upon Sam's eyes, which were filled with hopeless terror.

Telling the slaves to hold their ropes taut to keep Memnon suspended, Jim joined the three ropes in the way his father described. Normally, in that configuration, the noose would have slipped under his jaw bone, and Memnon's suffocation might have taken days. However, Jim made sure the noose rope would snap backward and break the man's neck quickly. At least, he wanted to be able to tell Sam that his paw had not suffered for long. When he finished attaching the rope to the wagon axle, Jim jumped back up on the flat-bed.

Then he heard a noise, a moan that crescendoed to a groan then a scream. Had it come from inside him or someone else? He could not tell, but its effect was transforming. When he glanced up, the figure dangling above him had become The Master, and Jim felt a sudden glee. He quickly grabbed the reins and pulled the wagon forward in a lurch, then stopped it with the hand brake. After that, he bounded to the ground.

Jim did not have to look back after he jumped, to know the state of his victim. The crackling sounds of the breaking bones and the gasps, cries, shrieks, and prayers of the slaves told him enough.

The tears in his eyes blinded him as he ran down the hill, past the slave shacks, and through the woods. Several times he stumbled and fell, cutting his face and arms, but he got up and kept running until he reached the swamp that bordered the plantation on the south.

There he sat, the prayers of the slaves for God's mercy and the sound of Memnon's bones breaking still playing in his head.

Jim knew their hysterical reaction was exactly what The Master sought from his chattel. Now, as he had after every seriously abusive act, The Master would send them candy and treat them lovingly for a few days, while he rationalized his cruelty.

"But will that work again," Jim pondered.

He knew that Memnon was a cherished leader among his people. Would The Master's cruelty toward him arouse enough hatred to overcome their fear of him? Would this be the time they realized that fewer than a dozen whites would be no match for them in their hundreds?

* * *

Hours later, Rezin P. found Jim at the edge of the southern swamp, reclining on a green grass knoll, under a line of huge bald cypress trees that dripped Spanish moss. The thick fern-green grass beneath him was like a carpet, and the trees stood in a line so straight they might have been planted that way.

Matching green Spanish moss hung from the tree's bent branches to the ground, like a woman's long hair, providing an arch-like ceiling over an enclosure open to the water. The incline of the knoll made it perfect for lying back and thinking one's thoughts.

Though easy to find, Jim thought of this as his secret, private refuge, perhaps because he believed that he was the only person living on the plantation that could still appreciate its beauty. Everyone else, he thought, had been hardened beyond human sensitivity by The Master.

"You look awful little brother. You been cryin'?"

"Go to hell Rez."

"Paw says to come on back. He ain't mad at you."

"Him mad at me? I hate that mean old son-of-a-bitch. Why can't he do his own hangin'?"

"He says that someday we will have to run things, and we have to learn how."

Jim thought his brother seemed unconcerned about the human life that had just been taken.

"Do you think it's right, Rez?"

"You mean us needin to learn?"

"No, I mean us ownin' them. What if they owned us? What if they beat us? What if they hung us?"

"I see what you mean. I never thought about it much."

"So think about it now."

"Well, Paw says they have a better life with us than they had in Africa. He says over there they fight and kill each other all the time. He says there is no God in Africa; they worship graven idols, so when they die, their souls always go to hell."

"Do you believe that?"

Though similar in size and two years older, Jim thought Rezin P. behaved like a younger brother. He seemed to lack the strength of personality and conviction most people had and never seemed comfortable expressing his own opinions until he knew theirs. Before answering, he propped himself up on his right elbow and looked into Jim's eyes as if he might find the right words written there. Then he winced.

"What's wrong?"

"Your eyes turned yellow, like a wolf. They're alright now. It scared me for a minute."

"Must have been the sun reflecting."

Rezin P. hung his head. "The other planters say the same thing Paw says. So I guess it's true. They say blacks are like children and not smart enough to take care of themselves."

"But don't you feel sorry for them sometimes?"

"I think they are happy most of the time. Sometimes Paw has to punish them to keep them in line. But he says they are not really human like us, and they don't have feelings like we have."

"I think paw is wrong, Rez. I think Sam, and his maw love me more than The Master does, and I know I love them more, and

Sam has been more of a brother to me than John J. or Stephen ever was."

"I guess you're right, Jim. Sometimes I think The Master would rather see us dead than disobedient. So you gotta learn to hide your feelings from him like the rest of us do, at least until we can get away from here."

"But why did he make me do it, Rez? He's the one who likes killin. Why didn't he kill Sam's paw himself?"

"Maybe it's like Paw said, he thinks you are weak, or maybe he thinks you are too close to Sam. Maybe you better stop letting Sam sit in our classroom and learn like he was one of us. You know he might take it out on Sam next time he feels like killin."

The two brothers lay side by side for a while longer, both staring into space, not saying a word. The wind was calm and the odor of rotting vegetation in the swamp crept in on them. Then Jim sat up, nodded toward home, and they both stood and turned in the direction of the main house.

"I still don't know how I can ever face Sam and his Maw," Jim said.

As they approached the slave-shacks, Jim noticed a crowd gathered outside the shack where Sam, his older sister Baucis, called Bettie, and his mother lived, now without Memnon.

"She be with Memnon and God now," Jim heard a slave woman say, as he joined the group. "Praise him."

"What are you talking about, Aurora?"

"They Maw, Sam and Bettie Maw, she done hang heself."

The news was almost more than Jim could stand. "I have caused two deaths today," he thought.

Jim had barely known Memnon, but he regarded Sam's mother, the woman who had suckled and raised him, almost as his own.

* * *

Inside Sam's shack, his mother was laid out on a cedar plank door supported by two wooden barrels, her considerable body covered by a stained homespun sheet. The stench of black-oil burning in a lamp upon a tree-stump table pervaded the room, and the walls were covered with its soot.

His sister, Bettie, sat upon the floor in a corner, bawling and shaking. Sam sat in another corner exercising his already muscular arms by raising and lowering large stones. When he heard the slaves outside talking to Jim, he stopped exercising and hid the stones behind him.

When Jim entered, Sam buried his face in his hands.

"I'm sorry, Sam; my Paw made me."

Sam did not raise his head out of fear that the look in his eyes would threaten Jim and lead to more violence. Memnon told his son never to let a white man know when he was angry. "If they gets feared of you, they kill you like they was mashing a cockroach."

Accordingly, Sam feared his young master would see the hatred in his heart.

Jim began bawling and pleading.

"I loved your maw. He made me. Sam, tell me you know it wasn't my fault."

Sam could not find it within himself to feel sympathy for Jim. He could only hide his face and think about getting even, and getting free. Without showing his face, he said, "You jus' go on now, master Jim. I gots to bury her. It ain't nothin for to worry on. We gonna be fine. Go on now."

Jim seemed stunned. "Ain't there nothin I can do, Sam?"

"They gone. It ain't nothin. We be fine. You go on now."

Sam just wanted Jim to leave so he could be alone with his grief and hate, and his thoughts of strengthening his body enough to make good the escape to freedom that his father could never manage.

"Alright Sam, but before I go, I have to tell you that Rez and I are afraid The Master thinks that you are becoming a threat to him, and that might make things dangerous for you."

Sam did not move or respond.

"We think it would be better if you stay out of the classroom from now on, and I can't give you anymore quills and parchment either. We can't let The Master think you might get sassy like your paw."

Still pleading, Bowie added, "Do you hear me, Sam? Do you understand?"

Again, Sam did not move or respond.

As if he lacked the maturity and experience to assign any deeper meaning to Sam's words and behavior, Jim seemed to interpret it literally, as he departed saying out loud, "Maybe Rez was right. Maybe they don't have feelings like us."

Sam heard Bowie's parting words and clenched his fists so hard that his fingernails dug into his palms. When he was certain that he and Bettie were alone again, he raised his head.

"Stop your bawlin, sister. Get the needle and twine. I'm gonna go get Daddy down."

Her crying stopped immediately, and the scowl on Bettie's face was replaced by wide-eyed open-mouthed incredulity. "You gonna what?"

"I'm cuttin Daddy down. Our mamma and daddy need to be buried together."

"Are you tryin to get yourself dead too, brother?"

"The master is gone so you can stop the pic-speak."

While growing up in the same shack, as Sam began to learn, he taught Bettie. Both learned to speak the English language correctly, but they were careful not to let others know.

Concealing that truth had turned into a kind of game they played when they were not alone. When others were around, be they white or black, sometimes she and Sam competed to see who could sound most ignorant. They called their game pic-speak, which was short for pickaninny-speak.

"Besides, it is dark outside and nobody will see me. The Master won't ever know who did it."

"He may not know it was you, but he will know it was one of us, and there is likely to be another hanging. Don't do it, Sam. I can't stand anymore dying right now."

"We can run away afterward. I know Daddy's route north up the big river to Canada."

"Daddy tried that three times and he was caught three times. I never did figure out why he kept trying. Our lives here aren't that bad . . . mostly."

"Wake up, sister. Can't you see that the good times are over?"

Sam looked at Bettie and snarled, but he felt protective of her, and allowed her to stare him down and continue. "We have it better than most. I hear stories. I'm not willing to go with you into the wilderness, and Mamma and Daddy wouldn't want you to leave me here by myself."

Sam shrugged stoically and together they sewed the cloth closed around their mother so no dirt would touch her skin. Then Sam carried her gently to the slave cemetery where he laid her by as he dug a deep grave and made a dirt mound beside it.

While he dug, the other slaves arrived in twos and threes. All were assembled when Sam handed the shovel up and climbed out, and their spiritual leader took charge.

"Lord God, today you brung our brother Agamemnon and our sister Cassandra to they new life with you in heaven, and even if they bodies ain't in this grave here together, we know that they souls is up there together with you. We hopes that our mother Mary and her son Jesus will help bring peace to they chillin Baucis and Samian hearts cause they know you has taken they maw and paw to they rewards, like you will do for them and us some day too. We pray that you will show your light into The Master's heart too and forgive what he done to he own son James today too."

As they departed, each man, woman, and child scooped dirt from the mound with both hands and cast it into the grave. Then Sam shoveled in what remained and patted it down

Walking back to his shack alone, Sam finally succumbed to the weight of the day's horrible developments. Tears ran down his cheeks as he was overcome by self-pity.

In a single-day, everything that supported his feeling of well-being had been destroyed. His parents were dead; his best friend had forsaken him; his sister made it clear that she was depending on him to remain a slave and take care of her. It was almost more than his fifteen years of being alive could assimilate.

He could not go on. He stopped walking, sat beside and leaned against his tree-safe, to be alone and think. Gradually, he realized that he was feeling fear. Then he remembered something his father had said.

"You have to make you head and you body strong so you is ready for anything, and when some bad thing come you has to practice beating it in you head, even if you can't never beat it for actual. When you believe in you head that you can beat it, you won't be feared of it no more."

Then he stood and reached into the hollow tree trunk to retrieve a copy of "The Odyssey" that he had sneaked out from the Bowie library and hidden there.

At home he spent the remaining hours of this terrible day reading while he exercised, holding the book in one hand, and one of his stones in the other while he raised and lowered it.

But he kept losing his concentration because his mind wanted him to think about ways he could prepare himself to avoid having another day like the one just ending.

Chapter 2

"Sam has gotten so big even the white-men are afraid of him. He's alive today because I've been here to protect him, and if I leave him, The Master will kill him or the slave hunters will do it when he runs. The Master looks at Sam and sees Memnon."

"I have to admit that I'm a little afraid of him too, Jim, but if we take him with us to New Orleans, I'm not sure we can afford to feed him. Bettie says he eats two chickens and a couple of catfish a day and drinks half-a-gallon of milk at each meal."

It was January, 1815, and eighteen-year-old Jim Bowie and his older brother Rezin P., were leaving their home to go south, ostensibly to help General Andrew Jackson fight the British. Truthfully, Jim just wanted to move beyond the day-to-day control of his tyrannical father, so he played to The Master's ego and convinced him that he wanted to follow in his father's footsteps by becoming a soldier.

When the brothers arrived in New Orleans and discovered that the fighting was all but over, they decided to stay anyhow and seek their fortunes. Being the sons of the owner of the largest plantation and the most slaves in Saint Landry Parish opened doors for them, to the inside of New Orleans elite financial and social circles, and their manners, classical education, and good looks enabled them to exploit the opportunities they found.

Foremost among these was a coincidental introduction at a casino that led to a business offer from larger than life pirate brothers, Pierre and Jean Lafitte.

Subsequently, at a sidewalk café on North Galvez Street, mid-morning coffee and beignets on the table before them, the awestruck Bowie boys listened intently as Jean outlined the proposed arrangement.

"You would be our brokers for the slaves from the ships we capture in the Caribbean Sea and the Gulf of Mexico, and bring to Snake Island."

"That's a Spanish island isn't it. Don't they call it Galveston?" Jim asked trying to sound intelligent.

Lafitte took a bite, then wiped the powdered sugar from his mustache before answering.

"Yes. Galveston. We have the blessing of Don Luis Aury, the military governor, to operate there and you will have first choice from every shipload at the rate of one dollar per pound."

Jim motioned for the waiter to freshen his coffee. Then he looked at Rezin P., trying to assess his reaction to what they were being told.

"You can bring them into the United States through Bayou La Fourche, Bayou Boeuf, or we will deliver at the mouth of the Mississippi River."

Rezin P. was nodding at every sentence.

"You can sell them through your connections in New Orleans and your father's connections further north."

Jim felt like the victim of a conspiracy. Ever since he killed Sam's father his focus had been on getting away from the plantation and the life that constantly reminded him of it. Now he felt himself being dragged back into that very life.

At their hotel Jim tried to convince Rezin P. that they did not need to be involved in the slave trade and could do just as well trading cotton, cane, and other commodities.

"Rez, I don't want any more to do with slavery or slaves. Paw wanted to put me in charge of all our slaves and I came down here to get away from that. If we do this deal with Lafitte, we will have to go to The Master for the money. We'll be right back under his thumb."

"So what are we going to do? Our money won't last more than another six months. Besides, you will never be free of slavery as long as you have Sam. You know you can't sell him, and you can't send him back home."

"I know, I know. But maybe someday I can set him free."

"You don't hold title to him, Jim; The Master owns him. The only way you could free him would be to take him north to Canada yourself and turn him loose. Where you gonna get the money for that?"

Jim began pacing while he talked.

"The Master's cotton agents have offered me a job, and they said they will pay me to use Sam on the docks. I figure in a few years I can make enough to . . ."

Rezin P. did not let his brother continue. "It will take you a lifetime of commissions selling cotton to make what we can make with Lafitte's deal right now. We can quadruple our money every ninety days. Then we can pay The Master back and be shed of him once and for all."

"You know that old bastard is not going to give us a damn thing. If we get money out of him, we can be sure there will be strings attached," Jim countered.

The brothers stared at each other for what seemed like an eternity to Jim, who finally relented. "Alright, Rez. You win this one. I'll go along for a while. But you have to deal with The Master and I don't think he will part with one damn dollar."

* * *

First, they asked their father for a loan of twenty thousand dollars for what they described as a business opportunity. As expected he said no immediately.

Jim had watched his father negotiate deals time after time and he knew The Master always began by maneuvering to strengthen his bargaining position.

"What kind of opportunity?" he asked them.

After they outlined Lafitte's proposal he said, "Sounds risky to me. You know bringing in new slaves is illegal now."

"More manipulation," Jim thought.

"Lafitte has it all worked out," Rezin P. said.

"I don't know Lafitte, but what I hear of him is all bad," The Master said.

"So, are you in or out?" Jim asked.

"Keep your place boy, I'm still thinking."

The Master leaned back in his chair. In a few minutes, he leaned forward.

"I'm willing to back you with the understanding that I run things. You boys are too young to be trusted with that much money on your own."

Jim looked at Rezin P. and both nodded. "Alright, what are your terms?" Jim asked.

"Get Stephen in here. He can write up our contract as I dictate. Fetch John J. too."

When the other brothers arrived, The Master began. "In consideration of the sum of twenty thousand dollars . . ."

Stephen's eyes were wide as he began to write.

The contract stipulated that each lot of slaves would be brought to the plantation in barges and wagons provided by The Master, and he would select the slaves he wanted to keep. The others would be transported on north and sold on the block in Alexandria.

After signing, Jim, Sam, and Rezin departed for New Orleans with a letter of credit on The Master's bank. Compensation for the two brothers had not been mentioned so Jim was already thinking about ways to put some of The Master's money in his own pocket.

* * *

Soon the brothers traveled to Galveston where they reached an agreement with the Lafittes to purchase thirty-five males, sixty-five females, and two male children, to be delivered by ship to the mouth of the Mississippi River. Then they sailed back to Plaquemines Parish to await the slave ship.

A captured Spanish barque that Lafitte had renamed Grande Terre, sailing under the flag of Cartagena, delivered this first lot of Bowie slaves on Jim's (and Sam's) twentieth birthday. The ship carried over four hundred black bodies, and several barges besides those owned by The Master sat in the river awaiting her arrival.

The Bowies brought Sam along as evidence for the new slaves that they would be well-fed and well treated. All three men rowed out and climbed aboard the Grande Terre to arrange with the captain for disembarkation of their part of his cargo. When Jim met the captain and beheld the crew, he wished he had come armed.

Every crewman had a knife or cutlass and a flintlock pistol stuck under his belt. Some had all three, and the captain had two of each in leather holsters, as well as scabbards on his belt and a beautiful silver and gold sabre, unsheathed and stuck in a sash around his waist.

"Our name is Bowie, captain. Here is our bill of sale for a hundred and two head," Rezin P. said.

"Yours'll be the last out, Bowie. We unload from the aft hatch, and yours is up in the focsle. I'll let you know when to bring your barges alongside. Now, move forward and stay the hell out of the way."

Just then the aft hatch door was swung open, and a well-armed crewman descended to the hold, a key in his hand, to unchain the people below. That done, two crewmen leaned down and yelled, "Out, out."

Soon the head of a black man emerged from the hatch. The head turned; the eyes looked all around and came to rest on Jim Bowie's.

His first thought was that he had never seen such a look of fear. All of the slaves on The Master's plantation were born in the United States, and Jim could not recall seeing such an expression of terror on any face, even when The Master was at his worst.

He thought he must be seeing the amalgamation of the man's anguish at being stolen from his family, the horror of his months at sea, and his longing for loved ones and things familiar. Jim swallowed and looked away.

The Grande Terre crewmen stood on either side of a path from the hatch to the rail. Weapons drawn, they yelled and motioned to the head to step on to the deck and run their gauntlet. When that slave did so, others followed, each behind the previous, still wearing a clevis shackle; right ankle, left, and right again.

The crewmen struck some of the slaves as they passed. "Probably troublemakers," Jim thought.

When a slave reached the rail, he jumped onto it, swiveled on his buttocks, and climbed down a cargo net backward. It appeared to Jim that they had done this before.

When one of them did not move fast enough to suit a crewman, he would be picked up and thrown into the waiting barge, thirty feet below. The first time Sam witnessed this, Jim saw his eyes grow larger, his nostrils flare, and his fists clench.

The Other Rose of Texas

In the barge, two armed men, each holding a cat-of-nine-tails, herded the slaves to the front, packing them in tightly. If a slave sat or fell down, he was beaten with a cat until he stood.

Then the women and children came up, following in their turn. The only time the line halted was to bring up the next barge.

It took two and three-quarter hours to load three hundred slaves into three barges. Then the crewman in the hold threw the ends of three ropes up through the hatch. With two crewmen to a rope, Sam, Jim, and Rezin P. watched as they pulled up the dead bodies of a man, a woman, and a child and threw them into the river on the side of the vessel opposite the barges.

"I'm sure they had more dead than that from the crossing. These must be since Galveston," Rezin P. observed. "I wonder if any of ours perished."

When their focus returned to the ship rail on the barge side, the captain approached them. In the distance, they saw the three loaded barges being pushed north by a stern-wheeled steam tugboat.

"Alright, Bowie, bring your barges up."

Rezin P. walked to the rail and motioned to his tug boat captain to push their barges up for loading. The Bowies had brought three barges for one hundred slaves, and Jim saw the Grande Terre captain laugh and point at the soft hay piled high in each one.

"Sam, go down and hand out the food and clothes," Jim instructed.

"When The Master finds out we spent his money to put new clothes on their backs, he'll bull whip us both," Rezin P. reminded Jim for the third time.

"Just make sure they are all here, big brother. I'll handle The Master."

Sam and an armed guard were in position below in the barge when the first Bowie slave stuck his head through the hatch. The crew gauntlet was still in place as Rezin P. stood by the rail to count heads.

"Hold it," Jim shouted, then turned toward the rail and shouted again. "Captain, tell your crew not to touch any of my slaves." Jim looked at him hard. "Alright, bring em on."

The captain just sneered.

When the slaves arrived in the barge waiting below, Sam handed each person a foot square cotton cloth, four corners tied together, containing fried chicken, fresh carrots, and bananas. The guard handed out the clothing, a homespun shirt and pants to each man and child, and a dress to each woman. In the bow of each barge, an open barrel of water and a gourd dipper had been placed.

Bowie's barge passengers were allowed to stand, sit, or lie down, as they wished. Most took water first, then ate the food as they sat in the hay.

Loading was nearly complete when an especially lovely young woman stepped onto the deck. She was of regal height, thin and shapely. Jim remembered her from Galveston and followed her with his eyes as she walked unhurried toward the rail.

Suddenly, a crewman jumped out of line, picked her up and threw her over the rail. Jim ran to the rail and looked down.

Fortunately, Sam had been looking up when she came sailing down, and had caught her in his arms. Her momentum forced him backward into the hay, where her curvy body landed full length on top of him. When they got to their feet, she smiled at Sam as he handed over her food and again as the guard presented her dress. Her teeth looked perfect.

On deck, Jim was livid. He grabbed the offending crewman by the shirt-front, pulled a knife from the man's belt, and held it to his throat. The captain rushed forward.

"Hold on. Hold on. He just lost his head. She been keepin her legs closed to him since we left the Ivory Coast. You're a man, Bowie; you understand."

Bowie shrugged, pushed the man down to the deck, then stuck the knife deep in the rail and broke it off at the tip.

Loading was completed with no further interruptions. As the barges started up the river, some of the slaves put on their new brightly-colored clothes and, from a distance, their flotilla resembled a Sunday picnic outing.

* * *

The Bowies were aboard the tug and Sam had taken a position in the middle barge of the three that were lashed together, so he could move from one to another. Glancing around, he could see that the slaves were fascinated by him. Especially the women, who looked at him and into his eyes often, as if they were seeking clues to reveal whether he was a slave, like themselves, or some kind of black master.

The barges pulled away from the Grande Terre at three-twenty in the afternoon for the ninety-two mile voyage up the river to New Orleans. The sky was bright blue and full of cumulus clouds, but none threatened rain. As the sun dropped lower, the air cooled, and Sam noticed the slaves huddled together for warmth. Seeing this, he picked up a hand full of straw and climbed upon the abutted barge gunnels.

He stood where he could be seen by everyone in all three barges and began to hold himself and shiver, trying to communicate that he was cold. Then he held the straw against his chest and stopped his motion, hoping to communicate that the straw had warmed him. But it didn't seem to be working.

Then the girl he had caught, now seated in the straw below him said, "Moto visha," and held a hand full of straw high. The people around her began to burrow under the straw. Then Sam turned and shouted the same two words in every direction, holding up the straw, and the people took up the chant as they covered themselves with blankets of it.

A smooth river, the warmth, the dark sky, and the steady chugging sound of the tug's steam engine combined to bring sleep to the slaves, but not to Sam. He was lost in thought.

The day had brought his first exposure to the cruelty of the slave trade, and the realization of how much his ancestors must have suffered. He thought of the contrast between his relatively comfortable existence and what he had seen these people endure.

Both he and they were called slaves, but no other label he could recall had practical definitions so opposite. He thought of his life in New Orleans, how different it was from the plantation, then thoughts of being aroused by the slave girl prompted memories of the woman who waited for him now, just up river.

"Portia."

Saying her name stirred deep feelings in Sam. Portia was the black maid of Miss Cleopatra, the mulatto accident of an indiscreet sampling of his own merchandise by a creole slave trader who used Cleo to pay a debt he owed Jean Lafitte.

When Lafitte was tired of Cleo, rather than waste her beauty by sending her to the block, he had her schooled in the skills of a courtesan, including reading and writing, then he put her in a house on Rue de Chenevert that he won in a Chemin de Fer game and passed the key around to his associates as a business incentive.

Part of Jim Bowie's arrangement with Lafitte was that he could occupy the house, including Cleo, rent free. As a bonus, Portia liked Sam and he liked her. Sam had experimented romantically, with the slave girls on the plantation, but twenty-two year-old Portia gave him his first experience with a mature and knowledgeable woman. She soon became the only living person, besides his sister, to whom Sam revealed himself.

"I am as well educated as those white men, and a great deal smarter than most of them," he remembered saying.

Almost nobody knew it, but being with Jim Bowie every day since birth had given Sam practically the same level of education as his master. Jim's mother, The Mistress Bowie, a classically educated Georgia belle from Savannah, made her husband import the finest of teachers and tutors from the east for Jim and his brothers. Their father indulged his wife in this way, also allowing her to give Greek names to the slaves and livestock born on their plantations, and by paying for a fine collection of books.

"For years I sat on the floor in the corner of their classroom, and nobody paid any attention to me," Sam had told Portia. "Then Bowie stopped helping me, and I had to eavesdrop from the hallway and memorize what the Bowie brothers could write down because they had parchment, quill, and ink, and I did not. The Bowies thought my education stopped there, but I started taking their discards from the trash and stole an inkwell and ink. I wrote everything down at night, wrapped my materials in oilcloth, and hid them in a hollow tree trunk."

Portia's eyes grew wider as Sam spoke. Then he began to brag.

"Thanks to Mistress Elve Ap-Catesby Jones Bowie, Jim's mother, I can read, write, and speak the same three languages as her sons. I am better at mathematics than Jim, and I have read every book in the Bowie plantation library that I could sneak out."

As a token of her affection, Portia gave Sam a pig-skin pouch that contained a Loa Shango amulet, and a small doll made of straw. A strong believer in voodoo, Portia claimed that these talismans would protect Sam and always bring him back to her.

The pouch now hung from a leather strand around his neck. The rawhide strand was long enough for Sam to open the pouch without removing it from his neck, and he used the pouch to store his money and other valuables. As he clutched it now, he felt a throbbing in his genitals. Visualizing Portia in his muscular arms and kissing her, he remembered his mood had turned dark when he thought of not having her.

"Someday, I will take us to freedom. I will kill as many whites as I have to, just as they killed my father and mother."

The bad moment had passed and he added, "But for now, I am trusting you to keep my secret. If they find out what I know, it could get me killed."

Then with a great feeling of self-satisfaction the memories brought him, Sam put them aside and let fatigue claim him. Leaning his head back against the barge gunnel, he began to doze. He was almost asleep when he felt pressure on his right inner thigh.

He lurched awake and saw that it was the slave girl touching him. She smiled and moved closer.

Sam could not recall ever mustering as much will power as it took for him to wag his right index finger in her face and say "No. No."

Her ample lower lip curled down as she pulled away and burrowed under the hay. Again Sam had to take hold of himself to keep from going after her.

* * *

By nine the next morning, the barges were tied up in a line at the wharf near Pauline Street in New Orleans. The sun was high and the air warm. Sam handed out food while Rezin P. told Jim about the elaborate scheme they would use to circumvent the law against bringing new slaves into the United States.

"Here's how it works. We walk into the customs-house and tell the officer in charge that we found some barges full of Africans that somebody abandoned on the river. He will immediately confiscate them for the government. Then we will buy them from the government. Then the government will pay us half the purchase price we pay as a reward for turning them in, in the first place. This will all take about fifteen minutes, and we won't even have to unload them from the barges."

Soon the slaves were documented, legal, and on the river again following the same route to Baton Rouge as the sea-born fertilizer the barges normally carried. As the crow flies, their destination was eighty-two miles away, but as the Mississippi meanders, almost twice that.

"I have scheduled stops for food in Convent and White Castle," Rezin P. announced to Jim, continuing to demonstrate his organizational skills, "and at Baton Rouge, we will feed again and transfer them to the cotton wagons."

* * *

It all sounded easy to Jim and it was until they reached the docks in Baton Rouge. After the slaves were fed and more than half of them had moved to the wagons, Jim suddenly found the barges surrounded by four men with rifles.

"Don't you know you can't bring in Africans no more? I'm a federal Marshall and these are my deputies. We're confiscating these Africans in the name of the government."

"Just a minute Marshall. I have papers that prove these slaves are legal," Jim said.

"Papers can be forged. Now you load em back on the barges and be on your way. We'll take em back to N'Orleans."

There was something about this man that struck Jim as odd. He was shabbily dressed and sounded illiterate, and none of his men wore a badge. Jim looked at Rezin P. and blinked three times. Then he looked at Sam and did the same.

"Alright, you caught us Marshall. We're smugglers and we got this lot sold to a planter over by Opelousas."

The man's eyes brightened.

"If you let us make delivery and collect our money, I can make it worth your while. We're getting top dollar and it would be easier for you than takin' em all the way back to N'Orleans."

"How much money are we talkin' about mister?" the man asked.

"I don't know. Let me sum it," Jim said as he pulled pencil and paper from his shirt pocket.

The man lowered his rifle and stepped in, looking at the paper as Jim began to write. All of a sudden Jim grabbed the man's rifle and hit him under the chin with the butt. Then he whirled and fired at the closest of the other men, hitting him in the chest.

At the same moment Rezin P. and Sam lunged for the other two men. One of the men was able to pull his trigger before he was hit, but the shot went wild.

All of the riflemen were on their backs on the ground when another man arrived on horseback.

"I heard the gunfire Jim, what's going on?"

"Glad to see you sheriff. These men claimed to be Marshalls and tried to take my slaves."

The sheriff looked down at the men on the ground.

"These men are slave hunters. They must have thought they had found an easy mark. This one's dead. Do you want me to lock up the others?"

Jim looked at Rezin P.

"Yes, we do."

* * *

After departing Baton Rouge Jim said, "We haven't used that three blink trick since we were kids. I'm glad you and Sam caught on."

For the remainder of the journey he enjoyed remembering his boyhood, when on these same wagons he traveled between the same two points, delivering fertilizer and supplies one way and cotton the other.

But then, roughly four days after leaving the mouth of the Mississippi River, his nostalgia gave way to angst as he came face to face with The Master who stood in the barnyard when he, Rezin P., and Sam rode in on horseback at the head of the wagon procession.

"Here they are, Paw, just like we promised; one hundred and two head." Rezin P. said.

"Line em up so's I can count em. Give Stephen your expense sums."

When assembled as directed, the line of slaves stretched from the horse barn, under the hanging tree, for three hundred feet down the road toward the cotton fields.

"Couldn't you get more bucks? Where did they get them clothes?"

"They were wearing rags when we got them, Paw. We covered them, so they wouldn't catch cold and get sick."

"Tell em to strip. I want to see what you got for my money."

"Sam is the only one who can talk to them."

"Then tell Sam to tell them to take off their clothes, damn it."

Sam was standing behind a cotton wagon, more or less hiding from The Master. When he heard the instruction, he stepped out and shouted, "Kivazi katika."

Standing near Jim, Stephen asked, "How do you suppose Sam knew how to talk their talk?"

"It must just be in their blood. Lord knows they're not capable of learning it," John J. replied.

The slave men were quick to obey Sam's instruction, but the women just frowned.

"Wanawake kivazi katika," Sam bellowed.

Hearing Sam give this last directive, The Master cracked his whip. The women slid their sleeves off their shoulders and let their dresses drop to the ground.

"Sam, come here."

Obeying promptly, Sam followed The Master to the left end of the line.

"When I tap one, tell him to step forward."

"Yes sir, master Bowie."

The Other Rose of Texas

The Master walked from slave to slave like a military officer reviewing his troops, sometimes tapping immediately, sometimes looking at teeth or feeling muscle, sometimes just walking on by. Reaching the end of the line, he had selected five men and one woman, the shapely girl.

"Feed em all, Sam, then put the six in empty beds and the others in tents until the auction. James, you boys join me in my study."

"Fuatana mimi," Sam said, and the new slaves followed him down the hill toward the slave quarters.

The brothers followed their father to the main house.

"When are we leaving for Alexandria, Paw?" Rezin P. asked.

The Bowie sons were seated in brown leather chairs opposite The Master, who sat behind the enormous beech wood desk that he had imported from the Black Forest region of Germany. The Master had also planted beech tree saplings that came with the desk, along the carriage path from the main road to his front road, but the high Louisiana humidity soon killed them all.

"You're not. We're holding the auction right here, and you two are going right back to New Orleans to bring up another lot. Now, what's this I hear from Stephen about all this money you spent on food and clothes, and what did you do with all that hay, did they eat that too?"

"We put the straw in the barges for them to lie on and cover with. We made sure they did not soil it, and we can re-use it. We had the clothes ready for them because they were all in rags and almost naked when we selected them in Galveston. We fed em well because that is what you taught us to do, and because we did all that, none of them got sick and we didn't have a bit of trouble with any of them coming up here," Jim replied.

"Alright, but see if you can find some used clothes for em from now on. Now, let's have some dinner. I want you on the road back down there in the morning. I'm keeping Sam here to tend the new bunch, since he's the only one that can talk to em."

Suddenly Jim rose from his chair, put his hands on the desk, and leaned forward as far as he could into The Master's face.

"I don't mind that you have taken over a business that Rez, and I started. I don't mind that we have not seen a penny of pay for our work."

The Master stood now too, but his other sons remained seated with their mouths wide open.

"Sam stays with me," Jim said. "I need him to help with the next lot, and I know what you will do to him, if I leave him here."

Then Jim stepped back, as surprised as anyone at his own behavior. As far as he knew, only once before had any of The Master's children ever tried to defy him, and that was Jim, himself, on the day he hung Sam's father. Now he was defying the old man again, for the same reason as before, trying to protect a slave.

He felt confused, but before he could ponder further, The Master exploded into his face.

"You're soft, James. I'm ashamed to say that I have not been able to make you understand that they are just livestock and no different from the mules, the goats, and all the other animals I own."

John J. and Stephen smiled as The Master's words pushed Jim back in his chair.

Then in a louder voice, he added, "That buck is just another head of stock that belongs to me, and I will do with him as I please."

Lowering his eyes, Jim did not respond.

"That's better. Now, The Mistress had a special dinner made up for her two wandering boys."

The Master stood and led the four Bowie brothers to the dining room where they were joined by their sisters Sara, Merry, and Martha, and The Mistress.

As usual, the master dominated the dinner conversation. "When you get back to New Orleans, draw what cash you need and get busy with the next lot. I will deposit the money from the slave sale to the trading account."

"When should I have the barges ready for the next bunch?" Stephen asked, directing everyone's attention to the new responsibility The Master had given him.

Rezin P. responded.

"Say a week to get back to New Orleans, two weeks to make arrangements with Lafitte, a month to get to Galveston and buy the slaves, and another month to get delivery, and a couple of weeks for contingencies, you should have the barges and tug waiting at the same place three months from tomorrow."

The Master resumed control. "That means we can only turn four lots a year. Why can't Lafitte at least deliver to the wharf in New Orleans?"

"Jim and I already asked him that. He says his ships can't maneuver in the river, if they are attacked."

"Well, we better bring up more head per trip then. I want to be operating at two thousand head a year within twelve months, so start buying every one that looks fit. We can polish em here."

"How long are you gonna keep Sam, Paw?" Jim asked.

"As long as I please, by God."

The Mistress had not participated in the discussion to this point, but now she raised her eyes to meet her husband's. "Do not blaspheme at my table, Master Bowie."

"You can have him back as soon as he teaches some of the others to talk that talk that the new ones seem to understand," The Master said,

Stephen added, "I'm not sure they can learn it, Paw; we may just have to keep Sam here permanently."

Satisfied that further interaction with The Master would produce no gain, Jim excused himself. Kissing all the women on the cheek, he retired into his room.

***

The next morning, Jim walked to the slave quarters and told Sam that it would be at least ninety days before they would be together again and that Sam should avoid contact with The Master. Then Jim and Rezin P. departed due east on horseback, for their two hundred-mile ride back to New Orleans.

They followed almost the same route down that they used coming up, along the east-side river road south from Baton Rouge. Their pack mule carried a good supply of The Master's best Kentucky bourbon that Jim appropriated, and he stayed drunk as long as it lasted.

Their trip took three days longer than usual because Jim drank until early morning, and Rezin P. was not able to get him moving before noon each day.

On the ninth day, they camped outside Convent. All the liquor was gone so Jim rode into town to buy more. When he returned his usually gray eyes were ablaze.

"WHAT DID YOU DO WITH MY DAMN MONEY, BROTHER?"

Rezin P. looked at him but did not respond.

"I HAD TWO HUNDRED DOLLARS IN GOLD IN MY SADDLEBAG, NOW IT'S GONE."

"When you stop yelling, I'll tell you where your money is. Otherwise, you can go to hell."

Amazed by his brother's rare defiant statement, Jim gasped between parted lips.

"Alright, but it was damned embarrassing when I bought that whiskey and couldn't pay for it. So where is my money? The man said he would hold the jugs for me til I brought it in."

"It's gone. Your money went south," Rezin P. said and grinned.

"What the hell do you mean?"

"I mean when you passed out last night, I gathered all the money from your pockets and your saddlebags and took it into town."

"Well you must have had yourself a fine time on that much money. I hope you plan to pay me back."

"I wrapped it up and gave it to a riverboat captain I know. You can pick it up in New Orleans."

"Why did you do a fool thing like that?"

"Because you've had enough whiskey. You never drank like this before."

"I never had the worries I've got, before. We're back working for Paw, and now he's got Sam too, like a hostage, against me."

After that day, they made earlier starts and more miles per day, but Jim was sick, trying to sleep as he rocked in the saddle.

Chapter 3

Early, on the morning of the thirtieth day after the initial lot of new slaves arrived at the plantation, when most of the resident slaves and the mules had departed for the cotton fields, Sam overheard John J. complimenting Stephen.

"I think we will see a good turnout for the auction today. Your idea to send out those hand bills saying that consigned slaves would be welcomed, should bring in planters from all over."

Stephen nodded and smiled, "We'll be closer than New Orleans for a lot of them." Then he turned to Sam.

"It's time Sam. Go down and feed them, give them privy time, then march them into the horse barn." Two hours later, Sam was watching Stephen place three to five souls in numbered stalls there.

"During the auction, I will give you a number and you will bring me the darkies from that stall."

"Yes sir, master Stephen."

As the prospective buyers arrived, they entered the horse barn to inspect the slaves. By eleven o'clock, Sam had mentally counted thirty planters when The Master sent him to tell the house slaves to begin serving drinks in the large auction tent where other Bowie slaves fanned the guests with huge palm leaves.

Behind the main house, under Sam's supervision, slaves had turned a three hundred-pound side of beef on a spit over a fire pit for two days. After confirming that the meat was fully cooked, Sam reported back to Stephen in the horse barn.

Looking at the slaves huddled together in the stalls, Sam thought that some looked confused but most seemed to sense what was happening. With him in charge of them during the past six weeks, their lives had been comparatively ideal. Most had received training in the cotton fields or the saw mill, and all had gained weight from the three good meals a day they received.

Sam was standing behind Stephen, awaiting orders when a planter approached them.

"Monsieur Perret-Gente, how are things in New Iberia?" Stephen asked him.

"Stephen, go get your paw. I want to make him an offer."

Thinking that Perret-Gente wanted to reserve a particular group of slaves, Stephen left and soon returned with The Master.

"I'm sorry, Henri; I cannot make any sales before the auction. It would not be fair to the others who might want the same group," The Master said.

"You misunderstand, Rezin; it is not any of these I want," Perret-Gente replied, making a sweeping motion with his right arm. "It is this one," he continued, pointing to Sam. "I want him for breeding, and I will pay any reasonable price you ask."

"Come here, Sam."

Sam stiffened and stepped forward.

"Stephen, what is Sam's value on the books?"

"I'd have to look, Paw," Stephen replied, narrow-eyed.

Sam listened closely, hands behind his back making angry fists, his face passive, revealing nothing.

"Do that, Stephen. Monsieur, I will give you the price in a few minutes, but I must tell you that I cannot deliver him to you for at least two months. He is teaching a new language to some of my other slaves."

"That will be alright; I can wait."

Lunch was served at noon, the auction began at one, and, by three in the afternoon, every slave in the Bowie horse barn, and a few that were brought by other planters, were sold and paid for, and every sold body but Sam's was en route to a new domicile.

The Bowie men sat around a table under the tent, with Sam standing close by.

"Give us the sums, Stephen," The Master ordered.

Grasping a stack of bank notes and promissory notes in his right hand and holding it high, Stephen reported, "From the sale of our slaves, our commissions on the other slaves, and the four thousand we got for Sam, I hold in my hand ninety-two thousand, four hundred and three dollars. That represents a net profit of four hundred and eighteen percent from our first auction."

None of the men looked at Sam as The Master said in a loud voice, "Sam, leave the tent and tables up til tomorrow. I think I'll have dinner out here tonight."

Sam nodded. "Yes, sir, master."

"You'd better get busy teaching that new talk; you only have sixty days til your new master comes for you."

"Yes, sir, Master Bowie. I go start right now, sir."

"That's only eight Sundays from now, Sam," The Master added, "just one hand and three fingers."

As he walked down the hill, Sam recalled that The Master believed his slaves had difficulty dealing with any number greater than the count of their fingers and toes. With little else to be grateful for this day, he was pleased to still be thought of as one of the ignorant mass.

He had already started teaching English to the new slaves, deciding that would be easier than trying to teach Swahili to any of the others. Among those he chose to teach was the shapely girl. Her name turned out to be Mamunch Ua which meant kiss flower or kiss petal.

She made it clear many times that she was available to Sam, but he resisted. Faced now with an unknown future, he decided to concentrate on his escape and avoid an entanglement that might make him want to stay. Then there was Portia.

"I use Daddy's map," he told his grandmother, aunt, and sister that evening, as they ate at a table apart from earshot of any other slaves.

Sam's father, Memnon, had acquired a crude map from a Mississippi barge slave. It was drawn with charcoal on a piece of white cloth. The map showed one solid line that symbolized the Mississippi River and one broken line marking a trail from its headwaters into Canada. Crosses indicated towns along the way.

His father made Sam copy the map onto a piece of parchment and write in the names of the towns that Memnon had memorized but could not write himself, including New Orleans, Baton Rouge, Memphis, St. Louis, Dubuque, and Fort Gibraltar. Using his familiarity with the distance between the first two towns, Sam judged the distance between the other towns to be great.

All three of his father's attempts to escape had ended in Memphis, and Sam intended to avoid that town, even if it meant going hungry.

"But I's wait for master Jim to be home. Mayhap he buy me back."

When Sam said these words, the women began to cry. He knew they were fearing that he would meet Memnon's fate, but all Sam could do was think about how much he already missed Portia, wonder if the day would ever come when they could be together and free, and try not to cry himself.

* * *

After delivering the first lot of slaves to the plantation and returning to New Orleans, Jim Bowie drank steadily for nearly a week. Much of the time, his lean, twenty-two-year-old body was entwined with Cleo's.

Bowie was the first more or less permanent occupant of Lafitte's guest house, and definitely the first tenant to fall in love with its gorgeous mistress. His previous romantic encounters had been brief, hurried by his adolescent fear that his partner would change her mind at any moment. Cleo was the first woman who took him in hand, then proved to him time and again that wanting could enhance the pleasure of having.

When the time came to go to Galveston, he drunkenly told Rezin P. to go without him, select their slaves, and send word of the date that they would arrive at the wharf. He promised to join his brother there for the trip north.

Days later, when he finally woke up sober, Cleo brought him a cup of coffee and asked, "Why did you decide to move into that bottle?"

He had come to know this older woman, two years his senior, as intelligent and insightful, and she had gained his trust. It was two in the afternoon, and they were still in bed.

"I don't know if it's having to kowtow to that old son-of-a-bitch, or having to leave Sam up there for him to kill."

"Do you really think your father would harm Sam?"

"I think the old man remembers what he made me do to Sam's father, and that Sam watched me do it. As big as he is, ten men together could not stop him, if Sam decided to take revenge,. The Master knows that the only thing that will control Sam is his own fear, so the old bastard has to either keep Sam one down or get rid of him."

"Don't you think Sam is smart enough to stay away from him until you get back up there?"

"I hope so . . . damn it, sometimes I wish I could just get away from the whole filthy business."

"Do you mean being a slaver?"

"Yes, that's what I mean. I have been around slaves all my life but I never gave much thought to where they came from or how they got here. Now I have seen for myself."

Cleo laughed and said, "So we're like the cotton, huh, you thought we just grew out of the ground?"

"You know how kids are. Anything they see around them, they think it has always been there and always will be, and they don't really care how it got there."

"I'll bet you were a mean little boy, always pulling the legs off of grasshoppers and putting them on top of ant beds."

He grimaced at the image she suggested.

"But you know, as cruel as The Master is sometimes, he always seems to care about his slaves in the same way he cares about me and my brothers and sisters, like they were his children too. It is as if all the creatures he owns are part of his family, and the slaves fit somewhere between the humans and the mules."

"What a sheltered life you have led, Mister Bowie," Cleo said and kissed him. "My mother taught me real early that I was put on this earth for the white man to use and I had better learn how to please him or I would end up pulling weeds in a cotton field or worse."

"You are so beautiful. I love you, and I promise you will never have to worry about that again."

Cleo pulled away, stood, and walked toward a window. "If you really mean that, Jim, you will take us to Canada."

Bowie was silent. For a moment, his blind desire for her produced a vision of the four of them together, living somewhere beyond The Master's reach. Then reality set in, and he realized that this was the first-time Cleo had ever indicated that she might want more than just to be with him. Could she have an agenda he wondered?

"Cleo, right now I don't have a cent that I can call my own. My father controls all the money, and I can't risk making him mad and being cut off. The really sad part is, I will have to keep on buying and selling slaves to make enough money to get free of him. In a way, I'm a slave just like you all."

Cleo returned to the bed and pressed the full length of her body against his. "I know, my love. You're my slave. Come here, slave," she whispered and rolled on top of him.

"You make me feel like a real man. I'll be your slave as long as you want me."

* * *

The next morning Jim's thoughts gnawed him awake early. He had the beginning of a plan. "Whatever I decide to do about Cleo or Sam; I need money," he considered. "I'm not going to get it from The Master, so I have to find another way."

Cleo slept as he bathed, dressed in his finest business attire and prepared to call upon his father's bankers. He had made a decision and was feeling good.

Jim had become friends with the nephew of one of the bank owners, and it was this young man whom he sought out. His name was Arden Marion, and Jim believed he could be trusted.

"Arden, I need a favor."

"Sure Jim. How can I help you?"

"I want to open an account in my own name and one for my brother Rezin P., and I don't want my father or anyone else to know about it."

"That would be fine with me, Jim, but I'm not sure I can get it approved. You know how careful we have to be not to alienate The Master."

"Tell your uncle it is an insurance account, Arden; The Master is not going to live forever, and someday you will need to keep me and my brothers happy if you want our money in your bank."

"That is a very good point, Jim," Arden replied, smiling. "Since you put it that way, consider it done."

Concluding his business with the bank, Jim walked to Baronne Street and turned, passing the high walls of the slave pens now mostly empty in the June heat. He entered the door leading to a familiar slave block and approached a man seated behind a desk.

A black female child fanned the man with a palm leaf and he stood as Bowie approached.

"I'm going to have about forty head to move in about two months. What do you think the rate will be then?"

"Man, woman, or child, sir?"

"Mixed."

"Trained or not?"

"Not."

"You couldn't pick a worse time, you know, the heat and all, but if they is healthy, I expect the men might bring five hundred, the women three, and the children maybe a hundred, less our commission, of course."

"Alright, I'll get back to you."

"We only open on Fridays til October first, and you'll have to bring em in a couple of days ahead so I can get em notarized. We'll pen em for you at no charge."

"I'll want cash-money from a New Orleans bank."

"That'll cost you an extra point."

Jim left the block with a frown on his face, partly caused by the man's last comment, but mostly by the smell about the place, a mixture of urine, feces, and the bacon that was used to quickly fatten the slaves in the pens, just as corn is used to fatten cattle in a feed lot.

On his way home, he stopped at Madam Girard's le Casino des Filles at the corner of Dauphine and Canal streets. "Just one drink," he thought, "to celebrate".

However, his positive outlook quickly gave way to thoughts about what could go wrong with his scheme. Depression overcame him and he ended up drinking and gambling until sunrise.

* * *

As Jim expected, Rezin P. Bowie arrived in New Orleans the second week of August with eight barges of slaves.

"The Galveston market was off because of the heat glut, and I got the Lafittes down to six bits a pound," his brother reported proudly, "and they all speak Swahili."

"Good work, Rez; now we need to select forty head and turn them separate from the rest."

"What the hell are you talking about?"

"I've arranged to sell the forty, twenty for you and twenty for me."

"But I already gave Lafitte a draft for four hundred and six head. Stephen is sure to pick up the shortage."

"We tell him that forty died on the ship, and we got Paw's money back on them. By Friday evening, the refund money will be in The Master's account, and the profit from the sale will be in ours. Stephen will never know the difference, and Paw will admire us for being tough negotiators."

"I don't know, Jim; it sounds dangerous."

"We'll make around seven thousand dollars each, and we can do that every time. I already opened a bank account for you and one for me, and the bankers agreed to keep them secret from Paw. We can make close to thirty thousand a year apiece and stop depending on the old man and his money."

"I don't know, Jim; let me think about it."

Jim was beginning to feel frustrated by his brother's timid behavior.

"There is no time to think about it. The block is only open on Friday and the operator has to file the papers tomorrow morning. We have to deliver the forty head to him tonight or wait a week for the next auction, and Stephen would surely report a delay that long to The Master. I think we can get away with waiting here three days."

The Other Rose of Texas

"What if we don't get away with it? What if we get caught? We could go to jail for embezzlement or fraud and you know Stephen would love that? What if you're not as smart as you think you are?"

"I have it all worked out and you'll just have to trust me." Feeling more aggravated and beginning to feel desperate, he said, "If you don't go along I will do it alone and make all the money myself. I'll leave you here in New Orleans and tell Paw you got sick."

Jim knew his brother well and could tell from his body language that he was weakening.

"Now, are you in or do I kick your ass?" Jim said and laughed, feeling regretful for harassing the only brother he loved.

* * *

Soon the brothers were busy selecting the slaves for the New Orleans block. They picked the forty best males, and Jim delivered them. Before the barges pulled away from the wharf on Friday evening, Jim had deposited four thousand two hundred dollars to The Master's account, and eight thousand nine hundred dollars each to his and his brother's accounts.

Though they had nearly four times the number of slaves, the trip to the plantation with their second lot was without incident. Jim took Sam's place in the barges, as Rezin P. had done during the first leg of the voyage. Both men had learned enough Swahili words to get by.

In the barnyard at the plantation when they arrived, Stephen was suspicious, as usual. "Tell me again why we are short forty head," he demanded after examining the documents and making a head count.

"Forty died and we got Paw's money back on them," Jim replied.

The Master smiled, but Stephen looked puzzled. "Didn't they look sick when you picked them in Galveston?" he asked.

"We bought the whole cargo, and we didn't unload them in Galveston."

Stephen continued his interrogation. "And why did you have an extra three Days of expenses in New Orleans?"

39

Jim had anticipated all of Stephen's questions. He looked at Rezin P. and smiled, believing he was making a fool of his baby brother and enjoying having at least one witness to it.

"We had to wait for Lafitte's bank to give us the refund money. You can see from the deposit that we got it in cash, so we wouldn't have to worry about his draft not clearing."

The Master smiled again.

"Now, how about a little gratitude for us saving two bits a pound on this lot?"

"Good work, my boys. Now, I don't want to keep any this time so I don't need to inspect them," The Master said.

"Alright Paw," Jim said and turned to Sam. "Let's hear how good you are with their language. Tell them what to expect."

Standing before the two lines of new Bowie slaves, Sam began to speak, but to Jim's surprise, Sam was speaking English. However, standing beside Sam and translating as he spoke, were five of the slaves from the first lot. Rather than trying to teach Swahili to some of the old Bowie slaves, Sam had apparently taught the new ones to speak English.

After Sam described their new lives and the training they would receive during their temporary stay at the Bowie plantation, Jim approached him. When their eyes met, Jim smiled a greeting, but Sam looked away.

Jim was expecting a happy reunion with Sam and he felt a little sad.

"Do you think we have enough tents for everybody, Sam?"

"Yes, Master Jim; I thinks we be fine."

"Alright, Sam. Let's take them down."

When they arrived at the slave quarters, Sam got busy directing his charges to the tables where food for them had been served. Jim stepped inside Aurora's house.

"Is Sam alright, Aurora? He looks like maybe he is not feeling well."

"He real sad, Master Jim. The old master done sold Sam and he be leaving soon now."

"I'm sorry, Aurora, what did you say?"

After she repeated her words, Jim felt incensed. He bolted out the door and up the hill. After a brief search he found The

The Other Rose of Texas

Master inside the horse barn examining the frog in the middle of Clytemnestra's right rear hoof.

Still enraged, but remembering his last clash with The Master over Sam, Jim calmed himself and walked in casually before he spoke. "It looks like Sam did a good job of teaching English to those new slaves."

"Uh-huh," The Master replied, without looking up.

"Good idea he had, teaching them English instead of trying to teach the others that African language."

"Uh-huh."

"Sam is gettin' pretty smart."

"Uh-huh. Too smart for a buck."

"I guess I can take him back with me now, since he did what you told him."

"I sold Sam. They're coming for him tomorrow."

Taking a deep breath, Jim chose his next words with great care. "I still need somebody who can talk their talk. Can I take one of the others?"

The Master's mouth opened slightly, as if he expected a different reaction from Jim. "I need all my slaves here. You seemed to manage alright without him this time."

"We found one of them who spoke a little English. What about Sam?"

"I got a good price for him."

The cat and mouse game was over, and Jim saw that The Master's chosen hammer in this conversation was money. "I'll pay you more."

"How? You don't have any money."

"That's what you think, you old bastard," Jim thought to himself, but he said, "I'll get it from Lafitte."

The Master turned his face toward Jim; his eyes narrow and upper lip curled down.

"But if I do have to get the money from Lafitte or anybody else, our deal is off, and you are out of the slave business."

Jim held his breath. This was the first time he had stood up to his father with conviction. He realized what happened next would define his relationship with this man for the rest of his life.

Then a feeling of elation flowed over him when The Master lowered his head, turned his face back toward the horse, and said, "Alright, James. Take Sam, but keep him away from me."

Chapter 4

During the four years after their first slave auction, the price of slaves and cotton stayed high. However, each time he came home from New Orleans, Jim could see that the health of The Master, now in his late fifties, had declined a little more. The old man seemed to have fewer and fewer lucid days.

No longer carrying his whip on the belt around his narrowing waist, he often spent his time roaming his plantation on foot. Jim observed that sometimes, when The Master encountered slaves, especially those he recognized, he walked up and hugged each wide-eyed man, woman, and child. Many days, he made a special trip to the slave quarters where he would sit for a time and watch the smaller children play.

Then, on May 1, 1821, The Master died. Moreover, according to Stephen, who had become the family keeper of records, he died intestate.

The day after the funeral, the family met to discuss matters, with their lawyer in attendance and presiding.

"As you know, Louisiana civil law is based on the Napoleonic Code. Since we cannot find a will, the law says that all of The Master's property passes to his sons."

The Bowie daughters gasped, but The Mistress sat passively.

With a smirk, Stephen said, "Don't worry, Mother. We will always take care of you."

Immediately, Jim realized why Stephen was always reading the law books in the Bowie library. Now he had used his legal knowledge like a lever on a fulcrum to usurp their mother's property rights. The other Bowie sons could only nod in amazement and agreement, but Jim was incredulous.

"What do you mean no will? This is bull. I know he left a will. There has to be a will. What about something for the girls?"

"The Master told me he didn't want the fortune hunters chasing his daughters for their money. He said he trusted his sons to do right by their mother and sisters," Stephen explained.

The lawyer added, "There is really not much more to say. I have what I need to do the filing in Baton Rouge, so I'll be going."

The women left the room with the lawyer, but the brothers stayed to talk.

"Did you burn his will or just hide it somewhere in case you need it later?" Jim asked Stephen.

"What the hell are you talking about?"

"We all know he wanted each of his sons and daughters to have something, and for everything else to pass to Mother. She was the love of his life. Are you afraid she would favor us over you?"

"Go to hell, Jim."

Jim Bowie rose from his chair and lunged toward Stephen, but the others tackled him and all three fell upon the floor.

"I want out of this deal," Jim said, rising from the floor and seating himself. "Cash me out."

"There is no cash. All the money is tied up in land and slaves," Stephen answered, smirking again.

"Then sell it. I want out, and I am through slaving. You and John J. can go down to New Orleans, and I'll come up here and run the plantation. I've had it."

"But you have all the contacts, Jim. I'm not sure Lafitte would deal with any of us," Rezin P. said sounding nervous.

"I don't give a damn. I'm tired of working my ass off to make money for you to put back in the businesses. I need money."

For the first time during the meeting, John J. spoke. "Alright, Jim. On the next lot of slaves we can pay you all of the profit in cash. How would that be?"

"That's not enough. I have some debts I need to pay."

"Then we will look into selling the land that isn't already planted. That should give you around seventy-five thousand, altogether. Will that satisfy you?"

"That will do for now. But I am serious about getting out of New Orleans and away from that dirty business. So you had better start thinking about some other way to make that money."

"Alright, Jim."

Jim was doing his best to not reveal the desperation he was feeling. He was afraid to let anyone know how serious his financial problems had become.

Caught in a downward spiral of drinking, gambling, losing, and borrowing, he was deeply in debt and Lafitte was pressuring him to pay.

* * *

After The Master's funeral, when they returned to their New Orleans house, Sam found a note from Cleo and handed it to Jim.

Sam watched Jim read, crumple, and throw the note in the fireplace, then walk to a bar-cart and pour a tumbler full of cognac. He drank and refilled the glass, and drank again.

"Lafitte would never have done that, if she had not asked him to," Bowie said. "I'll be at the casino, if anybody wants me," he added and walked out the door.

Sam went to the fireplace and dug the note out of the ashes, un-crumpled it, and read, "My Love, Lafitte has sold Portia and I. Don't try to find us. It's too late."

Sam's eyes moistened, then his tears began dripping spots on his leather pouch. In a corner of the room he sat upon the floor and buried his face in his enormous hands. He had convinced himself that Portia would have stayed, had she been allowed a choice by Cleo. He tried to think about something other than missing her.

His brush with obscurity in the hands of a new owner a year before had refocused Sam on taking control of his own fate. He needed a plan, even if only to give himself hope, so he began thinking about it as if it was a picture puzzle.

Staying in New Orleans and away from close supervision at the plantation was the first piece of the puzzle and Sam reasoned that one would take care of itself.

Jim Bowie had become a favorite in the casinos and among the other gamblers for his skill at losing most of the money he earned from slaving and shady business deals. Sam believed, as long as Jim stayed busy building on his reputation as a ruthless womanizing rogue, they would stay in New Orleans, and he would be oblivious to Sam's whereabouts most of the time.

For Sam the next puzzle piece was bringing Bettie to New Orleans so she would be there when the time came to escape.

* * *

Sam got Bettie to New Orleans by convincing Rezin P. that her cooking, together with Jim's affection for her, might help put more greens and less bourbon in Jim's diet. But when she came, her presence and her cooking had little effect on Jim Bowie's self-destructive lifestyle. He was never harsh or rude to her, just indifferent, and rarely appreciative.

However, Sam did not really care if she helped improve Bowie's condition or not. For him, having Bettie there meant that someone else could watch and serve their master while he sought money and searched for Portia.

He knew he could earn the money in a number of ways. He could load and unload cargo on the docks, or wash dishes at a restaurant, or whitewash a fence, but he could never receive the cash. The law stated that the earnings of a slave could not be given to him directly since they belonged to his master. So the money had to be handed to the master or his bank as agent. Nor, for the same reason, could a slave sell something to a white person, or gamble in a casino, and receive the money.

One evening when Bowie was out, while Sam and Bettie were eating their evening meal, Sam opened his pouch and laid two small gold coins on the table.

Bettie's eyes opened wider, then she asked, "Where'd you get those? You been stealin?"

"I think I found a way to make some money. I found these on the deck of the last slave ship we unloaded."

"What you mean, you found them?"

"I saw them on the deck and I picked them up. I figured if the sailors are that loose with their money, they must have a lot of it."

"So because you found two coins in six years, that's how you gonna make some money?"

"No."

"How then?"

"By rolling dice. I found out there is almost always a dice game going on when the ships are in port."

"That's sinful. Besides, what makes you think those white men are going to let you play dice with them?"

"They are not all white, and they don't care what color a man is as long as he brings gold for them to win."

"Well what makes you think you can make money"

Sam reached into his pouch again and laid seven much larger gold coins beside the two smaller ones.

"I've been going down to the docks every night for almost two weeks. It turns out, I'm a pretty good dice player."

Bettie smiled. Then she started laughing and Sam joined her.

"I'm gonna start callin you Goldie," Bettie said, and laughed more.

"As soon as I find Portia, we're leaving," Sam said.

"Where are we going?"

"I haven't decided yet. We can go up the river to Canada or down the river and around to Mexico? I speak both languages."

"How we gonna do that?"

"Don't you know who I am girl, I'm Bowie's giant slave. Everybody in Louisiana knows about me. I carry the authority of the Bowie name and I can go anywhere I want."

The more Sam thought about it, the more pleased with himself he became.

Chapter 5

In 1826, following an economic recession and "Panic" the previous year, England banned trade with the United States.

The British navy enforced the ban, and the demand for United States cotton tumbled. This was followed by a surplus of slaves for sale on the block as their owners tried to raise cash. The demand for newly imported slaves vanished almost overnight along with Jim Bowie's major source of income.

Again, he sought relief from his brothers, and again, Stephen seemed to take pleasure in denying him. "Where the hell is all the money we gave you before?"

Jim was sober and not in the mood to fence with his kid brother.

"I need more. You can buy me out for four bits on the dollar, if you do it today."

"We don't have any cash. We can give you a note."

"I need cash."

"I'm not willing to sell acreage or slaves in a down market to raise cash for you. We can give you a note, and maybe you can borrow against it."

"Stephen, if I didn't know better, I'd think I was listening to The Master. You're even beginning to look like him, with that whip on your belt."

Then Jim turned to John J. and Rezin P.

"And you two. Why won't you speak up for me? I'm your brother too. Are you afraid of him?"

"That's enough," Stephen said, "do you want the note or not?"

"I'll take it as a loan but I want all three of you to sign it as proof of your collusion against me."

"Done," Stephen said.

The Other Rose of Texas

With no hope of borrowing any more money in New Orleans, Jim decided to go to Alexandria and try his luck. Years before, he had stopped going there with the slaves to be auctioned, so his knowledge of local people, affairs, and politics was not current. He felt a bit uneasy about his prospects.

He felt humiliated as well. How had he gone from being a prince of New Orleans to being a potential consort of dirt-farmers in Alexandria in so short a time?

Reflecting on the sad state of his fortunes and reputation he blamed the economic times, his brothers, and Lafitte, but never himself.

* * *

At lunch on his third day in Alexandria, Jim's good friend Samuel Levi Wells, a colleague from the Louisiana Militia during the New Orleans campaigns, was giving him the information he sought.

"I hear this Wright fellow is the man to know here now," Jim said.

"He calls himself Major Norris Wright. He came here from Maryland two years ago. Apparently, his family has money."

"And he's sheriff?"

"Yes. He fell in with that new bunch and bought the office. They all seem dead set on taking over business and politics around here, any way they can."

Wells continued when Jim nodded his understanding.

"Wright is a braggart and a loudmouth, and he has started belittling you and me and Sam Cuny, and anybody else who has lived up here for a while."

"What did he say about me, Samuel?"

"He said that his friends in New Orleans thought you must have darkie blood because when you drink you can hold a bottle in each hand and one with each foot too, like a monkey."

Throwing his napkin in his plate, Bowie stood and pushed his chair back. He felt even more humiliated than before.

"Where can I find him?"

49

"He usually plays cards in a side room at the Bailey Hotel in the afternoon. Jim, be careful, he carries a pistol under his coat."

As predicted, Bowie found Wright at the poker table. Facing Jim as he entered the room, Wright seemed to recognize him. He immediately, stood, pulled his pistol and fired.

Jim reached inside his coat, touched his left chest just below his third rib, and withdrew three red fingers.

Considering himself a peaceful man, Bowie had come to seek a public apology from Wright, without bloodshed. Now, seeing his own blood, Bowie felt angry yet calm. Gathering himself he dived over the table and knocked Wright from his feet.

He purposefully straddled Wright, placed a knee in his groin, and began to pound Wright's face with both fists. Then Wright reached into his right-boot, and his hand emerged with a dagger that he planted in Bowie's left shoulder. Holding Wright by the throat with his left hand, Bowie pulled the knife free and raised it high above the fat man's left eye, preparing to plunge it deep.

Jim had never killed anything in anger but, at that moment, he intended to kill the sheriff. In a flash, one of the other card players grabbed and held his right arm while four others dragged him off of Wright.

Still angry, Bowie shook-off two of his adversaries and was preparing to kick one of them in the chin, when the other one drew a pistol and placed it against Jim's forehead. His anger turned to fear and Jim stopped struggling as the other two men pushed him against a wall.

"These men can probably get away with killing me here and now," Jim thought.

Then Wright sat up, gasping for air. "Put that son-of-a-bitch . . . in jail," he said looking toward his deputy, Alfred Blanchard. "I'll hang him tomorrow myself."

"You ain't hangin nobody," Samuel Wells said, standing at the head of a just arrived group of seven obviously armed friends of Bowie, including Rezin P.

"Come on, Jim."

The Wright man lowered his gun and the two others released Jim. The group accompanied him to Wells's home, where his seventeen-year-old daughter, Cecilia, and Bowie's doctor cleaned and dressed Jim's wounds.

"You're lucky to be alive, Jim," Samuel Wells observed. "You were foolish to confront an armed man, with no weapon of your own. Why don't you at least carry a knife?"

Bowie winced as Cecilia dabbed wood alcohol on his chest lesion. He looked at her face. She smiled and dropped her eyes.

"I'll tell you why." Rezin P. offered.

"Since we were kids, he thinks he is indestructible. He never carried a weapon even when we hunted. He used a rope or a snare or his bare hands. He never even loaded his musket when we fought the British. Sometimes I think he wants something or somebody to do him in."

"That's not so Rez. A man needs a good reason to take a life, even an animal's life, and it should not be an easy thing for him to do," Jim said.

Bowie was feeling strangely complete when they put him to bed. He had not solved his financial problem, and he was in considerable pain, yet he felt somehow satisfied.

"Maybe I like knowing that I still have good friends," he thought.

Soon Cecilia brought in his supper tray. Bowie looked at her face again, and again she smiled. This time, before she dropped her eyes he looked deep into them.

At first he thought he saw admiration. Then she looked back and he decided that she was feeling something more.

* * *

Two days later, Jim and Rezin P. Bowie departed Alexandria on horseback for the seventy mile ride south to the plantation. Making good time, that night they camped outside the new town of Ville Platte, more than halfway.

While lying on a horse blanket beside a campfire, after a meal of fried bacon and boiled beans, Rezin P. reached into his saddlebag and withdrew a long narrow object wrapped in oilcloth.

"I bought this off a blacksmith from Arkansas. He swore he made it from a hunk of metal that fell out of the sky and a piece of a tree hardened by lightening."

Jim felt curious as his brother peeled away the protective cloth.

"I was planning to keep it myself, but I think you need it more," Rezin P. said and handed Jim what turned out to be a knife in a dark leather scabbard

"I got mad and lost my head back in Alexandria," Jim said as he raised himself on his left elbow and grasped the scabbard, accepting and examining it as a courtesy to his brother.

"But I don't plan to need a weap . . ."

When he touched the knife itself he stopped in mid-sentence. He felt a strange tingle in his right hand as he grasped the handle and slid the knife out. About nine inches long, an inch and a half wide, with a single edge and slightly clipped point, the knife felt alive in his hand and seemed to become an extension of his arm. The leather-bound wood handle felt fused with his body.

"On the other hand, a man can always use a good knife. Thanks, Rez," he concluded.

Still sore from his wounds, Jim slowly sat up. Despite the pain he stood and slid his wide belt through slits in the scabbard, positioning the knife on his left hip. He began to practice reaching across his body and pulling the weapon quickly with his right hand.

Then he removed the scabbard from the belt, cut two new angled slits, and repositioned the knife over his stomach, tilted to the right. He practiced drawing again, and it was less painful.

Growing tired, yet strangely calm, Jim returned to his blanket. Observing that Rezin P. had gone to sleep, Jim reclined against his saddle and stared at the dancing flames of the camp fire. Then he focused on the wood and surrounding ashes.

"Ashes to ashes," he thought. "That wood is me. Those flames are my life, using me up, too soon."

Then he looked at the whiskey flask lying beside him and remembered how taking a few pulls from it the previous night had made the pain from his wounds go away.

Instead of reaching for the flask, however, he grasped the handle of his new knife and thought, "I've got to stop putting myself in the fire."

Then, without taking a drink, Jim Bowie closed his eyes and slept.

* * *

In August, 1827, Jim Bowie took a trip to Natchez, Mississippi, in response to a message that a banker there was willing to give him a loan.

When he arrived, he felt surprised to find Samuel Wells, George McWhorter, and Samuel Cuny, friends from Alexandria, awaiting him at the City Hotel.

"There is no banker here willing to loan you money. It's a scheme that Sheriff Wright cooked up to ambush you," Wells reported. "Some of his cronies are already here, Crain, Doctor Maddox, and the Blanchard brothers, but Wright has not arrived, so we have a little time to plan what to do."

"You mean they're going to just kill me outright?"

Feeling a little anxious, Jim touched the handle of his knife.

"From what we hear, Maddox is going to challenge you to a duel. You will choose the weapons, so they can choose the time and place. The place they choose will have lots of trees for their men to hide behind, and when you show up they will shoot you and anybody that is with you."

"How do you know all this?"

"That's the funny part. We got it from Wright's own daughter. She overheard her father discussing their plan, and she told my daughter Cecelia, because Cecelia told her she was in love with you. You know how young girls are, Jim."

At the mention of her name Jim felt a yearning to see Cecelia again.

"I think I should just leave town," Jim observed.

"Before we came over here, we talked about this a long time," Wells replied. "I knew you would say that and Cuny wanted to just send you a warning, not to come up here in the first place."

Jim looked toward Cuny, acknowledging his friendship with a smile.

"But I said that Wright would just try again, some other time, some other place, until he gets you. I heard him tell the Blanchard boys that very thing. I think he feels like you made a fool of him by getting away in Alexandria."

"I didn't exactly get away. I've got two scars to prove it."

The three men from Alexandria were passing a jug of whiskey around as they talked. When it came to Bowie, he just passed it on without swigging.

Glancing at the jug, then at Bowie, Wells continued, "I think he wants to kill you this time, and he wants to do it outside of Louisiana jurisdiction."

"I think we should just shoot Wright on sight," McWhorter said. "If we kill him, I think the others will back down."

"I don't think I want anything to do with a murder," Bowie said, looking at each man in turn. "I'd rather just go back to New Orleans and take my chances. Isn't there another way?"

Their discussion continued until after midnight. The next morning, Bowie and his friends were all seated at breakfast when Wright and his group entered the hotel dining room.

Rising immediately, Wells stepped in front of an overly surprised looking Maddox.

"I demand satisfaction sir for your defamation of my good name. What weapon do you prefer?"

Maddox looked at Wright, who also appeared surprised.

"Pistols, we want pistols," Wright replied.

"Assuming that you are his second, we accept your choice of pistols. We choose tomorrow at sunrise on the sandbar two miles downriver from the Vidalia ferry."

The Wright group all looked puzzled as the Bowie group all stood and walked out. Jim felt grateful that he would not have to face his enemies alone.

* * *

The following sunrise, with fog radiating where the cool air fell on the warmer water, the bows of five row boats carrying

Jim Bowie and fifteen other men slid onto the appointed sandbar. Located exactly in the middle of the mile-wide river, it was eighty yards long, fifty yards wide, mostly dry, and totally free of vegetation. Depending on where a man stood on the smooth surface, he could be within the legal jurisdiction of Mississippi or Louisiana or both.

From the banks, it was impossible to identify the figures on the sandbar with the naked eye, and the early-morning absence of traffic on the river eliminated the risk that anyone might be seen from a passing vessel.

Sunlight crawled over the eastern horizon as the seconds prepared flint-lock pistols then handed the guns to their principals. That done, the duelists, Wells and Maddox, took positions ten yards apart.

"Ready. Aim. Fire."

Both men fired and missed. Their seconds rushed forward and handed them other loaded pistols.

"Ready. Aim. Fire."

Both men fired and missed again.

From their militia days, Bowie knew his friend Samuel Wells was an excellent shot with a pistol, and he doubted that Wells, or even his opponent, could completely miss a target as large as a man twice in a row. He could only conclude that both men wanted an end to the violence, and they had somehow agreed to miss each other.

When the duelists walked forward and shook hands, Jim knew he was right. Feeling happy that no blood had been spilled he sprang forward to suggest to all parties that their honor was restored.

When Bowie approached Maddox with his empty right hand extended, Wright's friends rushed forward to join the group. However, unfinished business remained between others on the sandbar.

Stepping forward, Samuel Cuny shouted, "Colonel Crain, this is a good time to settle our difficulty" and fired his pistol. The ball missed Crain but struck Bowie in the hip, knocking him backward and to the ground, where he sat for a moment feeling confused.

Then both Cuny and Crain fired. This time, Cuny hit Crain, and blood spouted from Crain's left arm. But Crain had hit Cuny full in the chest, and the latter fell backward onto the ground and did not move.

Seeing this, Bowie rose to his feet without regard for his hip wound, drew his knife, and charged at Crain. Lacking the time to reload, Crain struck Bowie in the head with his empty pistol. The blow was so hard that it broke the weapon into pieces and sent Bowie to the ground once more, dazed and on his knees, confused again.

All the men on the tiny sand island, except Cuny and Bowie, began to run and weave defensively, trying to avoid being someone's target. Looking up Jim saw his bitter enemy, Norris Wright, aiming a pistol at him. Wright fired and missed then drew his sword cane, charged like a dismounted lancer, and stabbed Bowie in the chest.

Bowie heard a moan-groan-scream, a sound he had not heard since the day he hanged Sam's father. This time, Bowie knew that the sound came from inside him.

Fortunately, Bowie's breastbone steered Wright's blade away from any organs. As Wright attempted to pull the blade free to try again, Bowie reached up, grabbed his shirt, and pulled the sheriff down upon the clipped point of his drawn Bowie knife. Fate, skill, or both guided Bowie's blade between Wright's ribs and into his heart, killing him straight away.

Already shot and brained, with Wright's sword still protruding from his chest, Bowie was shot and stabbed again from the back by attackers whom his adrenaline charged mind could not identify. Somehow, he got to his feet and tried to pull the sword cane from his chest. As he did, both Blanchard brothers fired at him, and Alfred's ball struck him in the left arm.

He stood and moved close enough to them that, when Bowie extended his right knife arm and spun, he cut off part of Alfred's forearm. Reloading, Carey Blanchard fired a second shot at Bowie, but it was wide, then Carey himself was shot and wounded in the right leg by Major McWhorter.

After a little more than ten minutes of fighting, both sides had one man dead. The Wright contingent had three wounded.

The Other Rose of Texas

On the other side, only Jim Bowie was injured, with three mini-ball wounds, two stab wounds and a braining.

As his friends assembled around him Jim was lying flat on the sand, in overwhelming pain, yet he managed to look up at Wells and say, "You were right Samuel, I feel better knowing I don't have to worry about Wright anymore."

* * *

As soon as he was able to travel after the sandbar fight, his friends took Jim from Natchez to the Bowie plantation. During his first few weeks there, the doctor came and went as the slave women, Aurora and Calliope, minded him daily under the supervision of his mother, now in her sixties.

With her daughters, all married and moved away and her other sons traveling on business, The Mistress Bowie's only family on the plantation was Jim. When he began feeling better and staying awake, she began visiting him in the morning while the air was still relatively cool. Sometimes she read to him, sometimes they talked, and sometimes she sat quietly, knitting as he dozed.

He could not recall ever being alone with this woman before, and, initially, Jim felt uneasy conversing with her. He had only really felt comfortable around two women in his life, one a slave woman who raised him and the other a beautiful young slave he thought he loved. Gradually, however, his conversations with his mother became more natural and friendly, and, for Jim, one visit in particular was most enlightening.

Sitting up in bed for the first time, he had just finished a large breakfast. Calliope had taken the tray and left the room, leaving Jim still sipping a cup of coffee.

"You know mother, growing up I thought you were a queen who just happened to be living in my house. I only remember seeing you at special meals and church services, and you always seemed to be dressed in a ball gown."

The Mistress smiled, "That's the way The Master wanted it. I can say it now. I believe your father was afraid your sisters and I would be a bad influence on you and your brothers. That you would be less manly if you were around women. So he kept us apart."

"Did that work?"

"If you are you asking if I think my sons are masculine; the answer is yes. But at a price."

"What do you mean?"

"I mean you are all fine men, but I think I could have helped you be a little happier. When you couldn't meet your father's demands, I could have given you a little comforting love and understanding. As it was, I could see that you either met his unreasonable expectations or felt bad about yourselves for failing him."

"You mean you would have told us that failure was acceptable?"

"No, I would have said that failure was forgivable and you would be happier if you could learn to forgive yourself. That is something your older brothers have never learned. I think they both gave up on being happy a long time ago."

Water glistened in her eyes as she continued.

"It makes me sad to think that they avoid coming on this land because the memory of their failures here is too painful."

Jim felt fascinated. He had thought that only he in the Bowie family had the insight and sensitivity his mother now revealed.

"When he was just a boy, your brother David drowned trying to prove to The Master that he was man enough to out swim and catch a run-away slave in the big river."

Jim had not thought of his long-dead older brother for years and he felt sad.

"Saddest of all though is Stephen, who thinks he is happy because he has become even more mean spirited than The Master."

Jim did not often care about the opinions of others, especially what they thought about him. However, his mother's observations about his brothers had aroused his curiosity.

"What about me, mother."

"I still have hope for you. I have always thought you are more like me than like your father. I also sense a change in you recently."

"What kind of change?"

"You seem more at peace with yourself and I have been encouraged by the fact that you have not asked for whiskey since they brought you here."

"You may be right."

"If you work at it, you might be able to start forgiving yourself for being a mere human being, and that will change your life."

Just then Calliope knocked and entered, announcing that guests had arrived downstairs.

After The Mistress left to greet the visitors, Jim reflected on her words. What she said about her sons set Jim to thinking about his brothers in a new and more tolerant way.

Yet something else was impacting him more. Experiencing his mother for the first time as a flesh and blood human being, an intelligent woman, a source of comfort and compassion, not just another object that his father owned, was stirring deep feelings in him,.

Then she returned.

"Samuel Wells and his daughter Cecelia are downstairs. I asked them to stay for lunch. Do you feel strong enough to come down?"

Jim looked down and to the left.

"Yes, I think I do."

Still feeling discomfort from his gunshot wounds, but preferring not to accept any personal assistance from Sam, Bowie shaved himself, combed his hair, put on his best pajamas, dressing gown, and ascot, and joined his visitors in the dining room.

When he entered, Cecelia smiled, and Jim was less conscious of his pain.

* * *

After her first visit, Cecelia Wells, now eighteen, frequently came again to read to Jim in his sickbed. Each time, after she left, The Mistress praised the young woman and reminded her thirty-year-old unmarried son how lucky any man would be to settle down with her and raise a family. Soon nine months of convalescence had passed and Jim returned to New Orleans with nothing more to show from his sandbar fight than the scars on his body, or so he thought.

Then, at home, he began to open the mail that had accumulated during his absence, and he unwrapped the first of many dime novels he would see with his name on the cover, this one entitled "Bowie and His Knife, Death Born of Lightening, Forged From a Star". It described his sandbar encounter and compared his knife to Samson's hair, speculating that he drew his strength for it.

His mind and body returned to the business of making a living, but not his heart. Hungering for the easy life of the plantation that his recent memories produced, he began visiting his mother as often as he could. The Mistress always managed to invite Cecelia to visit at least one entire day during his stay.

Seeing what a fine lady she was becoming, at first Jim related to Cecelia as a kid sister, mainly out of respect for her father. She had a sweetness and innocence that Jim had never encountered in a woman, and he found himself revealing more than he wished to her, as if she had become his confessor and had the power of absolution. Soon, she was the first person since his brother Rezin P. that Jim took to his private refuge by the cypress trees, where they would talk for hours.

She had an innocent way of posing the most intimate questions. "Am I anything like the women you are with in New Orleans?"

Despite her youth, he felt comfortable responding to her in the same honest and direct way he did to everyone else. "I spent my time with whores. You are nothing like them. Your mother and father have raised you to be gentle and fine and clean."

"I think your mother must have raised you the same way, Jim. You seem gentle and kind too, at least when you are not fighting."

"But you don't know the truth. My mother had little to do with it. You never knew my father, and you don't know my brothers. They called my father The Master. He was the cruelest man I have ever known, and he tried to make us all just like him."

"I can tell from your voice that you have been hurt, and when you think about it, you feel angry."

"When I was fifteen, The Master made me hang a slave and then the slave's wife hanged herself. I guess I have been angry ever since. When I was eighteen, I left home to get away from The Master and ended up right back under his control."

"But your father is gone now. Why are you still angry?"

"When he died, I tried to forget what I did and get away from slaving, but my brothers wouldn't let me. Then I started drinking and gambling, and I became someone . . . I hate my life."

"Why don't you change it, change your life?"

Wondering if The Mistress had been coaching her, Jim's mouth opened and he squinted as he looked into Cecelia's eyes.

"Why are you looking at me like that?" she asked.

"It's odd. My mother said something like that, not too long ago. But I can't change."

"Why not?"

"I don't have any money, and the only way I know how to make any is by slaving or growing cotton."

"So why don't you leave New Orleans, live on your plantation, and grow cotton?"

"That's a good question."

"Did you ever wonder why God spared your life?"

"Funny you would ask. I was shot and stabbed and knocked in the head with a pistol barrel. I thought Wright would finish me, but then it felt like my knife had a mind of its own. It seemed to force my hand upward, guiding the blade between his ribs and into his heart. He collapsed and died on top of me. I was shot twice more and stabbed again. God could have taken me that day, and I'm still trying to understand why he didn't."

"I think God has a plan for you. Even though you have questioned and forgotten him, I think it is a sign that he has forgiven you and wants you to find happiness."

"How do you know that? Are you an angel?"

"Do you want me to be an angel?"

For Jim, Cecelia›s question cut to the heart of what he was feeling about her. During his mother's visits to his bedside, when he began to know The Mistress as a person, he also began to examine his attitude toward other women.

He finally admitted to himself that he saw Cleo and all the others he had been with as objects to be pursued, conquered, and owned, and to be taken out of their cloister only on special occasions. In this way, he thought, "I have become my father."

Now his feelings for Cecelia were growing strong, and, for the first time in his life, he resolved to try to have an open and honest relationship with a woman. He wanted to ask Cecelia questions and really listen to her answers, to know and consider her feelings and thoughts and opinions.

"My darling girl. You know who I am and I have told you about the terrible things I have done, yet you seem to accept me. So I want to accept you as who you are. Not an angel. Not anyone else, not someone you think your father wants you to be, or my mother wants you to be, or I want you to be."

Jim thought he saw admiration and affection in Cecelia's eyes and took that to mean that she liked what she was hearing.

* * *

The next time they sat under the moss canopy beside the swamp, she kissed him passionately and said, "I love you, Jim Bowie; I think I have since I bandaged your wounds in Alexandria."

Bowie sensed that her actions and words meant she wanted to give herself to him, but he resisted the urge. Then he made an announcement.

"My mother has convinced my brothers to let me move home and run the plantation. As a token of reconciliation, Stephen has authorized our bank to advance me enough money to pay off my creditors and leave New Orleans free of debt."

Cecelia smiled like a flower opening to the morning sun.

"Now we can be married, and I want you to save yourself until we are."

Saying that he pulled her body close to his and kissed her with great ardor.

"We can move into the big house, if you don't mind living with my mother, or we can build one of our own."

"I love your mother and she can be a big help when our babies come."

They chose the date of Saturday, September 19, 1829, for their wedding, at the Bowie plantation. That date gave them three months, time enough for Cecelia to travel to New Orleans and buy her trousseaux, and time enough for Jim to conclude his affairs in New Orleans and move himself, Sam and Bettie back home.

Thinking of the changes about to happen in his life, Jim could not remember feeling as hopeful since he and Rezin P. first moved to New Orleans.

"No more slaving with Lafitte," he thought. "No more corruption and dishonest dealing, no more drinking and gambling and whoring and depression, no more cruel ways."

* * *

"We should have run years ago," Sam said.

Since Bettie joined Sam in New Orleans, Jim Bowie was either drunk and insensible or out of town for months on end. For years while ruling themselves their daily existence seemed relatively carefree, and compelling thoughts of running receded. Until now.

"What we gonna do little brother?" Bettie asked.

Sam shrugged.

"We been livin here like we was free for so long, I don't think I can stand goin' back up there and bein' a slave again."

Sam felt helpless. He had known their easy life was over when Jim announced his plans to move home and marry Cecelia. He knew Bettie would blame him so he waited to tell her. Now it was too late to do anything but talk about it.

"We can try to run. I got two hundred dollars in my pouch."

"What about Portia?"

"It is hard to believe she has been gone almost seven years. By now even a fool would know that she doesn't want me to find her."

"Do you think we can get away to Canada?"

The years of good living and eating her own delicious cooking had increased her weight significantly, and as Sam spoke he was considering how well Bettie would hold up on the road.

"I'm beginning to wonder just how far we can get if we run north. The distance from Baton Rouge to Memphis is four times as far as it is from New Orleans to Baton Rouge, and Memphis is only a quarter of the distance from Baton Rouge all the way to Canada. I'm amazed more and more that Daddy made it all the way to Memphis three times."

"How long did it take him?"

"He said the shortest way was through the Arkansas Territory, but the safest way was along the river, because every little river town had a slave population, and they fed him and hid him during the day."

"So how many days did it take him along the river?"

Sam could hear anxiety in her voice. Was she also anxious about the physical demands that she would have to face, day after day? He thought so.

"He said in good weather he could walk about ten miles a night. His problem was that the walking paths followed the river, and the river was full of bends, so he really only made about five miles a night."

"Will you please answer me? How long did it take?"

Sam could see that Bettie was gritting her teeth and he decided to tell her the truth.

"He said it took him three months to get to Memphis."

"You mean it would take us a whole year to get to Canada?"

"Yes, and I'm not sure what we will find when we get up there."

"What does that mean?"

"Let's face it, sister, no matter where we go, we will still be black, and I don't know if we will ever be safe or happy in a white man's world. I wonder if the whites have it in their nature to allow us to live free, even if the law says they're supposed to. I think they will always stress our differences and say we are too stupid or childlike to take care of ourselves. They will keep trying to find excuses to control our lives, and they will always find one while there are more of them than there are of us."

"That makes me real sad, brother. It's like we have no hope."

"That's why, if we run, we might be better off going to Mexico. It would not take as much time to get there, and we could still go to Canada if Mexico did not work out."

"You mean they don't have slaves in Mexico?"

"Mexico is not part of Spain anymore, and their constitution makes slavery illegal. Nacogdoches, Mexico is a little over two hundred miles away from here, and we could make it there in less than two months, even if we just made five miles a night. Since I am still pretty free to travel in Louisiana, we might even be able to walk some in daylight too, and get there sooner."

"I'll go wherever you say."

Sam thought Bettie seemed to relax a little.

"I know. But I'm still worried about the problems we will have when we get there no matter where we go. We have to eat, so we will have to work and make a living."

"Well I can always cook, and you can always work cotton."

"I know, but we will need money to get started, and my two hundred dollars is not enough."

"How can we get more?"

"The only way I know is gambling on the ships."

All of a sudden Bettie's eyes twinkled and she seemed to turn whimsical.

"I'm gonna miss bein here, havin parties for our friends, you teachin them to read, like we was all white. I been feelin like a proper lady."

"I know. I'll miss it too."

The corners of Bettie's mouth turned down.

"But if you want to go to Mexico, I'd better start looking for dice games and you better start putting together enough food for a couple of weeks. We can hunt and fish on the trail, but it won't be enough."

However, their run to freedom never even got started. Bowie kept them busy packing and preparing to move and they were rarely out of his sight. Soon it was their last day in New Orleans and Jean Pierre Lafitte was stopping in to say goodbye and get the house keys back from Bowie.

Then they were aboard a boat steaming north against the current. When they got off at Baton Rouge, Sam knew their chances of escape were lost.

* * *

The atmosphere at the plantation could not have been more festive. The Mistress had summoned all her children home, and they made a fuss over their brother who was to finally to be a bridegroom at age thirty-three.

Likewise, when Jim visited the slave quarters he saw that Sam and Bettie were receiving a festive welcome too. He noticed that the unmarried females smiled broadly at Sam, especially Kiss Petal, whom everyone now called Kizzie.

On the morning of the day before the wedding, Jim anticipated the arrival of the Wells family and the bride-to-be. However, only Samuel Wells arrived, his eyes red. After Jim sat him down and handed him a glass of bourbon, he began to weep.

"Her mother said that on the boat trip back to Natchez, she began having chills and back pain, and she had a fever," Wells began explaining. "A doctor on board examined her and said it was yellow fever."

Jim sat patiently as Wells mind began to drift. "I should have sent her to Memphis to buy her clothes, they don't have near the fever as they do down south."

Samuel swigged his glass empty and Jim re-filled it.

"They tried to get her home quick, but during the wagon trip, her skin turned yellow and she couldn't keep her food down."

His tears began to roll down both cheeks and Cecelia's distraught father bent over with his hands covering his face. Jim crouched beside him and put his arm around Samuel. Then Wells said, "She died beside Catahoula Lake."

Jim continued to re-fill Well's glass and after a few more drinks Samuel explained that his physician in Alexandria had ordered the immediate burial of his daughter's body, so there would be no funeral, no chance for Jim to say goodbye.

Seated nearby, her face wet with tears, The Mistress said, "The minister is already here and I would like to ask him to bring us all together and bless the memory of that sweet child."

Jim could see that his mother was looking to him for approval of her suggestion but he looked away. The Mistress rose and walked out of the room.

The Other Rose of Texas

In the afternoon all of the family gathered in the ballroom for a brief memorial service, but Jim was neither there or anywhere else on the plantation.

* * *

Before noon, after Jim learned of Cecelia's death, he saddled a horse and rode out toward New Orleans without saying a word to anyone, leaving Sam and Bettie at the plantation. Although his heart was broken for the second time by the loss of the woman he loved, he was not willing to feel anything but anger. He just wanted to be alone to hate everyone and everything.

Arriving in New Orleans he took a cheap room in the French quarter near his favorite casino. But he neither drank nor gambled, or partook of any other vice.

He ate his meals at inexpensive cafes. He slept little. By day he read books from the library, mainly escapist literature by Voltaire, Cooper, and others.

He was reading a book of poetry by Robert Burns when he suddenly stopped and said aloud, "Why did you take her? I was paying attention. I was behaving myself."

Then he realized he was talking directly to God for the first time in his life. He tried to continue reading, but his tears prevented his eyes from seeing the page and he buried his face in a pillow.

That evening he walked the streets, sometimes talking to himself, continuing to try to assign blame for the loss of the thing he cared for most.

"Are you dooming me to sadness as my mother said my brothers are?"

"Accept your humanity. That will change your life," mother said.

"Change your life yourself," Cecelia said.

Then he found himself passing Lafitte's house, his recently vacated home for over twelve years. He looked in through the open street gate at the lighted windows beyond the courtyard and saw the old pirate's son, John Pierre, talking with a man who was holding a broom.

Bowie entered the gateway. As he approached, Lafitte the Younger glanced his way then turned and smiled a greeting.

"I thought to never see you here again my friend," Lafitte said, extending his hand. "Has your wife allowed you to return to our sinful city already. Is she with you? I hear she is a fine lady and it would be my honor to meet her."

Jim noticed how exquisitely dressed Lafitte was, including a beaver hat and silver tipped cane. At the same time he realized: how wrinkled he must appear to Lafitte, that he had not shaved in a few days, and how badly he smelled.

"It didn't work out. The fever took her before the wedding."

"I'm sorry Jim. Truly I am. Why don't we go inside and have some of that liquor you left behind."

"Alright."

As Jim entered the house a rush of memories, good and bad, gathered in his mind and he felt tempted to accept the whiskey he was offered. However, "I'd like some water," was what he said.

Jim thought Lafitte looked surprised at his request.

"So tell me, what are your plans now? Are you ready to resume our affiliation ? This place is clean and ready for you to move back in tonight."

"I don't know what I want, except to take some time to figure it out."

"You mean you didn't come here tonight to pick up where we left off?"

"No. I was walking by and saw the open gate."

"You don't have to play me for an advantage. You know what I think of you, what we all think of you. Just tell me what you want and it's yours."

"Right now all I know is what I don't want."

"The best thing for you is to get back to work, using your knowledge and connections, doing what you do best."

"You mean slaving."

"Yes. Get your mind off your troubles. I'm ready to turn my whole operation over to you and make you an equal partner. I'll be the silent partner and you can run things your way."

"I can't stay in New Orleans. I've made too many enemies here."

"That's fine. I still have a slave block in Galveston. The ships still deliver there. The market in Texas is booming."

"I have an agreement to cut my brothers in on anything I do."

"That's fine too. I don't care how you divide your half."

For the first time in months Jim was beginning to feel more than just dead inside.

"Will you finance a trip for me to go and see your Galveston operation before I decide?"

"I'll have one of my ships take you and bring you back, and you can live on board while you're there."

Jim knew that Lafitte was offering to transport him aboard a slave ship and he wanted to avoid that.

"Let me talk with my brothers. They may be willing to pay my expenses, if they want in on the deal."

"Alright."

All the way back to his room that night, and for days after, Jim considered that a fresh start in Texas might be what he needed, even if it involved slaving. Maybe there he could begin to find the happiness that his wonderful blonde angel had said that God intended for him.

* * *

The day-after Jim road out alone for New Orleans, Sam was returning to the slave quarters when he spotted Stephen talking with Aurora while she stirred a large pot of green-beans over an open fire. Knowing Stephen's temperament, Sam was not surprised to see him wearing some of The Master's clothes, including his whip.

Having no interest in dealing with the youngest Bowie brother, Sam waited behind a barn until he was gone. Then he walked down and joined Aurora.

"He's turnin out to be jus' like his paw. We be jus' a bunch of sows and boars to him. He tol' me to look at some of the females an tell him when is the best time to breed them. If he gonna be doin what I think he gonna be doin, it ain't right, an I ain't gonna do it."

"But he carryin' he daddy's whip now. What ifn he whip you bad like The Master done? Master Jim ain't here now to stop it."

Soon Aurora and Sam were standing in the library of the main house and Stephen was demanding her report. While Sam listened, she gave Stephen the dates when each of seventeen women he had identified would be ovulating. She added that twelve of the women were married.

As she spoke, Stephen made a list. When she finished, he looked at the list and said, "I see that Nemesis is ripe. Go tell her to report to me now. Sam, you stay here."

"Yes, sir, Master Stephen."

Concluding earlier, from Aurora's comments, what Stephen was up to, Sam's role in the proceedings now became clear to him, and he probed his mind for a way to avoid it.

"I could say I have a disease," Sam thought, "but he would look and whip me for lying."

Sam was still mentally searching for a way out when the slave woman called Nem arrived.

Stephen led the two slaves to the second-floor bedroom where his sisters formerly slept. It was secluded at the east end of the hall. Inside the room, he ordered both of them to take off their clothes. When they seemed to hesitate, Stephen placed his hand on his whip, and they obeyed.

When they stood naked before him, he started to give them instructions. "Nem, when I say . . ."

Before he could finish the sentence, the door opened and The Mistress walked in. "What do you think you are doing, young man?"

Visible to Sam, but not to Stephen, Aurora stood quietly in the hall, listening.

"I'm beginning my new breeding program, Maw."

"Your new what?"

"I'm using Sam to improve the strength and stamina of our slave line just like that planter who bought Sam planned to do. You remember."

"I remember you were a nasty little boy, but I thought you had outgrown it. Do you know that Nem is a married woman?"

"You mean that silly ceremony they go through down there before they couple?"

"I shall say this to you only once, so I ask that you listen carefully."

"Yes, Mam."

"In his wisdom, your father left the moral welfare of our people in my hands. Never in his life did he even consider such blaspheme as you are attempting to undertake here today. In the eyes of God, Nem and the others are as married as they would be if our own minister had performed the ceremony and registered the nuptials with the parish. You are not the master here, and if I hear any more about you trying to force anyone into sin, I will ask your brothers to hold you down while I spank your bottom. Do you understand?"

"Yes, Maw."

"I am concerned for your soul, son, and I am wondering if what you call your breeding program is an adult manifestation of the voyeurism you seemed to enjoy as a child."

"Maw, not in front of the slaves."

"Sam, you and Nem put your clothes on and run along. I think everything will be alright now."

Nem, now in tears, ran ahead while Sam and Aurora walked back to the slave quarters together.

"You ain't no prize bull. Yo' mammy and I raised you to be God fearin' and God say we can't do no dultry," Aurora said in a way that reminded Sam of his long dead mother.

"I mo' worried 'bout what some of them husbands gonna do if I go messin' round they wives," Sam replied.

Actually, Sam's real concern was with how he would survive now without Jim's protection. He suspected that Stephen felt very embarrassed and was already plotting revenge on the three slaves who had witnessed his scolding.

* * *

In March of 1830, Jim returned to the plantation and arranged a meeting with his brothers. Six months had passed since the death of Cecelia Wells and he was still grieving, however he had taken Lafitte's advice about trying to bury his troubles under his work.

He opened the meeting saying, "Junior Lafitte has offered to give me half of his slave operation, if I will run it for him."

"What does old man Lafitte say about that?" Rezin P. asked

"Junior is running things now. People say the old man and his brother are dead, but Junior says they went to Maracaibo and they're not coming back."

"If Junior offered the deal to you, why are you telling us about it," John J. queried.

"Because you are my brothers and we have always been partners, and because you all agreed to let me come home and run the plantation when mother asked you. I want to show you I appreciate that."

Jim thought Stephen looked skeptical. He cleared his throat and continued.

"I think we can all profit from this. If Junior is willing to give me a half for nothing, he probably thinks the whole of it is worthless. My contacts in the trade tell me that the American and British Navies are both out to stop the slave ships altogether, so Junior is probably planning to just abandon his interests unless he can make some kind of deal."

"How can we profit from that?" Stephen asked.

"The cotton market has still not fully recovered from the panic in twenty-five so the demand for new slaves through New Orleans is non-existent and we're not making any money down there. We need new buyers, and the stories I hear about the population explosion in Texas makes it the logical place to look for them."

"We have survived bad times before without trying to spend our way out. Besides, we don't have any ready cash to give Lafitte for his block," Stephen stated.

After years of dealing with the negative position that Stephen always took on an issue, Jim was ready for this one. "I hear the market for slaves in Texas is strong and getting stronger.

The Other Rose of Texas

The land is prime and a lot of people are planting cotton and cane. I've seen the shipments on the docks in New Orleans."

Jim looked directly at his kid brother and added "We may be able to take over Lafitte's block in Galveston, or open one of our own, without paying him anything. That way we can start making money immediately. We might even find a few head down there for your breeding program, if Maw doesn't mind."

Stephen jumped to his feet and glared at his brothers as all three laughed out loud. "Damn you Jim," he said.

Jim had regained some of his old swagger and was feeling good about himself as he continued, "I need to go and take a look to decide and I need financing for the trip."

He did not bother to inform his brothers that, for him, seeking a new market for slaves during the trip would be secondary. What he wanted was to investigate and explore in Texas, to see if there might be a different kind of life for him there, on a different path, in a different place.

Therefore, when the vote was taken everyone but Stephen favored the trip and supported a promise to reimburse his expenses.

Immediately after the meeting Jim walked down and found Sam alone in his shack.

"I'm going to Texas, Sam, and I think you better go along."

"Where bouts is that, Master Jim?"

"It's in Mexico, across the Sabine River to the west. If you go with me, you won't have to worry about Stephen making you take your clothes off in public," Jim said and laughed until he bent over.

Sam grinned as Jim continued.

"The look on Stephen's face when Maw walked in on you must have been a sight. I'll bet it was like that time she caught him behind the barn with that sheep. He must have nearly wet his pants. I hear she called him a voyeur, that's someone who likes watching naked people together."

Sam smiled, still without comment.

"Seriously Sam, we better get you out of here. I've never seen Stephen in such a state. Usually he is just words, but if he can get at you, I think you will have to break his neck to keep him from hurting you."

73

"Do you think he gonna hurt Bettie or Aurora?" Sam asked.
"I think Maw and Rez will watch over them."
"How soon we goin?"
"As soon as we can pack up."

Part II - 1830 - 1835

Chapter 6

Jim Bowie entered Texas with a new feeling of optimism. The moment he crossed out of the United States, he gave himself permission to be a new man, a man without a past, a man with a bright future in a new world, no longer obliged to be or do what others expected.

This is how Bowie, with his slave Sam, their horses and pack mules, and the strong scent of pine trees in his nostrils, rode into Nacogdoches on a beautiful February day in 1830.

Bowie would begin his exploration of Texas by trying to bring Sam into Mexico as his slave. His bankers had told him this was the place to try that.

"They're gonna make us into Mexicans here," was all he told Sam as they entered army headquarters.

"My name is Bowie and this man is my slave. I would like to live in Texas," he announced.

"You may do so, Senor Bowie. You must pledge allegiance to Mexico here and join the catholic church in the parish where you settle," the Mexican army major said.

"Good, where do I sign?"

"Unfortunately, your slave may not do the same."

"What do you mean, Senor?"

"I mean that, in Mexico, slavery is not legal."

Jim had heard that bribery of public officials was routine in Mexico, so he tried that approach. "Major, it would be worth a lot to me if I could have my man with me. Could you not make an exception to the law for me?"

"I'm sorry, I cannot. No slaves are allowed."

"But I have friends who say they have done this."

"I am sorry, Senor; you have been misinformed."

Bowie was becoming concerned that he might have to take Sam back home. Had he been misinformed? Then he had another idea.

"What if this man were not my slave, and he wanted to live in Texas of his own free will?"

"That would be a different situation, Senor. Let us say you have a written contract with this man to work as your servant, and you plan to live within the state of Coahuila y Tejas. In that case, there would be no problem for either of you."

"Thank you, major. What I meant to say earlier is that my name is Bowie, and this is my valet, Sam."

After becoming Mexican citizens by swearing and signing their allegiance, Jim and Sam took a good road due south. After forty-seven days and a steam-powered ferry ride across the Bolivar Roads of the Gulf of Mexico, they arrived on the east end of Galveston Island.

* * *

Bowie planned to spend a few weeks in Galveston relaxing and observing daily commerce. Preferring to avoid recognition and contact with local society, he signed the hotel register, "John Smith, New Orleans."

The morning of the second day, remembering the location of the slave blocks from a previous visit, Bowie left the hotel and walked east with Sam on a street everyone called The Strand, after another street in London.

The early April weather on the Island was almost ideal. The humidity was still low and quite bearable. Perspiration was evaporated from the body quickly by a stout, tropical sea-breeze, even from the glistening, black bodies of hundreds of slaves who loaded and unloaded the shallow draft, sailing vessels tied up at the wharfs on the bay side of the island. If slavery was illegal in Mexico, it was not apparent here.

Traffic on Galveston Bay was brisk. By day, the ships arrived to deliver all manner of consumer goods, building materials, and farming tools. They departed with cargos, mostly of cotton, and some sugar cane, and rice.

The Other Rose of Texas

Jim knew that at night, an occasional slave ship was berthed and quickly unloaded.

At the slave block, Jim asked around and was directed to Lafitte's man.

"Yes sir, Mister Bowie, Mister Lafitte said you was coming. How can I help you?"

"Tell me about your operation," Jim replied.

"Well, each broker has different days of the week," he told Bowie. "We hold the Lafitte auctions twice a week, every Wednesday and Saturday, beginning an hour after sunrise and again two hours before sunset."

"You mean you let other slavers use your block?"

"The city owns the blocks. Anybody can buy time."

"How about sales volume?"

"We average about ten head per auction, many more when one of our ships docks. Lately we're seeing more planters bring slaves here to trade with each other. I collect our commissions either way."

After Lafitte's agent promised to send word to Bowie about his next ship load of slaves, Jim turned to Sam and said, "Let's go find some seafood."

They were walking back west on The Strand when Jim saw a crowd gathered ahead at Sixth street. When they were closer, he heard shouting and the periodic crack of a whip.

When he saw what was happening, Bowie told Sam to go on back to the hotel alone, just a block further, "quickly and quietly."

Sam obeyed and Jim watched until he entered the hotel.

Then, turning and standing behind the gathered men, Jim's height enabled him to see over them and look at something he had never seen before, not even in New Orleans. A stocky man dressed in dirty homespun was cracking a whip near the bare buttocks of five black women.

The women were naked and shackled, their wrists tied loosely to a hitching post. One of the women held her head back and screamed, though the man never touched the skin of any of them with his whip.

"What's going on?" Jim asked the man in front of him.

"Oh that's just Wade showin' off the lot he brung for the auction this afternoon," the bystander replied, then turned his face toward Bowie and grinned. "He only brings young ones with big teats."

"Does the law let him get away with this in public, in daylight?"

"The block operators don't show em naked long enough to suit Wade, so he does this to kind of advertise. Besides, slavery ain't legal, so they ain't no laws about it."

This was the first time in years that Jim had encountered the cruelty he used to see every-day, as a slaver. Yet he could not recall ever seeing people gather on a street anywhere and seem to enjoy watching others, even slaves, endure abuse and humiliation. "Is the rest of Texas like this?" he wondered.

His appetite for food was gone and his stomach ached a little as he walked back to the hotel, remembering that he was in Texas to try to escape life as a slaver for good, and considering that a way out might prove harder to find than it was to seek.

* * *

On the fourth Saturday after arriving in Galveston, Lafitte's man sent word that their restored brig, the General Victoria, had docked with a load of slaves. Bowie had their horses delivered to the hotel just after breakfast.

Feeling a little annoyed that it had been necessary to wait so long for a Lafitte vessel to arrive, but well refreshed and a little restless, he planned to observe the morning auction then ride out to explore the west end of the island.

At outdoor slave auctions, Bowie liked to stay mounted and take a position behind the crowd, to give himself a panoramic view of the proceedings. However, after taking that position on this morning, he dismounted. Handing his reigns to Sam, he said, "Sam, you stay here. I'm going to ask when the auction will start."

Bowie had walked almost beyond summoning distance from Sam when he heard a man shout, "Get off that horse, you black bastard. No buck is gonna look down at me from no horse."

The Other Rose of Texas

He turned around in time to see a man grab Sam's leather belt and drag him from his horse. Sam hit the ground hard. His hand opened, and the reins of Bowie's horse slipped out. Then both horses reared and ran.

Jim was instantly angry with himself for leaving Sam alone.

During his first long stride back to Sam, Jim pulled his knife from a leather scabbard under his long coat. He wanted the knife handy, in case someone pulled a weapon on him. In a second, he was halfway back to Sam, and he could see that the abuser was standing off-balance with his right-boot on Sam's neck.

Then he saw the man's face. It was the man called Wade, the man on the street with the whip from the second day.

He knew that, even from Sam's penned position, his tremendous strength could have freed him, but the sight of a black man making an aggressive move against a white-man, even to defend himself, would have incited mob rule and probably an immediate lynching.

Events had happened very fast, and Bowie thought that Sam might still be dazed and reflecting on how he had ended up on the ground. Regardless of the reason, Jim felt thankful that Sam had not yet moved.

Then Sam no longer need to move because, at that moment, the abuser's own neck seemed to snap when the weight of the knife in Bowie's hand, multiplied by the velocity of Bowie's powerful right arm, impacted the back of his head, just below his knowledge knot. The man's boot on Sam's neck rose three feet in the air above him, and Wade's body tumbled through the air. When it hit, it skidded to a stop, face down in the sand, and lay in a heap.

The crowd was quiet. As Bowie reached down to help Sam up, he said, "This man is a friend of mine."

As he returned his knife to its scabbard, a short man in a blue frock coat murmured, "Look at that knife, that must be Jim Bowie."

"He's still breathin'," another man said. Some of the men in the crowd had rolled Bowie's victim over on his back. Wade did seem to be breathing, but his eyes were closed.

Within minutes, a man wearing the uniform of a Mexican army captain arrived. He walked over to the booted man on the ground, knelt beside him, rose and said in English, "Looks like his neck may be broke."

Then he turned to Jim and said, "I hear your name is Bowie."

"That's right."

"You know, Mister Bowie, around here we don't damn near kill a man just for bad treatin' a Indian or a slave."

"I'll tell you, Captain; this negro man here is my servant and my friend, not my slave. Besides, I thought slavery was illegal in these parts."

The captain's eyes opened wider.

"Estoy en el hotel de la ciudad," Bowie said in perfect Spanish, then turned his back on the captain and walked away.

Bowie and Sam found their horses at a water trough up The Strand toward their hotel. However, instead of riding along the beach as planned, they returned to Jim's rooms where Bowie wrote a letter to his brothers outlining the progress of his trip, mainly to remind them of their pledge of money. A few sentences were enough to do that.

"So far, I am of two minds about this place. The market for slaves seems fairly strong and growing, but I am not certain that Lafitte has anything to sell. The city owns the block, and we can operate on different days from him without asking Lafitte's permission. All we need is suppliers. I am leaving Galveston soon for San Felipe to look into the political future for slavery in Texas."

* * *

The following day, the Mexican captain called at the hotel. He informed Bowie that Sam's abuser did not have a broken neck. He said that, if Bowie contributed toward the man's medical bill, the altercation would be forgotten by all. Bowie surmised that most of his money would remain with the captain, but handed over a draft on his New Orleans bank for twenty-five dollars.

However, to avoid feeling completely cheated, Bowie gave the captain some advice to pass on to Wade with his share of the money. "When you pay him, I want you to tell that cowardly bastard that I have seen Sam hold a six foot gator by the snout with one hand and tear off its legs with the other. You can't always be sure that oppression will vouchsafe forbearance. He is lucky that Sam held his temper."

"Gracias, Senor, Bowie, I will tell him." The captain bowed slightly then turned to walk out before saying, "I hope that I have not made a bad impression on you."

Lost in thought, Jim did not respond to the captain's parting words.

Normally, Bowie was close with his money and would have argued a little before surrendering it, but now he was deep in thought and relieved to be free of worry about the man he attacked.

He was also puzzled about becoming so violent; he had not experienced that much rage since the sandbar fight. He could have simply talked the man into releasing Sam, and he wondered why he had not.

That afternoon, Bowie visited a second-floor veranda overlooking the street where he ordered a brandy to enjoy with a cigar. Rummaging through a stack of newspapers and magazines, he noticed a six-month-old copy of The New York Courier and Enquirer with a front-page story about him and a block-print of his distinctive knife. The headline read, "Famed Weapon of the Famous Killer."

"No wonder I was recognized by the locals yesterday," he murmured.

Within minutes, he heard the voice of a boy hawking the local single sheet newspaper, "Crazed Knife Fighter Injures Local Man," over and over.

Feeling like a fool for thinking he could get away from his reputation, Jim returned to his room and had his dinner served there.

***

The next morning Sam was summoned from his room in the stable to Jim's hotel room. When he arrived Sam found breakfast waiting on a table.

"I feel bad about what has happened to you here so I thought we would eat together and talk about it," Jim said and motioned for Sam to sit down.

Dean Kirkpatrick

Sam sat, his hands folded in his lap, feeling anxious.

"Go ahead and eat Sam," Bowie said as he picked up his own knife and fork.

"I was hoping the folks in Texas would be friendlier, especially toward their slaves, and I still hope they will be more considerate outside of Galveston."

Chewing his food, Sam nodded silently. He was recalling similar hopes he had when Jim told him they would be making the trip to Texas. He remembered his delight at learning that he was going to get a good look at Texas and Mexico without the risks a runaway slave would face. Now his optimism had faded.

"And I'll do my best to protect you from any more abuse," Jim added.

"Yes sir Master Jim. I'm thankin' you for that."

When they finished eating Jim moved the dishes to a nearby breakfront and spread a map before them on the table.

"Do you remember a man we met in New Orleans about seven years ago named Stephen Austin?"

"Yes sir, I thinks I does."

"Well, he lives in Texas now at a place called San Felipe, and we're going there to see him."

"Yes sir," Sam observed.

Pointing at their place on the map with his right index finger he said, "We're here in Galveston."

Then his finger moved across an area with nothing drawn on it except a single crooked line going north, that ran past the names, San Felipe and Austin's Colony, "and this is where we're going, along the Brazos River," he added.

"This is virgin land that I want to see and we only have two problems. First there is no trail. We rode down here over roads and pine-needle trails, but this time we'll be breaking trail through open country covered with overgrown brush and cactus."

"That be harder," Sam observed, covertly patronizing his owner.

"That's why I got us these chaps," Jim said, reaching under the bed and handing Sam a thick cow-hide garment that resembled pants. "These will keep your trousers from getting ripped up."

"Thank you Master Jim."

"The other problem is Indians."

"What is Indians, Master Jim?" Sam asked, feigning ignorance.

"They are red skinned savages that travel in groups and kill everyone they see."

Sam had read about Indians in the New Orleans Library books that he checked out using Jim's card, and he thought his master's description of them a little extreme.

"We'll have to look for sign and be careful so they don't see us."

Sam felt more curious than afraid.

"After San Felipe, we'll go to San Antonio de Bexar," Jim said, following another line on the map with his finger. "Over this road."

"Looks like a heap of ridin' Master Jim."

"In San Antonio I'll decide where we go next."

"Yes sir."

"Now, let's go down and load up the supplies I bought."

"I can do that myself Master Jim."

"We'll go together. I'm not taking any more chances with these lunatics here."

The sun was barely up the following day, in a cloudless sky, when they mounted their horses and headed for the ferry to the mainland that embarked from the north side of the island. The stern wheel steamer churned the shallow bay dirty brown as it carried Bowie, Sam, their horses and mules smoothly across the two miles of calm water.

For the first time during their journey Sam felt unsure of their fate.

*   *   *

A hazard that Jim had not anticipated proved more threatening than Indian attack. After the sunny crossing of Galveston Bay, Jim Bowie and Sam lost more than four days crossing the winding Brazos River five times. Swollen from heavy spring rains each crossing was made treacherous by fast currents.

By the time they arrived at the home of Stephen F. Austin, Bowie was ready for some dry ground and shelter. He was there to get Austin's take on the future of slavery in Texas for his report to his brothers. He was confident, if any American could accurately predict that future, it was Austin.

In their late twenties when they first met, at a New Orleans ball in early 1823, each had recently lost his father. Austin, carrying on with the work of his father, Moses, was in the city to organize financing for his first Texas colony.

Their first encounter included a lengthy discussion of slavery during which Austin, though morally opposed to it, tactfully agreed with Bowie's argument that slavery was necessary for success in an agricultural economy.

Ever the diplomat, Austin now received Bowie and Sam graciously into his home. He offered Bowie a room in his double pen log house and instructed his house-keeper to find indoor accommodations for Sam. That evening, Bowie and Austin dined on smoked pork-ribs, roastin' ears, and fresh tomatoes, in a room where Austin was sure their conversation would not be overheard.

"What are you doing in Texas, Jim?"

"I'm a Texan now, myself, Stephen. Sam and I came in through Nacogdoches, and we took the oath."

"You mean they let you bring a slave in with you?"

"No, Sam swore too. He came in as a freeman, but he's still my property outside Mexico."

"So, are you planning to settle in my colony? You know you will both have to join the Catholic church to do that."

"We may look into that later, Stephen. Right now, I'm here just to look around and see what opportunities might exist for me and my brothers."

"Do you mean to trade in slaves, Jim?"

"That's one possibility, but not the only one. There's land trading and raising cattle, and of course, there's planting."

"What would you plant?"

"Cotton is what we know best, but the land I've seen so far isn't suitable for it. Where is all that cotton I saw in Galveston coming from?"

"A little of it comes from southwest of here, but the best place for a man to grow cotton is further north, that is if he can keep his scalp. But won't you need slaves for cotton?"

Jim was trying not to grin at Austin. He knew he had come to talk about slavery and now he sensed that Stephen knew it too, all along. Jim felt amused that his friend had given him the perfect opening, as if reading a line from a script.

"I suppose we will. Do you think Mexico will ever allow open slavery like we have in Louisiana?"

"You know how I feel about that personally, Jim, but I also realize that none of my colonists want to work for wages for somebody else. So I guess slavery will have to be the answer here too."

"Where is the manpower coming from now?"

"From slaves. Believe it or not, I tried to get slavery legalized in my colonization law but, Mexico City would not accept it. However, they were willing to provide a way around the law against it."

"And how is that working for you?"

"It works the same way that you brought Sam in. As long as the slaves swear loyalty to Mexico, you can bring them in as indentured servants, and unless you tell them, they never know they are not slaves anymore. They still work for you, you can still buy and sell them on the block in Galveston, and they are still your property outside Texas."

"What about chattel with the banks though?"

"What do you mean?"

"I know the banks in New Orleans won't accept anything as loan collateral that they can't repossess, and the Texas banks probably won't consider indentured servants as collateral in the first place."

"I see what you mean."

Feeling pleased with himself for making a point so solid that Austin had to agree, Jim reinforced it.

"You need to legalize slavery to facilitate financing if you expect business in Texas to grow."

But Austin took another tack and Jim felt deflated.

"Well, I'm not optimistic about that, and even if it was sanctioned by one administration, the next one might repeal it. Leadership and philosophy change pretty often down there. However, when it comes to slavery, I am certain about one thing. You need to be careful about discussing it. If the wrong people get the idea that you are in Texas to promote it, they will run you out, or lock you up."

"I know and I'll be careful. I appreciate the advice."

"So where do you go from here?"

"I have letters of introduction to Senores Seguin and Veramendi in San Antonio de Bexar. I guess Sam and I will head out in a few weeks, after we look at some of that cotton country you mentioned. That is, providing there is a place around here where we can stay for a while."

"You know you are welcome here, Jim. Both of you. But when you do head west, it would be best for you to travel with a group, in case you encounter Comanches. If you are interested, there is a traveling party stopping here now on their way to Bexar and Saltillo. I'll introduce you, and I'll give you a letter of introduction to Andrew Ponton too. Gonzales would make a good stop on the trail to Bexar, and Andrew is my alcalde there."

"Thanks, Stephen. I owe you."

"Let me give you one more piece of advice, Jim."

Saying this, Austin reached into a stack of papers on his desk and, after handing Bowie the latest copy of The New Orleans Bee newspaper, he continued, "This came yesterday."

The headline read, "Deadly Knife Claims Galveston Victim."

Reacting to the copy, Jim said, "I didn't kill him. I didn't even cut him. I just hit him real hard."

"I know. I read the article. What I'm saying is, watch your back. You're getting pretty well-known, and some young hot-head may want to start building a reputation on your grave."

* * *

The next-day, Austin introduced Jim Bowie to the William Wharton family, Isaac Donoho, and C.K. Ham, the sojourners he mentioned the previous evening, and they invited Jim to dinner with their group.

"We're planning to depart for San Antonio on July twentieth, Mister Bowie. We will stop along the way to examine the suitability of the land for farming, and expect to reach San Antonio around the first of October. Then we will continue on to Saltillo. You and your slave are welcome to travel with us, if you wish. By the way, I think you know my good friend, Governor Houston, late of Tennessee."

"That's very kind of you Mister Wharton. I think we will join your party, at least as far as Bexar, and yes, I do know Sam Houston; we met on a riverboat a couple of years ago."

When Wharton made introductions at his table, there were smiles and nods of approval all around it, especially from three young women, who turned out to be unmarried daughters, one from each family.

"Mister Wharton, I notice you folks brought a few slaves with you. Do you mind if I ask you about how you plan to use them?"

"I wouldn't mind a bit, Mister Bowie, if you wouldn't mind telling us a little about that famous knife of yours."

Jim felt a little embarrassed. He preferred not talking about himself, especially when he sensed that people were seeing him as some kind of superior being. But the ink was on the page, he thought, and the stories about him were rapidly becoming folklore.

"Well, there isn't much to tell, except to say that most of what the newspapers say about it is exaggeration. A few years ago, my brother gave me this knife for protection."

Bowie reached under his coat, removed his knife from its scabbard, handed it to Wharton handle first, then continued his comments. "I got used to carrying it, and now I use it to cut kindling for the fire, to butcher game, and for many other things. But I can tell you, this blade will never touch a man again, if I can help it."

"It's quite a knife, sir," Wharton said as he handed it to Donoho. "Now, what can I tell you about our plans?"

"I guess I'm mainly interested to know why you came to Texas and what you plan to do, now that you're here."

"That's pretty simple, Mister Bowie . . ."

Bowie interrupted Wharton, saying, "Please call me Jim."

"Then you must call me Wil, and he is Isaac, and he is Caiaphas," Wharton said, pointing to the other men. "As I was saying, I'm a lawyer, originally from Virginia. We all came here from Tennessee to find some good land to farm. We plan to go in together. I brought my slaves with me, and my partners plan to send for theirs when we get settled."

"Do you know what crops you will raise?"

"We saw some land just below Harrisburg that is ideal for raising rice, and farther south we saw some that would be good for sugar cane. We understand from Austin that the best land for cotton is pretty far north. We are going to Saltillo to find out from the government where grant land is available, before we decide what to raise."

"What about the status of your slaves? Are you willing to free them and hire them back? You know the banks here won't loan you money on them."

"Jim, I'm enough of a politician to believe we can get that slavery law changed, if there are enough of us who work at it."

Bowie liked Wharton and his ideas, and they continued to talk long after all of the others said goodnight.

Finally, Jim had risen to leave when a young man emerged from the shadows behind Wharton and began to speak. He was equal to Jim in size and similar in stature.

"Your women will na be safe if you let this bastard travel with us, Mister Wharton. I have heard about the things he does to them."

Jim thought of Austin's warning and felt himself growing tense.

Wharton stood and turned to face the intruder. "You'll have to forgive Alexander here, Jim, he's a young Scot I hired to drive a wagon, but he acts like he's the wagon-master."

"Where did you hear about me young fella," Jim asked.

"I've read those stories. The ones about you and those whores in New Orleans. King of the whores they called you. I saw how you looked at our girls and how they looked at you. You think all women are whores."

Wharton responded, "Don't pay him any mind, he's sweet on the Donoho girl and he has let his Scottish temper get the better of him. Now you apologize to Mister Bowie, he is my friend and I won't have any more of this."

The young man clinched both fists and stepped toward Bowie. Instinctively, Jim reached inside his coat to draw his knife and realized it was lying on a table, ten feet away from him.

Reacting to Jim's motion the challenger scowled and said, "I thought so Bowie. You're na a man without that knife. Put it aside and let's see who the real man is here."

"My knife is over there. I don't need a weapon to take care of you, boy."

Jim's Scottish temper was up too. As he was removing his coat, Wharton stepped between the two men. "You're fired Alexander. Gather your belongings and get out now."

The young man looked at both men and frowned, saying, "I'll see you again knife fighter. Maybe next time there won't be anybody to protect you." Then he walked back into the shadows.

"I'm sorry Jim," Wharton said. "I'll bet you get a lot of that."

"More and more," Jim replied.

* * *

"I wouldn't go up there alone," Sam heard Austin tell Bowie, "and neither would you, if you had seen the things I have. It's not just the Comanche. None of the tribes want us here and they kill every man they can catch, in a horrible way as a warning for the rest of us. They turn the women and children they capture into beasts of burden and work them to death."

Despite Austin's warning, Bowie and Sam spent the next few weeks exploring the land to the north. Just above San Felipe, the Brazos and Colorado rivers formed what was almost a delta.

"We'll ride between the rivers," Bowie told Sam.

Most of the land they crossed was unsettled, especially outside the limits of Austin's colony. But Sam had to agree when Bowie said, "The land looks mighty good for planting cotton and the rivers and creeks look like they get enough rain to grow it. I think we can bring the fertilizer up one of the rivers like we do back home."

Venturing well into Indian country they killed small game and cooked it during the day to avoid building fires that might be seen at night. Nor did they use a fire for warmth, as the weather remained warm and dry.

When they began to see Indian sign, they turned around and rode back toward San Felipe, pacing themselves to arrive in time to depart with the Wharton party. They were still a hundred miles north when they came upon a grove of oak trees surrounding a small log house.

The house was ablaze and the dismembered remains of what appeared to be two black men, were strewn about the grounds.

"We ought to bury them," Jim said to Sam.

"What we gonna dig with, Master," Sam replied.

"You're right. But we can at least cremate them, so the varmints can't eat them."

"You mean burn them?" Sam asked.

Sam wondered if Bowie would be so quick to burn the remains of white men, instead of giving them a proper burial.

"Yes."

"Yes sir," Sam nodded and both men began throwing body parts into the fire.

A first arrow whizzed by Jim's right arm and lodged in a lower log of the house wall, the stone arrow-head completely buried. A second arrow and then a third flew at them but missed as Sam and Jim sprang for their horses and guns.

With a loud scream a naked red-skinned man came running toward them, holding a bone handled knife in each hand. Bowie side-stepped him, and as the Indian continued on toward Sam, Bowie drew his own knife and buried it in the man's back and through his heart, driving him to the ground.

As the savage went down, one of his knives cut Sam's right chap leg, but did not pierce it. Now the Indian lay motionless.

"Did you hear someone crying jus' before the arrow come," Sam asked.

The Other Rose of Texas

"No."

"I think I did," Sam added. "Over there," he said and pointed in the direction from which the Indian came.

At that moment a little negro boy toddler walked into the clearing, rubbing his eyes with crooked index fingers. Then he looked up and, seeing the two men, he began screaming, "ma-ma, ma-ma," and ran back into the woods.

Sam, then Jim followed the sound until they found the baby draped over the naked body of a black woman staked out spread-eagle on the ground. When she looked at Jim she began to scream too. However, when she saw Sam she stopped screaming and seemed calmer.

"Praise be, praise be," she repeated as Sam untied her ankles and wrists.

Then she sat up, clutched the little boy, and cried for several minutes. She stopped crying when Jim returned with a shirt and trousers for her to wear. She put on the clothing and after that she began talking.

"We was clearin' the land, cuttin' down trees and burnin' em when they come. They was five. They killed my husband and his brother outright. They made me watch while they chopped em up and ate they hearts."

Sam felt nauseas. He wondered if the telling was somehow therapeutic for the woman. "Why else would she want to relive the horror she saw?" he thought.

"They all left but one after they took what they liked from the house and set it on fire. I guess the one stayed for me," she concluded and began to clutch her son and cry again.

"What were you all doing all the way up here alone?" Jim asked. Didn't they tell you about the Indians?"

"We come from Mississippi and all we knowed is cotton. We wanted to get a little land and plant, but we didn't have no papers."

"You mean you are runaways?" Jim asked.

"You a slave catcher mister? You fixin to take me back there?"

"No woman. You don't need to worry about that. Now go on and tell your story."

"Well pretty soon our money near run out and we couldn't find work."

All of Sam's questions about making a life in Texas for he and Bettie were being answered by this women and he did not like what he heard.

"Then somebody tol' us 'bout the land up here, that nobody much cared 'bout who was on it, so we spent the money we still had on supplies and seed and come up here."

"Weren't you afraid of the Indians?" Bowie asked.

"We heard they was killin white folks, but we was hopin' they would leave us dark folks be. All we wanted was to live free and raise a little food and cotton, so we decided to trust the will of Jesus. Praise be."

"Well you can't stay here now," Jim said. We can take you and your boy back with us to San Felipe. I think you can find work there. Do you know where I can find a shovel?"

After burying what remained of the two black men and the body of the Indian, the party departed for a week long ride back to civilization.

With Bowie leading, the woman rode the Indian's horse and carried the boy. Occasionally she turned and smiled at Sam, riding behind her.

Her smile reminded him of Portia and Sam wondered if there would be time for them to be together before he had to ride west.

Chapter 7

The Wharton party, Jim, and Sam made the eighty mile ride from San Felipe to Gonzales in just over two weeks. Jim sent Sam on ahead with instructions to camp with the group on the east bank of the Guadalupe River. After introducing himself to Andrew Ponton, Austin's man there, he checked into the only room of the local hotel and took a bath.

The next morning, Jim rode out to eat breakfast with Wharton. They had finished and were talking U.S. politics when Bowie heard a voice behind him.

"Hey, Bowie, where's that bloody knife of yours?"

The voice had a Scottish accent and Jim realized it came from Alexander, the wagon driver that Wharton fired in San Felipe. Without turning his head or rising, Bowie replied, "It's at the hotel. I don't carry it all the time."

Jim felt exasperated but he tried to sound calm and soothing. "Would this knife business never end?" he thought.

"Well, you better bloody get it cause I have one just like it that I'm gonna stick in your bloody gut."

Then Wharton whispered, "About eight feet directly behind you. Knife in his right hand raised high. I think he's drunk."

"Alright, let me go get mine so we will both have one."

As he said the words, Bowie stood, whirled, lowered his head and ran at his adversary, planting his head in the man's stomach so hard that he retched and folded up. The reactive jerk of his right arm brought his knife down toward Bowie's back. In an instant, Jim stopped the motion by grasping the raised wrist with his left hand and driving the rosy nosed man backward until he fell on his back, dazed and semi-conscious.

Wharton stood, walked over, and picked up the knife that the Scotsman had dropped. "Looks just like yours. Wonder where he got it."

Jim produced his own knife and held it beside the copy. "Yes, it does. Must have cost him something. You know, I'm getting pretty sick and tired of all these knife-smiths making a living off of my name."

"Want me to get the alcalde?"

"No, I don't need any more stories goin around. Just let him sober up and give him back his knife after I'm gone."

Bowie was feeling very discouraged.

"You mean you're leaving?" Wharton asked.

"I think that's best. Alexander may have friends and I don't need any more trouble."

"What about the Indians?"

"I'll be careful. We haven't seen any sign, so I think we'll be alright."

"Take care of yourself my friend."

"I'll see you in Bexar and maybe go on to Saltillo with you," Jim said.

After crossing the Guadalupe he and Sam followed a good trail almost due west. Riding along Jim reflected on his hope of finding a new and better life in Texas.

"What was that?" he thought. "Oh yes, I'll be a new man, without a past. I'll find a bright future in a new world. No longer will I be obliged to do or be what others expect."

Now it seemed ridiculous, almost comical, he thought. "So far my past has run me out of every town I have visited, my bright future is the sun in my eyes as I keep riding and hoping the people are different in the next town, and I may as well walk around with my knife in my hand because they all expect to see me cut somebody."

* * *

Bowie and Sam rode into San Antonio de Bexar on the sunrise rays of an October Wednesday that promised to be hot and humid.

Already dressed for his call on Vice-governor Veramendi, Bowie wore a green frock coat over an ivory colored silk shirt, black cravat, and tan waistcoat and breeches, all of the latest continental style in New Orleans. His knife was well hidden under his coat, but still easily accessible.

The town was referred to by most simply as Bexar, properly pronounced "bay-har" but Anglicized to the single syllable "bear." Bowie and Sam entered Bexar from the east, passing through the cottonwood tree-lined Alameda. On their right, the first structure they passed was the former Mission San Antonio de Valero, known to most, as the Alamo. Crossing the San Antonio River over the Calle del Potrero footbridge, they continued east past numerous adobe walls and buildings, to Soledad Street. The morning air smelled of fried breakfast and bowel movements.

Soledad was the eastern boundary of an open area called Main Plaza, which marked the geographic center of Bexar. Like most of Bexar, it was without grass or trees. At Soledad, the two men turned right and quickly arrived at the Veramendi Palace, an "L" shaped hacienda edging on the San Antonio River.

The Palace wall on Soledad contained five windows and handsomely carved wooden double-doors that were large enough, when opened, for a mounted rider to pass through. Smaller, pedestrian doors were inset in the center of the equestrian doors.

Upon arrival, Sam dismounted, walked to the door, and swung the brass knocker, striking the wood three times. When a servant opened the door, Bowie addressed him from horseback. "Me llamo James a Bowie. Estoy de aqui ver a Gobernador Veramendi."

"Espere por favor Señor a Bowie."

Soon the servant opened both equestrian doors, and Bowie rode through to the courtyard. Sam walked behind, leading his horse, leaving the pack mules tied to a rail outside.

Inside, Sam took charge of both horses, and Bowie followed the servant down a flag-stone walkway bordered by large terra cotta pots containing yucca and cactus. At a table under three enormous cypress trees by the river Juan-Martin-Del-Carmen Veramendi-Granados, vice-governor of the Mexican state of Coahuila y Tejas, was having his morning coffee.

When Bowie first saw him, he wondered if Juan was as splendidly dressed every morning. Veramendi's full beard and mustache completed the distinguished countenance that his formal morning coat suggested. A smallish man, his voice was authoritative yet kind.

"I have been expecting you Mister Bowie," Veramendi said in perfect English.

"It is an honor and a pleasure to meet your excellency," Bowie said, observing his host's du jour choice of English.

"Let us dispense immediately with the formal address. Please call me Juan. May I call you Jim?"

"Please do, Juan."

"May I offer you coffee, Jim, or something stronger?" Veramendi said and motioned toward a nearby cart.

"To be perfectly candid, Senor, I have heard that your local mezcal is very good for cutting through the trail dust."

"Pablo, mezcal para el Señor Bowie. To what does my country owe the honor of your visit, Jim?"

"Juan, I am now a citizen of Mexico, and I am here to explore the opportunities available in my new country."

"Allow me to ask you, Jim. The negro standing beside your horse, is he your slave?"

"He is my slave in the United States, yes, but I understand that he cannot be my slave here."

"Is it your plan to use Mister Austin's law to bring other negroes here in the same way that you brought this man?"

Bowie thought he must have looked surprised to Juan, because his host quickly added, "I apologize for being so abrupt, Jim, but I know of your reputation as a trader of slaves and your recent visit to Galveston, as well as your association with the pirate Lafitte."

"Do you know Lafitte, Juan?"

"I once loaned him money, which he did not repay."

"I'm sorry." Bowie feigned concern. He knew of many men that Lafitte had defrauded in this way and the news of it no longer interested him.

"Frankly, I was advised to not receive you by important people who spoke of the violence that usually follows in your wake.

They believe you are in Tejas to promote slavery. But I like to make my own appraisal of a man. It is not necessary for you to respond, but allow me to share a few thoughts for your consideration over time."

Bowie was amazed at how quickly his meeting with Juan had arrived at the matters he came to discuss. He was prepared for a long discussion, perhaps more than one, where each man would delicately probe for information about the other's interests and intent. Under the circumstances, he might have considered Juan a fool, or at least a bad negotiator, for revealing so much so soon, without gaining something in return, yet all Bowie could be certain of was that he liked this man very much.

"Please do, Juan."

"I think the time will come, and I hope it is soon, when all men of dark skin who were brought here from the United States will be given land and informed that they, and their women and children, are free citizens of Mexico."

Bowie looked concerned. He had not expected Juan to take such an extreme position.

"I know that this will cause a catastrophe for anyone who has invested heavily in slaves and brought them to Tejas, and I hope that you personally will not make that mistake. I also hope my words will not discourage your ambitions here, because I think there are many business opportunities in Tejas that will interest you, and many good people already here who are willing to be employed, so slaves will not be needed."

When his host spoke again, Bowie realized that Juan had carefully planned for his arrival in Bexar for some time. He felt out-maneuvered yet flattered.

"I have a specific proposition in mind for you, Jim, and its success would prove that I am right about what I believe. But for now, let us dispense with talk of business. I have a room ready for you and a place for your man, and I hope you will be a guest in my home for as long as you care to stay."

"Thank you, Juan. I am honored by your kind invitation."

"I have also organized a small dinner affair in your honor, con su permiso, for the evening of Saturday next."

"You are most kind, mi amigo."

Jim left his meeting with Veramendi feeling more valued and optimistic than he had since the last time he sat with Cecelia in his secret place.

* * *

Bowie spent Thursday walking around Bexar while Sam cleaned and pressed their trail-soiled clothes and cared for their horses and mules. Around town, Bowie introduced himself in Spanish simply as "James de los Estados Unidos", trying to delay public knowledge of his presence in Bexar as long as possible.

On Friday morning, still finely dressed with his knife scabbard concealed in the small of his back, he entered the San Fernando Cathedral, located on the south side of Main Plaza. A poorly dressed couple knelt on the steps to the chancel with another couple standing behind them and a black-robed man with a book standing before them. Obviously a wedding, Bowie took a seat in the nave to wait until it was over, and the priest was free to talk.

As the padre walked back up the aisle after escorting the wedding party out, Bowie stood. "My name is James, Father."

"I am Don Refugio de la Garza, the parish priest, Senor Bowie. I had word that you might be coming by."

"You have a beautiful cathedral, Father."

"Thank you. It was built by the hands of settlers who were sent here from the Canary Islands by King Philip the Fifth, almost a hundred years ago."

"Father, I am here because I wish to perfect my Mexican citizenship. I understand I need to join your church." Bowie handed over the documents he received in Nacogdoches.

"That is certainly possible, my son. Tell me, are you a baptized Christian?"

The Bowie boys had all been christened as babies, and their mother had included religious instruction as part of their education.

"Yes Father. I think it was done in a Methodist church."

"Very well. You may begin your catechism classes immediately. They will be followed by your initiation into the church, your confirmation, and first communion. With diligence, you should be a full member within six months."

"I had something a little quicker in mind." Bowie said and handed Father de la Garza a bank draft for five hundred dollars. "I hope this will help my new church."

"The poor will be grateful," the priest replied as he looked at the draft amount. "I think we can conclude the entire matter here this morning, Senor Bowie. Please follow me."

Before noon, with yet another official-looking document in his pocket, Bowie walked from the cathedral down Commerce Street to the footbridge and stood staring down at the river. Compared with most rivers, this one appeared as little more than a ditch or, at best, a creek. However, closer examination revealed that it was deeper than it first looked, and Bowie thought the loose soil of its steep banks might be difficult to climb, even for a horse.

Then he noticed a man wearing all black linen and a wide straw hat with a red band, fishing with a bamboo pole from the bank. He sat in the hot, noon-day sun, though there were shade trees close by. Bowie walked over to the man. "¿Cómo el pesquero hoy es?"

"I speak American, senor, and the fishing, she is not good."

Bowie was curious about how such a pitiful stream could contain any fish worth catching. "Where does the water come from, senor?"

"It comes from the holy grotto, about one league that way," the man replied, pointing north.

"What do you mean?"

"I mean it comes out of the ground and that is why is it so green."

Bowie had not realized before. Now, in direct sun-light, the water did appear green, almost the color of emerald.

"The color comes from the limestone formations under the holy grotto. The peons say it matches the color of the robe Our Lady wears. But they are mostly fools."

"Do you sometimes catch fish?"

"Si senor, I catch many things, but the day is hot and these fish are lazy."

"Do you earn your living this way?"

"No senor, I do not have to earn a living. People give me that which I need."

"And why do they do that, senor?"

"I am the seventh son of a seventh son, and I see and tell people things about themselves."

Bowie handed the man a peso coin. "Do you see anything about me?"

Laying his pole aside, the man accepted the coin, and then he stood facing the river. "Stand before me and look into my eyes."

Bowie stood about three feet in front of the man. As he did, the noon-day cannon was fired in the former mission.

"Ere ye be two score, a thing behind ye will loom largest before ye." As if possessed, the man spoke the words with a Scottish accent.

Bowie felt a sudden chill and gave the man a weak smile. "Gracias amigo, adios."

Thinking this had to be one of the most bazar experiences of his life, he walked back to the footbridge, then across it. He stood for a time looking at the Alamo, estimating the distance to it from the footbridge at about three hundred yards. He noticed the green, white, and red flag of Mexico flying from a pole above what appeared to be the main entrance. Unaware that the structure had housed a Mexican military garrison for years, he wondered why a catholic mission would fly a government flag.

Then he pondered the fisherman's prediction. He was pretty sure that two score meant forty, so whatever was coming would arrive within the next five years. But what single thing behind him would impact his future? His knife? The footbridge? The river? The mission? The flag?

Jim Bowie smiled again and turned toward the Veramendi Palace. Still mulling the fisherman's words, Jim looked for him as he walked, but the man had disappeared.

* * *

In the southern-most room of the Veramendi Palace, on his first Saturday afternoon in Bexar, Jim Bowie lay naked on his bed, smoking a New Orleans cheroute, while Sam laid out their formal clothes. The heat of the day was oppressive, dissipated only slightly by a breeze that entered the room through an eastern door transom, exited through a western window, and swirled the cigar smoke in French-curves in between.

At eight o'clock in the evening, the sun was well down when Bowie and Sam left the bedroom and walked a flag-stone path to the main parlor, two doors away. Sam walked a few feet behind Jim, carrying a rosewood case with brass hinges and padlocked brass hasp.

When Bowie entered the room, his focus was immediately drawn to an imposing eighteen-foot-high wall.

"It is, fossiliferous limestone," Juan said, shaking Jim's hand. "The panels are two-meter squares I had quarried from cliffs above the Colorado River to the north. The panels contain the shells and impressions left by millions of floral and faunal beings that have been trapped in the calcium carbonate for eons."

"Very impressive," Jim said.

"That wall is the principal reason why people call this residence a palace."

Still carrying the case, Sam walked to the left corner of the room beside the wall, turned, and stood awaiting direction from Bowie.

"My dear, this is Senor James Bowie," Juan continued, leading Jim toward her. "Senor Bowie, my wife."

A handsome woman a few years older than Jim, Maria-Josefa-Candida Navarro-De-Ruiz Veramendi-Granados wore a dark blue, off-shoulder gown that complimented her ample breasts. Her hair was pulled back and pinned up, behind a tiara ablaze with diamonds.

"Senor Bowie, it is a pleasure to meet you at last."

Curiously, during his comings and goings for days, Senora Veramendi was the first female member of the family that Bowie had met, or even seen.

"The pleasure is entirely mine, Senora, and may I thank you for the excellent accommodations that I have enjoyed here in your beautiful home."

"Con su permiso Senor, my husband informs me that your Spanish is excellent, but we all decided to practice our English upon you this evening. I hope that you do not consider this offensive."

Bowie smiled and nodded his approval.

When Bowie entered the room they all rose from their seats, even the women, as if they expected some kind of physical activity to ensue.

He had seen this before but had not yet decided if his reputation brought people to their feet, ready for action, or if he had unintentionally inherited his father's knack for making strangers feel afraid.

Taking his left arm, Senora Veramendi led him around the room and introduced him to the other guests.

"Senor James Bowie of the United States, I would like you to meet our Alcalde, Jose Salinas, and his wife, Theresa, and this is Commander Rafael Manchola of Presidio La Bahía, his wife, Marie, and sister, Antonia, and this is Juan Almonte of the City of Mexico."

Bowie and the other men bowed slightly at each introduction, and each lady curtsied. He was discussing the weather with Almonte when all other conversations around the room stopped. His back to the door, he turned his head slightly, then completely, and his body followed. Standing in the doorway, he saw one of the most beautiful women his thirty-five-year-old eyes had yet seen. Her dark hair hung in corkscrew curls over her green velvet, conical skirted gown.

Senora Veramendi quickly took Bowie's arm again, leading him and saying, "Let me introduce my eldest daughter, Ursula."

The pair practically walked over Juan Almonte, who lunged toward the doorway, trying to reach Ursula ahead of Bowie, and failing.

"Ursula, this is the famous Senor James Bowie."

"It is a pleasure, Senor."

Ursula curtsied, her eyes downcast, making her regal stature seem smaller, and dispersing her expensive Paris scent about the room.

"The pleasure is all mine, Senorita."

The Senora disconnected herself from Bowie, and then he bowed, took Ursula's gloved right hand, and kissed it. In her seemingly shortened state, Bowie felt that he towered over the young beauty.

The Other Rose of Texas

After both of their bodies straightened, Ursula stepped obliquely left, out of the doorway. Her gaze stayed down and she spoke no more.

"She does not need to talk," Jim thought, "all the men in the room have gathered around her and each woman has raised her ventilador to her mouth, probably to cover a catty remark."

The moment seemed awkward to Bowie, so he signaled Sam to bring the rosewood case to him. As Sam presented the case with both hands, Bowie retrieved the padlock key from his vest pocket. He unlocked it, then turned toward his host.

"Senior Veramendi, it is my pleasure to present this small token of my esteem and admiration to you." Sam opened the case to reveal a highly polished knife, similar to Jim's, but with an ivory handle, and brass cross-guard curled toward a deeply clipped point.

"Thank you, Senor Bowie. I have heard of your famous knife, and I will be proud to own this one."

Just then, a liveried butler stepped into the doorway and said, "La cena es servida".

Juan Veramendi rushed to his daughter's side and offered his arm. Following them, Bowie and the Senora, and the others in pairs, all made their way to the dining room.

The main wall of the dining room was made of the same limestone as the parlor wall, but was only twelve feet high. The room furnishings and the crystal, china, and sterling silver that decorated the long table were as fine as any Bowie had seen, even in New Orleans. He wondered which Veramendi had such discerning taste.

Bowie was seated to the right of his host, with Senor Salinas to the right of Senora Veramendi at the opposite end of the table. Ursula sat across the table from Bowie, two chairs down.

After the wine for the fish course was poured, Senior Salinas stood. "May I propose a toast to our new vice-governor, our host and good friend, Juan Veramendi."

All glasses were raised, then everyone began chatting. Apparently Ursula wanted to be heard, so she practically shouted when she said, "You are here to trade slaves, Senior Bowie?"

Bowie had been conversing with her father. He stopped in mid-sentence and stared at Ursula, his mouth slightly open.

"Is slavery not your business, senor?" she said more softly as the room became quiet.

Ursula seemed intent on proving that she was her father's daughter regarding the issue of slavery, and Bowie wished she would be less public about it. He was about to respond when Senora Veramendi spoke.

"Ursula! Senor Bowie, please forgive my daughter. She was born beneath the sign of Libra and is sometimes more outwardly expressive than we might wish."

Ursula lowered her eyes again, and her face turned red as she reacted to her mother's scolding.

"I apologize, senor," Juan added.

"Please Juan, your daughter has asked a fair question, and I don't mind giving her an honest answer," Jim said.

Bowie's feeling of surprise changed to gratitude when he considered that Ursula had afforded him the opportunity to earn some compassion from her father and possibly from others in the room. He wondered if she was performing for her father or trying to impress his guests as he chose the words of his response carefully.

"The answer to both questions is no. I am not in your country to trade slaves; therefore, my business in your country is not slavery. Since I came here, I have recognized many opportunities that I did not expect, and none of them involve slavery. Partly thanks to your father's good advice, I am seriously re-evaluating my interests."

The crisis passed, and the red was gone from Ursula's cheeks when she raised her face and briefly looked directly into Jim Bowie's eyes.

Bowie thought that Ursula's glance toward him had gone unnoticed. Then a comment by Juan Almonte, who was sitting directly across from her, changed his mind. "I find Ursula's directness most admirable and her topic most timely."

Jim had noticed Almonte studying him and Sam during the knife presentation. Now, listening to Almonte, Jim concluded that he had used a sterling intellect to overcome his Aztec lineage and peon-like features. Had he decided to use his wits to seize an opportunity to gain ground with Ursula, Jim conjectured?

The Other Rose of Texas

Almonte looked directly at Ursula as he started to speak again. Then he switched his gaze to Bowie.

"The north Americanos are attempting to corrupt the principal of liberty for all men that we fought for against Spain. I am happy to hear Senior Bowie say that he is not one of these corrupters, if he is sincere. Slavery is a despicable institution and a flawed economic practice. All the major nations around the world have condemned it, except the United States. We do not need or want it here."

Looking around the table, Bowie saw a look of approval on each face, especially Ursula's and her father's, and he felt a tinge of envy. Yet he felt confident that he could regain any stature he might have lost in the eyes of the Veramendis.

The important thing was he now had most of the answers he came to Texas to get. First, he had discovered that slavery had no future in Texas as long as it was a possession of Mexico, no matter how Stephen Austin might disguise it. Next, he had good prospects here. An important politician had practically adopted him and promised to offer him a bright future without the need for slaves, bought or sold. Finally, he had met a beautiful and spirited young woman who might turn out to be the best discovery of all.

Chapter 8

After cognac and cigars for the men in the dining room, sherry for the ladies in the parlor, and a polite amount of conversation when they rejoined, the dinner guests departed.

Ursula was in her room, already in her nightgown, when her mother entered without knocking. "I thought you had some sense, young lady, and then I witnessed your display of utter idiocy tonight. Have I not always taught you to flatter an eligible man, not challenge his values in public?"

Her mother's accusatory tone put Ursula in a defiant mood.

"What makes you think there were any eligible men in that room tonight?"

"I can see how you might feel so about that hyena Juan Almonte, but Senor Bowie is rich and handsome. He will soon be very important here."

" Senor Bowie is an old man. He must be as old as you."

"He told me he is thirty-two, and may I remind you, Maria Ursula, that your father is fourteen years my senior."

"What makes you think that he would consider marriage at his advanced age? He has escaped it so far."

"He was ready a year ago, but his intended died two weeks before the wedding. He said he wants a home and a family."

Although she was curious about this man, she wanted to avoid giving her mother the advantage of knowing it, so she tried to re-direct the conversation.

"You seem to know a lot about this man. How do you know so much?"

"He told me himself. He seems to be trying to win my regard."

"Then, if you find him so appealing, you take him to your bed. Don't try to put him in mine."

The Senora raised her hand as if to slap her impertinent daughter, then lowered it.

"Why do you hesitate? Are you afraid of leaving a mark on my face and making me less saleable to Senor Bowie?"

Ursula knew she had driven her mother to the limit of her patience when the Senora pushed her against the wall. Ursula felt her mouth fly open and a gust of air burst forth. Then the Senora pushed her again, this time with a question.

"Do you want me to tell your father that you are no longer chaste?"

"What do you mean?"

"I know you are not a virgin. I know of your affair with Rodrigo before his father sent him back to Spain, others do as well. Fortunately, this man Bowie is not among them, at least not yet, and I would urge you to lure him into a marriage, before he learns."

"You seem to care more about your own public embarrassment than my broken heart. I loved Rodrigo and he loved me. We wanted to make a child so his father would have to consent to our marriage."

"Unfortunately for you, all you made was a reputation that will prevent you from making a good marriage into a respectable family. Pay attention, my daughter, this Americano may be your last chance."

"How do you suggest I entice this Senor Bowie?

"I think you can find ways to do that."

"What if I do not want to marry him?"

"If I were you, I would first maneuver him to a point where such a choice will be relevant. After your marriage, you can take a lover, as I have. The important thing now is to get the proposal."

Ursula's mouth opened again in surprise. "I had no idea. Are you not afraid I will use that knowledge against you with father?"

"I think he already knows. Some years ago, your father's desire for me seemed to wane. Then I met a man in Tampico."

Ursula felt faint and sat on the edge of her bed, stunned by her mother's confession.

"I believe your father is not fool enough to think my frequent trips down there are because I like the beach. We have never spoken of it, but he encourages me to travel as I wish."

Ursula felt a sadness growing inside her. She did not know if it was for her mother, or from the thought of a similar fate for herself.

***

Bowie and the Senora were at breakfast the day following the dinner party, when Ursula, her duenna, and the other three Veramendi children appeared in black riding clothes.

During introductions all Bowie could think about was that Ursula looked as beautiful in the morning light as she had by candlelight the previous evening. He felt aroused by her for the second time.

"On Sunday the children ride for an hour or two then they change their clothes and we all go to mass," the Senora began explaining.

"Why do you not ride with us, Senior Bowie?" Ursula was quick to add with a faint smile.

"Yes, please senior," her brother Marco exclaimed.

"With pleasure Senorita," Bowie replied.

"Good," the Senora continued, "then we will make today special.

"In what way mama?" Juana, a sister asked

"You may ride a little longer today and when you finish you will ride to the holy grotto. Senior Bowie asked about it last evening and I have asked Father de la Garza to join us there for lunch so our guest can see where God gives birth to the river of Saint Anthony."

"That is very kind of you Senora," Jim observed. He felt flattered by the special attention. "Perhaps being a little famous has some advantages after all," he thought.

"And since the ground is consecrated," the Senora continued, "he will say mass for us so we need not go to the cathedral today."

When the riders departed, they were followed by two vaqueros carrying muskets and pistols. Bowie carried his Lancaster rifle, two pistols, and his knife. Since they would be riding north, they could be seen by Indians, and the sight of armed out-riders would discourage contact.

First, the group trailed east. At the footbridge, each rider dismounted and led his horse across it. When all reached the east side of the river, they re-mounted and rode north, passing in front of the west wall of the Alamo.

A dry, weather changing line had passed through Bexar earlier, and the morning air was cool and crisp. Ursula's hair began to play on the cool breeze when she cantered her horse. The allure of her beauty that began for Bowie the previous night was compounded by the glow of her ivory skin against the cloudless, blue sky. He wanted to spur his horse up beside her, look into her agate colored eyes, and begin the conquest of her body.

However, he knew he must wait. This was his first encounter with her siblings and his first exposure to a duenna. The diplomat in him dictated that he should win over the family before seducing its daughter. Soon, however, he could not resist and he maneuvered his horse up to the left of hers.

"Senorita, please tell me of this woman who rides with us this morning. I believe she is called a duenna."

"Yes Senior, her name is Consuelo and she is the cousin of my father. She lived in Veracruz and when her husband died she came to be duenna to me and my sisters."

"And what does this mean that she is your duenna?"

"She is like a chaperon, but more. She is supposed to prevent interaction between me and males who are not of my family."

"Like me?"

"Yes, like you Senior. And when she cannot prevent this interaction, she is supposed to at least prevent physical contact."

"Do you mean she would attack me if I touched you? Does she have a weapon hidden somewhere?"

Ursula threw her head back and laughed, and Bowie noticed her perfect white teeth for the first time.

"No Senior, you need not worry. There are ways that one may be touched when one wishes to be."

Bowie concluded that this ravishing young woman had mastered the art of the double-entendre and he was hearing one now.

As he was reflecting, Bowie felt a nudge and Consuelo pushed her horse between he and Ursula. Then, as if jealous of Bowie, eighteen-year-old Juana, a pretty girl too, and ten-year-old Josefa steered in to Bowie's left and thirteen-year-old Marco, pushed in, between Bowie and Consuelo.

"Do you always carry your famous knife, Senor Bowie?"

"Why yes, Marco, I do."

"And you have it with you now, Senor?"

"Yes, I have, Marco." Bowie paused, then anticipated Marco's objective. "Would you like to see it?"

The eyes of the children widened as he reached under his coat with his right hand. Normally, he threaded his belt through the scabbard, but today he had tucked the scabbard down the small of his back, under the belt. When it emerged, showing his dexterity, he flipped it into the air, caught the blade end of the leather scabbard, and held it out for Marco to examine.

Marco hesitated. Then he looked into Bowie's eyes. Bowie nodded toward it, then Marco dallied his reins on his saddle horn and grasped the knife by its handle in both hands, as though it was a living creature that must be handled gently.

"Careful, Marco. It's a little heavy."

Then Marco looked back toward the vaquero guards and held up the knife. Both smiled broadly.

When Marco offered the knife back to him, handle first, as he had offered it to Marco, Jim felt warmed by the adulation in the boy's eyes.

The group continued riding north for three leagues until it reached the hills above the town. On a high hill, they stopped their horses abreast. Behind them, the riders could see the town, the Alamo, and the river that separated the two. Before them, they could see even higher hills.

Again Bowie positioned his horse beside Ursula. As they surveyed the scrubby terrain and breathed in the scents of wild cedar and mesquite, she turned toward him and said, almost in a whisper, "Farther to the north, there are many springs that have created arroyos and grottos. There are also secret caves."

Her glance at him the previous evening together with her last sentence were all Bowie needed to confirm his feeling that this girl found him interesting, and he began fantasizing about what might happen between them in one of those secret caves.

* * *

During the next few weeks, Bowie rode with Ursula and the others almost every Sunday. Despite the approach of winter, the weather gradually warmed and the humidity rose.

On a Sunday when all of her siblings were in bed with chicken-pox, and Consuelo was required to nurse them, Jim and Ursula rode south, where no armed guards were needed. As they rode, the couple talked freely for the first time.

Bowie had already realized she was a special young woman. Now he wanted to know more about her. Moreover, he wanted her to know more about him, and he began to kibitz with her casually.

"Tell me how you became so smart young miss. Where have you studied."

"If you must know old thing I studied in Madrid until Mexico gained independence from Spain. Then father sent me to Cambridge for three years, then to a convent in the City of Mexico, and I finished at the church school in Monclova. What about you?"

"Impressive," Bowie observed.

"And what of you old thing. Where did you get your learnin'?"

Jim was aware that Ursula was taunting him with allusions to their age difference, but her feisty jabs just added to her allure.

"My mother brought professors to our plantation until I was eighteen. Then I moved to New Orleans and my real education began."

"You attended school their?"

"Yes, the university of reality where I studied cruelty."

"I assume you are referring to your work as a slave trader."

"Yes."

"If you feel that way, why do you still do it?"

"There is nothing bad about slavery, only with those who do it badly. Even the bible supports it."

"I fear you are wrong there old man. In Acts, the bible says, God hath made of one blood all nations of men for to dwell on all the face of the earth."

"Yes, but in Ephesians, God said 'Slaves, obey your earthly masters with respect and fear,'" Bowie countered.

"Yes, but in the same chapter, he said, 'You know that he who is both their master, and yours is in heaven,'" she quoted.

He had initiated their discussion of slavery as little more than casual conversation, but the fire in her eyes told him she was deeply invested in it. As she spoke, her pronunciation of the English words was flawless, but they had the staccato edge of Spanish, as if sharpened by her passion for the subject or for winning what had become a debate, he was yet unable to decide which.

"Yes, but in Peter, he said, 'Slaves, submit yourselves to your master with all respect,'" he replied. "You know your bible well, but I do too," Jim added.

"In his letter to Philemon, Saint Paul asks a Christian to free his slave. This is proof that owning slaves violates Christian principals," she continued, leaning back in her saddle and thrusting her breasts forward. She gave Bowie a smug look that he thought was born of self-righteousness.

In return, he gave her a small tip of his hat.

"Senor Bowie, did you not say that your father fought for liberty from the British?"

"Yes, he did."

"If that is true, I find it difficult to understand how you can support liberty for yourself and deny it to other human beings."

Bowie had heard his father respond to that statement a hundred times by saying that blacks were not human, but he had never felt that the old man was right. As a baby, Jim had been suckled by a black woman; as a boy, he spent more time with black families than with his own; and as a man, his constant companion was a black slave.

"Why are you so concerned about slavery, Ursula? From what I can see, you and your family have never owned any slaves or even been around them."

"I knew a former slave woman in England. She cried every night for her lost husband and children. She did not know where they were, or even if they were alive. She made me realize how wrong it is for one human being to own another or possess the power of life or death over another."

"I see." Jim was feeling drained by their debate and made no other reply.

They rode back to the Veramendi Palace in relative silence, while he reviewed their conversation in his mind and speculated about Ursula's regard for him.

***

The following Sunday, Bowie emerged from his room at the time he expected the Veramendi family to depart for mass. No one was in the courtyard, and he decided they must be behind schedule. He lit a cigar and paced the grounds, waiting.

Suddenly, Ursula on her black horse bolted over the riverside wall of the Palace, all alone, without duenna, family or guards.

"Why is she riding alone? Where is she going?" Bowie wondered and his pulse quickened with anticipation.

Following her, when he dismounted to cross the footbridge, he could barely see her in the distance. He realized she had run her horse across the bridge and was now at least a mile ahead of him, heading north.

He decided not to tire his horse by galloping after Ursula. If he lost sight of her, he would be able to track her in the short, moist grass. Besides, he felt certain he knew where she was going.

By the time he reached the northern hills, he had made up most of the gap between them. When he paused on the top of a hill, he saw her below in a wet arroyo. Now she walked her horse. Clearly, she wanted him to be able to see and follow her.

"Wanting can make having even better." Jim thought of the lesson that Cleo had taught him and decided that Ursula learned it too, or was it a concept that women understood instinctively?

Regardless, he was definitely feeling the wanting and hoped he would soon have the opportunity to know the enhanced having.

As he rounded a bend, he saw her pause then ride on and disappear behind a waterfall that flowed over a pink granite shelf.

When she did not emerge, he knew there must be an opening in the rocks behind it.

He rode through the opening, into a narrow passage that opened further into an enormous natural room full of stalactites and stalagmites. As his eyes adjusted to the darkness, he heard a horse broadcast an alarmed whinny from a few feet away.

"Clever," he thought. "Kind of an equine watchdog."

Warm and wet, the cave had the slight odor of bat guano. Bowie looked around for a clue to where she might be. In his vest pocket, he carried several friction matches, one his favorite new inventions. He scratched one across a rock and, in the light it provided, he glimpsed several tunnels leading out of the room. His match lasted until he reached the third tunnel, and he scratched another and walked on. When that flame died, he thought he noticed light coming from a tunnel he had already passed, so he walked back.

Jim had never seen anything like this place. He had been inside a salt mine in Louisiana, but he had never seen anything that rivaled the geo-beauty of this cave. The light from his matches danced on crystal formations embedded into the limestone walls, creating a karstic fantasy world.

"Aphrodite herself could not have arranged this better," Jim thought. "Could Eros be fluttering around here somewhere?" he whispered and looked up. "I think one of your arrows already got me pal," he speculated.

Finally, Bowie found her, reclining in candlelight, propped up on both elbows on a blanket spread over a flow stone that had to be millions of years old. He was certain he had not seen a blanket tied to her saddle, so he assumed it was already in the cave.

He removed his coat and sat down beside her on the blanket. Then he took her in his arms, and kissed her several times with great ardor. Breathing rapidly, her breasts heaving, she laid back invitingly and allowed him to remove her clothes.

He wanted to believe that her apparent willingness meant that she had come to care for him and was offering herself as a gift. Jim had not been with a woman in over three years and he was feeling nervous. He concentrated on using his amorous skills and delaying his urge to thrust himself into the ecstasy offered by the vision that lay before him.

When he did finally take her he knew that he was not the first. Deciding that she would expect their encounter to be over quickly, as those with a teenage lover had probably been, he concentrated on giving her an unhurried and gentle experience.

Satisfaction filled him when her body shuddered beneath him, time and again. He had inspired such responses in women before, but hers seemed especially intense. He chose to believe she was finding unspoiled passion, exclusively for him.

Afterward, as they lay exhausted she asked, "Where did you learn to do that Senior James? I did not know such feelings could happen in my body."

"I don't know. You inspired me and it just happened. It all felt very natural."

Jim knew what he said was not exactly true and he was not certain she would believe him. However, he did feel confident that she would appreciate his effort to woo her with flattering words that were equal to his passionate deeds.

They stayed in the cave all morning and most of the afternoon, making love many times.

* * *

When Bowie rode back into town separately from Ursula, he discovered that the Wharton party had finally arrived in Bexar from Gonzales. Wharton told Jim that he planned to depart for the state capital in three days.

During that time, as Jim prepared to go with them, Ursula had her meals served in her room and he did not see her. He rode out wondering if she had changed her mind about him.

In Saltillo, using contacts that Juan provided, Bowie acquired grants to a large amount of land. But he still needed Stephen Austin's endorsement to perfect his titles. So from Saltillo, he and Sam rode to San Felipe.

When they arrived and Austin saw the grants, he seemed annoyed at best and livid at worst. "How in hell did you get your hands on so many grants?"

"I made a lot of new friends, mainly thanks to letters of introduction from Veramendi."

"That's not the way this is supposed to work. I won't be a party to this, it's dishonest."

"I need this land. I'm abandoning the slave trade. Besides, I'm planning to sell most of it."

"This is outside the intent of the law, for one man to control all this. After Mexico City finds out, it will be a lot harder for other Americans to get grants. They may even repeal the law altogether."

"I don't think so. I have the blessing of the vice-governor of the state."

Austin examined the grant documents and calculated the land area.

"We're talking over twelve hundred square miles of land here, Jim. I won't do it."

Bowie did not really want to spend time away from Ursula, but he had to have proof that he owned the land, and following the death of his Land Commissioner, Baron de Bastrop, in 1827, Austin was the only man in Texas the Mexican government had empowered to provide that. So he had to find a way to gain Austin's favor.

"On top of that, Veramendi and I are opening a textile mill in Saltillo that will use Mexican labor to weave Tejas cotton into Mexican cloth. That should make you happy, Stephen."

"Did you expect your grant land to be contiguous?"

Bowie took Austin's question to mean that his opposition was waning.

"Well, I was hoping it would be, yes."

What Bowie really wanted was some land along the gulf coast and the remainder between the Brazos and Colorado rivers. That it be one contiguous tract was not necessary, but he knew how to recognize serendipity.

"You should not do it that way, Jim, not even to the far north where the Indians are still in control."

"Well, what should I do?"

Bowie took Austin's twisted expression to mean he was trying to resolve an inner conflict. He finally responded, "Alright, I'll show you. Look at this map."

The Other Rose of Texas

When Bowie and Sam returned to Bexar, Bowie held the title to prime land that would be worth over forty-thousand dollars, even if it brought just five cents an acre. Now he was ready to concentrate on his next acquisition, the one with flashing eyes and corkscrew curls.

* * *

Ursula could not get her experience with Bowie out of her mind, her new giddiness both intense and distracting. She feared that if she appeared in public, someone, probably her mother, would observe her unusual and capricious behavior, so she spent as much of her time alone as she dared. When she attended family meals, she ate quickly, then excused herself and exited with sideways glances, trying to detect suspicious or probing eyes.

Before their first encounter in the cave, she had accepted that her fate was to be the wife of this old man in a loveless marriage. She was not prepared for the overwhelming feelings and fantasies that had come to her instead. Could she actually care for this man? She didn't know yet, but after their Sunday together, she couldn't stop picturing him in her mind and anticipating their next rendezvous.

The first Sunday morning after Jim returned from San Felipe, she saw him waiting to follow when she rode out in the direction of the same secluded cave.

Again, he found her in the flickering candlelight and sat beside her on the flow stone. From an inside breast pocket of his coat, he produced a small book with the stems of two red roses inserted between the pages.

"There's a poem in this book that I especially like. It's by a Scottish poet. I'm Scottish, you know. It begins 'O my Luve's like a red, red rose.'"

He pronounced the words as Robert Burns had written them, affecting a Scottish accent, like his father's. "I'd like you to read it sometime," he said, then he took one of the roses from the book and inserted the stem in her hair, above her hanging curls.

"You know the rose was Aphrodite's favorite flower. Shall I call you Aphrodite, or shall I call you Venus?"

She did not reply, but when Jim kissed her passionately as before, her body responded. She relaxed into his arms once again. She was his as before and her experience this time confirmed the accuracy of her memory of the first time.

Riding alone back to town she felt confident that Bowie was ready to propose and she began to seriously examine her situation.

"Is it just the sex I want?" she pondered.

"Will that change after we are married?"

"Is he too old for me? Will I end up like my mother?"

"What do I really know of this man?"

"Only what he wants me to know?"

Before arriving home Ursula decided that she must learn all she could about this man Bowie, from whatever sources she could find, before it was too late to change her mind about accepting his proposal of marriage, when it came.

* * *

Bowie had been away again, this time for three weeks and on the Sunday following his return, he met Ursula in their cave.

"I have good news. Your father and I will be opening a textile mill together in Saltillo, and we have agreed upon your bride-price. Will you marry me?"

"You are a devil, and I will never marry you."

"I have acquired a great deal of land in Tejas. As soon as I sell it, we will be rich."

"You have used many women for your own pleasure and cast them aside."

"You are my rose, the only woman I will ever love."

"You buy and sell human beings. You will burn in hell."

"I am returning to Louisiana tomorrow to raise some money. I will be selling all of my interests, including my slaves. We will use local labor in the new mill."

"You are interested only in what my father can do for you."

"I can do as much for your father as he can do for me."

"You are a dangerous man who kills other men with his knife. You will not be alive long in Mexico, and my children will be fatherless."

"Where are you getting these ridiculous ideas?"

"I have had a lot of time to spend while you have been away neglecting me. I have been reading about you and your evil life."

Bowie sat down laughing. "And you believe that tripe?"

Ursula thrust her chin forward and blinked in affirmation.

He almost laughed again before saying, "You say you have read terrible things about me. Well, some may be true, but most were thought up by writers and others who made money using my name without my permission. There is no way that any mortal man could have survived all that made-up ballyhoo."

Chin still forward, she blinked again.

"Yet I will admit that one thing you said is true, but you seem to have the wrong reason in mind. I am interested in what your father can do for me, but not in a material way. I have come to regard Juan as the father I wish I had. I was never close with mine and I have come to love yours as my own."

"I cannot marry you."

"I understand, but I think you are not telling me the real reason."

Ursula looked down.

"I have received a letter from Rodrigo. He was my lover before you and as soon as he graduates from University, he is coming for me."

Jim felt as if a stalactite had fallen from the ceiling and pierced his heart.

"And how soon will that be?, Jim probed.

"He has three more years of studying the law in Toledo. Then he will be in a position to ask father for my hand."

"But your father has already agreed to our marriage."

"I know, and I must ask you to tell him you have changed your mind."

Jim looked away, then back again at Ursula. He put his index finger under her chin, raised her eyes to his and said, "I am just a man, my darling. But I promise that I will love and protect you and our children as long as you all live, including the time after my death."

She looked away.

"I'm leaving early tomorrow and I want you to think about your decision. If you still feel the same when I get back, I will speak to your father and call off the wedding."

Then Bowie kissed Ursula tenderly, stood and walked out.

***

Ursula slept late the next morning. She had spent most of the night trying to decide what to do and what to tell her parents.

When she awoke she put Jim's red rose in her hair and a broad smile on her face before walking to the dining room for breakfast. Everyone but the Senora had already come and gone when she arrived.

"What makes you so cheerful this morning?" her mother asked. "Where did you find that beautiful flower?"

"I am to be Maria Ursula Fructosa Veramendi Bowie. I will wear a beautiful white dress from Paris, my sisters will be my brides-maids, my brother will stand with the groom, my father will give me away, and you, my mother, will share my happiness, which is more than I can possibly bear alone."

She was trying to sound convincing.

"And when did you decide this?"

"Yesterday."

"So where is your gallant suitor now?"

"He has gone to Louisiana to settle his affairs, and he promised to sell his slaves too."

"I saw him leave this morning and he did not look happy. What makes you think he will come back?" the Senora said.

Ursula had not considered that possibility and she felt her face droop as she searched for a flippant reply. Her mother was right, aside from her, Bowie really had nothing in Bexar to return to, and she had rejected him. Perhaps he would get to Louisiana and decide to not return.

The Other Rose of Texas

She had not found a respectful retort for her mother before Juan Veramendi entered the room, sat down, and poured himself a cup of coffee.

"Our Ursula is going to marry the north-Americano," the Senora said.

"I know, Senora, I traded her for a textile mill," Juan replied.

Juan and the Senora laughed.

"I have scheduled the wedding with Father de la Garza for the afternoon of Monday, April twenty-fifth, of this year."

"That is less than two months away father, are you in a hurry to get rid of me?"

"One less mouth to feed," Juan replied, continuing to joke.

Disappointing her father was the last thing Ursula wanted, so she decided to continue to act as if there would be a wedding. She would let Jim Bowie deal with it all when he returned, if he returned.

Chapter 9

Believing he could still win Ursula's heart, Bowie was in a hurry to get back to his new life. On the well-traveled San Antonio-Harrisburg-New Orleans road, he and Sam made an exhausting thirty miles a day, seldom camping, eating hardtack and jerky mounted, and sleeping in the saddle.

In Vermillionville, Louisiana, a waiting letter told Jim that his brothers would meet him at their eighteen hundred-acre Arcadia sugar plantation near Thibodaux. However, rather than turn south and go there immediately, Bowie continued riding to New Orleans. He wanted to confer with his bankers, before confronting his brothers with information for which he knew they would not be prepared.

Being away slightly more than a year gave Jim much to tell his brothers. Finally arriving in Thibodaux he felt excited and hopeful.

Before giving his report, he presented an itemized list of expenses from his sojourn that totaled four thousand, four hundred dollars. His first concern was collecting on his brother's promise to reimburse him.

But Stephen, ever critical of his older brother, set the tone for the meeting with intimidating questions about Jim's expenditures.

"What are chaps and why did they cost a hundred dollars?"

Jim sighed. "Chaps are heavy leather pants that cover your breeches. They keep the brush from ripping holes in the cloth. I had a pair made for me and a pair for Sam."

"Don't they have roads in Texas?"

"We had to ride cross-country and break trail when we left Galveston. Some of the brush was thorny and neck high on a horse."

Stephen grimaced then asked, "What is this twenty-five dollar doctor fee?"

The Other Rose of Texas

This time, Jim felt less accommodating. He did not want to explain every line on his list. "I hurt a man in Galveston."

"You mean you lost your temper again and cut him up," Stephen stated. "We saw the headline in the Bee."

"He attacked Sam. Besides, I didn't stick him. I just hit him and only once."

John J. and Stephen finished examining the list, then John J. said, "The market is way down, Jim, so we can't afford to pay you all cash. You'll have to take slaves too and try to sell them; we can give you clear title to Sam and Bettie, Josephus and Charon, and three-thousand dollars."

"I don't need any more slaves. As a matter of fact, I want to sell my share in the ones I already own, except Sam and Bettie."

Jim had not yet given his report, so his comment brought puzzled expressions to the faces of his brothers and a question from Rezin P.

"What the hell's going on, Jim? I thought you went to Texas to expand our interests in the slave trade, not vacate them."

Jim looked directly at each man, and then replied, "As I recall, brothers, you authorized me to go to Texas to investigate the future of slavery there and to look into buying the Galveston block from Junior Lafitte. Is that not right?"

Stephen stood, then said, "We all expected you to identify every opportunity there might be for us to make money in Texas, regardless of how or where."

Jim smiled and nodded, feeling that he had tricked Stephen into giving him the perfect opening for his next statement. "That's exactly what I did, dear brother. I'm here to tell you Lafitte has nothing we need to buy, furthermore the future of slavery in Texas is doubtful.

Jim paused and looked around again, for dramatic effect, then said, "But we can make a fortune selling Texas land."

As if on cue, Jim thought, John J. joined the debate, saying, "But we don't own any land in Texas."

Jim felt almost ecstatic, reveling in the brilliant way he was leading his brothers toward the conclusions he wanted them to reach.

"But we do. I'm now a Mexican citizen and a member of the Catholic Church. When I go back, I'm going to marry the daughter of the Vice-Governor of the state of Coahuila-Texas, and I own almost seven-hundred and fifty thousand acres of prime land, on or near good water."

"And how much is that worth to us?" Stephen asked.

"I am more than willing to keep our partnership together in Texas just as it is here. We can use as much money as we can raise to buy more Texas land, so I propose that we sell the Arcadia sugar-plantation and all our slaves except those we need for cotton on the home place."

Stephen folded his arms and studied his brother. "And if we don't agree?"

"Then I plan to liquidate my part of our partnership, and I will give you first option to buy me out."

Again, Stephen took the lead. "I'm sorry to spoil your dream of being a Texas land baron, but since you left, our financial position has gotten much worse. The price of cotton has gone to hell, with land and slaves close behind. Cane is doing slightly better, and we have already made a deal to sell Arcadia for ninety-thousand dollars."

Jim was still feeling enthusiastic.

"Great, we can use that money to buy more Texas land."

"Sorry, brother, but we need that money to pay against our loans, so we don't lose everything else."

Jim's head began to throb and he felt temporarily stymied. He had expected resistance, but not this much.

"I don't think you understand. I'm on the verge of making a fortune for us all. People will be moving to Texas by the thousands. We can sell them some of our land and use some of it to raise cotton, cane, rice, and cattle, and I'm convinced we can do it all without a single slave."

The brother's opposition appeared to weaken when Rezin P. asked, "What is the least you can get by with, Jim?"

"I spent every dollar I had on this land, and I need money to buy a textile mill and reassemble it in Mexico. I also need my expense reimbursement and my share of the Arcadia sale proceeds. I've got to have it, brothers, whether or not we remain partners."

"Do you have to operate the mill in Mexico?" John J. asked. "With cotton the way it is, there are hundreds of vacant mills right here in Louisiana. We could probably find a good one at a tax sale."

"Having the mill in Mexico is the key to the whole enterprise. My future father-in-law strongly believes there are plenty of capable and willing Mexican workers, and we don't need slaves. The mill is his way of proving his theory and my way of proving my worth as a business partner and son-in-law. He has agreed to count my investment in the mill as my bride-price for his daughter."

"Where is the mill coming from?" John J. asked.

"Angus McNeill in Natchez has one that is almost new. He has agreed to have it dis-assembled, crated, shipped, and re-assembled in Saltillo, Mexico, for twenty-thousand dollars."

"Will he take a note?"

"No."

"Can you borrow against the Texas land?"

"I just tried. Mexican law prohibits their banks from loaning against a land grant, and the bankers in New Orleans say the grants are not legal instruments in the United States."

Stephen threw a hand in the air. "Well, if your own bank won't back you, why should we go along?"

"It's like I said, I already own a lot of land, but right now I need cash. If you get in on this deal you will see a return on your money right away, as soon as I can get back to Texas and start selling the land."

"What if you can't sell it?" John J. asked.

"Then you can put slaves on it and raise crops yourself."

"Why don't you do that now?" Stephen asked.

Jim began feeling that he had lost control of the negotiations and everything he had gained was now falling away.

"I can't have anything to do with slavery. The Veramendis are against it."

"Does that mean we get Sam back?"

"No, Sam stays with me and he wants Bettie with him."

"How will you explain that to your in-laws?"

"I'll think of something."

"Let us sleep on it Jim, and we'll let you know in the morning."

* * *

As usual Jim's brothers were less than generous. When he returned to Bexar all he had to bring was a bill of sale for a textile mill, some promissory notes signed by his brothers, and four slaves.

He felt defeated yet he remained hopeful. He still had his land grants and a chance that Ursula had changed her mind about the wedding. Rezin P. had accompanied him back to Texas to serve as best-man, in case she had.

After hearing of Jim's financial set-backs his father-in-law-to-be was understanding and agreed to let the wedding take place anyhow. He even told Jim he would arrange a family loan to pay for a New Orleans honeymoon.

Ursula's attitude was not as accommodating. The day-after Jim's return, they rendezvoused in their secret cave, and she exploded.

"You promised to sell your slaves and return with much money. Now you are here with even more slaves, and you have to borrow money from my family for my honeymoon."

"My financial condition is temporary. I will begin selling my land immediately and as soon as the mill is operating, I will plant cotton."

"What of the four slaves?"

"Legally they are not slaves here. They can work and I will pay them."

"Where will we live?"

"Your father has insisted that we remain in Bexar at the Veramendi Palace, until there is a need for us to live elsewhere. Why are we even talking about this? I thought your knight of La Mancha was coming to carry you away."

"I decided that three years is too long to wait."

"So you want to get married?"

"Yes."

Jim took a deep breath through his nose, trying to conceal his surprise by keeping his mouth closed. He felt elated, but he wanted to hide that too.

"So your parents convinced you to abandon your girlish dream of deferred bliss?"

"No. Not exactly. Something else has happened."

For Jim the air in the cave became heavy with curiosity. "What is it? Tell me."

"If you do not want me, I will seek refuge with the nuns in Monterrey."

Jim sensed that Ursula was scared and having a hard time telling him.

"I am," she hesitated, "I am with child."

"Is it mine?"

After he said it, Jim wanted to take it back. He knew immediately that he could not have said anything worse.

"You don't want me. I will go to Monterrey. My father will die, " Ursula sobbed.

"I'm sorry Ursula, of course I want you. I love you and I want our baby."

When he began to whisper promises of love and to kiss her ear, she melted into his arms. To Bowie her passion for him seemed just as strong.

After they made love, they began to make plans.

"My gown has an empire-waist and I ordered a large bouquet to cover my stomach when I walk down the aisle."

"At least she is acting like things are alright between us," he thought. Then he said, "We can stay at my home place for a year so nobody knows when the baby comes."

"We can ask father to turn the room next to mine into a nursery for when we come home," Ursula replied.

"So you're planning to tell your parents that you're expecting?"

"I wasn't thinking. I don't want anybody to know."

"I think it will be good to live at the Palace and have the help of your mother and sisters with the baby. Do you want a boy or a girl?" Bowie asked.

"I think I want a girl, so I can teach her to avoid rogues like her father."

Ursula laughed, but water came to Jim's eyes. "She got me back," he thought.

Ursula immediately stopped laughing. "I'm sorry my darling," she sobbed. "I know you love me and I believe you are a good man."

Her apology sounded insincere to Jim. Then he realized, though his brain believed what she was telling him, she was not convincing his gut.

"Is it all contrived, just to get her out of this mess?" he pondered.

* * *

Again, they returned to Bexar separately from different directions. Two weeks remained until the wedding, and a mountain of gifts in the parlor was growing steadily.

Ursula resumed writing thank-you notes and daydreaming about the special day to come. She told Jim that she planned to wait for the day of the ceremony for the final fitting of her wedding dress.

While Ursula wrote notes, Bowie sought Juan Veramendi and found him reading in his study, a scowl on his face. After he acknowledged Jim's presence with a wave, Veramendi continued reading for a few minutes, and then he looked directly at his soon-to-be son-in-law.

"By the expression on your face, you must be reading bad news," Jim said.

"I fear the news is far worse for you than for me. According to this two-week-old dispatch, the government is afraid there are too many north Americanos in Tejas, and President Bustamante has decreed that immigration must stop immediately."

"How will that hurt me?"

"There will be no new buyers for your land."

Jim felt that Juan was underestimating the determination of his countrymen. "Do you seriously believe that a decree will stop Americans from crossing the border?"

"It doesn't matter. They cannot become citizens of Mexico; therefore, they will not be able to perfect their ownership of land."

"I see what you mean." Bowie felt cut to the bone, but he tossed it off with a shrug. "Well, it looks like I'll be planting a lot of cotton. Do you know where I can hire a few hundred field hands?"

"The situation will be much worse than that. The government is sending troops up here to seal the border and imposing new taxes on us to pay for them. I am afraid too many politicians in Mexico City have forgotten the lessons of the American revolution, and too many Americans in Tejas will remember. We may soon hear the phrase, what was it, taxation without representation?"

"It appears I will not be rich as soon as I had hoped. Does this change anything between you and me?"

"Not unless you think it does. We still have the mill, and you have plenty of land for crops."

"What about Ursula?"

"Ursula will do as her mother and I wish, and we both think she needs a strong husband, like you, to control her childish impulses. My wife says Ursula is looking forward to being the wife of a famous man and having many children."

Jim was now quite familiar with Ursula's quick temper and rebellious nature. Their last exchange in the cave convinced him that she had gained self-confidence and wanted more control of her own life.

Then, remembering his misgivings about her true feelings he asked, "What if she changes her mind, under the circumstances?"

"At this late date, she would be disgraced, and though she is still virginal, it would be a long while before she could find another suitor. But, just to be safe, her mother and I will talk with her again, tonight."

Jim shuddered when he realized that Juan did not know his darling daughter had become a woman, before her proper time. Furthermore, he knew Juan would blame him for the deed and the public embarrassment if everyone else found out.

He worried that such a realization would cost him the trust and approval he needed, and had worked so hard to earn from this man; this man whom he had grown to love as a friend and surrogate father.

"Considering this new development I think Ursula and I should spend our first year on my family plantation. I can ship cotton from there down the Mississippi and around to the Rio Bravo for the new mill. Maybe the government will ease up on immigration in a year."

"That sounds wise. We will miss you both my son. But perhaps the Senora and I can visit you there."

Chapter 10

The Bowie's wedding day dawned overcast and cool, but the thin layer of clouds evaporated as the sun rose higher. By one in the afternoon, the April winds were calm, and the temperature was comfortable as Jim entered the San Fernando Cathedral from Main Plaza. He was greeted by the scents of burning candles, incense, and fresh-cut flowers, and he took a deep whiff.

Everywhere he looked he saw perfection and he felt happy to be joining a family that understood beauty, good taste, and gracious living.

Along the center aisle of the church each pew was decorated with pure white daylilies arrayed against deep green colored ivy. A high Spanish arch framed the sanctuary where a simple carved wooden crucifix hung on the wall behind the apse.

Spotlighted by a solid ray of light shining down through a high, octagon shaped window, a prie dieu stood in the chancel in front of the alter, flanked at each side by candelabra with a white taper in each of eight arms.

Jim walked beside the candles and into the sacristy, joining Rezin P. and Marco who had already begun to don the black dress suit, white linen shirt, black cravat, and white gloves that Sam had laid out for each man.

When they finished, Jim thought that young Marco looked a little nervous wearing his first formal attire. Trying to put him at ease, Jim said, "Marco, today you have the job of a man and I know you will do it well."

As he spoke a string quartet imported from Monterrey opened its program with Mozart's *Ave Verum Corpus*.

"Now, my future awaits," Jim said. Putting his arms around his old and new brothers, he led them to the sanctuary.

Guests had been invited from as far away as Mexico City and the cathedral was full. Jim scanned many unfamiliar faces before making eye contact with his former rival for Ursula, Juan Almonte, who wore the uniform of a Lieutenant Colonel in the Mexican army. Each man nodded in recognition as Jim thought that both their lives had changed dramatically in the few months since they first met.

The Mozart piece was followed by Schubert's *Ave Maria*, which accompanied the walk of Ursula's sisters, Juana and Josefa, and cousins, Juana and Gertrudis Navarro, to a place before the candles on the left, each dressed in a lavender colored gown and carrying a bouquet of purple African violets.

Remembering her words about going to the convent in Monterrey to have her baby, Jim was not absolutely certain that Ursula would show up until the violins and cellos began Pachelbel's *Canon in D*, and she appeared on her father's arm. Wearing her mother's diamond tiara, dressed all in white she carried an enormous bridal bouquet of white roses, baby's breath, and trailing white ribbons.

Beauty and youth and flesh and blood were the words that dominated Jim's thoughts, as he looked toward Ursula and smiled. But Ursula's eyes were downcast and her expression without joy. In fact, of all present, to Jim only Juan Veramendi seemed to be having a good time.

When the hour long ceremony was over, decorated carriages transported the wedding party to the reception at the Veramendi Palace, within sight of the church, while most of the guests left their own carriages and horses in Main Plaza and walked the short distance.

In the receiving line, Ursula positioned her body where no one could see her silhouette and kept her gigantic bridal bouquet positioned over her slightly protruding stomach. Then she sat on a chair in a corner and held the flowers over her disappearing lap and Jim stood beside her.

At the reception, the wedding quartet was replaced by a son group from Guadalajara. Though the music was lively the guests were standing around instead of dancing.

"Shall we dance?" Bowie asked his bride.

"Maybe later," she replied.

"None of the guests will dance until we do," he cajoled.

The Other Rose of Texas

The musicians began a waltz. Ursula stood and Jim led her to the middle of the dance area. With the bouquet between them, they began to dance. Then Juan and the Senora joined them, followed by several other couples.

When the song ended the bride and groom returned to the corner followed by the Senora.

"You look ridiculous trying to cover your bump with those flowers. You are not showing that much and when your father asks you to dance, I suggest you let Jim hold the bouquet."

Ursula glared and Jim almost laughed, but thought better as his mother-in-law continued.

"You think your own mother cannot tell that you are pregnant. Silly girl."

As the Senora predicted, Juan asked his daughter to dance and as suggested, she handed her bouquet to her new husband.

"I have a headache," she said when she returned to her chair. "I want to go to my room."

"Aren't you going to throw your bouquet?" Jim asked.

"I don't think I can. It's too heavy."

Jim smiled but Ursula did not.

"You should at least try."

Ursula nodded, acquiescing, and Jim asked Juana Veramendi to gather the eligible females. When they were assembled, Ursula faced them, walked to Juana and handed her the flowers, then turned and walked out of the parlor. It was barely six o'clock and the sun was still well up.

* * *

When all of the guests had departed, Jim joined Ursula in her room. She was already in bed, staring at the ceiling, with the covers pulled up to her chin.

"You looked very lovely today, my darling wife."

"I am a cow. Everyone noticed. They will talk of it all over town."

"It is all your imagination. No one noticed and no one said a thing."

"Except my mother."

"I'm sure she guessed it long before today."

"She will tell father."

"I think it is in her best interest not to tell anyone."

Jim sat on the bed and tried to change the subject as he pulled off his boots.

"Your father introduced me to many rich and important men today."

"Is that how it is to be, always business before me?" she said and looked directly at Jim.

He decided that her head must still hurt and tried to humor her.

"You were not even in the room. I would have stayed by your side."

"You could have left with me, to take care of me."

"If you had asked me to I would have, but I stayed with our guests to be polite. Besides, I needed to meet those men. I have to restore my fortune. Just give me time to get a few things going, and I will spend time being a husband."

"So, you neglect me from the very beginning of our marriage."

Jim thought the conversation was becoming absurd.

"Ursula, tell me what is wrong. Why are you acting this way?"

"Nothing is wrong. My baby has a father and a name and you have me," she said and turned her face to the wall.

Bowie decided that she was not ready to be rational and concluded that the changes in her body were already affecting her mind. He finished removing his clothing and slid into bed naked.

That night they lay together but did not make love.

* * *

The next day, with Sam driving the large, closed carriage that Juan had imported from Mexico City, they departed for a leisurely trip to New Orleans with overnight stops scheduled at the Seguin ranch, at hotels in Gonzales, San Felipe, Harrisburg,

Vermillionville, and Baton Rouge, and at camp sites they would select along the way.

Jim hoped that Ursula's attitude and behavior would change when they got away from Bexar. As they arrived his friends made a fuss over her in the towns where they stopped. But she seemed to still be in a foul mood when they reached New Orleans and checked into the hotel on Saint Ann Street.

"I feel like a ripe watermelon and I have to pee all the time."

Jim thought her condition still did not show very much, but she seemed obsessed with it.

"You become more beautiful every day, my love."

"Am I as beautiful as all those whores you know here. Are you planning to visit them, now that my body repulses you?" she said almost shouting.

"You are as desirable to me as you have always been."

"Then why have we not made love since we were married."

"I have been thinking the same thing and waiting for you to give me a sign or something, that you want to."

"It would not be good for the baby," she concluded softly.

Jim could not surmise how to deal with her erratic behavior and he began spending more time away from her, meeting with bankers and businessmen, trying to put together any kind of deal that might turn a profit.

Without telling Ursula, he even reopened discussions with Jean Pierre Lafitte about a Galveston slave enterprise. Sometimes he was away for days, leaving her to shop for maternity clothes or sit alone in their hotel room. Their bickering increased.

"How can you treat me like this? I am not even twenty, and I feel like an old shoe that you have cast aside. Is it because I am getting fat with your baby growing inside me? Do you love me or did you marry me for my father's money and influence?"

"Don't you see that what I am doing is because I don't want to depend on your father? Can't you give me just a little more time?"

As Ursula seemed to grow more irrational, Jim felt more hurt and defensive. Resolved to make their marriage work, however, he continued to try to appease her, hoping her behavior would become normal again at some point.

* * *

When Bowie was in town, the couple spent several evenings at dinner parties, balls, and other soirées, given for them by friends of his or of her father. Ursula usually remained seated with Sam standing behind her, and Bowie usually circulated as he praised the benefits of doing business in Texas to anyone who would listen.

Since immigration from the United States was no longer legal, he was proposing partnerships whereby his business prospect would provide the money for Bowie to grow cotton on his land in Texas and receive a share of the profits, without ever crossing the border.

During a ball at their hotel, one such business prospect turned out to be the husband of Jim's former lover, Cleopatra; a French planter who had bought her from Lafitte then freed and married her. In his eyes for the first time in ten years, Bowie thought Cleo was still quite beautiful.

From his smile, Bowie could tell that Sam thought the same of Portia when he saw her still attending Cleo.

"Ursula my dear, may I present Madam and Monsieur Jaques-Dalcroze …. My wife Ursula."

Cleo curtsied and the monsieur took Ursula's hand and kissed it.

Ursula looked at Jim, then at Cleo, and said, "Is this one of your whores Jim or one of the married women you dallied with?"

Jim could not believe his ears. The mouths and eyes of Cleo and her husband flew open and he feared for a moment that the Frenchman would demand satisfaction.

Instead, arm in arm, the couple turned abruptly and walked away.

"Ursula, why did you do that? That man was interested in doing business with me."

"And she was interested in doing something with you too. I saw the way you looked at each other. You used to know her didn't you?"

Jim was puzzled. Had he somehow revealed his familiarity with Cleo, or was Ursula's rudeness a product of her state of mind? He did not want to compound her suspicion, nor did he want to scold his wife in public, so he said, "You seem tired my darling, shall we go?"

On their way out of the ballroom Jim thanked their host and hostess.

* * *

When Sam saw Bowie approaching with Monsieur and Madame Jaques-Dalcroze to introduce them to Ursula, he was surprised by the sight of Cleo. However, when Portia emerged from behind her, he felt euphoric.

With the quick departure of her mistress and the Bowies, Portia was left standing alone. Seizing the moment and her arm, Sam escorted her out a side door, into the hotel garden and behind a tall hedge. Suddenly, in his mind, they had never been apart. He embraced her and said, "I have two hundred dollars in gold for us, are you ready to go north to freedom?"

She kissed him warmly and answered, "Two hundred dollars won't even get us to Memphis. We gots to get to Canada. That's over two thousand miles upriver, and the man say it cost a thousand dollars for each. The man say."

"But we can go overland on our own without paying anybody, and we can leave tonight. My paw told me about a way by the river."

"You tol' me your paw got caught and hung, and you want to go his way?"

Portia's comment revived memories and fears Sam had not experienced since moving to Texas. Suddenly he was back in the Bowie plantation barnyard looking up at his father dangling from a rope and swinging dead in the breeze. Sam's body felt cold and he shuddered.

"I'm not as strong as you, and I don't know if I could make it on the road. I want to get away, but I want to be safe doin' it. The man say he would hide me and feed me all the way on his cattle boat," Portia said.

Until that moment, Sam did had not realized how strong his fantasy was about leaving New Orleans with Portia immediately. Desperate to prevent her from vanishing again he asked, "Then will you wait for me? I'll get the money somewhere. Where will you be?"

"I can't wait forever. If I gets the chance, I gots to go. You sees, don't you?"

"I understand. But tell me how to find you and promise you will leave word about where you'll be if you go north."

"Alright. My cousin Samuel always know where Miss Cleo and me am. He belong to the owner of this hotel and he work in the kitchen usual."

"Here, you take this money and keep it for us," Sam said as he brought all of the gold coins up out of his pouch and handed them to Portia.

She looked at the coins, then back at Sam.

"Don't worry. You wait. I'll come for you," he said.

"I gots to go. Miss Cleo be lookin for me."

They embraced again and parted with Sam dreaming of the day they would be together again. However, Sam had no intention of waiting patiently. If money was needed, he would go to Canada and make some, then send back for Portia. She had told him how to get there. He needed to find a cattle boat. Apparently, cattle boats went all the way.

* * *

After watching Portia until she disappeared into the darkness, Sam went to his room by the hotel kitchen. He changed out of his formal attire, put on his warm coat, gathered the belongings he could get into his pockets and pouch, and headed for the river.

At the familiar wharf near Pauline Street, his nose led him to his objective; a floating cattle pen, over two hundred feet long, twenty-five feet wide, and packed with longhorns. Sam's emotion-clouded reasoning told him that the barge was ready to go north, and a push boat would arrive in the morning to begin the voyage.

The Other Rose of Texas

He quietly made his way to the corner rails of the corral, farthest from the gate, removed and folded his coat for a pillow, and leaned back against a post. He had been asleep about an hour when the moving cattle awakened him.

He stood, but before he could realize that he needed to flee from the barge, every steer had run out and on to the dock where three men on horses herded them down the wharf. Almost upon him, he saw a short, fourth man with a lantern in one hand, and a long metal tipped pole in the other.

"Hey you. What you doin there? You lookin for a free ride or you just like the smell of cow shit?"

The man pressed the metal against his throat. Sam was frozen with fear and could not move.

"I bet your master will pay me a lot for catching you. You look like you can do the work of two or three easy."

The cold pole tip cut Sam's flesh and warm blood ran down his chest. He looked down and saw that the blood was staining his pouch.

For the first time in his life, he showed anger in the presence of a white man. With one swipe of his right arm, he swept the pole aside and out of the man's hand. Then he lunged and hit the man with his massive right fist square in the nose, sending him sliding on his back along the well lubricated deck.

Not stopping to examine the man, Sam vaulted over a rail and ran down the wharf in the direction opposite the cattle.

The next morning, Sam was summoned to the hotel dining room where Bowie sat alone. As he entered, he noticed four uniformed policemen at the next table. With his shirt buttoned all the way up to cover his neck wound, Sam's hands shook behind his back as he stood before his master.

"Were you surprised to see Portia last night?"

"Yes, Master Jim."

"They said you were out past two. Did you enjoy your visit with her?"

Sam glanced down. Open on a chair, he saw a copy of The New Orleans Bee. "Longshoreman Found Dead On Barge," the headline said.

"Well, I'm sorry to have to tell you this."

The policemen rose from their chairs, and Sam jerked his gaze from the newspaper back to Bowie. He thought of trying to escape, but, again, he was too scared to move.

"But we need to leave for Natchez in the morning, so you probably won't see her again for a while."

Trying to appear calm, Sam took a deep breath and said, "Yes, sir. I get ever thing packed." Then he turned and walked out of the dining room behind the four policemen.

In his room, he had to sit and let his hands stop shaking and his breathing become regular again. He felt sorry that the man he hit had died, but grateful that he would be out of New Orleans before the killing could be traced to him.

"I was lucky last night," he thought. "I let my emotions cloud my judgment. I've got to be smarter. How can I be with Portia, take care of Bettie, and get us to freedom, all at the same time?" he pondered silently.

All at once the solution came to him. His lingering fear was replaced by excitement and he ran to the kitchen to find Portia's cousin Samuel.

"Tell Portia that Sam said he is going to get his master to buy her from Miss Cleo and when they get back to Texas they will escape to freedom together," Sam told him and Samuel promised to deliver the message.

* * *

The carriage ride to Natchez took two weeks. When they reached the outskirts, Jim pointed out the sandbar where he had successfully defended himself. This time, however, Natchez was not lucky for Bowie, and after a few days, he told Sam to prepare for the trip to the plantation.

From Natchez, they traveled south back to Baton Rouge because the roads were better and Ursula had been complaining about feeling sick. Now nearly three months pregnant, traveling on rough roads by carriage had been increasingly hard on her.

Over the last few miles Ursula began crying and screaming. Bowie was scared and as soon as they arrived at the main house he sent Sam to get the two best midwives on the place to attend her, one his paternal grandmother, Aurora, and the other his maternal aunt, Calliope.

They tried to ask her about her pain but had trouble understanding Ursula's heavily accented English, and she had trouble translating their colloquialisms. So Jim stayed to interpret.

"She havin' a miscarriage Master Jim," Aurora said, after examining Ursula.

"Can you help her?" Jim asked.

"I can't stop it but I can help her have it. Do you want to stay?"

"Yes, I'll stay. What can I do?"

When the worst had passed, Ursula went to sleep. When she awakened, the strangeness of her surroundings seemed to frighten her and caused an outburst.

"¿Dónde estoy yo? ¿Dónde está mi bebé? Mi bebé no está dentro de mí. Dios ha tomado a mi bebé. "

Hysterical and raving in Spanish, Ursula repeated the same phrases over and over.

"She said, 'Where am I? Where is my baby? My baby is not inside me. God has taken my baby," Jim translated. Then he said, "I am here, Ursula. Everything will be alright."

Jim felt confused about what to do next and Aurora must have sensed it. She sat on the bed, enfolded Ursula in her arms, and began to rock her.

Ursula reacted by curling her body, pressing her right thumbnail against her lower lip and leaning into Aurora's considerable bosom. She became silent and seemed to calm down.

"We take care of her now, Master Jim. You go on now; she be fine. Don't you worry."

"Thank you Aurora," Bowie said and walked out. His fear for Ursula had been replaced by anxiety for a different reason. He wanted to think so he headed for his knoll by the cypress trees.

His fretfulness now was the product of indecision. His last compelling imperative for continuing the marriage and returning to Texas was gone. His business opportunities there had disappeared and it was obvious that Ursula had married him to secure legitimacy for her baby.

Since there was no longer a baby she could return to Bexar, claim the marriage was not consummated, and have it annulled in the eyes of the law and the church.

She would be a virgin again, as far as anyone knew, and she could wait for her Spanish paramour to come for her or she could marry some other man.

At that moment, Jim did not consider that he still loved her. He just sat for several hours pondering what Ursula might decide when she reached the same conclusions about her alternatives that he had.

* * *

With the help of the midwives, Ursula's young body seemed to be recovering quickly from her miscarriage. Aurora told Jim that his wife appeared physically strong enough to attend the burial of the aborted male child, if she was careful.

Due to the heat, it was not practical to wait for a Catholic priest to sanctify the event so on the third day Calliope removed the tiny creature from the spring house, wrapped it in linen, and placed it in a minature pine coffin.

Sam carried Ursula from her room to a chair beside a small open grave in the family cemetery, behind the main house. She sat by as Bowie read the twenty-third psalm and Sam shoveled dirt back into the grave, over the coffin. Then Sam carried Ursula back to her bed.

While Ursula slept, Jim sat in a large downstairs room to the left of the vestibule that was built as a ballroom for Elve Bowie. It was his classroom and the center of his world for many years; the place where he learned to think.

Around him, the big house smelled of wood, whale-oil, mildew, paint, and soap, and except for Jim and Ursula, it was empty of residents. The Master was long dead and The Mistress was away visiting her daughters.

The Bowie daughters had all married and moved out. The sons had fled too: John J. to Chicot County, Arkansas; Rezin P. was still in Bexar; and Stephen was in New Orleans for an indefinite period. The only other non-slave on the place was the overseer, and he had his own house.

Sitting in the big empty room, with his wife acting indifferent toward him since their wedding and his son now in the ground Jim felt overwhelmingly alone. When Aurora entered he began to bawl, as if her persona granted him permission to be weak.

"Did you see him Aurora? He looked just like a person, like a little bitty man."

"Yes Master Jim."

"I should have brought her straight here. Going to New Orleans and Natchez first was too much for her."

"T'was the will of the lord," the slave matriarch said.

"I was stupid. It is my fault," Jim replied.

"God's will. God's will."

"Is he punishing me for killing Memnon, for killing your son?"

"T'aint our place to figure why God do what he do Master Jim."

"What can I do?"

"If you thinks you done wrong, then try to do right after now."

"Will Ursula be alright?"

"I ain't sure yet. She in God's hands too."

*　*　*

While Ursula recuperated, Aurora never left her. Calliope did the cooking and serving.

Aurora told Ursula of her experiences with women who had successful pregnancies and those who did not, and with delivering babies who had lived and those that had not.

"It be God's will."

Soon, following a thorough physical examination, Aurora advised Ursula that she thought the young bride could have more children.

The next day Calliope had just delivered lunch and was turning to go when Ursula said, "Tell me what Jim was like as a boy."

Before Aurora could speak, the younger slave woman responded.

"He had a soft heart for us folks and for the critters. He weren't feared of nothin but his paw. He was always bringin home a wild thing he found. One time, he brought home a bear cub and didn't know the mama bear was right behind him. I never seen a boy run so fast."

Ursula smiled for the first time since her arrival.

"Then he dragged home a full-grown alligator by the tail. Nearly scared us all to death. James would have took it back to the bayou, but his paw made him kill it and skin it to make him some boots."

"Was Jim's father a cruel man?" Ursula asked.

Tears came to Aurora's eyes as she responded. "His paw made Master James hang my son, Memnon. Memnon was Sam's paw. Then Sam's ma kill heself."

"Do you think that Jim feels bad about that?"

"Yes I does," Aurora replied. That be why he take care of Sam and Bettie so good, cause he kill they paw and think he kill they maw too. But it ain't he fault."

"I think he should set you all free."

"That be mos danger, Miss Ursula."

Aurora spoke her name for the first time and Ursula felt warm inside. "Why?" she asked.

"Slaves is slaves and white folks ain't gonna let us be nothin else, even if we got papers. What we is mos feared is fo' Master Jim go away for good and Master Stephen be by his se'f with us."

Ursula looked down.

"But they is one thing," Aurora continued.

Ursula looked at Aurora.

"If you can sometime, help Sam. I be mos appreciate."

Ursula grew tired and the conversation ended, but their talks continued the next day and for several days after. Ursula began to believe that Bowie might not be as dreadful a man as she had read and, with this thought to focus on, the psychological sting of her miscarriage started to recede.

* * *

After two weeks, one morning Jim was at breakfast in the dining-room when Ursula appeared.

"Calliope heated some water and I took a bath in that gorgeous bathtub," she said.

Jim thought she sounded almost cheerful. "You look beautiful my darling."

"She also showed me how to use that convenience."

"They call that an indoor toilet'," Jim said, using French inflection. It was designed by a man The Master brought over from England. It is connected to what he called a cesspool. The slaves actually built it."

"When we get home I'm going to ask father to get one."

After eating she made a request. "Show me your farm."

"You mean plantation. The Master would horse whip anyone who called it a farm," Jim replied.

They started in front of the main house, located on a hill facing away from the barnyard. "It is as close to being a colonial mansion as the slave carpenters could make it," Jim said.

Then they toured the barns and stock pens, viewed the slave shacks, slave cemetery, and the saw mill, where two slaves were riving a twelve-foot loblolly pine log. Finally, they sat upon the grass in Jim's secret refuge.

"Why is everything painted white? Is that not a lot of work to maintain?" Ursula asked.

"After the war, The Master was decorated during a ceremony at Mount Vernon, and he promised himself that he would have a fine place just like it someday. Everything there was painted white too."

"Mount Vernon was the home of the American President Washington, was it not?"

Jim nodded.

"Tell me of your family," Ursula said. "Aurora said that your father was a cruel man."

"Yes, he was cruel. Everyone called him The Master. He made me hang Sam's father."

Jim looked away.

"I'm not sure I ever loved my father, but I am sure I never did after that. His cruelty rubbed off on three of my brothers, but not on me or Rezin P."

"What about your mother and sisters?"

"The Master treated them like a queen and her ladies in waiting. My mother was not an intellectual, but she was well-educated, and she made sure her sons were too."

"Did your mother not want an education for her daughters as well?"

"The Master opposed it. He thought all they needed to know was how to make a good home for their husbands."

"Did your mother not realize the value of her own knowledge and protest his position?"

"As far as I know, except on matters of religion, he never asked her opinion, and she never volunteered it. In a way, that was best because he tried to anticipate her every wish, and she got more of what she wanted in the long run."

"I could never be like that, Jim."

"I know, my love, and I would never want you to be. You are an intelligent and educated woman, and I value that."

Then Ursula smiled and asked, "And what of the other women you have known, the woman you were going to marry before me, for example? Was she intelligent and educated?"

"Her name was Cecelia, but there was another woman before her, when I was barely a man; a slave woman in New Orleans who was beautiful and bright. You met her. Cleo at the hotel ball."

"So I was right. You did have feelings for that woman."

"Yes I did then. She was very skilled and convincing, but all she really wanted was for me to take her to Canada, and she left me when I wouldn't oblige her."

"And what of Cecelia?"

"Cecelia was the first woman I ever knew who seemed to feel things as deeply as I did. She was good and pure and chaste. We planned to live here and manage the plantation. But when she went to New Orleans to buy her trousseaux, she caught yellow fever, and then she died."

"So you think I am a whore like Cleo, because I gave myself to you freely?"

The Other Rose of Texas

"What I think . . . what I feel is as the second verse of that poem I gave you says, 'as fair art thou, my bonnie lass, so deep in luve am I; and I will luve thee still, my dear, til a' the seas gang dry.' You are a perfect combination of beauty, intelligence, spirituality, and passion. I am the most lucky man in the world to have you as my wife."

He took her in his arms and kissed her passionately. She clung to him.

"Do you think you could ever be happy living here with me, Ursula?"

Looking down, she paused for a long time before she raised her head and answered. "I, too, have deep feelings, my husband. I want you to know I now have a different perspective on you and on your slaves. Clearly, they love you, and since your father died, they are treated with kindness and compassion. However, I still believe that God does not want one man to own another, and I could not be happy with anyone who denies freedom to a fellow human being as you do here."

Jim looked up at the Spanish moss canopy over his head.

"I have asked my brothers to buy me out so I will no longer own any slaves except Sam and the three who are in Bexar."

He lowered his eyes and looked into Ursula's.

"I have tried to sell Josephus and Charlie, and I will continue to try. But I cannot part with Sam, and he cannot part with Bettie. I have to take care of them. But I promise I will never buy another human being as long as I live."

"I understand, my husband. I will try to be patient because I now know that you have a good heart."

* * *

That night, Ursula asked the three slaves to return to their own slave-shacks to sleep. She dressed in her most alluring negligee, placed a red rose in her hair, and walked into Jim's room.

"I think God took our son to punish me for my sins, and I have promised him that I will try to be a better person. I want to start our marriage over, and pretend that no one but us has ever lived and no time but ours will ever pass."

Jim closed the book, he was reading and laid it aside.

"But I hope he will forgive me for one final act of vanity. I want you to make me pregnant again. If my baby is born nine months from now, that will silence the wagging tongues at home."

"You could just go home without being pregnant. That would accomplish the same thing," Jim observed.

"That is true, but I saw how sad you were when I lost your son and I want to give you a child."

"Why would you want that? I thought you believed I would be a terrible father."

"Because I love you. Now cease speaking and make love to me."

After that night Jim's angst was gone. He could not imagine a crisis worse than the one that had played out over the previous six months and with it resolved, he felt certain that their relationship and marriage were on solid ground.

Jim and Ursula remained at the plantation for another two weeks, making love often. By the time they departed for the trip home to Bexar, the plantation fields had bloomed into a sea of white cotton.

Chapter 11

By late August, the Bowies were back home in Bexar. When Juan asked Jim why he changed his mind about spending the year in Louisiana, Jim said, "Your daughter wanted to be with her family, especially her mother, during her pregnancy."

"Splendid," Juan said, and Jim felt good about pleasing him.

A party was given by the Veramendis where Jim announced the impending arrival of his first child, due at the end of March.

Both Ursula and her mother were beaming and Jim decided it was because they knew that everyone was calculating that the expected birthdate was fully eleven months after the wedding.

Jim was happy too when word arrived that their Saltillo textile mill had been delivered and assembled, and awaited the first shipment of cotton.

A week later, he departed for Saltillo to see for himself. However, when he returned, he brought discouraging news.

"There is no cotton at the mill, and the American planters I visited on the way back say they are afraid the government will confiscate any shipment they send down there. They think the renewed crusade against slavery by the government will extend to the cotton that is produced by slave labor. I'm not optimistic, Juan."

"They have to sell their crop somewhere, do they not?"

"Yes, but they prefer selling it for a lower price in Galveston to the risk of losing it altogether."

"Then it seems we had better get some seed and start planting ourselves. Have you the land in mind?"

Despite the setback, Jim was still feeling positive.

"Yes, I can use some of my grant between the Brazos and Navasota rivers, about a hundred leagues north of San Felipe."

"I know that area. It should prove perfect and there is plenty of water," Juan commented.

"I agree, but we still have one big problem. I couldn't find anybody willing to come and work our cotton. They say they hear that fighting between the government and the rebels could break out up here any day."

"Let me make some inquiries in Mexico City to see if I can raise a work force. How many men would we need to start?"

"If they have experience with cotton, we could use around two-hundred hands. If they are not experienced, we will need half again as many."

"And when do we need them?"

"We have already missed the growing season for this year, but we will be alright for next year if at least half of them arrive by March first. We can use women and children, too, if necessary."

"I shall see what I can accomplish with the help of President Bustamante, and I will keep you informed."

"Good. But I think we need an alternative plan in case you are not successful."

"What do you have in mind?"

"I can bring in some of my slaves from Louisiana until I make enough money to buy some in Galveston."

"That would be illegal."

"I know. But I have no choice. I cannot sell any of my land and none of your people will come up here to work it. What else can I do."

"Using slaves would be the worst thing you could do. You would lose the respect of the friends you have made here, not to mention what it would do to Ursula."

"Are you saying I would lose your support?"

"I cannot condone the use of slaves."

"Then let us hope it does not become necessary."

* * *

For the next few weeks, with no prospective buyers for his land or hands to make it productive Bowie felt aimless. When his thoughts turned to slaving, the only endeavor that had brought him financial success, he felt conflicted. He did not want to renege on his promise to Ursula but his ego would not let him accept financial failure.

However, he had no operating cash, and he knew he did not dare ask Juan for a loan to buy an inventory of human beings. He considered taking Josephus and Charlie to the Galveston block to raise a little operating capital, but decided to wait a while longer for results from Juan Veramendi's efforts to recruit workers.

Then he received a fateful invitation from Juan Seguin to join a weekly poker game at the ranch of his father Erasmo, east of Bexar.

The poker game involved one and sometimes two tables of five. A chair might be occupied by a Mexican, Texican, or Tejano from anywhere on the map, as long as he was fluent in English and brought something of value that could go into the pot. It was dealer's choice for table stakes which might be currency from any one of a dozen banks or a bill of sale for anything that could be bartered.

Bowie broke even the first night and considered not returning, but the mention of a lost silver mine by Xavier Losoya caught his interest. He went back the next week to learn more.

"I'm curious about this silver mine, Xavier. Where is it supposed to be?"

Losoya, half grinning, looked around the table before replying. "Mi amigo, the mine is a legend. Many foolish men have searched, but none have found it."

Bowie persisted. "What does the legend say?"

Juan Seguin joined the conversation. "I am one of those fools, Jim."

Losoya's face paled. "I am sorry Patron, I meant no insult," he said.

Smiling forgiveness, Seguin took up the tale. "The legend says that, many years ago, the Lipan Apache worked a silver mine near the ruins of an Aztec temple about sixty leagues northwest of here. The Spanish took over the mine and built a mission to convert the Indians to Christianity and a presidio to quarter troops to protect the mine and the mission. The mission and the Presidio are still there."

"That doesn't sound like a legend to me. Why would the Spanish invest so much if there was nothing to protect? What happened to the mine?"

"The location of the mine was lost after the Indians revolted and drove the Spanish from the area in 1758."

"That's seventy three years ago. Has no one found anything in all that time?" Bowie queried.

"The Indians are thick up there. It is not safe for a man alone."

"It sounds like it might be worth taking the chance."

"Your own father-in-law can tell you more than I. Whether he would be willing to speak of it and risk having his new son-in-law turn his daughter into a widow is another question."

Bowie had heard what he came for. Now anxious to get home and ask Juan Veramendi about the lost mine he excused himself early, again breaking even in the poker game.

***

The next day at breakfast back in Bexar, Bowie could barely contain his excitement about the mine. "What better way to restore my fortune than finding a lost silver mine?" he thought.

"Juan, what is this business I hear about a lost mine near here?"

His father-in-law looked surprised. Then his eyes narrowed, and his expression changed to understanding as he said, "That's right, you have been spending time with Juan Seguin. Now I see."

Juan looked toward Ursula, as if he was deciding whether or not to continue. Jim was reminded of what Seguin had said about making her a widow.

"The mission was called Santa Cruz de San Saba; the Presidio was called San Luis de las Amarillas. The mine is referred to as Los Almagres."

"Is there truth to the story?"

"On the one hand, no evidence of a smelter was ever found in the area. On the other, I doubt that the Spanish would have wanted to transport large quantities of ore very far, so a smelter may be hidden somewhere."

The Other Rose of Texas

Juan took a deep breath and looked at Ursula again.

"I am inclined to think the mine is there, somewhere, but I am not sure how rich it is. Yet people still talk of Indians bringing silver and even some gold to nearby trading posts from time to time."

The more Veramendi said, the more energized Bowie felt. He rose from his chair and began pacing.

Veramendi continued.

"You know, Juan Seguin and I have talked about mounting another expedition to search for the mine. There are still men in Bexar who accompanied him to the area several years ago. Would you be interested in leading such a group?"

Ursula's eyes widened and her mouth fell open. "But Father, I need my husband here with me. My baby."

"Now Ursula, you have your mother and your sisters to help you, and a man like Jim needs adventure."

When Ursula looked at Jim, he looked away. Each day his ego made him less inclined to depend upon Juan to feed him and he felt desperate to find a way to reclaim his pride, no matter how dangerous the means.

"I think we should proceed," Bowie offered, seating himself. "What terms would be acceptable to you for financing the trip?"

"I think I could offer you the same deal I gave Seguin. Half to me, a quarter to you for recruiting and leading the men, and the other quarter to the men who go along."

"I know I can get my brother and Caiaphas Ham, how many will we need?" Jim asked.

"There were ten men last time, including Seguin. You should take Xavier Losoya to show you the way, and I think we can get six more as soon as word circulates."

Within a week the food, medical supplies, clothing, weapons, powder, and shot were assembled and ten men and two servants were ready to depart. Then on November 2, 1831, after a birthday celebration for Ursula the previous day, Jim Bowie and the men of the Los Almagres Mine Expedition rode out of Bexar.

* * *

To keep her mind from dwelling on her husband's absence, Ursula spent her days in her room directing local craftsmen to cut a doorway to the adjacent room and convert it into a nursery.

In daylight she fantasized about being a mother and on more than a few nights, she dreamed about being in Jim's arms.

Gradually, she felt more neglected and resentful. She did not want riches from a silver mine; she wanted her husband with her when she had his baby.

Four weeks had passed without a word of the mine expedition when Ursula was summoned by her mother to a family meeting in the parlor. When she entered the room, the first thing she noticed was the presence of Pablo Luis Ramerez, the family curanderismo practitioner.

Her father was standing when she entered. "Sit down, Ursula. I am afraid we have some bad news."

Feeling more curious than anything else Ursula sat between her sisters on a sofa near the fire place. Their quizzical expressions matched their mother's, making their faces appear as copies of hers, when their father began to speak again.

"A small band of friendly Comanches arrived here this morning. They had passed through San Saba a week ago, and they reported that they saw Jim's group on a hill surrounded by hundreds of Indians of many tribes. The Comanches said they were sure that Jim, and the other men, were all dead by now."

When her father spoke, it became clear to Ursula that Ramerez, the pseudo-doctor was there to sedate her, if it became necessary.

Juana and Josefa both hugged Ursula and began to cry, while dry-eyed Ursula put an arm around each sister.

Feeling angry now Ursula looked around the room. Her mother put a lace handkerchief to her mouth and tears welled in young Marco's eyes.

"Is this the adventure you had in mind for my husband when you sent him away, my father?"

Senora Veramendi rose from her chair. "You must not speak with disrespect to your father in this way."

A married woman now, who considered herself well beyond the control of her mother, Ursula stood and walked out of the room. She walked to the shed where Sam slept and knocked on the door. When he opened it, she stepped inside and quickly closed it behind her.

"Mister Jim is dead and you may have a chance to get free. I promised Aurora that I would help you when the time came so here is some money."

She handed Sam a handkerchief that was tied at the four corners.

"It is one thousand American dollars in gold. It is all I have," she added and was out the door before Sam could speak.

She appeared at dinner that evening dressed in mourning black. She ate little and said nothing.

Juan broke the silence.

"I will not believe that Jim is dead until I see it. So I visited the Comanche's camp on the river again this afternoon. I offered them one horse for each identifiable body they brought back for burial. They agreed to go back up to San Saba immediately."

Ursula did not react, nor did she remain for the traditional after-dinner family evening in the parlor. In her room, she sat alone thinking. "I am a twenty-year-old girl, five months pregnant, and now a widow."

She glanced at the hole in the wall that was to become the doorway to her baby's nursery. "Now I must raise my baby without a father or give myself to a kindly gentleman who is willing to raise another man's child."

She rose from her chair, crossed to the bed, and lay across it. "Oh, Jim. You promised to take care of us," she said and cried herself to sleep.

***

Six days after the bad news first arrived, her brother Marco rushed into Ursula's room. When he opened the door, she heard the cathedral bell ringing.

"A priest was in the cathedral bell tower repairing a rope when he saw a line of riders slowly approaching the west side of San Pedro Creek," Marco said breathlessly. "He counted eleven horses with upright riders, and a twelfth horse carrying a bundle draped over its saddle that hung like a man's body. Each of the three riders in the lead grasped his reins and saddle horn and swayed slightly from side to side. When the priest recognized the wide-brimmed brown hat that Jesse Wallace always wears, he began to ring the cathedral bell."

"What are you trying to say, Marco?"

"Senor Jim has come home safe. They have gone into the house of the curanderismo."

When she heard that, Ursula ran out to the hitching rail, where she mounted the first horse she saw, wheeled, and spurred it to a gallop. She quickly arrived at the home of Ramerez on Flores Street and, despite being almost six months pregnant, leapt from the horse and ran through a gathered crowd and into the house.

She felt elated when she saw Jim, apparently unhurt, cutting away the trouser leg of David Buchanan with his knife, revealing a bullet wound. The other two wounded men, James Corriell and Matthew Doyle, slumped in chairs nearby, while the dead body of Thomas McCaslin lay upon the floor between them, wrapped in homespun cloth.

Jim continued cutting as Ursula embraced him from behind and laid her head on his right shoulder. He turned his head toward her and his lips parted in a slight smile.

When the wounded men were treated Bowie motioned to Ursula to precede him out of the front door. Outside, they found Juan and Marco waiting in an open carriage.

Bowie lifted Ursula into the back seat of the carriage, tied the reins of their horses to the back, climbed in, and collapsed into the seat beside her.

"Let's go home," he said.

* * *

In the Veramendi Palace Jim Bowie ate his first hot meal in weeks, then went into his room and slept.

The morning of the second day, he rose, bathed, dressed, and joined the family for breakfast. Marco barely gave him time to take a bite.

The Other Rose of Texas

"The Comanches told father you were surrounded by Indians and you were probably dead," the boy said in an excited, high pitched voice.

Recalling the event from his memory for the first time since it happened caused a little of his initial fear to return, and Jim concentrated on making his own voice sound calm.

"On the trail we encountered two Comanche and a Mexican captive who lived with the tribe. That night the captive rode into our camp and told us we were being followed by over a hundred and fifty Twowokana, Waco, and Caddoe."

The entire family had gathered close around him, including Consuelo, and Jim thought they all looked tense.

"We didn't see any Indians all the next day and that night we camped in a large cluster of live-oak trees and bushes with water nearby. We were only three leagues from the old fort, and the next morning as we were about to depart they were on us."

"Were you scared?" Josefa asked.

"Yes, and I was most scared that I would never see you again," he said and tweaked her nose.

Ursula smiled and the children laughed. But, in spite of the levity, Bowie felt anxious all over again when he recalled seeing the large number of savages arrayed against his small group.

"There were so many. How did you escape?"

"We didn't escape. All day long they fired arrows and balls at us. Then they tried to burn us out. We just kept picking them off one by one. The next morning they saw that we were ready to fight them again and they rode away."

"How many did they lose?" Juan asked.

"When we reconnoitered we counted over forty blood spots. I think they lost many more than they expected. They seemed more intent on gathering their wounded than on mounting a successful attack against us."

"Did they not return?" Marco inquired.

"We waited for eight days to make sure they were really gone."

After breakfast, Jim joined Juan in the study. Closing the door, he said, "I found the mine, Juan."

"What did you say?"

"When so many Indians attacked, I knew they had to be protecting something. I bribed the Mexican captive. He admitted there was a mine and drew me a map to it."

Juan was standing now.

"While we waited for them to come back, I slipped away and located it. It's about two leagues north of the mission. The entrance is hidden by rocks in a box canyon. You have to be right on top of it to see it."

"How do you know it still has value?"

"The Mexican said that every tribal chief up there knows where it is, and they have agreed to share it. They take out small amounts of silver for ceremonial jewelry but from the veins I could see, there is plenty left. I even found a small smelter stored inside. I'm going back as soon as I can with some equipment and more men."

"Are you certain that is wise?"

"I need fifty thousand dollars, Juan, and I think I can smelt enough silver for your share and that much more for me and the men in a couple of months."

"Aren't you afraid the Indians will come back? What about Ursula and the baby? What is the money for? Perhaps I can advance it," Juan questioned.

Jim thought that Juan sounded a little frantic.

"I promise there will be a need for your participation later, but right now I have to do this on my own. I have accepted too much from you already."

Jim wanted to avoid hurting Juan, but it felt good to refuse another handout.

"Let me ask you this, though. Have you had any luck locating workers for the cotton-plantation?"

Juan looked away. "I was planning to tell you. It does not look promising."

"I figured that. I had a lot of time to think up there while we were waiting for those savages to come back, and I believe I have the solution to all of our labor problems. "

Juan looked back at him.

"Have you heard of the underground railroad in the United States?"

"Yes, I believe it exists to help slaves escape to Canada."

"That's right, and I think we can build a connection to it that will bring many of those runaways to Texas. That is why I need the money."

Jim felt more excited with each word.

"I also plan to hire every experienced free-man from every cotton farm that I can find in Texas. Then we will have an experienced labor force that we can work for wages. I think they will be more productive than slaves, and that will prove that what you said to me a year ago about slavery in Texas is right."

The excitement in Bowie's voice manifested as a proud smile that spread across Juan's face like a sunrise. "Why did I not think of that? It is so simple, and we might even be able to gain government cooperation. Have you told anyone else about your plan? Have you told Ursula?"

"I'm doing this for Ursula. But I want to surprise her by having everything in place and working smoothly before I do."

"How long will that take?"

"I don't know yet. I have to proceed cautiously. There is a lot at stake."

"You mean with the other slave owners here?"

"Yes, they will see it as a threat. They could organize against it and petition Mexico City to stop the runaways at the border."

"President Bustamante is a friend of mine. I think we can convince him to support your plan, or at least to consider it. I will send a letter right away to arrange an appointment."

Suddenly Jim realized that, in his effort to impress Juan, he might have said more than he should.

"Are you sure Bustamante can be trusted? Could he be someone with interests that might be threatened by my scheme?"

"I have known him for many years. He is a man who opposes slavery."

Jim stared at him for a moment, then Juan said, "I understand your concerns. When I request the appointment with the president I will explain that we want to discuss the textile industry. That way you can make the decision about what to tell him."

"Good, our other potential problem is the reaction of the slave owners in the U.S. We have to be careful not to encourage the slaves to run, but to just re-direct them to Mexico when they do."

When they parted, Jim wished even more that he had not let his ego tell Juan so much about his plan.

* * *

While Jim continued to recuperate from his Indian fight, the Bowie, Veramendi, and Navarro families celebrated Christmas and New Year's together.

Then in late January, Jim promised Ursula, "I'll be back before the baby comes," and was gone again, first to Gonzales where he formed a twenty six man ranging company and next, reportedly, off in search for the hostile Indians who had attacked him near San Saba.

By the time he actually did return to Bexar, his daughter was three weeks old, Jim had delivered over a ton and a half of silver to his New Orleans bank, and each of his rangers had his own personal cache in exchange for swearing to keep the mine location a secret, and agreeing not to return there without Bowie's permission.

His reception at the bank was sterling compared with the greeting Ursula gave him when he finally returned home.

When he arrived he embraced and kissed her tenderly, yet she felt stiff to him.

"Are you alright? Was the birth difficult? I tried to return in time."

"I named my daughter Maria Elve, after my mother and yours. Had you been here, as you promised, you could have participated in her naming."

Jim was ready to grovel if he had to.

"I like the name. May I see her?"

"I think you should be punished a while longer before I allow that," she said.

Had Ursula no red rose in her hair, Jim would have taken her words to mean he was really in trouble.

"I am sincerely sorry, my darling, but I can tell you that my journey was a great success."

Then Ursula walked to the crib, picked up the newborn, and held her up for Jim to see. "Would you like to hold her?" she said and smiled.

Jim thought of his hands and clothing, still dirty from the trail.

"I'm not sure how. I've never held a baby."

"Like this," she said, showing her husband how to support his daughter's back and head.

He cradled her head on his left elbow and her tiny body along his arm. When she opened her eyes and looked directly at him, his breath grew short and tears flooded his eyes. "Coyote," he said and sat upon the bed. "She is so beautiful." He could manage no other words before handing the baby back to Ursula and breaking down.

For Jim, it was something like what people had said about the moment before dying. The evils of his past seemed to parade before him in his mind's eye: The hanging, the ships of slaves, the drinking, the gambling, and the fighting. Now however, holding his own daughter, he was overwhelmed by the feeling that he had finally accomplished something good and worthwhile.

Ursula put baby Elve back in her crib, sat beside Jim, and held him.

"I know, I know," she said. "Now don't you wish you had not been away so long?"

He sobbed.

"I feel it too. A kind of forgiveness. As if God is saying, I give you this child as a sign that you have one more chance to get things right."

"Yes," he said, and looked directly into Ursula's eyes, his tears still flowing. "Yes."

Chapter 12

The three travelers from Bexar arrived in the Mexican capital on a beautiful morning in late May and settled into an apartment that Juan Veramendi kept on the Zocalo. Their meeting with the president was scheduled for the next day in the National Palace, a building they could see through a window, across the plaza.

Not much could be said for the beauty of the building. By day, it qualified as a palace architecturally because it was as boring to see as the Palais du Louvre in Paris. At night, however, Jim thought the lighted torches every twenty feet gave it the appearance of a medieval castle in Spain.

The next morning, while Sam remained in the apartment Jim and Juan decided to walk, rather than ride, across the square to their meeting.

In Bustamante's spacious office, after Bowie was introduced by his father-in-law, the three men were served coffee and fruit, then all doors were closed, and Juan began their discussion.

"Senior President, as you know from my letter, I see a bright future for the textile industry in my state based upon the production of cotton on the plains, and later raising sheep in our western mountains. My son-in-law and I have opened a mill in Saltillo that is ready to turn the cotton we grow into cloth for the clothing factories that we plan to build."

"Yes, Governor Veramendi, I recall our correspondence on the matter."

"Your excellency has been kind enough to endorse our efforts to find workers that we can hire to come to Tejas and raise our cotton. However, we have encountered the same obstacle that has troubled the government for centuries. None of our countrymen are willing to live in Tejas, due to their fear of hostile Indians."

"Yes, I am familiar with the problem."

"I think Senior Bowie has authored a solution to that problem, and we are here to seek the opinion of your excellency."

Bustamante smiled. "Please, Senor Bowie, tell me of your plan."

Bowie was feeling uneasy. The exchange between Juan and the President seemed stilted and uncomfortable, not at all like a conversation between friends.

"Thank you, your excellency. First let me say that our failure to recruit laborers from within Mexico may be a blessing in disguise. Cotton could become a significant new revenue source for our country. Since few of our Mexican nationals have experience, it would take years for them to learn the finer points of planting, nurturing, and harvesting cotton, without help."

Paying particular attention to Bustamante's body language and facial expression, Jim saw no negative signs and thought the man looked interested.

"This is knowledge the slaves in the United States already possess. We need to bring those people and their skills to Mexico and have them teach our people."

Now Jim saw hostility in the President's eyes.

"You do not need to go any further, Senor Bowie. If I had known you were here to campaign for slavery in Tejas, I would not have agreed to this meeting."

"I am sorry, your excellency. That is not my purpose. Please hear me out."

"Alright, but no more talk of using slaves in Mexico."

"I agree, Mister President. I think the institution of slavery is doomed throughout the world. It is being destroyed from without and from within by governments and by slave rebellions. As your excellency knows, among the leading nations around the world, the United States has the only government that has not banned slavery."

"Yes, and I am proud to say that I personally plan to free every slave who is already in Mexico, indentured by contract or not."

Bowie was feeling comfortable now and decided it was safe to reveal his plan to Bustamante.

"Yes, your excellency, and I think my plan will help you do that. As you know, in the United States, the abolitionists in the north are encouraging a slave rebellion in the south. I think the only thing that is delaying such a rebellion is what they call the underground railroad. It helps southern slaves escape to the north, and it works like a safety valve on a steam engine to let the most rebellious of them out of the boiler, so to speak."

"Go on, Senor Bowie."

"Your excellency, my plan is this; we simply expand the Mexico connection to the underground railroad and offer incentives to the runaways to come here instead of going to Canada. Some who come here will want to work their own land immediately, and some will be willing to work for wages for a while before they acquire their own land. Either way, they will be freemen producing cotton for our textile industry and our people can begin to learn from them."

The President had been leaning back in his chair with his right hand pulling at his goatee. Now he leaned forward and placed his arms on his desk.

"And how do you propose to expand this Mexico connection?"

"All over the United States, the network already exists that helps the slaves reach the north. We need to make it worthwhile for the operators of that network to tell the slaves about the good life they could have in Mexico and how to get here. If we offer the runaways liberty and a chance at free land, I think many will choose Mexico over Canada, or over the risk of being captured and returned to their masters, if they stay in the United States." Bowie paused and studied the president's gaze. Seeing sustained interest, he continued.

"Our first connections will be along the Mississippi River. This will give us an immediate flow of people coming down the river and into Tejas by boat along the gulf coast. Then all we need is a link between the Mississippi River and Nacogdoches. I have the contacts and the money necessary to get this started. All I need is the blessing of your excellency."

"What do you mean by my blessing?"

"All you need to do is have your generals tell their garrison commanders not to stop the slaves at the borders and to tell them where to look for work. Everything else can be taken care of where the freemen settle."

Then Juan added, "We realize that your support will require an expenditure of resources, and we would be honored to have you accept the large number of shares in our enterprises that we have set aside for your Excellency's use and distribution."

The president suddenly seemed more passive than Bowie expected in response to Juan's offer of compensation. He stood, walked to a window behind his desk, and turned.

"I am curious about one other thing, Senor Bowie. I know that you have been a planter, a slave owner, and a slave trader with Senor Lafitte. Why are you proposing a scheme that will abolish your means of making a living, and how can you be so sure it will work? Is it just the thought of making even more money that drives you?"

Bowie sensed resistance and wondered if he was hearing the president's real concerns.

"It is pure economics, your excellency. As many have already stated and written, an economy based on slavery is unsound and sure to fail. The Romans proved that."

"You mentioned that your plan would help me to free the slaves who are already in Mexico."

"Yes, your excellency. I plan to employ as many of these freemen as I can, and I will demonstrate to the other planters that I can be more successful paying wages than they are using slaves, and doing so with a lot less heartache. I also think the negro freemen will show the slaves they can have a better life if they leave their oppressive masters. I think I can convince the people in Tejas to adopt my plan because, even now, a clear majority of them just want to be successful and live peacefully."

"This plan could flood Tejas with Americans, or worse, give the United States an excuse to attack Mexico. At any rate, I cannot decide on this today."

Jim believed he was finally getting at the truth and he presented the feature of his plan that he thought would be most appealing to Bustamante.

"One last thing to consider, your excellency. As you know, government opposition to slavery is a major issue among our political activists in Tejas. I think you can reduce their animosity if you show that your government recognizes their particular needs and is at least exploring possible accommodations."

"Thank you, Senor Bowie. Juan, we will be in contact with you soon." Bustamante stood, bowed, and walked out.

"Do not be discouraged, my son. If the president can find a way to make money from your plan, we will have his cooperation," Juan said.

But on their way home from Mexico City Bowie was feeling discouraged and in his mind he again questioned the decision to reveal his plan to this politician.

During a stop in Saltillo they learned of an altercation between a Texican militia unit and the Mexican garrison at Anahuac on Galveston Bay, involving a young lawyer named William Travis.

Jim feared that this event might be the beginning of the rebellion everyone was talking about. He did not share this feeling with Juan but he did begin to consider how his underground railroad scheme would fair in a Texas that was not a part of Mexico.

* * *

Finally back in Bexar Jim was feeling strangely content. He still had problems, but he could not think of a good reason to feel unhappy.

"I want to stay home and enjoy being with you and our family," he told Ursula. "I want to take you out and show everyone how proud I am to be your husband."

"Jim Bowie, the famous explorer and killer, a househusband. Are you sick," she replied.

"I promise to attend family meals and go to mass. I want to take you to every social event, fandango, and fiesta you fancy."

"I would love that."

"And I want to spend a lot of time watching you care for our baby."

They both laughed, almost hysterically, at the incongruity of his statement.

Except for a couple of peace keeping trips with his militia unit, Jim kept his word to Ursula. He kept himself happy by finding time for work. Anticipating Mexican government cooperation with his plan, he began tracing possible underground railroad routes to Mexico on his maps and identifying places and people that he would try to involve in his scheme.

Traveling in his mind, he selected good locations for stations along routes through Pennsylvania, Ohio, Indiana, Illinois, down the Mississippi River, then through the Arkansas Territory and across the Red River into Mexico. Along the Gulf of Mexico, he marked potential stations in Florida, Georgia, and Louisiana. He expected to have President Bustamante's endorsement soon after the end of 1832 and planned to leave then and begin making personal contact with the underground railroad operators.

Meanwhile, even without official government support, a trickle of runaway slaves escaped from the United States into Mexico. They crossed the border from Louisiana or the Arkansas Territory, or they arrived in boats small and large along the gulf coast.

Some of these people started turning up in Bexar because, without making his overall plan known, Jim Bowie had managed to spread the word that he was offering work for wages on a cotton-plantation and a chance to earn land to any interested person, black or white. After obtaining their mark on a document that promised their loyalty to Mexico and an employment contract that paid them a reasonable wage, he sent them on to Rezin P., who was organizing and building their Texas cotton plantation.

* * *

In November, Ursula announced that she was pregnant again. Clearly, both Jim and Ursula were now getting what they wanted from their relationship.

"We have the money now and I can buy us a house if you like, my dear, but I would be overjoyed if you want to stay here with your family. I have been very happy here living with people who love each other."

"I am happy here as well," Ursula said.

"It's settled then," Bowie said feeling satisfaction.

Jim had returned to work at the desk in the study when Juan delivered bad news.

"Bustamante has resigned and fled to Europe. Pedraza has assumed the presidency, but it is Santa Anna who is really in control."

Bowie, jerked his head around at the sound of Veramendi's voice, then stood abruptly in reaction to his statement. "What will this mean for us?"

"I know little of Santa Anna personally, but I have heard that he tends to be tyrannical and vindictive."

"That means we cannot hope for support from the government," Jim said.

"Will you continue with your plan?" Juan asked.

"I don't know. I wanted to do this and surprise Ursula with a fait accompli. Now I think I need her participation in deciding what to do."

"I think you are a wise man. I will summon her."

Ursula joined the two men and Jim gave her a detailed description of his plan, including all of the pros and cons. He concluded by saying, "I think, regardless of any changes the government might make affecting immigration or slavery, Texas will always be open to any man who is willing to work and help grow the economy."

Jim could see his wife's eyes narrowing as he explained the details. She did not interrupt even once, but when he finished, she revealed her concerns.

"How long would you be away from us?"

"I think it will take about nine months, but I would not consider leaving until after the new baby comes."

"Clearly this will be dangerous. The slave owners on both sides of the border are rich and powerful men. If your plan is successful and they learn that you are responsible, you will never be safe. I will always be afraid for you."

"Then I will not go on with it. I will find the workers I need some other way."

"But you must go forward with it. This will be such fine work, God's work, for everyone, for Tejas, for Mexico, for the planters, and most of all for the slaves who will be free. You must go forward. This could change history and I cannot be selfish."

Jim could tell that Ursula meant every word. It gave him a warm feeling to recognize that she had grown from self-absorbed, scheming teenager to mature, caring woman, wife, and mother.

Then he looked at Juan who said," I agree Jim."

"Then I will," Bowie asserted.

***

Her mother and sister Juana joined Ursula when her contractions and labor pains began in the early morning of July 18, 1833. Her youngest sister Josefa tended baby Elve in the nursery, while Jim, Juan, and Marco paced in the parlor.

Bettie stayed in the kitchen boiling water and Sam stayed busy carrying it, and a supply of clean linen, to the birthing bedroom.

After three hours Ursula's labor pains became much worse than those she experienced with the birth of her daughter. Soon they rivaled the pains of her miscarriage and she began to rave .

"Santa Madre. Santa Madre. No llevar a mi hijo de nuevo."

"Your baby will be fine. No one will take your baby," the Senora said.

"Aurora, donde es Aurora?" she screamed.

"What is aurora?" Juana asked.

"I do not know," her mother replied. "Go tell Jim that she wants aurora."

Juana left the room and quickly returned.

"Jim said Aurora is a slave woman who helped Ursula through her miscarriage."

"He said that in front of your father?" the Senora asked.

"Yes. I did not know that Ursula had a miscarriage," Juana replied.

"Neither did your father."

"Aurora, donde es Aurora?" Ursula repeated as Jim entered the room.

"Aurora is not here my darling," he said.

"Do not let them take my son again."

"No one will take your baby my darling."

After three more hours of labor, as she had seemed to foretell, Ursula gave birth to a boy. The baby appeared to be healthy and by evening, her ordeal all but forgotten, she was ready to introduce the newest Bowie to his extended family.

"Jim and I have decided to name him James Veramendi Bowie," Ursula said as everyone including the two slaves gathered around her bed. "Con su permiso, father."

"I am honored, my children," Juan replied.

Then Jim looked at Sam and asked, "What do you think of our new little man Sam?"

"I thinks he be a Bowie cause he hair red like you," Sam replied in his best pic-speak.

When they had all gone Ursula said a prayer of thanks. She ended it by asking God to protect her husband after his departure which, she feared, would now happen soon.

* * *

On the morning of Thursday, August 1, Sam had two mules packed, two horses saddled and was ready to ride east. Jim was at breakfast when Ursula entered the room, still wearing her night gown. She seemed uncharacteristically frantic.

"Baby Elve is very stricken. She has a fever and will not respond when I try to feed her. I have sent for the curanderismo."

The medical man arrived and examined the sixteen month-old child. "At best, it is a simple infection that will pass. At worst, it is cholera. There have been rumors of outbreaks to the east and south."

Ursula began to cry. She leaned against Jim, and he put his arm around her.

"My babies."

"Sam and I will not leave until she is better. Thank you, Senor Ramerez."

"Keep trying to feed her, and I will come back this afternoon," Ramerez promised.

By afternoon, little Elve was awake and feeding, and her fever was gone. But the threat of cholera had frightened Jim. He and Juan conferred and decided on a course of action designed to deal with the risk without alarming the family. A meeting was called in the parlor where Juan presented their plan.

"Though they still call me Vice-Governor, with the death of Governor Letona I am now Governor Veramendi, and my new duties require a trip to Monclova. I think this would be a very good time for a vacation in the cool mountain air for us all. We have not visited our villa there in some time, and I want to see if it is being well maintained."

Everyone seemed to favor the trip except the teenagers, for whom Juana spoke.

"Father, there is absolutely nothing to do in Monclova, and we have fandangos and the fall fiesta coming soon, here. Besides, we want to attend school here this year, not there. May Josefa, Marco, and I please stay? We will be careful about our food, and we will always boil the water."

Jim knew from her comment that Juana was aware of her father's real motive for urging his family to accompany him to the new state capitol.

Ursula was seated upon a sofa beside Jim. Both were cradling a baby; she, their daughter, and he, their son.

"I will cancel my trip and go with you," Jim said.

"Your work is too important. You can join us in Monclova as soon as your business is concluded," Ursula replied.

Juan continued. "Then it is agreed. The Senora and I, Ursula and the babies, will depart for a vacation in Monclova as soon as possible. The children will remain in Bexar for school under the supervision of cousin Consuelo."

"Thank you, Father." The other children echoed Juana's words with smiles.

Jim glanced at Senora Veramendi and her expression told him that she supported her husband's decision.

Dean Kirkpatrick

The day after seeing the family off to Monclova, Bowie and Sam departed Bexar for New Orleans.

* * *

Ursula entered the parlor just as the Mexican army lieutenant was beginning his report to Governor Veramendi.

"Your excellency you have six eighteen-foot-long Conestoga wagons to be driven by my men, and two armed outriders to accompany your two vaqueros."

"Very good lieutenant."

"The first two wagons are fitted with board seats suspended on leaf springs. They will carry your family and servants and their bedding. The remaining wagons are loaded with luggage, fresh and dried foodstuffs and sixty-four barrels of spring water."

"Very well."

"Will there be anything else before we embark, Governor?"

"It seems you have thought of everything. We are all ready to go."

During the first part of the trip, the hot dry days made the trail dusty and the babies cranky. Averaging ten miles a day, the party reached the banks of the Rio Bravo by the middle of the month. After crossing the river, they camped, giving everyone a break from the daily jostling and rocking of the wagons that reminded Ursula of her honeymoon trip.

"The vaqueros brought in a white-tail buck and we shall have a good dinner tonight," Juan told everyone. "I may even open a bottle of Chianti to go with it."

The river crossing marked the halfway point of the three hundred mile journey and the beginning of a gradual fifteen hundred foot increase in altitude for the travelers.

This climb was accompanied by a gradual decrease in the ambient temperature, especially at night. The babies began to sleep longer. Ursula did too, and pictures of Jim entered her occasional dreams.

Then, after twenty-two days on the trail, when the Veramendi family arrived in Santiago de la Monclova, Mexico, they were greeted by the jefe politico who was waiting at the Veramendi villa with news for Juan.

"The first case of cholera was diagnosed here five days ago. Somehow the water in the town acequia has been infected."

"What about the river water?"

"We don't really know, but we can't take the risk."

"What about the wells?" Ursula asked.

"One well seems to be alright, but it will not be enough for the whole town."

"Did you isolate the sick ones?" Juan asked.

"We put the first ones in the jail. But when they started to die, people began leaving town. I'm afraid things are out of control."

"What about the Royal Hospital?" the Senora asked.

"It is filling up, and the doctors are overwhelmed."

"Thank you, jefe. Please keep me informed."

After the wagons were unloaded, Juan released the army detachment and advised the lieutenant to monitor the health of his men closely during their return to Bexar. Then he asked everyone, including the servants, to gather in the parlor.

"You have all heard of the sickness here. I thought we were leaving it behind in Bexar."

The cook and her helper began to sob.

"There, there, we have no reason to panic. We brought plenty of good food and water, and we will be alright."

Juan's intonation seemed overly stern to Ursula, and she thought she saw doubt in his eyes, as if he was saying one thing while thinking another.

"But we still need to be very careful. We must not bring water into the house from anywhere in the town."

"Do you think that water from the good well might be used to wash the diapers for the babies . . . if we put in much soap?" the Senora proffered, cocking her head.

"Yes, but only for that, and it must be boiled first," Juan said. Then as an afterthought, "and only when the people have enough water from the well for drinking."

He cleared his throat and continued. "Does anyone feel sick? Has there been any vomiting or diarrhea?"

No one responded.

"Here is what we must do. We must drink water only from the barrels we brought."

Everyone nodded.

"We must wash our food with the same water."

They nodded again.

"We must wash our hands with soap and good water after we go to the out-house, and after we change diapers."

He looked around the room with what Ursula considered a sad expression. "It is my fault that we are here, and I am sorry."

"Could we not return to Bexar, my husband?"

"I have considered that. But we might find the same sickness there, or we might somehow take it with us if we flee."

"It is not your fault, father. You did what you thought best for us."

"We are in the hands of God. If anyone feels sick, tell me immediately."

As often as she could after that, Ursula walked to the nearby cathedral to pray and talk with a nun she knew.

**

Two days later, the cook began visiting the outhouse frequently. Ursula and the Senora put her to bed and began checking her condition regularly.

"I can't think of a worse person to be infected. We have all eaten the food she has handled," the Senora said.

"Perhaps it is something else. I'm sure she has not used bad water," Ursula replied.

But the classic symptoms of cholera continued to show in the cook. She became too weak to walk to the privy and had to be carried. Her skin took on a blue cast; her hands began to wrinkle, and her pulse quickened.

Juan could no longer deny her condition. "She has it, and I'm afraid we brought it with us in the food or water, or she was carrying it."

"My babies," Ursula gasped.

"We cannot trust our food and water now."

"What can we do?"

"I am sending the vaqueros to the high mountains to bring back game and water from the melted snow. But I don't know how long it will take."

"What will we eat?"

"I think the vegetables from our own garden will be alright."

"Mother, if I am infected, will my milk be bad for Elve and James?"

"I don't know, Ursula."

Two days later, in the morning, the cook died.

Ursula felt overwhelmed and helpless. Walking alone by the river so no one would see, she allowed herself to breakdown and cry.

After sundown, Ursula smelled a fishy odor coming from the diaper of seventeen month-old Elve, and the sick room vigil began again.

Chapter 13

Disembarked from the ferry that carried them across the Sabine River, now on the road to Vermillionville, Sam was quiet and contemplative. As if there was something in the soil of Louisiana that caused it, his thoughts turned to Portia and freedom.

Continuing east, they arrived in the city on the shores of Lake Pontchartrain amid talk of dry weather, a dwindling mosquito population, and the reduced incidence of yellow fever and malaria.

When they dismounted at their hotel, Jim said, "We have some good work to do after dark, then we'll be leaving New Orleans in the morning."

Distressed, Sam pleaded to be allowed to see Portia. Two years had passed since their rendezvous in the hotel garden, and they had not communicated. Still, he felt confident that she was waiting for him.

"How will you find her, Sam? Last we heard, they were on a plantation somewhere, and we don't have time for any side trips."

"She done tol' me 'bout a cousin what always know her bouts," Sam replied in his best pic-speak. "Ifn he say she ain't in N'Orleans, I come right back."

"What will you do if you find her? There's no time for lollygagging either."

"I's gots to see her, Master Jim. Please, Master Jim," Sam replied, clutching his pouch and the thousand dollars in gold that Ursula had given him inside it. "When I finds her, I wants you to take this money I gots and buy her from her master."

Sam was sweating. He had just made the boldest statement of his life and he held his breath, awaiting Jim's reaction.

Bowie quickly turned. He looked hard into Sam's eyes and Sam met his gaze. From Bowie's expression Sam hoped to divine his master's thoughts, but thought that Jim's face, especially his turned up mouth, had never looked quite like this before. Then, in a voice Sam considered most gentle, Jim said, "Alright Sam, but you be back here by sundown. We have work to do. And tell Cleo I'll send her a bank draft for Portia."

Beginning his search, Sam learned from her cousin that Portia was still with Cleo. The cousin reported that Cleo's rich husband had died from typhoid fever, and Portia was more a companion to her now than a servant. The cousin added that the two women divided their time between a plantation across the lake and a chateau on Royal Street.

As Sam walked to the chateau through the French Quarter, the smell of baking pastry was strong. He felt almost giddy with anticipation.

When he knocked, Cleo opened her own door smiled and invited Sam inside. The smell of expensive French perfume replaced all others as he entered.

"She's not here, Sam. I sent her north."

Sam felt staggered by the news.

"She hadn't heard from you in over two years, and she figured you were either dead or didn't care anymore. I paid a cattle boat captain to take her to Canada."

"Will she be safe? I mean, will she be took good care of?"

"Don't worry, the captain used to work for my husband. I told him I would ruin him if anything happened to her." Cleo patted Sam's hand.

"When he gets back, he is supposed to give me a note from her with the name of the town where he left her. Portia said if you showed up to give you back this gold and tell you to start looking for her up there."

Cleo handed him the gold coins he had given Portia.

Through the fine lace curtains on the windows, when Sam noticed the light dimming outside, he knew he had to either return to Bowie or begin his run north to Canada and Portia, there and then. He began to feel scared and confused.

As the reality of his situation became clear, a voice inside his head started asking questions. "What if it costs more than twelve hundred dollars now? How can you know who to trust on the river? Who will take care of Bettie in Texas if you run now?"

Sam thought of asking Cleo if she knew a captain who could take him north and what it would cost. Then the same inner voice asked, "What if Jim Bowie comes here looking for you? You know they are friends. Can you trust her not to tell him where you went?"

Finally, he told Cleo that he would try to come back to find out where Portia would be in Canada. Then he left.

Sam was in agony. The sun was not yet below the horizon, so he sat on the cobbles beside a fountain. Putting his face in his hands, he leaned back. Suddenly, a stream of water hit the back of his head.

He stood and turned to see another stream of water shoot from the penis of a naked cherub in the center of the fountain bowl. Slowly he began to walk toward the hotel and Bowie, his head down and his shoulders rounded.

* * *

When Sam returned just after dark, Jim did not ask about Portia. Perhaps he saw anguish in Sam eyes.

Bowie had their horses saddled and waiting. From their hotel on Canal street the two men immediately rode to a house at the west end of Magazine Street by the levee.

When they arrived, Jim told Sam to knock on the back door of the house and tell the woman who opened it that he wanted to go north. If a man opened the door, Sam was to ask for food.

Bowie added that he expected Sam would not be in the house long because the people would want to move him along in the dark, in a hurry. So if it appeared to Sam that they were stalling, he was to leave.

Was Bowie trying to involve him in some new white folks game. Or was he trying to catch white folks who helped slaves escape. Sam wondered, but he felt more curious than fearful.

When Sam knocked, the back door was opened slowly by a grand-motherly woman whose expression was a combination of cordiality and caution. Upon looking at Sam's face, the caution was replaced by determination as she swung the door wide open and motioned for Sam to enter quickly.

"Go tell Abraham to come here," she said to a negro boy who walked into Sam's view.

"I wants to go north," Sam said, trying to look confused.

"Are you hungry, friend?"

Sam shook his head.

Soon the back door opened again, and a young negro man wearing a black patch over his left eye entered. The woman explained that the man would be Sam's guide to the next place, and they would be walking all night. She handed each man a bundle tied up in oilcloth.

"Eat this along the way. They will give you breakfast when you get there."

"Thank you, mam. Why you doin this for me, mam?" Sam asked.

"Have you never heard of the underground railroad?" the woman questioned.

"No, mam, I ain't."

"Well, don't worry, I'm a Quaker. We think slavery is wrong and I will help you get free of it."

Sam had been in the house less than an hour when he and his guide walked out. Bowie joined them outside and within a few minutes, Sam was knocking on the door again..

The woman's eyes grew wide when she opened it and saw Sam and Abraham with a tall white man standing behind them.

"Don't be alarmed, mam. I'm here to help you and these men."

Without being invited, Bowie urged the two men forward. "Someone may be watching, mam," he said.

When everyone was clear, Bowie closed the door. "Mam, my name is Bowie, and Sam, here, is with me. To make a long story short, mam, we live in Texas, and we are here to convince you to tell the slaves you help that they can have their own land and a good life as freemen in Texas with us."

With Sam nodding his confirmation as he began to understand what was happening, Jim went on to explain the details of his program. He ended by saying, "All are welcome, and I will see that they are as free and prosperous in Texas as they would be in Canada."

The woman's expression remained passive until Bowie handed her the map and the money and told her there would be more money to come. Then she became cooperative and gave Bowie the location of the next stop north on the underground railroad. In that instant, Sam realized that his master was inadvertently taking him north to Portia and freedom, and his urge to run was assuaged.

Then it occurred to Sam that they were doing what Bowie had called good work. He had become part of something that might help many people like himself? For the first time he felt a modicum of admiration for his master.

But Sam still had questions in his mind. What was Bowie up to exactly? How far north were they going? Was Jim concerned that he might use what he was learning to try to escape, or just taking it for granted that Sam would stay loyal?

Sam's ultimate focus stayed on inching up the river line of his father's map to join Portia. In his mind, however, the solid line had changed to railroad track and he pictured himself riding in a train car. Now, he was finding it harder to suppress his joy than it ever was to hide his anger.

* * *

The next morning, they rode north to the house the Quaker lady told them about. Assuming the password she provided would get them in, Jim stood beside Sam at the door and knocked.

This time the door was opened by a middle-aged man, with mutton-chops and a receding hairline, who was dressed in a suit but not wearing the coat. "Yes, what do you want?" he asked.

"Sympathy," Bowie said.

"Sympathy for what," the man asked.

"That's the password," Jim responded.

"What? Oh yes, the password. Come in."

The man turned away and walked toward a chair where he had laid his coat.

As he was putting on the coat he asked, "Are you helping this buck run north?"

"Not exactly," Jim replied.

When the man turned around, Jim saw a bright silver star attached to his coat lapel and he was immediately glad he had not revealed himself.

"Well then, what are you here for?"

"We just wanted to get a drink of water."

"Scared the hell out of you, didn't I friend?" the man said, laughing.

"What do you mean?"

"I saw y'all's mouth fly open when I flashed my badge at you. That's how I tell whether folks is sincere."

Bowie did not respond.

"Turns out I am the sheriff here. But I am also the station master, so I'll ask you again, are you aimin' to send this man north?"

"Can you give me some proof that you are who you say?" Jim asked.

"You said sympathy. That means you was sent here by a Quaker lady in New Orleans who has a helper named Abraham, and Abraham has an eye patch."

"Which eye?"

"What day of the week was it?"

"Wednesday."

"The left."

Feeling great relief, Jim smiled. "You had me goin' their sheriff. Actually, I'll tell you why we're here."

Jim gave the same explanation that had convinced the lady and the man caught on quickly. After he accepted the map and money and gave them the next station and password Jim and Sam prepared to be on their way again.

"Before I go, let me ask you. If I had seen Abraham on Tuesday, would his patch have been on his right eye?" Jim asked.

The sheriff snickered and said, "No son, his left eye is the bad one. I was just havin' a little more fun with ya."

* * *

By the end of October, Jim and Sam reached Natchez after leaving maps and money in La Place, Baton Rouge, and West Feliciana Parish. They went no further, however, as Jim appeared to be seriously ill with a high fever. A local physician was called, but Sam also sent for the Bowie family doctor in Alexandria, a three-day ride to the west.

"It's yellow fever. He probably contracted it in Baton Rouge. There's an epidemic down there," the local man said.

The doctor's diagnosis proved accurate. However, by the time his colleague from Alexandria arrived a week later and confirmed it, the crisis had passed.

When he was sure that Bowie was recovering satisfactorily, the family doctor returned home. Apparently, when he arrived in Alexandria, the physician circulated news of Bowie's whereabouts, and within a few days, Jim received a letter from Ursula posted the first of September in Monclova and forwarded from the Louisiana plantation. Tears filled Bowie's eyes as he read.

"Our little Elve has gone to God. It was the cholera. I sought Sister Angela's help in dealing with her death. I could not stop crying."

Sister Angela, Jim recalled, was an Ursuline nun at The San Francisco de Asis Parish Church in Monclova. She had been Ursula's teacher in the school there.

"Sister helped me accept that God took my precious child to save her from further pain and suffering, but still I cried for days more. Then we began to talk of my continuing grief, and Sister helped me consider that I believed God had made me miscarry before, and had taken my baby girl now, to punish me for punishing you. As we talked, I realized that I have been punishing you, and as I accepted that possibility, I began to feel somewhat better, and I could stop crying. The truth is, I have never allowed you to know how completely I cherish you. We have so much to talk about, my husband. Please come to me as soon as you can."

Ursula's letter told that the weather was cool, clear, and dry near the mountains, and that everyone else was healthy and feeling good, including month-and-a-half old James.

Ursula closed her letter with, "Receive Thou the Heart of Thy Wife," and these words spoke volumes to Jim about her feelings toward him. To him, it meant she had forgiven his insensitive ways, and was willing to love him unconditionally, despite all his inconsiderate and neglectful behavior.

The news of his daughter's death devastated him, but Ursula's closing words boosted Jim's spirits higher than they had been since he left Texas, and all he wanted was to go to her and comfort her.

Though he still felt weak, he began making plans for a trip to join his wife and family. However, within a week, in another letter, this one from Juana Veramendi in Bexar, Bowie learned that the letter from Ursula would be her last, and she would not be waiting for him.

"I am so sorry to inform you, my brother, that our family have died from the cholera in Monclova. My mother and father, my sister, and your daughter and son are now with God in Heaven."

Bowie was overcome with grief. When Sam found him crying, Jim gave him the shattering news, and Sam began crying too. For the first time since the death of Sam's parents, they shared an emotional moment.

* * *

Leaving Natchez a few days later, Sam and Jim crossed the Red River and rode into Alexandria where Sam heard the doctor declare Jim fit to travel.

They left Alexandria with the sound from the whistle on a new steam-powered riverboat in their ears, they rode south to the Bowie plantation for fresh horses, mules, and provisions, then south again to pick up the road to Texas.

The enticing smell of crawfish boiling in a spiced pot was strong as they rode through Vermillionville, but they did not stop.

Normally, on their cross-country rides, they talked from time to time, mainly about their days as young men in New Orleans, when both seemed to be living a charmed life. But this trip was different. It seemed to Sam that all Jim wanted to talk about was Ursula.

"Tell me what you remember best about Miss Ursula, Sam."

"Bestest I members Master Jim is the time she say she sorry for us four bein slaves, like she to blame fo' it. Ain't no white folks every say something like that I hear."

"I think she really cares about you and Bettie, especially."

Jim immediately realized he was still talking about his wife in the present, as if she still existed in the world.

"She say she even try to get her daddy to buy us and set us free, but he say that make you too mad."

"That's true. It would have made me angry. Nobody seems to understand it would not be safe for you to be free and alone in Texas. Until it is safe, I have to take care of you."

Sam did not reply.

"What else do you remember?"

Sam smiled and said, "I members how funny it was, them first times when Miss Ursula and my Gramaw Aurora try talkin', one 'ther. Granma say what you like to eat chil' an Miss Ursula say I like shekin and feesh an Gramaw say we ain't got no Mescan food an Miss Ursula sit up an flap her arms and say shekin, shekin, cluck, cluck, and Gramaw say oh, chicken, we got that."

Jim rocked in his saddle laughing. Then water came to his eyes and he realized he was sobbing.

"She can't be gone Sam. Why would God do that? Cleo left me, then he took Cecilia and now Ursula. Will it ever stop? Have I been that bad? Maybe the cholera will take me too when we get to Monclova."

Bowie seemed to be hysterical but, again, Sam did not reply. As he rode on without talking Sam contemplated his own personal predicament. Twice in the last three months, he had stayed with Bowie when he should have run. Why had he allowed his feelings for a white master to lead him, and his grief for a white family to draw him on? Even now, why was he allowing Jim to take him to a place that might bring death to both of them, without even asking Sam if he wanted to go?

Then he remembered a conversation with Portia. "Sometimes I think you don't mind being Bowie's slave as much as you put on," she said.

"I guess it's all that fine book learning I got," he replied. "It has made my life seem richer. I have to admit that I enjoy understanding when the whites talk about literature or music or painting. I like knowing who Mozart was and being able to recognize his music when I hear it. In those moments, I feel more white than black, and I wonder if I would find that kind of stimulation living in a black world, even as a freeman in Canada. Sometimes, I curse God for making me black and teaching me to think white."

Remembering his words, Sam did not know if he would give Portia the same answer now. For the moment though, he continued riding west with his owner, leaving a clear road to freedom further and further behind him, and wondering how he would ever be able to get back to it.

* * *

Stopping in Bexar, as Juan Veramendi's executor, Bowie had to make financial arrangements for Ursula's brother and two sisters. While there, he told his slaves, Bettie, Josephus, and Charlie, to stay on at the Veramendi Palace and watch over the children.

Continuing their ride west, he and Sam arrived in Monclova on Christmas day. They immediately rode to the Veramendi villa and found it completely empty.

They searched the grounds for new graves, but found none, not even in the old family cemetery that had apparently not been used for many years.

"Maybe they ain't passed, Master Jim. Maybe they just real poorly somewheres."

"I'm going to walk over to the church, Sam. You stay here and unpack. Don't eat anything, unless we brought it with us or you get it from the garden and wash it, and boil the water good before you use it for anything."

The church was named for Saint Francis of Assisi, and the architecture was almost identical to the San Fernando Cathedral in Bexar, where Jim Bowie and Ursula Veramendi were married less than three years before.

Jim was not ready for the sight of it and as he approached he halted on the street outside the surrounding adobe wall, sank to his knees, and did not move for several minutes.

People passed by. Lost in thought, he did not move. The bell in the single tower, announcing vespers, finally brought him back.

Dazed, he stood and looked toward the mountains and the sun going down behind them. Then he turned and walked back toward the Veramendi villa, as if, by not entering the church, he could keep Ursula alive.

* * *

The next morning, Jim forced himself to walk back to the church. The mountain air was amazingly warm for a winter day. Under an overcast sky, keeping his focus on the ground in front of him to avoid seeing the familiar shape of the cathedral, he entered and asked a novice to announce him to Sister Angela. The novice asked his name and directed him to wait in the side-yard beside a fountain.

When she appeared, Sister Angela was not at all like the picture Ursula had painted in Bowie's mind. He had always thought of the nun as a woman of imposing size, and he was not prepared for the petite figure who emerged from the chapel door and approached him.

As if she read his thoughts, she said, "The priests decided to bury them at the Royal Hospital along with the other victims."

When she spoke to him, in her deep, almost base, voice, he understood immediately why, to Ursula, the Sister had always seemed so large. Listening to what sounded like the authoritative voice of God must have distorted the child's vision of her diminutive mentor.

"The recent epidemic brought the first cholera victims we have had here in many years. It lasted thirty-one days, and we had over four hundred and fifty deaths."

This time her Irish brogue registered with Bowie.

"These are for you." After handing him five death certificates signed by a doctor and the parish priest, she continued. "Everyone in the house died. We know they were told about the sickness, and Ursula told me they were very careful to avoid exposure. We don't know if they brought the cholera with them in their water or food from Bexar; or perhaps the cook or baby Elve carried it. There were deaths before they came and after, so they were not to blame for our epidemic."

Bowie had removed his hat and was nervously moving it from hand to hand.

"Would you like to visit the grave, Senor?"

Bowie nodded, and she led him to a carriage. As they traveled beside the river, neither spoke. When they arrived, she led him around to the back of the hospital, to a three acre-cemetery on the east side, bordered by four foot high walls built of un-mortared basalt stones.

"There were so many deaths, and they had to be buried so quickly, we put many in the same grave, but I saw to it that your children were placed in the arms of their mother."

Touching Jim on the sleeve, she said, "I will wait for you in the carriage."

After Sister Angela walked away, Bowie began bawling uncontrollably. He knelt, then fell, prostrate on the mound of the grave. The vision of Ursula lying just below him with their daughter and son laid upon her breast, her arms folded over them, would not leave his mind.

He laid there for a long while, then he stood and sought out Sister Angela. As they rode back to the cathedral, they talked.

"Her last letter made me believe she forgave me for being a bad husband and father. In the letter, she said that she had talked about it with you."

"That is true, Senor Bowie. As a girl, Ursula had always been able to confide in me and, after your daughter died, we spent many hours talking about your lives together. Then she and the others became ill and died quickly."

"I had so much to make up for, Sister; I wish there had been time."

"Ursula wished the same thing. She felt that she had much to make up for too. She told me that she loved you deeply, but she had never allowed herself to express it fully because she feared for your immortal soul, and she did not want her expression of love to encourage your blasphemous ways."

"She was probably right."

"She also expressed a feeling of sorrow for maneuvering you into marriage."

"She was wrong about that. I knew what was happening all along, and I wanted it too."

"That knowledge would have helped her."

"Sister, it took me three weeks to ride here from Bexar. I spent my time thinking about all the terrible things I have done in my life, especially how I hurt my family, and I promised God that if I found them still alive, I would try to be a better man and make it up to them."

"She said she felt her behavior had caused you to spend time away from her, and she wanted to make a home that you would want to come to and stay."

"I should have been home more anyhow."

"I'm sure you are feeling many regrets and I hope you will come to forgive yourself. I was happy to see that Ursula had ceased to be the spoiled girl who was my student. She had become a mature wife and mother, and I feel I must give you some of the credit for that. I hope that God and time will bring you peace."

Bowie blushed.

Their carriage arrived back at the church and Jim had come around to help the nun step out.

"Now I'm sorry, but my other duties make it necessary for me to leave you, Senor."

"May I come again, Sister?"

"Certainly, but before you go, there is one thing more that I must tell you."

"Yes?"

"Ursula believed that her most difficult challenge would be to convince you to separate yourself from everything that had to do with slavery by any name and in any form, not foremost because of what it does to the slaves, but because of how it corrupts their masters."

At least a head taller, Bowie stood looking down at her upturned face.

"She said she believed that slavery was the only act for which God would not forgive you, and you had to abandon it and devote the remainder of your life to ridding society of slavery as a penance to save yourself from hell."

"She told me how she felt, but I never realized how deeply she believed it," Jim said.

"You know, when Ursula was ten years old, she attended school in England. Her school employed a negro woman from central Africa as a cook, a Christian woman whom Ursula grew to love. The woman's name was Victoria, and she had been a slave in the West Indies. She was freed through the efforts of a leading abolitionist and worked at his home for a time. This man taught Victoria to read, and she practiced by reading his books to Ursula."

"I was never willing to really listen to her arguments about the morality of slavery and discuss them with her in a serious way."

"Ursula believed, to paraphrase our lord, if you do an evil to the least of mine, you do it to me, and if you do an evil to me you do it to everyone, and if you do an evil to everyone, you do it to yourself."

"This cuts me deep, Sister. I couldn't just quit slavery and tell everyone else to do the same. I was afraid to show my hand while we were still trying to work things out with Mexico."

Jim was suddenly stricken with the realization that he sounded like a man who believed owning slaves was a bad thing for everyone but himself. Tears returned to his eyes and he looked away from the sister.

"The anti-slavery work I have been doing for the past few months is the result of her influence on me."

"Do you mean you do not own slaves?"

"No, Sister. I mean I have been working to rid Texas of the need for slaves. But I have kept my four personal slaves to protect them. My slaves in Louisiana belong to my brothers too, not just to me. I have done all I could."

"Senor Bowie, I'm not sure you believe your own words," the nun said, then she produced a book from the pocket of her habit.

"Ursula brought this home with her from England. It is called "A Letter on the Abolition of the Slave Trade" by William Wilberforce and, just before she died, she asked me to give it to you. She said she wanted you to read it, then ask yourself how you would explain slavery and your part in it to your children."

Bowie accepted the book and read the cover.

"Ursula said the slave women at your plantation told her what a sweet and tender-hearted boy you were until your father forced you to kill a slave. She said after that, your behavior toward them became like your father's, not as cruel, but as insensitive and indifferent. Ursula believed that you feel guilty about what you did, and that you cannot begin to forgive yourself until you free your own slaves and openly renounce slavery. Vaya con dios, Senor Bowie."

The sister turned and walked away, leaving Bowie seated by the fountain; head hung, deep in thought.

Chapter 14

Lost in thought too, Sam was in the kitchen frying a chicken they brought with them, and boiling some potatoes and greens from the Veramendi garden when Bowie arrived back at the villa. As the door opened Sam heard the church-bell, again announcing vespers.

"I made sure everything washed real good in water we brought, Master Jim."

After eating the food, Jim said goodnight and walked to his bedroom carrying a book. After cleaning the dishes, Sam retired as well.

During the night, a weather system passed. Sam felt a chill and arose to stoke the cook-stove fire. Closing the inside kitchen door to keep the heat in the room, and returning to his bedroom, he noticed that light still showed under Jim's door. He reasoned that Bowie must be reading the book he carried.

The next morning, when Sam entered the kitchen, he saw Bowie through the window, briskly pacing back and forth at the river's edge and occasionally opening the book and reading.

After putting their breakfast on the table, Sam opened the top of the outside Dutch door and called to him, then closed it quickly as cold air struck his face. Bowie responded immediately.

The room was still toasty warm from the fire as the men seated themselves. Bowie laid the book on the table, face up, and looked at his slave.

When Sam saw the book title, it occurred to him that through all the pacing and reading and pacing, Bowie must have been trying to reconcile his life as a slave owner and trader against the abolitionist arguments he had obviously been reading most of the night.

Sam felt curious and silently speculated that to hold Bowie's attention for so long, the book must contain a powerful message. He hoped he would get a chance to read it.

Then Jim interrupted his thoughts, "Ursula told the nun that I will be miserable forever if I don't forgive myself for hanging your paw, and I will burn in hell if I don't stop slaving, and free my slaves. I'm not sure if this was the prognosis of a perceptive and caring young wife, or the idealistic rants of an unhinged mother grieving for her dead child."

Sam thought Bowie's gaze was penetrating and his words harsh, and he was using words that Sam was not supposed to understand. Sam was suddenly afraid that his master had at last discovered his subterfuge and pic-speak game and was playing a game of his own. Then Bowie looked away and continued without pausing for a reply from Sam.

"Sam, I have always tried to take care of you and Bettie, especially since your maw and paw died, but I realize now I have always assumed that I knew what was best for you, better than you did yourself, and it was my job to protect you. I never really asked you what you wanted your life to be like. Now I would like to understand how you see things."

All of his adult life, Sam fancied having a conversation of this nature with his white masters. He wanted them to tell them how it felt to live everyday as a helpless, hopeless victim.

Sam considered that Jim was probably struggling to understand some new concepts, and hoped that might cause him to be receptive to an honest interchange of feelings and ideas with a man whom he had always ruled.

However, in a flash, Sam's fear took control. He did not want to waste this opportunity to educate Bowie, because the chance might not come again, but he still needed Bowie's protection, and his inner-voice reminded him that white men did not take well to criticism from black men.

His fear was compounded by his continuing confusion about how Bowie could spend so much time and money on his underground railroad scheme to replace slavery in Texas, yet not change the way he treated the slaves he owned one bit. Again, he reasoned that there must be something he did not know or understand about the man or the situation.

The Other Rose of Texas

Reasoning that Jim had never been so receptive to the wishes of another human being as he was at this moment to Ursula's last wish for him, Sam wanted to at least instigate a conversation. He felt that seizing the moment might give him a unique opportunity to help Jim look at slavery as a personal, moral issue.

But in the end, he could not find the courage to take the risk, and his timorous pic-speak let Jim off the hook.

"Bettie and me has had a good life. It ain't been like we was slaves. We has always been took care of good."

"That's the way I always felt too, Sam. You know, all these people who condemn slavery don't seem to care that most of us treat our slaves like family."

Sam scowled and clenched his jaw, thinking: "I hated your father because he used to beat my family behind your back. That is why my father ran time after time. He wanted to get free, and then find a way to rescue us all. My father had more spirit and courage than any of you Bowies. I hated you for hanging my father even if your father made you do it. The Master had to destroy him because he could not break my father. Then my mother could not bear the sight of him hanging from that tree or the thought of having your father's whip laid on her again."

After a deep breath, Sam said, "That's true, Master Jim, but not all of them slaves has had it as good as me and Bettie."

"Sam, you have been more of a friend to me than my own brothers, John J. or Stephen, ever were."

Sam's thoughts rose up again, even stronger this time: "Not even one day of my life have I been able to live where I want, eat what I want, or do work that I like. I could never take a woman for my wife and have children, for fear that they would be sold away. You call me friend, but you make me carry out your chamber pots and shovel your horse shit. I wonder how you would like being forced to act or speak, because another man is pulling your strings as if you were his marionette."

"Most slaves don't get to pick nothin, not even whether to live or die," he answered instead.

"I always felt bad about what I had to do to your paw, and then what happened to your maw. The only thing I could do after that is keep you with me and do what was best for you."

Sam silently thought, "I had to sneak around to get an education and around you whites I have to pretend to be stupid. Are those examples of how you took care of me?"

Handing Sam a folded leaf of parchment, sealed with red wax, Bowie sighed. "Ursula thought that slavery is wrong and wanted you to have this document. It tells everyone you are a freeman. It says that Bettie, Josephus and Charlie are free too. Put it in your pouch and don't ever lose it. It also gives the name of my bank in New Orleans, and as soon as we get back to Bexar, I will send some money there for you with instructions to the bank to help you go north. I'll put in enough to pay for all of you to go to Canada on a boat and more money to help you get started up there."

Sam had thought himself into an irrational and bitter state of mind that prevented him from appreciating the gravity of the change in Bowie's behavior that was taking place before his eyes.

Sam frowned and thought, "Why make your dead wife responsible for this? Why can't you admit that slavery is wrong? Besides, I am already a freeman in Mexico. I understood every word that army officer said in Nacogdoches, and I signed an X on the servitude contract because I didn't want you to see me sign my name. If you really wanted to free us, you would take us all to Canada yourself, right now."

Forcing a smile, he said, "I's thankful, Master Jim, but I ain't gonna have to leave right now, is I?"

Sam knew he was lying, but he still needed Bowie's protection until he got free of men in Texas who could claim to own him. It actually felt good to continue his deception, like angrily mistreating a cruel enemy, after he has surrendered.

"No, Sam. You have a home with me as long as you want."

Yet after Bowie went to bed that night, Sam began to feel cowardly for not revealing more of himself.

He took the Wilberforce book from the table to his room and read it. He had heard that there were white people in the north who were genuinely opposed to allowing one man to own another, but he had never imagined there were so many anti-slavery arguments as this book articulated. He had never dreamed that such thoughts existed in the white world, or that there was literature expressing them.

Reading the book seemed to reduce his feeling of shame. He had reason to be hopeful. After all, he had begun the day as a slave and ended it as a documented freeman. Then his demons returned and asked, "So why does calling myself free seem like a joke?"

When the sun came up he had resolved nothing. He rose and walked into the kitchen to prepare breakfast. Later in the morning he went with Bowie to visit Sister Angela.

"Sister this is Sam. I just freed him and all the other slaves I own in Texas," Bowie told her.

"That is a good start, Senor Bowie," she replied.

* * *

Because the capital of the state of Coahuila y Tejas had been moved from Saltillo to Monclova the preceding March, Bowie was immediately able to actuate Juan Veramendi's will with the death certificates that Sister Angela had given him. Filing the documents made him a very wealthy man, at least on paper.

In addition to his money in the New Orleans bank, the Louisiana interests he had not sold to his brothers, and his Texas land and cotton-plantation, he now owned the Saltillo textile mill outright, and Ursula's one fourth share of her father's considerable fortune.

However, when he tried to appraise his holdings that were under Mexican jurisdiction, foreboding overtook him, as he quickly realized their value depended more on politics than on finance. In a stable Coahuila y Tejas, with a steady stream of immigrants from the United States, his assets could be worth millions, but in a rebellious or conquered state, it could all be taken from him.

"I needed a political strategy," he said out-loud and thinking about that gave him a temporary respite from mourning Ursula.

His dread returned, however, when he considered that he was out of touch with the rapidly evolving relationship between Tejas and Mexico City. Again his thoughts turned to Stephen Austin, the man on whom he could always count for a sound assessment of political matters.

Jim needed to see Austin, face to face. However, rather than pack up and travel east on the chance that he would find Austin somewhere in Texas, Bowie decided to write a letter to his friend William Wharton in Bexar, whom he knew to be politically active, inquiring about Austin's whereabouts.

After four weeks, Bowie was glad he had waited in Monclova when a reply to his letter reported that Austin was in Mexico City to petition the Mexican Congress for repeal of the laws that were impeding commerce in Texas. Bowie decided that a trip to the Mexican capital might be more productive than waiting for Austin to return north, so he planned a trip south.

He and Sam waited until late March to depart so there would be plenty of grass for their horses and the two mules that would carry their equipment, provisions, and Jim's wardrobe, including his formal attire for state functions.

After a stop in Saltillo to inspect his cotton mill, and in San Luis Potosi to rest, he and Sam arrived in the Mexican capital and settled into the Veramendi apartment almost exactly two years since Jim's trip with Juan to see President Bustamante. Bowie expected to find Austin in his quarters in the same building, but did not.

The next morning, he began making inquiries and, after two full days going from office to office, he found Austin imprisoned in a cell in the basement of the Customs-house, located on the east side of Santo Domingo Plaza.

The building resembled a church bell tower, flanked by a three-story barn to the right and a two-story hacienda on the left, all with a reddish, tezontle-based facade. However, the tower was not for bells. It was for observing the volume of people on the streets and in the plaza waiting to pay taxes and duties on their goods.

Inside, the building smelled of parchment, money, and manure from hundreds of dray animals that had visited outside for decades.

"What in hell happened to you, Stephen?"

A thin and frail looking man in the best of times, to Bowie Austin appeared especially haggard.

"My first mistake was learning how to write," Austin replied sarcastically.

"What do you mean?'

"If I had not written that letter to the authorities in Bexar, they would not have arrested me in Saltillo on my way home."

"What letter?"

"My letter recommending the formation of a separate Mexican state of Texas. Vice-President Farias called it treasonable."

"I see. So when will they be hanging you?" Bowie asked, smiling.

The prisoner did not smile back. Instead Austin's expression convinced Jim that his friend was silently cussing him.

"After my trial, I guess. They had me in a dungeon until two weeks ago, don't ask me where, then Santa Anna took over and had me moved here."

"You mean Santa Anna is president again?"

"He has been president for over a year, but he was letting Farias run things. That little tyrant had scheduled my execution, but Santa Anna rescued me. Now Santa Anna keeps me alive, but at arm's length, so he will not be identified with my treason. Still, I am a lot better off than I was."

Jim tried to look more concerned as he asked, "Seriously Stephen, don't they hang people for treason down here?"

"I don't think Santa Anna will let it go that far. He arranged for the nuns of La Encarnación convent next door to bring me food, and my guard takes me over there once a week so I can take a bath. He seems to want me alive and in relatively good condition, for some reason."

"What can I do to help you?"

"There is not much anybody can do right now. We just have to let things die down. Now, tell me, what brings you to Mexico City, amigo?"

Knowing him to be a master of the political arts, Jim reasoned that there were details about his predicament that Austin could not or would not share, so Jim allowed him to change the subject.

"As usual, I need your advice. I lost my family to cholera, and I am trying to decide what to do now."

"I'm sorry, Jim. I had not heard. You mean your wife and children?"

"Yes, and her parents too."

"Assuming Juan named you executor, that puts you in control of a whole lot of money and property. Are Ursula's siblings looking to you for guidance."

"Yes, and what I do to guide them depends on what Mexico is going to do about Texas."

"I can't really predict what will happen on that. Santa Anna is an unpredictable political opportunist and a tyrant. But I can tell you what I want to happen."

Before continuing, Austin looked around. Bowie looked around too.

"As I said in the letter that got me in trouble, Texas must separate from Mexico. Santa Anna's government plans to free all the slaves, and I think that would be disastrous for the Texas economy. If I ever get back home, I'm going to declare independence and try to get the United States to annex Texas as a slave state."

"Your position has certainly changed from the first time we talked about slavery, Stephen. Back then, you thought I was the devil himself for being involved with it," Bowie said.

"I'm still opposed to it morally, but as you said years ago, it's expedient in an agricultural economy like ours."

"I can't believe my ears," Bowie replied. However he was not ready to debate slavery with Austin again, especially since each man had literally reversed his position on the subject, so he let the opportunity pass. He had what he came for, now all Jim wanted was to be alone to think.

"Is there anything you need, Stephen? Anything I can send you?"

"Yes, as a matter of fact. Send me some writing materials and clothing from my apartment. Oh yes, and some liquor. Have you lost weight Jim? You look tired."

"You don't look so great yourself, Stephen."

Both men laughed.

After he exited the Customs-house Bowie walked around the Distrito Federal, coughing occasionally, thinking about what he wanted and planning how to get it.

* * *

The Other Rose of Texas

The following day, using the news about the death of Juan Veramendi as a door opener, Bowie began calling on every politician who would see him and evaluating each man's views about what most of them called the Tejas problem. Then, believing he was ready, he sought a meeting with Santa Anna. It took a few bribes and promises of political support to secure the appointment, but he finally succeeded.

Entering the offices of the Mexican president in the National Palace for the second time, Bowie was struck by the appearance and smell of freshly cut yellow roses everywhere.

"As you know, Senor Bowie, Senor Veramendi and I were of the same political party, but I did not know him well, and frankly, I am seeing you today only to get a look at that famous knife of yours," Santa Anna said.

Bowie reached under his coat and produced his knife, saying, "This is the original that was given to me by my brother." Then he reached around to the small of his back and produced a scabbard containing an almost identical knife, saying, "I took the liberty of having one made for your excellency, which I hope you will accept with my compliments and admiration."

Santa Anna was clearly delighted.

"Thank you, Senor Bowie. You are most generous. Now, my time is limited. What may I do for you today?"

"Senor President, I am here to offer you my support in Tejas."

"And why would I need support from you or any other North Americano?"

"Your excellency, I am a loyal Mexican citizen, and I now control the Veramendi interests. I see my future in a Tejas that could become one of the leading states of Mexico and of enormous benefit to you and your government. Together, I think you and I can achieve that goal."

"Senor, should I need such help, I will let you know. For the moment, all I need is my army to enforce the law among the fools who think they can steal Tejas from me and turn it into Texas. However, I acknowledge your offer, and I will be watching to see if you are as loyal as you say you are. Thank you for the knife and good day."

The door behind him was opened, and Bowie was escorted out. The next day, he and Sam departed for Texas, with Bowie feeling angry and resolved to make it more advantageous for Santa Anna to deal with him than with a full-fledged Texas rebellion.

Chapter 15

By 1835, a year had passed since Bowie's visits with Stephen Austin and President Santa Anna in Mexico City. Now the Mexican president was busy dealing with threatened rebellion in ten other Mexican states and mostly ignoring Texas, even though Texas citizens had experienced three more minor confrontations with the Mexican army, hinting of rebellion there too.

A prosperous year, including the arrival of hundreds of runaway slaves, had moderated Jim Bowie's desire to cause trouble for Santa Anna. He was visiting Rezin P. at the plantation and discussing year-end results as they awaited dinner.

"Didn't I see some of our Louisiana slaves here when I arrived?" Jim asked.

"Now don't blame that on me little brother. They just showed up like all the other runaways," Rezin P. said. "So I freed them too and now we don't have slave one on this land."

Jim thought to himself, "Ursula would be pleased," but he asked, "What will you tell Stephen?"

"I don't know yet, but I'm going to love every minute of it."

Both men laughed.

"So, I hear we had a bumper crop," Jim announced.

"Yes, we improved our pounds per acre by thirty-five percent. The weather was good all year and our negro overseer got more work out of those people than I ever could."

"The people at the mill said your deliveries have been steady except when you had that trouble."

"You know we never did find those drivers the slave hunters took. I expect they were sold direct to a plantation or taken to the Galveston block. Now I put two armed guards on every wagon and I was thinking about sending the finished cloth to the docks at Tampico instead of El Copano."

"That sounds workable. We can have our supplies and equipment shipped there just as easy and the drivers will be safer on El Camino Real," Jim concurred.

Just then a negro woman entered the room carrying a souptureen. Jim recognized her as Kizzie, the slave from the first group they bought from Lafitte, years before.

"Hello Kizzie. How are you?" Jim asked.

"I's fine Master Jim. My husband and me is free here now," she said in accented English.

"That's fine Kizzie, and you know you don't have to call me or anyone here master ever again," Jim replied.

"I knows," she replied, beaming. Then she ladled the soup and left the room.

Rezin P. resumed his report. "We've had people stopping by about the land too. You know there hasn't been an Indian raid south of Parker's Fort for over a year and I've had good offers on ten square leagues."

"As far as I'm concerned you can sell it all. Just make sure you get cash and register everything with Austin's people in San Felipe."

"I will. Now tell me what's happening in Bexar. Are the women still chasing you?" Rezin P. asked grinning.

Though Ursula had been gone for almost two years, the mention of women instantly brought her lovely image to Jim's mind.

He coughed for the first time since arriving. Then he said, "between looking after my nieces and nephew, overseeing the mill, and leading my ranging company, I don't have time for anything else."

"It's been almost two years Jim. That's a respectable amount of time to wait."

"I know, but I still miss her and think about her every minute. When I get too lonely, I go see Cleo in New Orleans. That's all I need for now."

Feeling an overwhelming sadness Jim hung his head and coughed again.

"How are Sam and Bettie?" Rezin P. asked.

"They're all four still with me. I offered to give Sam some land and money to get him started on his own place, but he said no. I give them room and board and five pesos a month, and they seem happy with that. I think they will always do whatever Sam does."

"I think you're right."

They sat quietly for a moment, then Rezin P. broke the silence. "Why don't you stay a few days and rest up. You're looking tuckered. Have you lost weight?"

"I've lost a few pounds, but I needed to. I never could resist Bettie's cooking."

Jim attempted to rise from his chair but fell back into it.

Then he added, "I think I will stay a couple of days before I head south. I hear Austin is finally back from Mexico City and he's talking open rebellion against Santa Anna. I've got to go down and find some way to shut him up."

That night Jim awakened several times covered with sweat. As he had with his more frequent coughing, his weight loss, and every other ailment he had, he blamed these night-sweats on his harried lifestyle.

* * *

Jim Bowie found Stephen Austin at home in San Felipe, wrapped in a shawl and sitting by a fire, despite the hot September weather.

"Santa Anna is a de-facto dictator, Jim, pure and simple, and soon he will be de-jure. If he stays in power, we can say good-bye to the constitution, government by law, and any special dispensation for Texas. If he gets his way, he will free all the slaves, and his army will run every American who opposes him back across the Sabine or the Red, or worse."

"How can he or any man down there have that much power?" Jim asked.

"It's Mexican politics as usual. Whoever controls the army controls the country. That bastard is an experienced military leader and a tyrant. They are all afraid of him."

Both men experienced a brief coughing spell before Austin continued making his case.

"Our only hope is to form a government and break away from Mexico, then pray that President Jackson brings us into the union before Santa Anna comes up here and kills us all."

To Jim, Austin seemed manic and he was hoping to calm the impresario down before he could begin to incite a revolution. If too many people listened to Austin, Jim could lose everything and so could every negro man, woman, and child Jim had lured to Texas who could not produce authentic freedom documents that were valid in the United States.

"I can't let that happen. It would cause a war for sure. Nobody wants a war," Jim said, trying to sound forceful. "Are you sure you're not just mad at Santa Anna for keeping you in prison so long."

Austin shrugged and scowled, then looked defiant. "I can think of at least five influential men besides me, who would welcome a war for independence," he replied.

"We can't fight a war against a professional army without help from the United States; we have no artillery," Bowie countered.

"There is Mexican artillery all over Texas, especially in the Alamo. We could capture it."

"We can't win a war. There is not a professional soldier among us."

"Sam Houston fought at Horseshoe Bend and Fannin went to West Point. A lot of us served with Jackson against the British."

This was the first time Bowie had put these thoughts into words and his argument seemed weaker now.

"Why can't we just work out our differences with Santa Anna," Bowie queried.

"I can't think of one good reason why Santa Anna would even consider negotiating with us."

"Slavery is the only real issue. Only the slave owners would favor a war. I can show them how productive my freed slaves are and convince them to free their own."

"It would take years for you to convince the planters to free their slaves and pay them wages, and what makes you think the slaves would stay around and work for the cruel masters who beat them and treated them like animals?"

"A large majority of us don't own slaves and don't want war. I will organize them and show Santa Anna that Texas is loyal to him. Somehow, I have to stop this from turning into a war."

"You're no politician, Jim, and I am. I have the skills and influence to beat you at every turn," Austin threatened.

Bowie rode out of San Felipe knowing that Stephen Austin could not be deterred and wondering if he had lost the debate because his friend's resolve was stronger or his position more viable.

Yet Bowie still considered his own position more just and by the time he crossed La Llorona Creek on his way back to Bexar, he had concluded that his wisest course would be to work from within the system until he could negotiate with Santa Anna from a position of strength. So he decided to keep his own counsel while he waited for that opportunity.

* * *

From his trip to San Felipe, Jim arrived in Bexar just in time to gather his rangers and ride back east.

As they rode into Gonzales on the morning of October 3, Bowie thought the town looked deserted. After he and his men dismounted and staked their horses, he saw Colonel James Fannin, militia commander at Goliad, walking toward him.

"You missed all the fun Jim. A Mexican captain named Castaneda with about a hundred mounted came to get their cannon. Yesterday we hung a banner on it that said *Come and Take It*. Then we ran em off."

"Anybody hurt?" Jim asked.

"We killed two of theirs. One of ours fell off his horse and got a bloody nose. I felt like a minute-man at Lexington."

"What now?" Bowie asked.

"More men are on their way. Austin's in command and he says the war is on. He wants us all to hang around."

By afternoon the volunteer Texas rebel force in Gonzales had grown to over five hundred, and Stephen Austin, the elected General over all the militias, invited the individual militia commanders to a council of war.

"Our informants tell me those dragoons we routed yesterday are part of a new Mexican army led here by Santa Anna's brother-in-law, General Martin Perfecto de Cos. After that last incident at Anahuac in June Santa Anna sent him up with orders to regain control of us."

"I thought I was feeling out of control," Fannin said, and everyone laughed.

Austin paused, looked around, and resumed his remarks.

"According to my reports, even with this new army there are less than fifteen hundred Mexican troops still east of the Rio Bravo, and this may be our best opportunity yet to run them all out of Texas for good."

Austin paused and looked around again. Bowie wondered if he was inviting comments.

"A provisional government will be formed within a few days, and Texas will be declared an independent state of Mexico, but I don't think we have time to wait for that. I think we should march to Bexar now and attack Cos."

Fannin responded. "I agree, General. Some of their troops are still down around San Patricio and Goliad right now, but I think Cos will order them to join him in Bexar when he hears we are approaching. So we should be able fight them all in one place."

"What about food and ammunition?" Colonel John Henry Moore from the De Witt Colony asked. "We may be in Bexar a long time, or we may have to chase them a ways."

Bowie thought that, during his remarks, Austin had looked at him more than anyone else, perhaps in anticipation of an objection or argument against becoming the aggressor.

But Bowie was sticking with his plan. He had no intention of revealing himself to these men. For the time being he wanted Austin to believe his support could be counted on.

To that end he was now ready to become a leader and facilitator.

"I have a cache of dry goods and ammunition stored on Juan Seguin's ranch that should last us a month or more," Bowie said. "I stole it from the presidio in Bexar in July just for fun."

The men laughed again.

"I have a stock of carrots and potatoes and ten of beeves to give," Jared Groce added.

Austin closed the council saying, "It is agreed then. We will leave for Bexar, as soon as we can. Commanders, prepare your men."

* * *

In December, 1835, Jim Bowie and the other Texicans and Tejanos had been in Bexar for almost two months when Edward Burleson, an emissary from the new provisional government of Texas, arrived.

"The government is already broke General Austin. They want you to go to New Orleans to raise some money and I'm here to replace you," Burleson announced at a commander's meeting.

Bowie felt relieved to know that Austin, his main political opponent might be out of the picture for a while.

"Before you take command General, I think you should know that the men are grumbling. We've only had two minor encounters with the enemy since we got here, and they say they want to either fight or go home," Austin replied.

That afternoon, Burleson called the commanders together again to discuss strategy. Fannin spoke first. "I move that we go home for the winter then come back in the spring and attack."

His was the only motion and it was approved unanimously. Bowie felt confident that the delay would give him enough time to advance his own agenda and perhaps even prevent an armed conflict altogether.

But when the announcement was made to the other men, a grant impresario named Ben Milam was having none of it.

"Who will go with old Ben Milam into San Antonio?" he said.

Bowie felt amazed when more than half the men volunteered to go with Milam, and decided his best choice was to go along with the majority.

Yet Jim liked Milam immediately and was by his side as the Texican and Tejano rebels assembled on Soledad Street for an attack on the Mexican soldiers in Main Plaza and Military Plaza.

"That was a courageous thing, going against the commanders like you did. I admire that," Bowie said.

"I just want to get done with this business so I can get back to work. I have land to sell and a family to feed," Milam replied.

"Come with me," Bowie said to Milam. Then he motioned for Frank Johnson, Henry Karnes, and Sam Maverick to come along too. He led them to the nearby Veramendi Palace, flung both large doors open and guided them through to the parlor room, where he produced a crock jug of peach brandy.

"This is my place Ben. We'll have a fandango here after we whip these bastards," Bowie promised.

Each man took a swig. Then Milam announced. "Come on. I need to see if they have a lookout in the cathedral tower."

Milam led the group into the courtyard then to the doorway. As he raised a telescope to his eye Bowie heard the sound of a shot from the direction of a large cypress tree on the other side of the river.

Bowie turned toward the tree and when he turned back he saw Milam lying in Maverick's arms, blood spurting from the left side of his head.

The other three men turned and fired their rifles toward the tree, but they missed the sniper, and he jumped to the ground and ran away before they could re-load.

Bowie could only stand still, with tears in his eyes, looking down at his now dead friend.

Word spread and all three hundred Texicans took the loss of their inspirational leader hard. Many vowed to personally make the Mexicans pay for Ben Milam's death. Now energized, during three days of house to house fighting, they drove the Mexican army forces out of the plazas, down Commerce Street, across the footbridge, and into the Alamo.

Thereafter, two solid days of bombardment by rebel cannons convinced Mexican General Cos to give up the Alamo, and on December 9, 1835, inside the only adobe structure in La Villita, he and General Burleson negotiated the Mexican's surrender.

Bowie and the other militia leaders stood around the table as Cos silently read the Castilian version of the surrender document.

The Other Rose of Texas

Then Burleson said, "I want to be sure you understand that, by signing this document, you agree that you and your army will never again come north of the Rio Bravo River."

"Si, Senor."

"And we agree that you may keep a four pounder cannon and enough weapons to defend your troops against Indians as you leave Texas."

"Si, Senor."

"Finally, I want to reiterate that we will care for any wounded that you may wish to leave in Bexar."

"Si, Senor."

Bowie thought the Mexican general sounded condescending and insincere.

After Cos signed the surrender and led his men west across the Rio Bravo, the now separate Mexican state of Tejas was completely free of the occupying Mexican army.

Not a single Mexican soldier remained and, thinking there would be no need for them to return and fight again, most of the Texican and Tejano volunteers finally went home.

* * *

Soon after the battle, still grieving for Ursula, and now for Milam too, the only close friend he had allowed himself for years, Bowie was again residing in the Veramendi Palace.

From correspondence addressed to Juan Veramendi he learned that a new Mexican constitution had established a centralist government, and all the Mexican states had been replaced by a smaller number of government departments. This was centralized government taken to the extreme, Jim thought.

Now there was no longer a Mexican state of Coahuila y Tejas for Tejas to be separate from. Bowie knew the change meant the freedoms provided by the Constitution of 1824 were a thing of the past and Santa Anna had absolute power, just as Austin predicted. Now the President-General was free to use his army to enforce his will throughout Mexico.

This meant that, if Jim stayed in Texas, he and Santa Anna were destined to collide.

Part III - 1836

Chapter 16

Saying he felt sick and did not want to infect anyone, on January 19, 1836, following a trip to Goliad to meet with Sam Houston, Jim Bowie moved himself, Sam, and Bettie out of the Veramendi Palace and into the Alamo.

The truth was that he just wanted to hole up and be left alone until he felt better. The problem was that now, sixteen days after the move, he felt worse, and as he slept, his brain rode a high fever to a time when his dead wife still lived.

"Ursula. You are here, my Maria."

His delirious mind saw her as she was the last time, her lovely raven hair splayed across a white satin pillow. He heard her clear, soft words spoken in his ear, and felt the warm, sweet breath that carried them. His skin felt her hard, young body pressed against him - it all seemed real.

"You alright, Master Jim?" Sam queried.

Bowie did not stir.

"Master Jim, Master Jim. You alright?"

Their room occupied the southeast corner of a rock-shed that was attached to the south wall. Fifteen feet above them, the roof was reinforced from below to support cannons and riflemen standing on it. Called the Low Barracks, the structure also housed the main gate.

This early in the morning, Bettie was asleep in an Alamo chapel room with other women and their children. Bowie's other two freed slaves, Josephus and Charlie, remained at the Veramendi Palace across the San Antonio River. Though Bowie had freed all four of his negroes more than two years before, they refused to leave him. Likewise, he refused to make them leave, although having them around was a constant reminder of something he was trying to forget.

Bowie was groggy but coming awake now. Sam rose from his pallet on the floor and knelt beside Bowie's cot.

Jim coughed, then said in a raspy voice, "Damn it, Sam, I've told you and told you not to call me master any more. You are not my slave now, and I am not your master. You should call me Mister Jim or just Jim, but not master."

"But Mister Jim, I ain't want for you to send me away. 'Tain't safe," Sam said, still pic-speaking his fear of trying to cross Texas alone.

"You know you have a place with me as long as you want, but I have given you your freedom too, just in case."

"But I don't wants no freedom. I wants to stay with you."

Since Ursula's death, Bowie had been trying to discharge her final wish for him by detaching himself from slavery in all of its forms. His first act of separation was to free the last of his own slaves, but that did not seem to be enough. For over two years now, nothing seemed to be enough. Without knowing it, Ursula had tapped into an enormous reservoir of guilt in Jim that was slow to drain.

"Sam, do you remember the day in Monclova that I gave you that document, and you put it in your pouch?"

"Yes sir, I does. I members."

"Do you remember that I said there is money in the bank in New Orleans for you all?"

"Yes, sir, I does."

"Well, if anything ever happens to me, that document tells people that you and Bettie and Josephus and Charlie are free, and it tells the name of the bank. If you lose that document, Sam, you will go back to being slaves again, and your new master might not be as good to you as I am."

Explaining everything to Sam again brought back sad memories. Bowie's eyes moistened, as did Sam's. "Sam, the time may come when it is not safe for you all to be with me, and I may have to send you away for your own good."

"Why can't you jus' takes us back home, Mister Jim?" Sam asked.

"I have something to do here, something else I promised Miss Ursula."

The Other Rose of Texas

"We loved Miss Ursula, Mister Jim. Can't we help?"

"Miss Ursula loved you too, Sam, and it was important to her for you and Bettie and all the slaves in Texas to be free. Now a bad man may be coming here who might kill you if he finds you with me, and you will never live free."

"Don't that mean he might kill you too, Mister Jim?"

"Yes, it does mean that. But, I'm going to try to do something about it, before he does. Do you understand, Sam?"

"Yes, sir, I does."

"Then tell me."

"I is not supposed to call you master, and I is not supposed to lose that document in my pouch, and I is supposed to leave here when you tell me or if the bad man gonna kill me."

"That's right, now let's go back to sleep."

Obediently, Sam returned to his pallet.

However, wide awake now, Bowie rolled over on his right side, pulled his fine wool blankets up under his chin, and began to think about his strategy for a meeting he had scheduled later in the morning with Colonel Neill, the Alamo commander. Bowie planned to notify the Texas governor that he would make a stand against Santa Anna at the Alamo, and he wanted Neill's endorsement.

Bowie knew that, even to a close friend like Neill, he could not reveal the truth about his intention to delay the Mexican army at the Alamo and negotiate a truce with General Santa Anna. He knew he had to make the false case with Neill that his purpose was to engage the Mexicans in battle and he needed some good military reasons.

He stared at a fire-pit that had been dug in the floor where two blocks of limestone were removed. It was aglow with embers but not ablaze, so he wrapped a blanket around himself as he rose from his cot and walked to a small desk by the wall.

"Let's see", he said out loud, then looked at Sam, who rolled over but appeared to continue sleeping. In his head Bowie reviewed each reason he would give for defending the Alamo and hoped that Neill would consider them sound. Then, convinced that the reasons comprised a logical and defensible military strategy, he set about writing them down.

The morning light beginning to come through a window was adequate for writing, so Bowie did not fire the candle on the desk.

Laying before himself a leaf of parchment from a small stack, he dipped a goose quill pen into an inkwell. He tried to memorize the main points of his argument by writing them. He wrote the word "dictator," then looked down to his left. A running mouse caught his eye. Then a cat seemed to materialize and pursue the rodent.

During the next sixty minutes, he pondered and wrote more words: delay, rear, plan, troops, artillery, signature, mad, defeat, and December. Then he repeated the words in a whisper, over and over, until he was sure his groggy mind would remember each one and what it represented.

The sun was full up as Bowie folded the parchment and placed it under the inkwell. He did not feel particularly sleepy, but he did feel tired. He was coughing deeply, and his head ached. He lay down on his cot without intending to sleep, but he did.

When Bowie awoke again, Sam was walking out the door carrying a chamber pot. In what seemed like a single second, Sam returned, and Bettie was with him.

Bowie squinted, pretending to sleep, as he watched Sam quietly set about building a good cook fire while Bettie, like a painter squeezing oils onto a pallet, assembled the ingredients for their morning meal. While the animal fat melted in her cast-iron skillet, she chopped a large onion. When the lard began to smoke, she cast in the onion.

Suddenly, the room was filled with an irresistible aroma. Soon Bowie began to stir, then he sat up, smiled and asked, "What's for breakfast"?

* * *

When he stood again, Bowie felt dizzy, however, his headache was less grating than in the early morning and his cough not as deep. He had also planned to see the doctor this day but now decided not to. Instead, he took a long squirt of tequila from a sheep gut pouch hanging on a peg in the yellow limestone wall high above and to the right of his cot.

After pulling on his Wellington boots and hooking his suspenders on his shoulders, he walked to a small oak table near the fire, and sat in one of the two chairs, beside a steaming cup of chicory coffee Bettie had just placed there.

Finishing the beverage, Jim thanked Bettie then told her he would return for breakfast, and they would have a guest as well. After that, he rose, put on a wide-brimmed felt hat, and walked out the doorway, turned left, walked under a Spanish arch then straight ahead toward the officer's latrine, where he stopped to relieve himself.

Next, at the quarters of the Alamo commanding officer near the dry acequia, he knocked, announced himself, and walked in. The room was almost identical to Bowie's but twice as long. Windows on the east wall flanked either side of a door made of cedar and hung on leather strap hinges. The north end of the room was used for sleeping and the other end for meetings.

The south end had a desk and chair, and a large meeting table with six equipale chairs. It smelled like cigar smoke. The walls and floor were made of yellow limestone. The ceiling was mesquite vigas beams running east and west, and covered with Spanish tile, supported by cedar planks. The north end, where the two men stood, had a bed and pegs in the walls, like Bowie's, to hang belongings.

Bowie addressed Lieutenant-Colonel James C. Neill as the good friend he was. "You know, Jimmy, what we talked about yesterday might be a pretty good idea, after all."

"Man," Neill replied, "a good night's sleep sure straightens you out. Yesterday you told me there was not a way in hell you would even consider violating Sam's order to take the artillery east and blow this place up. What changed your mind? You must have found yourself a senorita in Bexar last night."

"Something like that," Bowie responded, momentarily remembering the physical sensations he had felt during his dream.

"So, hermano, what changed your mind?"

In a corner, leaning against the limestone wall while he talked, Bowie stared down at the floor of the small room. Then, feeling slightly dizzy again, he bent his six-foot one inch frame at the waist, reached for a post of Neill's bed, swung around, and sat on the Spanish moss filled mattress.

"Are you feeling alright, Jim?" Neill leaned closer. "Jim?"

"I'm alright, Jimmy. Just a little too much senorita last night, I guess."

"So why are you reconsidering? This place isn't exactly a tactician's dream."

"Well, first, I think we have time to prepare. Santa Anna couldn't possibly be here before spring. Today is February fifth so we have almost two months to get ready."

"Get ready for what, though? It's not going to be like December, with General Cos and a few hundred untrained and unmotivated peon soldiers. This time, it's the whole Mexican army, thousands of professionals, and what if there is an early spring? What if you don't have two months?"

Bowie looked directly at Neill. "I think we can do it."

"You know that after Cos surrendered, most of the men decided the war was over and went home. The rest went with Fannin to invade Mexico. When you got here, seventeen days ago, I was down to seventy-five men. Your thirty volunteers raised the count to a hundred and five, but that's still nowhere near enough."

"Yes, I know."

"If Cos couldn't hold this place, what makes you think you can?"

"That's my whole point, Jimmy. We don't have to hold the Alamo." Bowie began to cough.

From his canteen, Neill poured water into a leather cup and handed it over. Bowie swigged it down, handed the cup back, and cleared his throat.

"I want to send a dispatch to Governor Smith, Jimmy, and tell him we will make a stand here. Will you support me?"

"Are you sure, Jim?"

Bowie nodded and went into a coughing spasm, now as deep as earlier. He tasted blood in his mouth.

"Jim, you need to be in bed. Let's talk about this later, when you are feeling better."

Feeling worse by the minute, Bowie knew he would only be good for a few more minutes of conversation, so he pressed Neill.

"Will you sign it?"

"Frankly, Jim, I think you're wrong. But I have to tell you I can't sign anything because what happens here is not my decision to make anymore."

"What do you mean?"

Neill hung his head slightly. "Most of my family is poorly, and I have to go back to the colony for a while. I'm turning command over to Travis. He's the one you will have to convince."

Jim knew William Travis by his reputation as a trouble maker and felt shocked by this news from Neill.

"Does it have to be that cock of the walk?"

Neill nodded. "He has the rank now, thanks to the governor."

"When?"

"Any day, not more than a week. So you see, I don't have the authority to sign it."

"Will you sign it anyway, Jimmy?"

"I can't, Jim. I don't think we have a chance here."

Bowie stood and began to cough deeply.

"Alright, Jimmy." Frustrated and disgusted, but not angry, he walked out, still coughing.

"God be with you all," Neill uttered as Bowie passed him.

* * *

Bowie returned to his room. After taking another long pull of tequila, he sat in the chair at the small desk, now well lighted by the inside window.

Occasionally wiping the perspiration from his forehead with a red bandana, he wrote a long letter that complimented Colonel Neill as a commander and gave the detail behind each word on his list as a reason why the salvation of Texas depended on standing and holding San Antonio de Bexar and the Alamo against the soon to be advancing Mexican army.

Then, knowing the words to be untrue, he also wrote, "Colonel Neill and myself have come to the solemn resolution that we will rather die in these ditches than give up this post to the enemy." However, his purpose was not deception for he believed in his heart that this, and any other such lie, was justified because it would serve to prevent bloodshed on both sides.

At the other end of the room, Sam washed a pair of red, long winter, underwear in a basin, and Bettie fried beef strips with onions and peppers, and corn tortillas in hog lard, in cast-iron skillets over the fire pit.

As billowing smoke escaped the room through the doorway, it carried a bouquet of delicious cooking smells.

"Sam, you and Bettie eat some, then you go find Mister Bonham and ask him to come for breakfast."

After bolting down the food, Sam left in a fast walk.

Then Bowie lit the candle and dripped wax on the folded letter to seal it closed. In addition to the writing materials, the desk held a flesh-out, cow-hide dispatch case, into which he placed the letter.

Bowie felt faint again. He squirted another line of tequila from the pouch, then reclined and dozed on his cot.

Awakening and sitting up minutes later, Bowie watched rotund, middle-aged Bettie dish up two plates of food just as twenty-nine-year-old James Butler Bonham of South Carolina entered the room with Sam behind him.

Bowie gestured toward the small oak table, saying, "Sit down, Bonham. Have a bite."

The steaming plate of food before him, Jim thought that Bonham's eyes began consuming the sumptuous-smelling fare, even before seating himself.

"Try rolling everything up in the tortilla," Bowie said. "It's a recipe Bettie got from a woman in Bexar."

Bonham assembled the food with his fingers, then licked them and took a bite.

"Um."

"I hear Travis is relieving Colonel Neill," Bowie ventured.

Bonham hesitated for a moment, chewing a large bite of food, then replied, "I hadn't heard."

"Travis is your cousin, isn't he?"

"Second-cousin," Bonham said, ruefully.

Bowie thought he detected indifference in Bonham's tone.

"You don't like him?"

"I understand him; he thinks like a lawyer."

"You're a lawyer too, aren't you?"

"Yes, sir."

"How's the food?"

"Best I've had since I got here."

"Good. Lieutenant Bonham, when you finish I've got a mission for you."

"Yes, Colonel."

Bonham took the last bite and stood, still chewing.

Extending the dispatch case toward the tall, handsome Bonham, Bowie said, "I want you to take this to Governor Smith. If he is not in San Felipe, try Washington-on-the-Brazos. After you deliver it, await his orders."

"Yes, sir."

"Don't open it or surrender it to another soul except me and the governor."

"Yes, sir."

"If you encounter Travis or anyone else on the way or when you return, do not divulge any information about your mission, and continue on your way immediately."

"Yes, sir."

Believing that Bonham was a man who would always complete his mission, Bowie added, "Do you understand?"

"Yes, sir."

"Then tell me."

"I am to deliver this case to the hands of Governor Smith without fail, to await and deliver the governor's orders to you, and not divulge my mission to anyone."

"That is correct. Now be on your way and return as soon as you can."

After Bonham's departure, Bowie collapsed on the floor. It took Sam and Bettie together to lift him back onto his cot.

* * *

By the next afternoon, Bowie had regained some of his strength. After another of Bettie's tasty meals, he peered through the window and said to Sam, "I think I'd like to sit in the sun for a while. Would you put a chair out for me, Sam?"

Obeying immediately, Sam placed a chair a few feet east of the main gate, in the sunlight coming over the west wall. The warmth of the sun felt good to him and Bowie had been napping in the chair for about an hour when the loud voice of the gate sentry awakened him.

"HALT! STOP! WHO ARE YOU?

From his chair, Bowie could not see who the sentry was addressing. However, he could hear the exchange of words and became mildly curious.

"I'm Captain William B. Harrison, and this is David Crockett. We are the twelve Tennessee Mounted Volunteers come to the aid of our Texas brothers."

Colonel Neill was quickly summoned. He approached in a brisk walk and extended his hand into the gate passage.

Bowie's interest waxed when he heard the name Crockett and he strained to hear more.

"Colonel Crockett, it is indeed a pleasure to meet you and your men. I'm Colonel Neill, the garrison commander."

"Colonel Neill, my militia unit in the great state of Tennessee elected me to lead them, and there I am a colonel. Here, I'm just another private and seek no higher station. Captain Harrison here is our commanding officer."

"That's fine. Let me welcome you men to the fight. My aide will see to your billeting."

Then Bowie heard Crockett's voice say, "Fight, you say? I thought all the fighting was over," and the group from Tennessee moved forward into his field of sight.

Bowie did not want to meet these new men in his present, weakened condition, especially not the famous Davy Crockett, so he turned his face away. However he immediately began to think about how he might arrange to meet this bear hunter, this teller of tall tales, this former U.S. Congressman, from a stronger looking, more flattering pose.

Chapter 17

The following Sunday, Bowie's former sisters-in-law, Juana and Josefa, made their regular weekly delivery of food and supplies to him in the Alamo. Ironically, the sisters were able to help Bowie because fate had kept them alive in Bexar instead of sending them to Monclova with their now dead parents.

Their brother Marco was away at school in California, but the sisters still resided in the Veramendi Palace, with Bowie's other two freed slaves as their paid servants. So far, on Sam's advice, the former slaves, Josephus and Charlie, had elected to stay in Bexar. They earned their room, board, and five pesos a month by caring for livestock and running various errands. This day, they carried what the sisters brought.

Bowie was feeling better, having eaten and slept well during the two days since his last collapse. He had made an early-morning trip to use the Alamo's only bath-tub, located in the hospital, and was now fully dressed in his finest business attire.

Over the fire pit, Bettie had every available skillet and pot full of something, together with three chickens on an ingeniously designed spit that Charlie turned occasionally. Outside comments that entered through the open door told that people were walking by just to breathe in the mixture of aromas.

Hearing that Jim had been down sick, the sisters had also brought along a traveling, Franciscan priest.

"We found Father Wright saying mass in the chapel and thought you might want him to hear your confession." Juana announced.

The padre introduced himself and explained that he had come to Bexar with a volunteer military group called the New Orleans Greys when they brought the eighteen pounder cannon to Bexar in December.

"We are happy to have you with us, Father," Bowie said and shook the friar's hand.

The room was getting crowded, but Bowie decided there was room for one more.

"Sam, go see if you can find Mister Davy Crockett. This time of the mornin,' I expect you will find him near the cattle pen. Ask him to come for lunch and tell him he has time to change his clothes, if he wants to."

In no time, it seemed, Crockett walked in the doorway. "I finds Mister Crockett by the chapel, talkin to the doctor," Sam said from behind him.

Apparently, Crockett had attended mass. He was dressed in fine clothing that rivaled Bowie's. He extended his right hand, then spoke with a Tennessee drawl thick enough to ice a cake. "You must be Colonel Bowie. I hear tell that you wrestle alligators in Louisiana. I'm David Crockett, and I'm here to tell you that I do the same thing with bears in Tennessee."

Bowie answered Crockett's wide grin with a rare grin of his own.

"It is an honor to have you join us, Colonel Crockett. It is not often that we meet such a famous personage."

"The honor is mine, Colonel Bowie, and I must say that your reputation far exceeds my humble accomplishments. I'm just a back-woods boy who traveled to Washington-on-the-Potomac a few times."

Anticipating having guests for lunch, the Veramendi sisters had brought a table top, four extra chairs, and dishes, goblets, and cutlery for six. Bettie directed Josephus and Charlie to turn Bowie's cot lengthwise in the room and lay the tabletop on the cot-posts.

Now the chairs and dishes were in position, and Bowie invited his guests to be seated. After serving all the guests, Bettie prepared plates for herself and the other blacks, and they carried them outside to eat in the plaza.

Bowie began his first group meal in months by asking Father Wright to give thanks, and then he made introductions all around.

The Other Rose of Texas

Crockett spoke next. "Colonel Bowie, I have heard many stories about your accomplishments in Louisiana, especially around New Orleans, and I am curious. Why did you leave there and come to Texas?"

Bowie smiled. Through the years, he had learned that getting people to talk about themselves was a good way to court their friendship. Obvious to Bowie, his terms in the U.S. Congress had taught Crockett the same lesson.

Though he recognized the ploy, he was feeling expansive, so when Bowie saw the faces of the ladies brighten in reaction to Crockett's question, he decided to respond in detail. In the women's eyes, he believed he saw admiration for their famous brother-in-law, so he concluded that hearing about his past life would be a special treat for them.

"Alright, I'll tell you, but if it gets too boring, you have to stop me, and please eat. Don't let Bettie's wonderful food get cold."

The ladies and Crockett smiled and nodded. The priest maintained a passive expression.

"By 1830, my brothers and I . . ."

"Were you close to your brothers, my son?" Father Wright asked, joining the conversation.

"I was close with Rezin P., but not with my oldest brother John J., and my youngest brother, Stephen, was my hair shirt. While we were growing up, our father pitted us against each other."

The priest flashed a tight smile. "Perhaps your father also taught you to be ruthless in business."

Bowie took a bite of chicken and looked around the table while he chewed. He was not sure he had heard the priest correctly, so he let the comment pass.

"As I was saying . . ."

"Did your father also teach you how to de-flower young women?" the padre interrupted again.

Jim took another bite and looked around the table again. The shocked expression on everyone's face confirmed that he had indeed heard correctly. However, Bowie did not want to spoil the ambiance of the gathering, so he decided to treat the priest like a heckler at a political stump speech, and ignore him.

"My brother, Rezin P., opened our meeting by telling us that Lafitte said we had to sell more slaves or our deal with him was off. Junior Lafitte was running things by then, and he said he was tired of being a business man, and he wanted to concentrate on being a gentleman. I said I thought Lafitte's real problem was the British and Spanish navies, and that what he really wanted was for us to buy his slave block in Galveston, so he could get out of the business."

Apparently, Crockett had been heckled a few times too and decided to ignore the priest's rudeness as well. Looking puzzled, he said, "I thought slavery was illegal in Mexico. I heard it was a hanging offense."

"True, but they didn't seem to be enforcing that law in Texas right then."

Bowie began to cough, and Juana quickly grabbed the tequila pouch from the wall and handed it to him. After taking a long squirt, Bowie continued his story.

"Excuse me, just a little frog in my throat. As I was saying, the opportunities in Texas looked promising, but I told my brothers I wouldn't want to get us involved unless there was a chance that the Mexican law against slavery could be changed, at least for Texas."

Bowie coughed again, but briefly. "So my brothers agreed to pay for my trip."

"Obviously, you made the journey, Mister Bowie," Father Wright observed. "How far did you travel?"

The priest seemed to be acting normal again.

"That's the interesting part. I went to Galveston, then to San Felipe to see Stephen Austin. My New Orleans bankers had given me letters of introduction to Senior Seguin and Vice-Governor Veramendi, so I came here to Bexar next."

The sisters both smiled when they heard their father's name.

"And then two things happened that changed my life. Senior Veramendi told me that the future of trading slaves, by any means, was doomed throughout Mexico, but as a Mexican citizen I could make a fortune trading Texas land."

Bowie spoke slowly, careful with his comments about slavery.

"Was Veramendi right?" Crockett asked.

"He was right at that time. But very soon, President Bustamante banned immigration from the U.S. and left me sitting on thousands of acres of land with no prospective buyers. Then last year, President Santa Anna repealed all the special laws we had up here in Texas, including the one we used to bring in slaves. As for the fortune, I'm still working on that."

"You said two things happened that changed your life. What was the second, my brother?" Josefa asked.

Bowie's eyes moistened as he answered, "I met my beloved Ursula," and then he began to cough again.

The expression of the younger sister seemed to indicate her satisfaction with his answer. The other young woman glared at her sibling as if the memory of another woman was the last thing she wanted to foster in Bowie's mind.

Jim noticed the exchange of looks between the two and was wondering what it meant, when the priest spoke again.

"And did your beloved Ursula know how many men you attacked with your well-known knife, how many men you killed?"

Father Wright was at it again, and Bowie had finally had enough. Jim's memory of his drunken and disreputable years had been clouded by time. Moreover, he had convinced himself that his good deeds and exemplary conduct since that time more than made up for his transgressions. It angered him to be confronted by a man who was either ignorant of his reformation or considered it insufficient, but he tried to tone down his response since his accuser was a man of authority and what he said was admittedly true.

"Are you drunk, Father, or crazy?" Jim said, not attempting to defend himself. "We invite you for a friendly meal and all you can do is insult your host."

"You obviously don't remember me, Mister Bowie. You saw me in Alexandria, Louisiana almost ten years ago when I went there to settle the affairs of my brother, whom you killed on that sandbar. I had a parish in New Orleans, and I have followed your infamous exploits first hand. Three of the men you ruined in business were members of my congregation, and I heard the confession of two of the virginal young women that you spoiled. You are the devil himself, sir, and I can see now that God has visited sickness upon you as retribution. Vengeance is mine, sayeth the lord."

Father Wright stood and walked out, leaving everyone with an open mouth and glazed over eyes.

"That fella reminds me of a man I knew in Tennessee," Crockett commented. "No matter how many drinks I bought him, I could never win his vote."

Bowie felt grateful that his amusing new friend was trying to restore the festive mood to the room.

The Veramendi sisters smiled, but Bowie could only cough and hold his chest.

Later in the day, his fever began to rise, and the sisters put him to bed.

* * *

During the two days since his Sunday luncheon party, Bowie had only been conscious a few hours, and Sam was becoming frantic. How sick was his former master? How much longer could he and Bettie depend on Bowie for protection?

They were washing dishes and laundry in the acequia east of the Alamo, where he was sure they would not be overheard, when Sam sought his sister's council.

"We'd better start thinking about what we're gonna do if Bowie can't protect us."

"What do you mean, brother?"

"I mean we've got double trouble, sister. If he dies, we're gonna end up on the block in Galveston, unless we can get to New Orleans, but I don't know how we can travel through Texas safely. There's no underground railroad out of here."

"But you still have our freedom thing, don't you?"

"The first white man I show that to is going to take it away from me and tear it up."

Bettie nodded her understanding.

"And Bowie said that a bad man is coming here to kill him. I think he means the Mexican army is coming back, but I don't know when."

"When I was cookin' at the north camp fire, I heard some of the men talking about that too."

"If you hear anymore, tell me. I'm gonna learn what I can around the commander's room. We need to make an escape plan, just in case."

* * *

After his conversation with Bettie, when he was not tending Bowie, Sam walked by Colonel Neill's quarters frequently, always carrying a garment to mend, boots to shine, or something else he could use to make it appear that he was working.

As he passed, if he heard voices coming from inside the commander's room, he squatted beneath the open window and listened. If anyone looked his way, he gave them his best "I's just a dumb ole slave sittin' an a'workin" smile.

At ten A.M. on Thursday, Sam's system produced results. As he approached, he saw a man enter Neill's room, followed by another man. A third man, a negro, stopped beside the door. The first man wore a blue cut-away coat with gold epaulettes over white trousers tucked into black Wellington boots. The red band around the crown of his wide brimmed Amish style hat matched the red sash around his waist. The second man was dressed in buckskin and carrying a flint-lock rifle. The negro man wore dark pants and an orange shirt.

Noticing Sam, now sitting on the ground below the window to the left of the door, the negro man sat beside him.

"I's Joe."

"Shush," Sam replied and tilted his head to listen to the conversation inside.

"I am Lieutenant-Colonel William Barrett Travis, and I have written orders from Governor Smith to relieve you of your command of this post, sir," he heard the first man say.

"I am relieved, sir."

Sam knew Colonel Neill's voice and thought he recognized anger in it. His observation was confirmed by the scowl on Neill's face when he walked into the plaza and turned toward Bowie's room without saying another word to Travis.

As Neill passed Sam heard him say, "I hope somebody slaps the arrogance out of that boy." Then he laughed and added, "He's in for a big surprise when he learns about your master's plans for this place," and walked on.

Inside, Sam heard Travis speaking again. "Private Despallier," he commanded.

"Yes, sir."

"After you unpack my belongings, find Colonel Bowie, extend my compliments, and ask him to join me here."

"Yes, sir."

Sam knew that the doctor was with Bowie and decided not to follow Despallier.

As expected Despallier returned within a few minutes. "Colonel Bowie is indisposed, sir."

"What do you mean, Private?"

"He's sick, sir. He cannot join you. He looks pretty bad, sir. The doctor is with him."

"Take me to him."

When Travis emerged into the plaza, Joe stood and followed him at a respectful distance, as Travis followed Despallier to Bowie's room.

Feeling amused as he followed Joe, Sam thought of the child's game, follow the leader.

Arriving, as Travis tried to enter Bowie's room, a man stepped in front of him.

Sam heard another familiar voice say," Are you crazy, man? This is a sick room and should probably be quarantined,"

"I'm Lieutenant-Colonel William Barrett Travis, your new commanding officer, and I need to see Colonel Bowie now."

"I'm Doctor Amos Pollard, Colonel, and you can see him from here."

"I mean I need to talk to him."

"He's out of his mind with fever. I doubt he would make any sense right now."

"I was sent here by General Houston to help him destroy the mission buildings and the walls. We are both in command now, and I am bound by my orders to confer with him and get the work started."

"Colonel, the only thing you'll be bound by is the fever you will get from him if you persist. It's probably typhoid, but possibly something communicable. I'm not sure yet."

Sam felt satisfaction as he listened to the doctor use facts and logic to repeatedly counter Travis's egotistical attempts to brow-beat him.

"Well, when can I talk to him?"

"If it is typhoid, his fever should break in two or three days."

"Very well, doctor. I'll expect you to notify me the minute he is lucid."

"If that means when he is not contagious and can talk sense, I'll do that."

Travis executed a military about-face and walked away. Before following Travis, Private Despallier said to Pollard, "I was born and raised a few miles from Jim's home place. Tell him Charlie Des said hey-ee."

Again following Joe, Sam heard Travis send Despallier to summon Captain Almeron Dickinson.

Then Joe stopped and turned to face Sam. "Why you dog my master round?"

"I's a spy. You wanna be a spy with me?" Sam asked.

Joe grinned and said, "Sho".

"Alright, you's a spy too. Now be still, us spies need to hear this," Sam whispered as Dickinson approached.

"Captain, order the men to assemble here."

"All the men, sir?"

"Yes, all the men, regulars and militia too. Let's use the bugle; I want them familiar with the calls."

Dickinson took two steps, cupped his hands and shouted toward the north wall. "MAJOR JAMESON, COLONEL TRAVIS HAS ORDERED ASSEMBLY. WITH YOUR PERMISSION SIR WE NEED OUR BUGLER."

Beyond Sam's hearing range, the major opened his mouth and gestured with his hand, then a youngish looking figure emerged from a hole in the ground beside him and reported to Dickinson.

"Colonel Travis, this is Albert C. Grimes; he's as close to a bugler as any man we have. Grimes, get the bugle and come back here and sound assembly. If the men don't mind the bugle, tell them to pass the word."

"But I don't know where the bugle is, sir."

"I saw it on a wall peg in the hospital."

"Yes, sir."

Within minutes, Grimes was blowing the shiny horn. Gradually, the men abandoned whatever task they were at and walked toward the call. Sam assumed that those who knew told those who did not what the bugle exhortation meant.

Preparing to speak, Travis turned toward Dickinson and asked, "Where are the others?"

"They're down by Colonel Bowie's room, sir."

"Are they stupid? Bring them down here to receive orders along with these men."

"I tried sir, but they said they report to Colonel Bowie, not to some damn shave tail politician . . . sir."

Sam thought to himself, "So Bowie is still in charge here. I'll be alright as long as he can give orders."

Travis's face had turned slightly red, still he began to address the assemblage. "Men, we have orders from General Houston to destroy the mission and transport the artillery east to him. Where we lite will depend upon where the General decides to stand against the Mexican army, if and when it arrives. Personally, I don't think the enemy will be here before April, if they come at all. We gave them a pretty good licking in December, and they may just let us be."

Travis turned to Dickinson and said, "I included those comments about the Mexican army to help keep the men from leaving Bexar and going home as the others did. I think we might be able to keep this command together, if the men see easy times ahead."

The men had begun murmuring and shuffling their feet, and when he turned back Travis yelled, "ATTENTION, YOU MEN. ATTENTION TO ORDERS."

The men stiffened and became silent.

"We don't have enough explosives, so all we can do is dig holes along the walls for the time when we do. We can also dismount the cannon and prepare them for transport. Major Jameson will be responsible for demolitions, and Major Evans will oversee preparation of the cannons and ordinance. They will assign you men to duty directly. Are there any questions?"

"Yea, what are those boys down there gonna do?" Grimes the bugler asked, pointing toward Bowie's men.

"They will work too, Private," Travis replied.

He motioned for Majors Jameson and Evans to take charge, and, followed by Dickinson, he entered his room and closed the door, but Sam could still hear him through the window.

"Dickinson, make sure that bugler digs a few latrines. I'll not tolerate that kind of insubordination."

"Yes, sir. What are you gonna do about Bowie's men, Colonel? You can't get near him, and they won't make a move without his order."

"I can wait a couple of days. I have to. But if he doesn't come around, I'll deal with his men some other way. I want you to watch Bowie and Pollard and let me know about things. Do you understand, Captain?"

"Yes, sir."

"You're dismissed."

Dickinson left.

Soon Travis left his room and turned toward the men who were assembled near the low barracks. Joe and Sam followed.

* * *

From the corner of his eye Crockett saw a handsomely dressed man approaching, followed at a respectable distance by two negro men. He had not been introduced but he knew the man was Travis.

"So I told them, you may all go to hell, and I will go to Texas," Crockett said, concluding a story. The men laughed, then applauded.

Since Crockett was not part of the regular Texas army, he reasoned that he and the other Tennessee volunteers should to be part of Bowie's command. They had seated themselves on the ground among Bowie's men who were clustered outside his room

When Travis approached the group, no one saluted or came to attention or bothered to afford him any other military courtesy, and when he sat beside Crockett, some of the men stood and relocated.

"My name is Lieutenant-Colonel William Barrett Travis, Colonel Crockett, and I am proud to meet you, sir."

"You don't need to call me colonel or sir. Here, I'm just another private soldier, and I am pleased to meet you too."

"Should I call you Crockett then?"

"Crockett will be fine."

"Well Crockett, first let me say how happy I am to have you and your men from Tennessee here with us. As you may already know, I am in command here."

"I heard you were sharing command with Colonel Bowie."

"Yes, that is true, but I was appointed by the governor and he was not."

Crockett felt like the only buyer at a horse auction as he sensed that a sales pitch was coming.

"I understand colonel, so what can I do for you?"

"Although you may choose to exercise no authority, we both know that your reputation affords you a great deal of influence over these men. So I want you to know that I would consider your cooperation on any matter of great value."

"I appreciate that, Colonel. I'll do all I can to help."

"I believe you were a politician back in Tennessee, were you not?"

"Yes, I had the privilege of serving my friends and neighbors that way."

"Then you will understand when I tell you that it is my goal to work in harmony with Colonel Bowie and his men."

"Yes, I believe I do."

"And I think that you could be most helpful to me with that and at the same time you could help yourself."

"What do you mean, Colonel?"

"To put it bluntly, Crockett, if you decide to continue your political career after Texas has won independence from Mexico, I think I can do you more good than Bowie can, so I am offering you a partnership."

"If you are saying you want me to be second in command to you and Bowie, I already told you I am not a colonel in Texas."

"That is not what I had in mind. I heard that you and Bowie have become friends."

"Yes, I guess we have."

"Well then. What I want is for you to keep me informed about what he tells his men and what he says about me. In the name of harmony and cooperation I want to be able to plan how to achieve our joint mission here."

Crockett was clinching his teeth to keep from grinning. In Washington he had heard enough of this kind of double talk to last him forever, from men who thought they were smarter than everybody else. Crockett found it amusing that Travis so obviously saw himself this way.

"Are you asking me to be a spy for you, Colonel Travis?"

"Not at all. Not at all. I would describe you as an unofficial liaison."

Crockett decided that his wisest course of action with a man like Travis was to keep every door open, so he hedged.

"I'm not sure I'll be staying in Texas. I didn't come here to fight."

Travis looked shocked.

"But if I do decide to stay, I'll consider your proposal. Now, if you'll excuse me Colonel Travis, I need to clean my rifles."

* * *

In Bowie's room Sam was stirring some beef broth in a cast iron pot that Bettie had placed on the fire embers.

"Colonel Bowie?" Doctor Pollard shook Jim's shoulder. "Colonel Bowie, you need to wake up and take some nourishment. You need to drink, so you don't dehydrate."

Pollard motioned to Sam and said, "Sam, help me raise him up. Bettie, make him take some of that broth."

Opening his eyes, Jim Bowie seemed semi-conscious most of the time that Bettie spooned soup down his throat. Then delirium claimed him again, and he did not see Crockett enter his sick room and sit cross-legged on the floor beside the fire pit.

"How's he doin' doc?" Crockett asked.

Doctor Pollard kneeled and rubbed his hands together over the fire. Then he leaned closer to Crockett, and Sam heard him whisper, "I think the typhoid has almost run its course, but his consumption seems to be getting worse. Do you know how long he has had it?"

Crockett whispered back, "I haven't known him for long doc, but I think Sam could probably say."

They both looked at Sam, who smiled back.

"I don't want Travis to know anything about this," Pollard replied. "He might start scheming on Jim. Can you find out from Sam, and let me know?"

Crockett nodded and Pollard rose, just as Bettie returned, carrying dishes she had washed in the acequia.

"Sam, I'll be back in a few hours. I think Colonel Crockett is going to stay a while though." Pollard closed his medical bag and walked out.

Crockett stood, walked over and moved the chair from the small desk to a place beside the cot. He sat down, then placed his right hand on Bowie's forehead. Bowie's eyes darted under closed lids.

"Sam, how long you been with Mister Jim?"

Sam tried to look a little confused when Crockett addressed him, so he could be slow to respond. "Well, sir. I been servin Master, I mean Mister, Jim since the day we was borned," he replied.

"What do you mean, Sam?"

After hearing his reply, Bettie turned her face to the wall, and Sam guessed she was trying to avoid laughing in Crockett's face in response to his pic-speak. Enjoying her amusement, Sam used his next reply as a hint to his sister that he was ready for a competitive round of their game, if she was.

"Well sir, I means my mammy say Mister Jim and I's borned on the same day, sir, and that day his paw, The Master, give me to him, and they puts me in his crib, beside him, and my mammy say she suckle us both."

"Well I declare, Sam, so you know Jim about as well as a man could."

That question really put Sam on his guard. He had seen Crockett talking to Travis, a man he had begun to fear. Feeling anxious now he did not want to reveal any information that might jeopardize Bowie. At the same time, he wanted to learn anything of value that he could from this famous Tennessean.

"Yes sir, I been beside Mister Jim ever day of his life. He even taken me with him when he move down to N'Orleans, when we's jus' boys."

"What kind of young man was Mister Jim, Sam?"

"He was a good man, sir. He and Master Rezin P. never beat me or Bettie either. All the brothers was better men than they paw though."

"Did their paw beat you, Sam?"

"No sir, Master Jim wouldn't let him hurt me, but he whipped my mammy and all. The old master was a evil man. He liked to kill a slave sometimes."

Just then, Jim Bowie sat upright on his cot and began to cough deeply. Eyes still closed; he pressed his solar plexus with both hands and bent over. A trickle of blood drooled from the right side of his mouth.

When the coughing stopped, his torso fell back upon the cot. He never opened his eyes.

"How long has Mister Jim had that bad cough?"

Sam hesitated and looked at Crockett blankly while he decided how to answer. So far he felt confident that he had not disclosed anything that could be used against Bowie, yet neither had he learned anything. Now, if he answered truthfully, he would reveal, perhaps to Travis, that Bowie had been ill for a long time. He became more nervous as he tried to decide about trusting Crockett. Then he decided to risk it.

"It started when we come back from Mexico, after Miss Ursula and the chil'ren died. But there weren't no blood til about a year ago."

"Sam, how come you keep calling Jim, master? He told me that you weren't his slave anymore, that he had made you a free man."

Sam took a deep breath. If Bowie had told Crockett that Sam was free, it must be alright to discuss the subject.

"That's right, sir. He did it after she was dead, said he had did it because he promise her. But I been saying Master Jim since I could talk, and I can't remember not to."

"If he promised her, then why did he wait until she was dead to make you free?"

Sam realized he had gotten himself in a trap, but he had decided he needed some information from Crockett, so, rather than feign stupidity, he continued.

"I mean he said he promise her after she was dead. It was after we got to Mexico to look at the graves, and he was talkin to the little lady at the church all day. I saw her once; she had on a black dress and all you could see was her face and her hands."

"You mean she was a nun?"

"Yes sir, like them ones in N'Orleans."

"And Mister Jim was talking to her all day?"

"Yes, sir. Then he came home and gave me my freeman thing with red wax on it."

"And what did he say, Sam?"

"Master Jim say Miss Ursula don't want him ownin no slaves and me and Bettie and Josephus and Charlie was free now. He say put the document in my pouch and don't show it to no man unless Master Jim dead too."

"So how come you're tellin' me this, Sam?"

"Master Jim say he like you, Mister Crockett, that you was our friend and we can trust you. He say if anything happen to him, that you the man to help us get to N'Orleans."

Sam hoped that, with this lie, he had gained Crockett's trust. He needed to learn what it was about Crockett's home state of Tennessee that caused Sam's father to be caught in Memphis so many times.

"You from Tennessee, ain't you, sir?"

"That's right, Sam."

"You got slaves up there?"

"The folks in the eastern part of Tennessee think slavery is a bad thing, and they don't own any. I don't own any slaves either, but most of my neighbors do. I live in the western part of the state, Sam, between Nashville and Memphis. A lot of men in Memphis make a living catching runaways that come up the river heading for Canada."

So that was it Sam thought. It is not safe for a negro to even be seen around Memphis. My paw was lost the minute a white man spotted him.

Sam nodded his appreciation for the information.

"Sam, I've got some things to tend to now," Crockett said. "If Mister Jim wakes up, you come and find me, or send Bettie. Do you understand?"

"Yes, sir. If Master, I mean, if Mister Jim wake up, you wants to know."

"That's right, Sam."

As Crockett emerged from the low barracks, Sam watched him through the window. He pulled a raccoon-skin cap from under his belt and positioned it on his head. Then Crockett walked diagonally across the plaza toward the hospital, located on the second floor of the south end of the Long Barracks. Sure that Crockett was on his way to report to Doctor Pollard, Sam worried that Crockett might visit Travis as well, later.

Then he fingered the freedom document inside his pouch and remembered what Crockett had said about slave hunters in Memphis.

"Would the underground railroad really be safe?" he pondered.

"Would it be better to travel by ship from New Orleans to someplace like Nova Scotia? Would there be enough money for that?"

Then Sam realized he was putting the cart before the horse. First he had to actually get everybody to New Orleans and if Bowie did not get better, he was not sure how he could do that.

* * *

When Bowie finally awoke and sat up on February 15, Crockett was in the room.

"Sam, go tell Doc Pollard that Jim waked up," Crockett ordered, then he asked Bowie, "How do you feel?"

"Like I been chewed up and spit out."

Crockett handed him a canteen of water. "Just sip this."

"I'd prefer tequila."

"Later. Let's see what Doc has to say first."

When Doctor Amos Pollard arrived, he asked everyone to leave the room, so he could examine his patient.

"You a real doctor, doctor?" Bowie asked.

"I attended medical school, if that's what you mean," Pollard replied. "In Vermont."

"What are you doing here? Aren't there easier places to practice medicine?"

"I knew they would need a doctor here."

As he helped Bowie remove all his clothes, the physician asked, "You get all these scars from those knife fights we heard about?"

"There was only one knife fight, Doc. Well maybe one and a half. I didn't have a knife myself for the first one. The other wounds are just from livin'."

"You mean that fight on the sandbar was the only one?"

"Yes, Doc, all the other stuff was made up by the newspaper people and hack writers. That one on the sandbar would never have happened either, if those clod-hoppers from Alexandria had the code and manners of a New Orleans gentleman."

"I heard you were outnumbered, and they almost killed you. Weren't you afraid of dyin' ?"

"I have a philosophy about that, Doc. When death comes, it will only take a moment's courage to face it, and until that moment comes, it is senseless to worry about it."

"And all those stories about the Bowie Knife?"

Bowie raised himself on one elbow, reached under his pillow, and pulled out a long knife. "You mean this?"

"Yes, where did that come from?"

"My brother gave me this one after another man pulled a knife, and I couldn't. Then we had a few other knives made like this one as gifts."

The knife Bowie handed to Pollard, handle first, was the weapon that Jim received from his brother, Rezin P. As Pollard hefted it, he said, "Nice balance. Heavy though. Sharp. I'll borrow it the next time I need to take off a leg."

Pollard handed it back, then continued poking, thumping, and pressing Bowie's chest and stomach, while he listened through his ear trumpet stethoscope.

Bowie returned the knife to his cache, then reclined his head.

"Roll over on your belly." Pollard said and repeated his probing and listening regimen on Bowie's upper and lower back.

"Alright, on your back again."

This time, Bowie needed help to turn his body over.

The doctor put his wooden listening device back in his leather satchel, then looked directly at Bowie. "You can get dressed."

"How'm I doin' Doc?"

"I think you already know that, colonel."

This was the first time Bowie had been attended by a physician since his stop in Alexandria on his way to Monclova, over two years before. Since then he had attributed his ailments to his harried lifestyle and refused to seek treatment.

"I want to hear it from you."

"You want it all?"

"Yes."

"Your body has been weakened by consumption, probably for at least two years. That's why you contracted typhoid fever so easy. The typhoid has not yet run its course and, together with the advanced consumption, will continue to weaken you. Your fever will rise and fall, and you will be in and out of consciousness. I've seen this before. You have little hope of recovery, and soon you will not be able to leave this cot. In fairness to your men, I think you should pass command to a subordinate."

"How did I catch it Doc?"

"Sam said you started coughing right after your wife died."

"Do you think I have made himself sick?"

"I don't know. I've heard explanations that are even more far-fetched than that, like it is caused by vampires."

Bowie felt angry. Until now he had successfully denied the seriousness of his painful and degenerative state. Realizing he was angry at himself and trying to avoid offending Pollard, he controlled his tone of voice.

"I like you Doc, and I appreciate your honesty. I promise, as soon as we get this business with Mexico taken care of, I'll take a long rest. Now, I would like to talk to Colonel Crockett."

"As you wish, Colonel. There is not much I can do to make you comfortable, but I will send Reynolds around with some quinine and laudanum."

"Thanks, Doc."

When Crockett re-entered the room, Bowie was awake with his eyes closed.

Crockett tried not to disturb Bowie as he moved the chair closer to the cot, but when he seated himself, Bowie opened his eyes.

"Well, Congressman Crockett, how are you liking Texas?"

Bowie knew his use of a title that Crockett no longer held would be a barb, but he wanted the man's attention. Then he noticed a light green Pitkin flask and a gallon crock whiskey jug on the table and assumed that Crockett had just placed them there. A slight twinge of regret pinched his insides for his sarcastic remark.

Crockett nodded toward the bottles. "The flask is full of mezcal, and the jug is half full of tequila. Doc said it was okay, so here," he said and reached for the two containers.

Bowie accepted the flask of mezcal and raised it up to look for the maguey worm. Then, after motioning for Crockett to put the jug of tequila on the floor beside his cot, he uncorked the flask and took a long pull. "Man, I'll take this over laudanum any day."

He held the flask out toward Crockett, whose expression declined the offer, then he took another long pull. "Doc says I'll be on my feet in a few days."

Crockett looked down.

"But I should pass command until I'm up and around."

Without looking up, Crockett queried, "I thought Travis was already in command too."

"Before we talk about that, I'd like to get something straight between us. What are you doing here?"

When they first met Bowie felt that Crockett had just stepped out of one of the many stories that circulated about him as the semi-literate, backwoods buffoon who earned his living with his mouth, could talk a pond out of its fish, and had talked the people of Tennessee out of their votes. Now Bowie sensed there might be more to this man than what he revealed to the public and he wanted to know if he was right.

Crockett looked up. "You mean, why am I in Texas, or why am I in this room?"

"Let's start with Texas."

"Haven't you heard? I lost my job in Tennessee, and I'm looking for another one."

"Yes, I heard. Did you really tell everyone to go to hell?"

"I lost my head, but by that time I didn't have much else to lose, after Andy quit me. You know Jim that reminds me of a story about."

Bowie cut him off.

"What makes you think you can do any better down here?"

Bowie pulled his blanket up around his shoulders, then Crockett stood and moved his chair to a place between Bowie and the fire pit that would not block Jim from the heat. Before seating himself again, he turned and placed two oak logs on top of the red, glowing coals, and two more at right angles on top of the first two, forming a square. Flames licked the logs immediately.

Then he turned the back of the chair toward Bowie, straddled it and said, "I'll be fifty years old in another six months, Jim. I'm the same age as my father when he died. It's getting too late for me to make a new start, and I sure couldn't do it back home in Tennessee."

Crockett reached down to his left, hefted the jug, and took a pull of tequila. Bowie stared at him intently.

"I heard there was free land down here for men willing to fight, so I come along with the others."

Bowie was silent, his eyes probing until Crockett peeled away a layer of his pretense.

"Hell man, I can't fool you. I heard the fighting was over. Besides, I know my best fighting days are over too, but I might still be able to run for political office and claim some property for my family. Lord knows, I can't afford to buy any."

"Can I call you Davy?"

"I favor David. My mother liked the bible stories about him."

"I had a brother named David. He drowned. Can I trust you, David?"

Although Bowie was not ready to accept the doctor's gloomy prognosis, for the first time since arriving at the Alamo he did admit to himself that he needed a confidant, and he was considering Crockett.

"Can I trust you, Jim?"

"The truth is, David, Doc says I'll never walk away from this bed for very long."

"What is it?"

"Typhoid laid me low, but it's the consumption that'll put me under."

"Can't you go to the dry air? I hear that helps."

"Doc says it's too late, but he doesn't know me very well."

"What you gonna do?"

"That might depend on you."

"What do you mean?"

"Well, you could take that information to Travis and probably get yourself a commission in the army of Texas."

"Yes, I guess I could do that."

Bowie took Crockett's response to mean that he was not already in cahoots with Travis. Encouraged by that, Jim continued.

"Or you could be my eyes and ears if the time comes when I can't leave this room."

"So you want me to be a kind of unofficial liaison?"

"I guess you could put it that way."

"Then I'll give you the answer I gave Travis when he proposed the same thing."

Jim was not surprised.

The Other Rose of Texas

"I said I'm not sure I want to stay in Texas now. I didn't come here to fight. But if I do decide to stay, I'll consider your proposal. Now, if you'll excuse me colonel, I need to go clean my rifles."

"I understand how you feel. You probably think Travis and I are acting like school boys fighting to be first in line. But consider this. Travis wants to lead his line into a war and I want to lead mine away from one."

"What do you mean?"

"That's all I can tell you right now except that you can trust what I say."

Chapter 18

In his Low Barracks room, it had been four days since Jim Bowie's temperature was above one-hundred four degrees, but Doctor Pollard had been unable to bring it below one-hundred one. His cough was worse, and his spittle showed growing traces of blood.

Sam spent every minute at Bowie's side, and Crockett seemed to spend most of his daylight hours there too. Crockett and Sam passed the time talking. Sometimes Bowie participated, with his eyes open. Other times he closed his eyes and pretend to sleep. Either way, he heard every word.

"You think we gonna have to fight here, Mister Crockett?" Sam asked.

"I don't know. I sure hope not. I've never seen a worse place to try to defend."

"You mean we ain't safe with all these walls around us?"

"The walls are the biggest problem. There's too much wall, and they're the wrong kind."

"What you mean, Sir?"

"I mean it would take about seven hundred riflemen to defend these walls, and we don't even have a hundred."

"But they's more men comin', isn't they?"

"I don't know. I hope so. But even if more come, most of the walls aren't high enough to protect us, and there are no holes for the men to fire through."

"What kind of holes?"

"The walls of a good fort have holes three or four feet above the ground that are just big enough for a man to aim and fire his rifle through. That way, the man is protected from the enemy firing back at him. On our walls here, the men will have to stand and fire over the top of the wall, and if the enemy is standing just below them, they will have to lean way over and fire down. So you can see that they will not have much protection, and they probably won't last very long in a battle."

"Yes, sir, I thinks I sees what you means."

"And most of the walls are not very high. The enemy could even jump over some of them and use ladders to get over others."

"But Mister Jim say we got lots of cannons. Can't we just keep shootin em so they don't never get close to the walls?"

"Mister Jim is right, Sam; we do have plenty of cannons. But sooner or later, we will run out of powder and cannon balls. And the enemy has cannons too, and if they get close enough, their cannons can blow holes in our walls. Then their soldiers can walk right in."

"It sounds like we got bad trouble, Mister Crockett. What we gonna do?"

"Well, according to Colonel Travis, as soon as Mister Jim gets better, we're gonna blow this place up and take the cannons east to General Houston."

Suddenly, as Bowie spoke, both Crockett and Sam jerked his head around.

"It sounds like you have served in a few battles, Senor David."

"Yes, sir, Senor James. I have defended a few frontier forts in my time, but most of them would fit inside the cattle pen here. The thought of trying to defend this place scares me."

"Well, I can tell you this. Last December, after Ben Milam died, three hundred of us took this place away from General Cos, and he had over seven hundred men and lots of artillery. So you are probably right."

"Who was Ben Milam? Have I met him?"

Bowie felt the loss of his dead friend intently. He needed Milam here to talk things over, to offer his opinions, to share the responsibility. Now Jim was trying to learn if Crockett could be his friend in that way.

"Bravest man I ever knew. He was killed during the battle."

"It sounds like General Houston made the right decision about abandoning this so-called fort, then," Crockett said.

251

"I'd say that would depend on how big an army they send up from Mexico, how many of our men we can get here before they do, and where we put em."

"Can we be sure the Mexicans are really coming?"

Bowie looked at Sam, wondering why he had stopped asking questions.

"That's a good question, David, but I think they are coming. If they just let Texas go without a fight, that could set off armed rebellions all over Mexico, not to mention what they could expect from other countries, if they showed that kind of weakness."

"So how many men will they send?"

"They will have to keep some of their troops in Mexico to maintain order, but I expect they could spare three or four thousand to come up here. Their biggest problem would be logistics."

"What is logistics?"

"Getting supplies, food, ammunition, up here. It is a long way from here to Mexico City, or even to Vera Cruz and Monterrey, places where they have substantial stockpiles. Up here, they will have to live off the land, and the land is not very generous until you get east of Bexar."

"Four thousand professional soldiers is a lot for us to fight."

"I agree, David, but we might not have to fight their most experienced soldiers all at once. Only about two-thirds of their army is trained; the others are barefoot Indians with antique weapons. I expect they will enter Texas in three or four columns separated by a few hundred miles. The land won't support all of them at once in a single army."

"It sounds like you been giving this some thought."

Bowie felt good about Crockett's understanding of their situation and he was ready to explore their relationship.

"Just passing the time, here on this cot. So tell me, David, what's Travis up to now?"

"He just struts around mostly, giving orders to his own men and trying to cajole your men into digging holes. Your men just smile at him, and his own men don't raise a hand when he is not around." Crockett said and smiled.

"He's got Major Jameson figuring out where to put the charges to blow up the walls and the buildings, and his men are dismounting the cannon, so he can haul them out of here. I think he is waiting for you to get back on your feet before he goes very far."

"David, I need to see Travis now. Then I need you to keep him away from me. I can't let him know how bad off I am for a while. Will you do that?"

"Sure, Jim, I can tell him, but then I think I'll be moving along."

"You mean you're leaving? Where will you go?"

"Anywhere but here. This place is a death-trap."

"You realize, if you leave most of the other men will too. And I don't mean just your Tennessee boys."

"Why don't you go with me?"

"Alright, I will. I'll make you a deal. You stay for my meeting with Travis. After the meeting, if you still want to leave, my men and I will go with you. We'll all go back to Goliad. They have a real fort and more men down there. Agreed?"

Bowie was gambling, but he thought he could win Crockett's support.

"I don't know. I'll have to talk to my men first."

"So that business about doing right by your family and running for office was a bunch of bull or are you just afraid of Travis?"

"Alright, I'll tell Travis you want to meet and I'll stay and listen to what you have to say," Crockett said angrily. "But in the meantime Bowie, you can go to hell."

Crockett stood and walked out.

Bowie liked Crockett's self-directed nature. Yet he felt satisfied that, with the man's help, his plan still had a chance to succeed.

Bowie rolled over on his right side and went to sleep.

* * *

"You did what?"

Travis sat in the chair opposite Bowie's cot. Crockett and Dickinson leaned against the wall on opposite sides of the doorway. Sam had gone to the cavalry courtyard to tend Bowie's horses.

Bowie repeated himself. "Fourteen days ago, I sent Bonham to Governor Smith with a dispatch that said we're going to defend this place, not destroy it."

"Who the hell gave you the authority to make that decision, Bowie? General Houston put me in command here."

"I sent it before you arrived, and you're right, Travis; Houston put you in command of the Army of Texas regular troops, but most of the men here are volunteer militia, and they elected me to be their commander."

"But General Houston said he told you to demolish the mission, and he ordered me to come here and help you do it."

Bowie chose his words carefully. He enjoyed getting the best of this young upstart, but did not want to overplay his hand.

"I don't report to Houston. I answer to the provisional governor and congress, and that is what I did." Bowie began to cough, but quickly put his red bandana to his mouth to hide any signs of blood.

Travis stood now, his face red.

Turning toward Crockett, Travis barked, "Colonel, will you and Captain Dickinson please leave this room."

Crockett looked at Bowie.

"They can stay," Bowie commanded, feeling assertive.

Travis's face contorted as he spoke again.

"Colonel Bowie, I happen to know you are a very sick man. Did you forget that the regimental surgeon reports to me? According to him, all I have to do is wait a few days, and you won't be able to command a damn thing."

"You may think you'll be in control, Travis, but my men won't follow your orders, unless I tell them to, and if my men don't follow you, none of the other men will either. You saw how Crockett deferred to me just now, and you'll get more of the same from every man here, unless I back you up."

Travis looked aside cunningly, and then his expression, especially his eyes, changed from intense contempt to surprise, then from surprise to solicitude, like a lawyer who has decided to try a different technique to manipulate a clever witness.

"So you really think that this is the best place to make a stand?"

Bowie tried to summon his list of reasons for holding the Alamo. Had they come to him from Ursula in his dream or had he surmised them? He couldn't remember now.

"We don't have to fight Santa Anna here; we can ambush him on the road, like the Minute-Men attacked the British at Lexington. We can hit them with their backs to the Frio River or the Medina, depending on which is the fullest. Then we can either drown em or pick em off, one by one. If we position the artillery right, none of them will ever reach Bexar."

Then Travis said, "Alright, Colonel. I understand what you plan to do, but I'm not sure I understand why."

Bowie looked down and to his left and said, "I know Santa Anna by reputation, and Stephen Austin knows him personally, after spending almost two years as his captive down there. Stephen and I agreed that, if we ever had to fight him, we should do it as far to the west as possible, because his armies will never advance any farther than he does personally."

"Why is that?"

"Two reasons. First, because of our victory over Cos last December, Santa Anna does not know what to expect up here. So when he arrives, he will wait a while to divide his force and send troops elsewhere that he might end up needing himself. That means we only have to fight him in one place, like with Cos."

Bowie felt like coughing again but cleared his throat instead.

"Second, his ego is so large that none of his general staff will dare to exceed or even approach his accomplishments in the field. They won't take the initiative or make a move without direct orders from him, and the farther away they get from him, the longer those orders take to reach them. So they wait and do nothing."

Bowie sighed, relieved he remembered the details of his strategy correctly.

Travis smiled.

"Delaying him here will give Houston time to prepare, in case the Mexicans get past us. That alone should earn some favor for you with Sam and you can take all the credit," Bowie added.

"So why not stop him outside Texas, west of the Rio Bravo, or at least at that river. That's what Fannin wanted to do?"

"We need a close fallback position, just in case. That's why we need to fortify the Alamo, then attack at a point where we can retreat to it if we have to."

"Why wouldn't Santa Anna just bypass Bexar and march on to capture the politicians in San Felipe first?"

"That's easy, Travis. He needs to show that General Cos's defeat in December was a fluke, and he needs the heavy artillery that Cos abandoned here in the Alamo for his own use. He can't leave an undefeated force at his back, and he cannot plan the rest of his campaign until he disposes of us, and Fannin's group, at Goliad."

The more Bowie said, the better it sounded to him, and the more he believed it would work. It did not matter if he faced Santa Anna at the Alamo or on the road, as long as his own position was strong and he could force the dictator to negotiate.

"That brings up another question: why don't we just move everything to Goliad? They have a real fort down there, and it would take fewer men to defend it," Travis questioned.

"I already answered that one. The Mexican army didn't lose a battle at La Bahi; they lost one at the Alamo."

Bowie was not sure he had finished the list, but he thought he had. Then he remembered the final item.

"Last of all, though, a major reason he is coming to Bexar with his army is that he is mad as hell at me. I'm a Benedict Arnold to him because I told him over a year ago that I would be his friend and ally up here."

Now Travis was nodding at every point that Bowie proffered. "Alright, Bowie. I've heard enough. You're probably right about all this, but I need to think about it. I'll have to get back to you. Meanwhile, I'll send Doctor Pollard around to check on you."

"Have him bring me more Mezcal," Bowie replied, now able to relax.

Dickinson departed with Travis, but Crockett stayed. "I like your plan," he said. "I thought you said you had no military training."

"I'm sorry I was so rough on you yesterday. Does that mean you'll stay for the fight?"

"Yes, but you can still go to hell," Crockett announced and laughed, "But I'll stay and go with you."

Then both men laughed.

* * *

James Butler Bonham rode back into the Alamo on the morning of Tuesday, February 23, 1836. Carrying the same dispatch case he had taken to Governor Smith he immediately reported to Jim Bowie's room.

Bowie was sitting up in his cot with his eyes closed and Sam beside him in a chair when Bonham walked in and asked for a cup of coffee. Then the young officer sat down to drink it and await his commander's orders.

Bowie opened his eyes and was about to speak when Private Despallier walked in. "Colonel Travis sends his compliments and asks that the lieutenant join him for a meeting."

"Charlie, you go tell the colonel that the lieutenant will be along bye and bye," Bowie answered. "Bring he some of that coffee Sam, then we'll open that case and see what the governor had to say."

Bonham still had the dispatch case strap slung across his chest like a bandolier. Sam watched as he removed his hat, guided the strap over his head, and handed the case to Bowie.

"As you ordered colonel, nobody but you and Governor Smith has opened this case," Bonham said.

Bowie accepted the case feeling proud that his plan to negotiate with Santa Anna from a position of strength was nearly complete. Momentarily he would know how many reinforcements the governor was sending to defend the Alamo and when they would arrive.

"Thank you Bonham. By the way, I'm promoting you to the rank of lieutenant-colonel as of this moment," Bowie said, smiling.

"Thank you sir."

"Now, let's see here." Bowie said and began to untie the three leather strings that kept the case flap closed.

At that moment Travis arrived in Bowie's room, accompanied by Crockett and Dickinson. "Well Colonel Bowie, it looks like we arrived just in time for the big moment."

Bowie looked up, then he untied the last string, raised the flap, and reached in. Feeling nothing with his hand he looked inside.

Bowie felt stunned and deflated. He looked around, then at Bonham. "Has this case been out of your sight since you left here?"

"Yes, Colonel. When I delivered it, Governor Smith took it into his office and closed the door. Nobody else was in the office and nobody came or went before he came out and handed the case back to me. Since then it has not left my sight."

"Gentlemen, the case is empty," Bowie reported.

"If there is no reply, that means General Houston has convinced the governor to not try to hold the Alamo, and Congress will not be sending any help here at all," Travis said.

Travis looked directly at Bowie and continued. "That puts you and your plans to attack the Mexicans on the road right in the old lavatrina, pardon my Latin."

Bowie thought Travis looked and sounded boastful and his anger began to grow.

"That was not my real plan. I told you that just so you would stay until Santa Anna got here."

Bowie had let his pride overcome his discretion and he regretted his words immediately after saying them. Now he could not think of any alternative but to tell the truth.

"You mean you think you can defend this place against the whole Mexican army?" Travis asked.

"That is not my real plan either."

"Suppose you tell me your real plan."

"I plan to negotiate peace with Santa Anna."

"Just how in hell can you do that?"

Bowie coughed deeply before answering. "The main problem between us and Mexico is slavery. If we can solve that one, we can work out everything else."

"And how do you propose to do that?"

"I have proven that using freemen to raise cotton is more efficient and more profitable than using slaves. I think I can convince the other planters to free their slaves and pay them wages to avoid a war, and I think I can convince Santa Anna to give us time to try."

"I think you're crazy Bowie. Congress will never go along with that. Most of those men own hundreds of slaves."

"That's my point, Travis. Most of us regular folks don't own slaves and don't want war. Congress will have to listen to us."

"Pollard told me you have been ranting in you sleep about some kind of promise to your dead wife. Does this have anything to do with that?"

Bowie was about to respond to Travis sarcastic comment when he began to cough deeply again.

Five minutes later he was still coughing and blood was running out both corners of his mouth.

"Sam, run and get doc Pollard," Crockett directed, speaking for the first time since he entered the room.

As Sam sprinted out the door, Bowie stopped coughing, grasped his chest with both hands and fell backward on his cot, apparently unconscious.

* * *

After the doctor arrived to attend to Bowie, Crockett and Dickinson accompanied Travis back to his quarters.

"So what will you do now, Travis?" Crockett asked. With Bowie incapacitated and the Alamo clearly vulnerable, the Tennessean was reconsidering his options.

"I don't know. But we can't let the men hear anything about this. If they do, the volunteers will leave. Thank God we have another three weeks before the Mexican army gets here."

Travis looked down to his left. "Listen, Crockett. I need you to come with me while I talk to the men. Dickinson, sound assembly."

"Most of them are not here, sir. Bowie's men spread the word about a fandango at the Veramendi house last night. All the volunteers walked into town and they are still gone. Our men are the only ones left on the walls."

Travis's expression turned sour. "Bring two horses."

Travis and Crockett rode out the main gate of the Alamo and reined their horses toward the footbridge.

Strangely, not a living soul appeared in their path as they rode over the bridge, past Presa, Navarro, St. Marys, and Soledad streets and into Main Plaza.

In Main Plaza, the two men dismounted and tied their horses in front of the cantina on the south side. Around him, Crockett noticed a few of the volunteers lying on the ground or leaning against the sides of the adobe buildings, asleep. Clearly, these men had indulged in the drink and festivities of the previous night and they were sleeping it off.

"Let's get some coffee," Travis said, motioning toward the cantina.

Though the front door was wide open, nobody appeared to be inside. Travis shouted, but there was no reply.

"I don't like this, Crockett. Where are all the people? I wonder if they heard something. Maybe we should put a lookout in the cathedral tower. I'll try to get one of the volunteers to go up."

They walked outside, and Travis kicked one of the men who was asleep against the wall. "Wake up, Private."

Just then, Crockett said, "Hold on, Colonel." He had spotted William McDowell, one of his Tennessee boys. Quickly Crockett sent him to the bell-tower with orders to ring the bell if he noticed anything suspicious.

The weather was unusually warm and humid, even for a late winter day. But inside the cantina was cool, so Travis and Crockett decided to stay for a while. Crockett found hot embers burning in a pot belly stove, so he decided to stoke them and boil some coffee.

By half past one in the afternoon, some of the volunteers had entered the cantina. In the absence of a proprietor, they helped themselves to the liquor. Even more of Bowie's men gathered outside, around the entrance. None of them seemed to be in a hurry to return to his post in the Alamo.

At two o'clock, Travis told Crockett he wanted to address the men. The cantina lacked the space to hold all of them, so Travis shouted for those inside to follow him out. Outside he mounted his horse.

"Men, I am here because your commander, Colonel Bowie, has collapsed and is probably dead by now. I'm here to take command of you volunteers."

Bowie's ranking subordinate, Captain William Charles M. Baker of Missouri, was the first to respond. "I'm afraid we will have to see that for ourselves . . . Colonel."

"I thought you would want it that way, Captain, so I would like five of you to join me in the morning for a meeting with Doctor Pollard."

"Why can't we see Colonel Bowie for ourselves?"

"Perhaps you can, but that will be up to the doctor. Just have your representatives meet me at the hospital in the morning at ten."

"Meanwhile, you are all familiar with my orders from General Houston and tomorrow morning we will all begin to obey those orders. I think we probably have a month, three weeks for sure, before we see the first enemy troops. The Mexican army will have to wait until there is enough grass to feed their stock on the way up here, and I heard they still have snow on the ground as far south as Monterrey."

"I ..." Just as Travis opened his mouth to continue, the cathedral bell began to ring.

Crockett ran to the sound. The bell tower was just a few feet away, but when he arrived, McDowell had already scrambled down and was standing by the cathedral wall gate.

"David, I saw Mexican cavalry crossing Alazan Creek, sir. A lot of them. It looked like the advance guard of a whole damn army," McDowell reported.

"How many and how far away now?"

"About a hundred. Maybe a mile and a half. They carried long lances pointing up."

Crockett ran back to the gathered volunteers. "Men, the Mexican army is here. I suggest we collect our belongings and get back to the Alamo, and I suggest we do that in one hell of a hurry. We have about fifteen minutes, even less if they charge us."

Noticing that Travis was sitting on his horse in the same place, with a glazed over look in his eyes, Crockett took charge. "You men with rifles form skirmish lines and block the streets."

Then he heard the faint call of a bugle coming from the south. "The rest of you head for the mission." As he said the words he turned and slapped Travis's horse on the rump and it bolted toward Commerce Street.

When Crockett saw that everyone was across the footbridge, he ordered the skirmishers to retreat.

Amazingly, everyone made it into the Alamo. No shots were fired by either side.

Now safe, for the moment, Crockett saw that every man had immediately gone to his assigned post.

* * *

In his room with Pollard and Sam, Bowie was sitting up with his eyes wide open when Crockett entered.

"What's all the commotion?" Bowie asked.

"The Mexican army is here," Crockett replied.

"Get me on my feet. Get my clothes. I've got to talk to Santa Anna."

"I don't think he is here yet. So far, all we have seen is about a hundred lancers. But he can't be far behind."

"Get me up anyhow. I want to see my men."

Everyone looked at Pollard, who nodded his approval. Soon Sam had Bowie dressed, for the first time in weeks, including a felt hat and his knife.

When a somewhat wobbly Jim Bowie emerged into the sunlight of the Alamo plaza, a cheer went up, like a wave traversing the Alamo walls.

The greeting from his men made Bowie feel like a man just dosed with a tonic. He removed his hat and waved it all around. Then he and Crockett joined Travis on the cannon platform built over the former Losoya house at the southwest corner of the compound.

Soon they were joined by Captain William H. Carey and Privates William H. Smith and Lemuel Crawford. All of the men were standing beside an eighteen pounder cannon, except Smith, who stood behind it holding a linstock with a smoldering slow match.

The Other Rose of Texas

Now, focusing his optical telescope, Bowie could see Military Plaza filling with mounted lancers who were dressed in blue uniforms trimmed with crimson, and other cavalry dressed the same.

Even closer, in Main Plaza, he saw a group of splendidly adorned men, obviously the Mexican general staff, led by an imposing looking figure on a milk-white horse, whom he recognized as Santa Anna.

Soon, a detachment of lancers crossed the footbridge and approached the Alamo under a white flag. They halted within earshot of Bowie and his group at the southwest corner.

Bowie recognized their leader, Juan Almonte, who began to address the Texicans. "His excellency, Presidente and Generalissimo Antonio Lopez de Santa Anna has sent me to inform the rebels presently encamped in the former Mission de Valero that they will all be put to the sword, unless they surrender at once."

As Bowie was about to step forward and request a meeting with Santa Anna, the eighteen pounder cannon discharged. Nobody was standing in front of the powerful cannon, but Crockett was close enough to the muzzle for the blast to set the fringe of his buckskins ablaze.

The cannon was pointed in the general direction of Bexar, but nothing indicated that any building had been hit.

Bowie turned toward Travis and asked. "Who fired that gun?"

A wide-eyed, Travis replied. "I don't know."

Then both turned to Smith.

"It was a accident, Colonel Bowie. I was lookin at them fancy soldiers"

After calming their horses, and without another word, the column of Mexican army lancers turned and rode back across the footbridge.

For the first time since boyhood, Bowie felt his stomach tighten with anxiety. What would he do to carry out his plan now? He thought of the fisherman's prediction over five years before, realizing he would not be two-score years of age until April tenth.

He remembered the noon-day cannon boom then, and he had to admit that the eighteen-pounder cannon shot loomed large before him now. The Mexicans obviously considered it a defiant reply to their terms, and Bowie feared it would cost him his only chance to reason with Santa Anna before hostilities began.

His anxiety turned to dread when he saw a blood-red flag that many of the men in the Alamo were pointing to. It flapped in the breeze from the cross atop the San Fernando cathedral bell tower. As they pointed he could hear some of them wondering aloud who had decided the Mexican army would not arrive until spring.

Bowie returned to his room planning to rest. Instead, when he arrived he sat in the chair by the small desk. "Sam, I'm gonna end this thing today. But first, I feel like eating. Go fetch Bettie."

When Bettie returned, Charlie was with her. "Josephus done run off, Master Bowie, but I's here fo' to he'p," the slightly built young man said.

"Thank you, Charlie. I'm glad to see you," Bowie replied.

Bettie still had some of the food from the last delivery made by the Veramendi sisters, and she prepared a fine lunch, which Bowie insisted on sharing with her, Sam, and Charlie. After they ate, Bowie dispatched Sam to summon Major Green B. Jameson.

During Sam's absence, Bowie wrote a note, sealed it and placed it in the dispatch case. The note read, "To His Excellency Antonio Lopez de Santa Anna, Presidente of Mexico and Generalissimo of the Army. Your Excellency, I regret the unilateral action taken today by my co-commander in response to your generous offer to discuss terms of surrender. I am in possession of certain information, which may enable us to avoid hostilities that can only produce tragic results on both sides. Signed, James Bowie, Colonel of Militia."

Jameson arrived, and Bowie was still feeling optimistic as he handed over the case.

"You speak Spanish, don't you, Major?"

"Yes, Colonel."

"Then take this case to the footbridge under a white flag, await a reply, and bring it to me. Let nothing or no one deter you. Do you understand?"

"Yes, Colonel."

"Then tell me what you are to do."

"I am to let nothing stop me from taking this case to the footbridge under a flag of truce, and I am to await a reply and bring it to you."

Bowie followed Jameson outside. He noticed Travis standing beside the eighteen pounder on the platform to his left.

Suddenly, Travis ran down the ramp toward Jameson, now mounted and carrying a white flag.

"HALT."

"I'm sorry, Colonel Travis, but I'm under orders from Colonel Bowie."

The main gate was swung open and Jameson rode out.

Travis shouted again. "CAPTAIN MARTIN."

In a moment, twenty-eight-year-old Martin stood before Travis.

"Yes, sir."

"Get a horse and follow Jameson. When the Mexicans come to the bridge, have Jameson tell them I am inviting Colonel Juan Almonte to a parlay inside the Alamo. I don't have time to put it in writing."

"Yes, sir."

Soon Bowie and Travis were side by side on the platform, watching the Mexican Officer of the Day ride to the footbridge accompanied by eight lancers. After delivering the case and the message, Jameson and Martin waited, as the lancers rode away.

"How do you know Almonte?" Bowie asked Travis.

"He was one of the officers that put me in jail in Anahuac. We talked and I got to know him a little."

In two hours, the same Mexican detachment returned. Through his glass, Bowie saw that words were exchanged, but the case was not handed back.

Returning through the main gate, the two emissaries reported to their respective commanders who were standing in the plaza together.

"Tell me what happened Major," Bowie ordered.

"Their OD told me that Santa Anna said to tell Jim Bowie the time for words has passed, and the time to die has come."

* * *

At sunrise, the next morning Bowie was standing on the west wall of the Alamo when he heard a cannon boom. Two seconds later, he saw a cloud of dust rise about fifty yards away. Another boom produced a similar plume half again as close. Yet another was followed by a cannon ball that bounced off the wall below him like a child's ball.

The next ten minutes were without cannon fire, then another boom was followed by a cannon ball that fell inside the wall, almost exactly in the middle of the plaza. Bowie retrieved the projectile, then walked back close to the west wall and summoned Captains Dickinson and Carey.

"Captain Dickinson, pass the word to the men to stay close to the walls when they walk, especially after they hear a cannon boom."

"Yes, sir."

Bowie coughed into a red bandana in his left hand then passed the three and one-half inch diameter ball he held in his right hand to Captain Carey and asked, "What do you make of this?"

"That is a cast iron cannon ball that was probably fired from a six-pounder, muzzle-loading Mexican cannon."

Two more booms came thirty seconds apart and Carey added, "There are two pieces firing." As if to verify this observation, Bowie saw two cannon balls fall inside the wall near where the first one hit, about four feet apart.

"Captain Carey, tell your men to gather the cannon balls from time to time and stockpile them for our use later. For the time being, we'll not try to discourage Santa Anna from adding to our supply."

"Yes, sir."

"After that, join me in my quarters and give me your assessment of their artillery strength."

"Yes, sir."

Bowie returned to his room and was sitting on his cot when Carey arrived. Carey took the chair by the desk. Sam was sitting quietly on the floor near the fire pit.

Carey began his report. "As you ordered, Colonel, I dispatched Lemuel Crawford to tell the men at our seven Alamo batteries to stockpile the incoming cannon balls. Then I climbed the ramp to the southwest corner to identify the location of the Mexican six-pounders firing at us. Using my optical telescope …"

Bowie interrupted saying, "You don't have to tell me how, just tell me what. I trust that you know what you're doing."

"Yes colonel," Carey resumed. I spotted two cannons that Santa Anna must have mounted during the night. They are just across the river, about five hundred yards due west."

"Go on Captain."

"Assuming Santa Anna is using all the artillery he has in Bexar, for the present we don't need to worry. To hurt us, they will have to get those guns across to our side of the river and a lot closer to the walls."

"What if he brings in bigger guns?"

"I doubt Santa Anna would try to haul in anything heavier than a twelve-pounder field cannon. Twelve-pounders could damage our walls, even from the Bexar side of the river, but there is no sign of anything that big here yet. Guns any bigger than that weigh over two ton apiece and would take months to haul up here."

"One more thing, Captain. Where exactly is the cannon fire coming from?"

"It looks like the cannons are in the side-yard of that big house on Soledad, the Veramendi Palace, I think it's called. In my opinion, there were better places to put those pieces. Say, isn't that your house Colonel Bowie?"

"Alright, Captain. Let me know immediately if anything changes, and I will expect regular reports twice a day."

"What about our artillery, Colonel? Are we going to fire back?"

"I will let you know, Captain. You may return to your duties."

Carey walked out and Bowie reclined on his cot. Within ninety seconds he began coughing deeply and he put the red bandana to his mouth. Five minutes later he was still coughing.

He felt something strange in his mouth and he pulled the bandana away. It was full of blood and some black material he had never seen before.

Dean Kirkpatrick

"Better go get the doc Sam," he said in a raspy voice.

* * *

Walking toward Bowie's room, as the roofless Alamo chapel came into view on his left, Crockett noticed some of Bowie's men gathered around the entrance. He turned and walked to the edge of the group. Through the doorway, he could see Doctor Pollard standing a few feet up the earthen ramp to a cannon platform at the east end. Crockett pushed his way inside the former church.

The smell of gunpowder from the magazine dominated as women huddled around side room doorways, and the remainder of the volunteers, gathered below him, stood quietly listening to their chief physician.

"Colonel Bowie does not have long to live. He has advanced consumption and this morning he began coughing up blood and lung tissue."

Captain Baker responded first. "It's not that we don't trust you, Doc, but Travis told us that Colonel Bowie was already nearly dead, and yesterday he looked just fine. We would like to see for ourselves."

"You can do that Captain, but his room is already crowded, with space for only one or two of you. If you like we can go there now. Follow me."

Pollard led the group out and away from the chapel, and when they arrived at Bowie's door, Crockett, Baker, and Lieutenant Eliel Melton entered behind him. Sam, and Bettie were already there.

Crockett thought the room had the feeling of a wake as he looked at Jim Bowie lying on his cot, blood running from the corners of his mouth and trickling down the wool blanket tucked under his chin.

Bowie's fevered mind seemed to be journeying backward, and he was ranting. "Ursula … I'm sorry." Cannon fire continued outside and his body seemed to shudder at each blast.

"Can't you help him, Doc?" Baker asked.

"I've done everything I could since he rode in. He's been sick for a long time."

* * *

When Bowie awakened an hour later nobody had left. He sat up and looked around the room, then at the bloody blanket. He touched his mouth with the middle three fingers of his right hand and looked at the blood on them.

"Can somebody help me clean up this mess? How can I entertain guests looking like this?"

Feeling much better now after sleeping, he was pleased when some of his visitors smiled. However, before anybody could respond to his request Travis walked in.

"Doctor Pollard, have you forgotten who your commanding officer is? Why didn't you tell me that my friend Jim Bowie was this sick? As soon as I heard I rushed right over to see if I could help."

Pollard was silent but Bowie was not. "What did you have in mind Colonel Travis?"

"I think it is obvious that you are too ill to perform your duties so as of this moment I am ready to assume your duties and take sole command of the garrison, volunteers and regulars alike. My first act as sole commander will be to write some very strong letters to the cowards who have left us here to die alone."

Everyone gaped at Travis with narrowed eyes but their eyes widened as if in abject amazement in response to Bowie's reply.

"I think we can work something out Travis."

Now Travis's too looked amazed, like a child who had just received the keys to the candy store.

"I think we have ourselves a pretty fine predicament here, don't you?" Bowie continued.

"Yes, I do, and it is all the fault of that son-of-a-bitch Houston for sending me here in the first place and not telling me I would have the whole damn Mexican army in my lap before spring."

"Things are what they are," Bowie replied. "Wishing they were different will not improve our situation. I think the first thing we should consider is getting out of here, and if we can't escape, we need to know what chances we have for reinforcements. If we do have to stay, what about food and water, powder and shot, and how should we use our artillery and riflemen?"

"I don't know about those things. I'm a lawyer, not a soldier."

"We have some pretty good men here who do know; they wouldn't have stayed if they weren't good men. Some of them have military experience and they can help figure things out. We also have some obstacles around us, natural and man-made, that can work for us against the enemy. So you see, we have some options."

"I can't argue with that," Travis agreed.

"Now here is my offer Travis. I will tell my men to follow your orders, if you will appoint Crockett and the six men on this list to your command staff and hold all of your staff meetings in this room so I can observe."

Bowie handed Travis a piece of parchment and Travis read the names of: Bonham, Pollard, Jameson, Evans, Carey, and Baker.

"You must think I'm an idiot," Travis said. "You're not relinquishing command you're saddling me with eight co-commanders. What if you are out of your mind sick and can't observe, are we supposed to wait for you to regain your senses?"

"My condition will be my lookout and these men will be your advisors. You will make the decisions."

"I need time to think about this."

"There is no time. This is the deal. Take it or leave it."

"What if I leave it?"

"Then I will pass command to Baker."

"Alright. I accept your terms. I will be in sole command and in charge of letters. I think you should know that yesterday I sent Doctor John Sutherland and John W. Smith east with a letter to Andrew Ponton in Gonzales, and I sent William P. Johnson with a letter to Fannin at Goliad. This morning, I sent Albert Martin to Gonzales with a letter I wrote last night to the people of Texas and all Americans in the world."

Until Travis's last comment Bowie was feeling good about his decision to work with Travis. Now he was concerned that Travis might be looking at their situation as an intellectual exercise rather than as the life and death struggle it was.

"That's fine, Colonel Travis. I hope your letters bring results. Meanwhile you should assemble your new staff for a strategy meeting as soon as possible? We may not have much time."

"Let's meet first thing in the morning. I have some more letters to write today."

"As you wish, Colonel. Captain Baker, pass the word to our men that they now report to Colonel Travis."

Bowie had no intention of giving up anything to Travis or anybody else. But he now had the means to command the Alamo defenders from his bed, for as long as he was able to think and talk, no matter how bad his condition became.

Chapter 19

At sunrise Bowie was awake and sitting up in bed as each member of Travis's new staff arrived. Sam and Bettie had helped him clean up the blood from another night of fever and coughing and he held a fresh red bandana in his right hand.

Bowie hoped the reports the men gave would help ground Travis in the reality of his dilemma, and that a demonstration of their knowledge and efficiency would soothe Travis and help him feel confident in the abilities of these men he had chosen for command.

When the reports were finished, Bowie asked Crockett to give a summary to make sure they had a common understanding.

"On the positive side morale seems high, we have around two weeks-worth of food and ammunition, a fourth of the enemy are barefoot Indians, and our sharp-shooters are keeping their troops from using the footbridge. Right so far?"

They all nodded as Crockett looked around.

"On the negative side they will soon have fifteen hundred men and eight cannons here and they are building breastworks so they can get their cannons closer to our walls, our gun-powder is poor quality but so is theirs, we need to fortify the main gate and palisade, each of our riflemen is covering seventeen feet of wall, we don't know if or when reinforcements will come, we need to plan a withdrawal just in case, and, oh yes, we are running out of firewood," Crockett concluded.

Each man nodded his concurrence again.

"Colonel Travis, I think we should seriously consider withdrawing from the Alamo tonight while we have a chance of getting out of here alive," Crockett added.

Travis immediately stood and began ranting. "I'll tell you boys, I don't think we have a thing to worry about. My letters have arrived by now, and I'm sure that thousands of men are marching to join us. So until I give the order, there will be no further talk of retreat from the Alamo. Is that clear?"

Now Bowie spoke.

"Colonel Bonham, how soon will we know about reinforcements?"

"I need five days for all the couriers that are out to get back."

Bowie was still hoping he could somehow arrange to talk with Santa Anna.

"I think we can wait five days. But we should build up the fortifications and keep up the pressure on the footbridge. Are there any other orders, Colonel Travis?" Bowie asked.

"No orders, but I do wish to report that I am sending more letters to Goliad and Gonzales and one to general Houston to shame him into sending us more men."

After the officers departed Bowie began coughing but no lung tissue showed up in his bandana. He began to shiver and Sam put another clean blanket on him.

* * *

Jim Bowie was still shivering on his cot when he heard the sound of many rifles firing above and around his room. He arose, wrapped himself in a blanket and walked out into the plaza.

Looking up to his left he saw Crockett, Carey, and Baker standing on the southwest corner cannon platform. By the time he climbed the ramp the firing had stopped.

"A sentry spotted a column of around three hundred Mexican troops marching down Commerce Street," Baker reported. "They have two horses pulling a caisson and a cannon. We've been firing but they're just out of range."

"The cannon is a the nine-pounder," Carey said. "Must have just arrived."

As soon as the Mexican column reached Presa Street, Baker yelled, "Keep them off the bridge," and the Alamo sharpshooters began firing again.

Looking through Carey's glass, Bowie could see splinters rising from the cypress plank bridge deck and oak rails as the mine balls fired from the Alamo struck the wood. The enemy column halted, obviously reacting to the same sight.

Soon the Mexican column executed an about-face, began to march again, and turned south on Navarro Street, followed by the horses and cannon.

"They may try to cross the river," Bowie said.

"Should we fire our cannon and stop them?" Carey asked. "If they get that nine pounder close to our main gate, it could do some damage."

Still entertaining the hope of a parlay with Santa Anna, Bowie replied, "No, let's see what happens. I think the crossing may be harder than they expect."

As Bowie predicted, the Mexican troops began crossing the river at a place people called the Old Mill Ford, immediately downstream from an earthen dam.

Next the horse-drawn gun assembly began to cross. However, when the horses pulling the cannon tried to climb the opposite bank, they slid back.

"It looks like the load is too heavy and the bank is too slippery," Bowie said.

Within a few minutes, Bowie saw some of the soldiers sitting on the ground removing their footwear. Then they waded into the water and took positions around the caisson and cannon wheels.

The narrow wheels seemed to be stuck deep in the mud. Men on either side began whipping the horses as the soldiers tried to push the wheels forward without success. A second effort failed too.

After another lengthy pause, the caisson was opened, and some of the soldiers carried powder kegs and cannon balls to shore, while others unhitched the field cannon carriage.

"They're lightening the load," Carey observed.

Then, with a mostly empty caisson, the soldiers manned the four wheels; the horses were whipped, and all advanced up the bank to dry, level ground.

Next, while one group removed the remaining items from the caisson and laid them out in the sun to dry, others began putting back the powder kegs and shot.

Yet another group unhitched the horses from the caisson, hitched them to the cannon, and with the help of other wheel-men, the horses dragged the cannon up the bank to a position behind the caisson.

Bowie was impressed when Carey proved his expertise by predicting the soldier's next activity. "They'd better make sure everything is dry. That cast iron will rust pretty quick and those fuses won't burn wet."

As if in obedience to Carey the cannon was swabbed inside and wiped down outside, and the cloth and the fuses were put back in the caisson, but the doors were not closed. When everything was reassembled in its pre-crossing configuration, the soldados fell in and came to attention. Then the formation began to march.

Baker slapped Carey on the back, laughed and said," it only took them two hours to go twenty-five feet."

Then, in an extremely rare moment of spiritual expression, almost just to himself, Bowie said, "Ursula told me that spot is where the river was named. Perhaps the difficult crossing was the river's way of telling them to renounce worldly pursuits as Saint Anthony the Great taught us."

Bowie continued to observe as the soldados soon arrived in La Villita, a collection of wood and straw huts that extended all the way to the main gate of the Alamo.

He could see that these dirt-floor shanty huts were surrounded by women and children, apparently family members who had followed their men north from Mexico. The soldiers had fallen out and were beginning to mingle with them.

"It looks like some of those men will be having a home-cooked lunch," Bowie said. "Maybe we should do the same while we can."

* * *

Just after one in the afternoon, an Alamo lookout shouted down, they're re-assembling Colonel," and the same four Alamo leaders resumed their watch from the southwest corner. Bowie was now fully dressed, including his knife.

Noticing that the caisson was detached from the cannon carriage, Bowie said, "They must be carrying cannon balls and powder in their back packs. That'll make it hard for them to move very fast."

Observing that four enemy troops positioned at the wheels of the cannon carriage were beginning to roll it toward the Alamo main gate, followed by the formation, Bowie said to Baker, "I think we'd better move half of our riflemen to the west and south walls."

The Mexicans had advanced two hundred yards to a point near Commerce Street when Captain Baker yelled, "FIRE," and sixty Alamo rifles discharged simultaneously.

Bowie saw blood spurt from multiple wounds as four Mexican soldiers fell immediately, and the remainder ran for the perceived protection of one or another of the huts.

Then he saw two soldiers stagger from huts and fall to the ground as another barrage of Alamo mine-balls easily passed through the straw walls and hit them.

"Now they're seeing what a man can do with a good rifle," Bowie said.

Crockett nodded.

Suddenly, below Bowie, the Alamo main gate flew open. Twenty Texicans emerged and started running for the abandoned Mexican cannon. However, the Mexicans were closer to it.

Two heroic Mexican artillerymen ran to the cannon and tried to aim it while other riflemen formed a standing skirmish line, protecting the cannoneers with their bodies.

"Brave men," Bowie shouted. Then he whispered, "On both sides."

Another volley was fired from the Alamo. Two men in the enemy skirmish line fell, and the line dissolved. But then the enemy cannon boomed, and the shot would have been effective had there been time for them to aim it at the gate accurately. As it happened, the ball fell harmlessly in the grass field to the east.

The Texicans had almost reached the cannon when a distant group of Mexicans began to pull on a rope that somebody attached to the gun-carriage, and it rolled back toward La Villita and beyond Texican reach. The Mexican soldiers followed the cannon in retreat.

"I think they've had enough," Bowie said and Baker yelled, "CEASE FIRE."

Before returning to the Alamo, the Texicans on the outside set about burning every hut in sight for five hundred yards. The first enemy attack had come dangerously close, but had been repelled. Now the Alamo defenders made sure there would be no structures for cover to help the enemy get that close again.

Soon an enemy detachment approached the main gate under a flag of truce. "I think they want their dead and wounded," Bowie said.

"They show us a red flag and expect us to honor their white flag," Baker said, aiming his rifle. "They can go straight to hell."

"Don't fire, there is still a chance we can reason with Santa Anna," Bowie said.

After the sun went down that night, a norther blew in and the temperature dropped into the thirties.

As Bowie shivered he had new reason to wish that reinforcements would come from Goliad. In December the Alamo's supply of winter clothing had been taken by Fannin for the doomed Matamoros Expedition and those warm garments were now with him, a hundred miles down the San Antonio River.

Then Bowie thought about the women and children in the La Villita huts with no protection from the freezing north wind, and he supposed that they had no winter clothing either.

Finally, thoughts of the day's victory made it a little easier for him to go to sleep. Although feverish, he slept until morning without coughing up blood.

* * *

On advice from Bowie, Ursula's sisters had joined their brother in California. After they left Bexar, and Bowie's former slave Charlie joined Sam and Bettie in the Alamo, Jim Bowie invited their Tejano cousins, the Navarro sisters to join him in the Alamo for protection.

Now with Sam carrying water to the men on the walls and Bettie cooking for everyone, twenty-seven-year-old Juana Navarro-

Alsbury and her twenty-year-old sister Gertrudis were looking after Bowie.

The morning after the battle at the main gate he was sitting up in bed with his back to the wall when Juana looked at her watch pendant and said, "You have not taken nourishment for a while. Could you eat some food, Senor Jim?"

Before Bowie could answer, Crockett walked in and said, "I don't know about him, but I could stand a bite."

The sisters smiled then stood and walked toward the doorway. "We will be back soon with some food for us all."

"How are you feeling there, James?" Crockett asked.

"Like the devil was camping on my chest."

"I came to talk about the fine mess you have got us all into," Crockett said and smiled broadly.

"It ain't my fault Santa Anna showed up early. You go on and get the hell out of here. I'll fight the bastard. Where's my knife?"

Bowie smiled back, and Crockett continued.

"You said we could wait five days to even consider getting out of here, and it doesn't matter that we will be outnumbered ten to one by then, the enemy artillery will be close enough to blow holes in the walls, and Sam Houston will prevent any reinforcements from coming because he knows this place is indefensible, and he ordered you to abandon it in the first place."

Crockett took a deep breath. "And we know the morale of the men is still high because we have not told them about of any of this. Did you say all that because you still think you can talk to Santa Anna?"

"Have you heard of any more contact with the Mexicans?" Bowie asked.

"Nothing. Now you answer me one. Did you really mean it when you said you decided to make a stand here because you promised your dead wife to abolish slavery in Texas, or were you talking out of your head?"

"Pollard told me I've been talking in my sleep. I guess he heard me say that too."

"Yea."

Bowie was feeling lite headed as if he was lingering on the edge of a dream. He shook his head and answered Crockett.

"Well, I guess I was a little delirious when I said it like that, but in a way it's true. Ursula got me thinking about slavery several years ago, and I decided that Texas would be better off without it. Then Stephen Austin told me that he was going to try to bring Texas into the Union as a slave state. By then, I had a lot of runaway slaves working for me. I didn't want them returned to their masters, and I decided I was the only one who could stop that from happening."

Bowie coughed, wiped his mouth and continued.

"I know how asinine making a promise to my dead wife sounds but, no matter how this thing turns out, I think Ursula played an important part in determining the future here. If I can somehow negotiate peace with Santa Anna, and we stay with Mexico, it will be because she convinced me that Texas is better off without slavery. Or, if we beat him and make a Texas Republic, my decision to stand at the Alamo and delay Santa Anna will be an important factor, and her memory inspired me to do that too."

"It sounds like you have become an abolitionist?"

"No, I think abolitionists oppose slavery on moral grounds. To me, it is a practical matter. Slavery divides people."

"What do you mean?"

"Your own state of Tennessee is a perfect example. People in the western half own slaves and people in the eastern half condemn them for it."

"I see what you mean, but what does that have to do with Texas?"

"Simply this. As long as we have slaves in Texas, it will be in turmoil, and the only way to stop it is to keep Texas as part of Mexico where slavery is illegal."

Crockett made no comment.

"That is why I want to talk to Santa Anna and I would have already done it if that damn cannon had not gone off."

"I understand what you are saying, Jim, and I appreciate your promise to your wife, but why have you staked your life, and our lives on this?"

"Most of what I own is in Texas, and I need things to be stable for it to have any value. I also think that Houston and the politicians are trying to start a fight that the United States will join and bring us into the Union. A war like that could go on for a long time. Most of us just want peace."

Bowie began to cough deeply, and Crockett handed him the Pitkin flask.

Then the sisters returned with the food, and the two men began to eat as Crockett continued their conversation,

"I don't think there is much hope now of talking with their main hombre."

Crockett grinned, and Bowie decided he was proud to have used a Spanish word. "The generalissimo has hung a red death flag on the cathedral; he put his first two cannons in the side-yard of your house, and he's got his band playing the cut-throat song. It seems pretty final to me."

Bowie cleared his throat and took another swig of mezcal. "It sounds final to me too, and I agree with you, if we want to live, I think we had better get the hell out of the Alamo."

The sound of rapid gunfire began outside, and Crockett ran out the door before responding to Bowie's words.

Chapter 20

The sound of gunfire on Friday, February 26, that caused Crockett to cut short his visit with Bowie came when a group of Jameson's men, out gathering wood, engaged a Mexican patrol near the Alameda. The day after that, Alamo sharpshooters fired, without effect, at an enemy group that dammed the acequia where it connected with the river to the north, leaving the well as the only source of water in the Alamo.

Now the day had arrived for the decision to be made about holding or fleeing the Alamo. However, none of the couriers had yet returned, nor had any reinforcements arrived.

Travis was still asleep when Bowie met with Crockett, Bonham and the others before dawn.

"I think I should ride toward Goliad and see for myself how soon Fannin and his men will be here. Yesterday a lookout reported that most of their cavalry rode out the Gonzales Road, so I think I can get out through La Villita," Bonham reported. "Maybe I'll meet Fannin on the Goliad road and we can attack their flank and run them back across the river."

"I agree," Baker said. "After the licking we gave em the other day, the men are ready to take it to em."

Carey nodded.

"At worst, I think I can get back here by Thursday night," Bonham added.

Bowie was growing fond of young Bonham. He saw him as bright and resourceful as his cousin Travis, but without the same devious nature.

"Have you got a warm coat? It's cold and wet out there," Bowie asked.

"No, but I'm wearing three of everything."

"Well take mine," Bowie replied.

After Bonham departed, Carey said, "I'll go report to Travis so he doesn't pitch a fit about us meeting behind his back." Then he and the others walked out, leaving only Crockett and Pollard with Bowie in the room.

Bowie began to cough and shiver. Doctor Pollard retrieved his stethoscope and listened to Bowie's heart.

"Beating like a drum. I wish all our men had a heartbeat that strong."

"Did I hear someone say there were eight hundred men here in December?" Crockett asked.

"Yes, and I think I must have treated every one of them for something or other."

"So what happened to them? Where did they go?"

"I can answer that," Bowie said. "After we won in December, everybody thought the fighting was over."

"That's what we heard in Tennessee too."

"A few stayed here; some went with Fannin to invade Mexico, but most just went home."

"But haven't they heard by now that the Mexican army is here? Why don't they come back and help us?"

"I expect some of them have come back, and they are with Houston somewhere to the east. The others are probably waiting to see what the politicians decide."

"What do you mean?"

"Since September, the two political parties have been arguing about what to do. Obviously, the war party wants war, and the peace party doesn't. Last I heard, neither one has a clear majority. Another problem is that the government is broke, and they can't pay for any soldiers."

The attention of the three was suddenly drawn to Private Micajah Autry, a fellow traveler of Crockett's from Tennessee, who stuck his head in the door. "Captain Baker asks that you join him on top of the chapel."

When Bowie and Crockett arrived, Baker was looking through his glass in the direction of the Goliad road.

"We just saw the Mexican cavalry gallop in on the Gonzales road then out down the Goliad road," Baker reported. "As you can see, that battalion of infantry there," he added, pointing, "is following the cavalry, and we can see more cavalry forming up in Military Plaza."

"What do you think it means, Colonel?" Carey asked

"It might mean that Fannin is close. For sure, it means that Bonham will have a harder time getting back in here."

"What if Bonham can't get back at all? What if he is dead? We have to decide about retreating very soon, before anymore Mexican troops arrive, and we can't get out at all," Crockett said.

"I think you're right, Colonel. If we are going to retreat, we should do it tonight while half their troops are gone from Bexar. Baker, go fetch Travis and meet us in my room."

* * *

When Travis arrived, Bowie saw that he was carrying a letter.

"This one will shame them," Travis said. Listen to this, 'if my countrymen do not rally to my relief, I am determined to perish in the defense of this place, and my bones shall reproach my country for her neglect.'"

"That's great, Colonel Travis, but right now, we need to figure out what we are going to do about staying alive and getting out of here," Bowie said.

"You men are cowards, Colonel Bowie. I'm certain that my letters to Fannin and Houston will bring reinforcements, if we just wait a few more days. We must hold the Alamo at all costs."

"Colonel, we don't have a few days. Seguin's spies reported another nine hundred men and six more cannons have crossed the Rio Bravo at Guerrero. They could be here in two or three days. Santa Anna just sent all his cavalry and a battalion of infantry toward Goliad, and if they find Fannin, they will stop him before he gets here. Right now, we figure Santa Anna only has around seven hundred soldiers left in Bexar and half of them are wearing white. We will never have a better chance to withdraw."

Travis was silently scowling at him as Bowie continued.

"I asked Major Jameson to prepare a plan for our strategic retreat, in case we needed it. Major, explain your plan to Colonel Travis."

"Thank you Colonel Bowie. Captains Baker and Carey will organize and supervise the withdrawal of the one hundred and seventy-nine souls now in the Alamo."

Jameson looked up, as if inviting comments from the others.

"Beginning at two in the morning, we will depart at twelve-minute intervals in groups no larger than ten, including women, children, and slaves. Each group will include at least one man who is familiar with the geography around here acting as leader, and no group will include more than one woman. The groups will head east and south, avoiding roads, and all will re-assemble at Gonzales."

Again, Jameson looked at each man present. Bowie nodded, and he continued.

"Since we do not have enough horses to go around, each group will be entirely mounted or entirely on foot except that all groups that included a woman will be mounted, and men with horses will be encouraged to give them up to women where needed."

Carey, Baker, and Evans nodded. Bowie thought that Travis seemed stoic.

"Colonel Crockett will be responsible for getting Colonel Bowie out, if he needs help, and his group will include Doctor Pollard and the slaves Bettie, Sam, and Charlie."

Crockett nodded.

"Major Evans will see to it that all the cannon barrels are packed to the brim with powder, and a twenty-minute fuse will be stuck in each muzzle. In the powder magazine, a keg of powder will be so fused as well. The major, Captain Samuel C. Blair, and Lieutenant Charles Zanco, will light the fuses and will be the last men out of the Alamo. Are there any questions?"

Bowie was pleased with the plan and said, "Excellent planning Major." He assumed they all thought Jameson got it right when there were no questions or comments.

Then Travis rose. "Just a minute Colonel. I have something to say." Travis was standing behind his chair now.

Feeling frustrated Bowie cursed mentally, then dipped his forehead toward Travis and blinked his eyes.

"What if Fannin, or anybody else comes and we are gone. They will be sitting ducks for Santa Anna with half the walls blown away and no artillery."

Bowie took a deep breath, preparing to reply, however, before he could Evans looked at him and said, "With your permission Colonel Bowie."

Bowie nodded and Evans said. "Colonel Travis, you have never seen or heard anything like the explosions I have planned for this place. For a good twenty miles everyone will hear the booms and see the glow in the dark sky. I think the Mexican soldiers will ride back here immediately and our people will not come any closer until they reconnoiter."

"You may be right Evans, but what about dividing our force. I'm no military genius but I have always heard it is bad to divided your troops."

Baker responded. "That principal would apply if we were facing a battle, but we are trying to avoid one by sneaking out of here."

Realizing that Travis was grasping for straws, Bowie said, "We'd better get busy, we don't have much time."

By ten o'clock that night, the group leaders were selected and informed. There would be eighteen groups, ten mounted and eight not. If everything went well, all the groups with women would be out by four o'clock, everyone else would be out before sunrise, and the powder explosions would serve as reveille for the Mexicans.

* * *

At midnight, Crockett, Baker and Carey called the group leaders together and told them to compare their planned routes, so there would be no conflicts or overlap. They were preparing to inform everyone else about the withdrawal and assign group departure times when they heard a shot from the main gate.

Crockett ran toward it asking, "Who fired that shot?"

"I did, Colonel. There's somebody out there, and not just one."

Crockett climbed a ladder and joined the sentry on top of the Low Barracks, over the main gate. The hoof sounds of many horses echoed in the darkness, then someone yelled, "Shoot the bastard," followed by the sound of a single horse running away.

The sentry shouted, "Who's out there?" and twenty rifles were aimed into the darkness.

Then a voice replied, "Don't shoot again. I'm George Kimbell. We're from Gonzales, and we have a wounded man."

"Show yourselves," the sentry shouted.

Crockett heard the horses approaching, then the riders materialized in the light from the black-oil torches. There appeared to be about thirty of them, and in the group, he recognized private John W. Smith and Captain Albert Martin, couriers that Travis had sent to Gonzales.

"Open the gate and fetch Doctor Pollard," Crockett ordered and climbed down.

Both of the nine-foot oak gates opened, and the Gonzales group rode through. One man had blood dripping from his left boot. Two others helped him down from his horse and sat him on a flat rock near the well. When Pollard arrived, the man was cussing. "Your damn sentry shot me."

Kimbell saluted and reported to Crockett. "We're the Gonzales Ranging Company of Mounted Volunteers. I'm Lieutenant Kimbell."

"What was all that fuss about out there, Lieutenant?"

"A rider intercepted us just after we came through the Alameda. He offered to lead us in. We couldn't see him very well, but his English was perfect, so we thought he was one of your rangers."

"We never send patrol riders out alone, just couriers."

"Well, I guess Smith knows that, and when he yelled for us to shoot him, the man rode off in a hurry."

"I'm sorry about your man's foot, but it sounds like things could have been worse."

"Your arrival may change things for us."

When Crockett turned to see who was talking he saw Travis walking toward him. Crockett's stomach tightened as he thought there could be no worse time for the arrival of reinforcements.

"I knew you men would come, Lieutenant. Was it my letters? How many men did you bring? A hundred? Two hundred? How many more are on their way?"

"There are thirty-two of us, Colonel. We came ahead because most of us have relatives or friends already here."

"That's fine. That's fine. Now how many more are coming? Wait, don't answer that. I want everyone to hear. Crockett send word to the staff officers to gather in my quarters."

"What about Colonel Bowie? Aren't we supposed to meet in his room?"

"I'm in command here. Now, do as I ordered."

When everyone had gathered Travis introduced Kimbell and said, "Now tell us how many men are on their way here."

"We heard that General Houston was heading west with five hundred men, and that Fannin had already left Goliad with his three hundred."

"By God, didn't I tell you that my letters would shame them into coming? This changes everything."

"It does if it's true, Colonel," Crockett said and the others nodded. "Are these facts or just rumors, Lieutenant?"

"That's just what I heard. I can't say for sure."

Crockett thought that Travis seemed to be getting very excited. "I don't care. I'm in command here, and I'm calling off the retreat. We'll have a thousand men here soon, and we can send Santa Anna to hell."

"Colonel Travis. We have everything ready to abandon this place as you were ordered to do by General Houston. Don't you think we would be smarter to leave here and join him? Tonight could be our last chance to get out."

Crockett looked around the room, hoping to get support from the others, but nobody spoke. His stomach tightened even more with fear as he realized he was losing control of the situation.

Travis glared at him but Crockett tried again to bring logic and reason into the discussion.

"What's more, I think that Santa Anna wants us to escape tonight, or he would not have sent so many troops away at the same time. I doubt that he will give us a second chance. If we stay and the reinforcements don't come, we're doomed. Less than two hundred men cannot hope to defend this place, and you know it."

"Private Crockett, didn't you hear the lieutenant say that General Houston is coming to join me? Me. That means the best military mind in Texas has decided that my plan is better than his."

Crockett could only frown when Travis added, "Captain Carey, I'm ordering you to remove the powder from the cannons and reload them with grape and shot. The rest of you make plans to receive eight hundred men who will be arriving soon and report your plans to me in the morning. I can see now that everything is going to work out fine."

***

Arrival of the reinforcements from Gonzales and the belief that many more were on the way, caused morale in the Alamo to soar. The following morning, even Crockett allowed himself a positive outlook.

As he watched the sunrise from the southwest cannon platform he saw Bonham approaching. He walked down the ramp and greeted the traveler who rode in the main gate.

"I would have been here yesterday, but I had to leave the Goliad road to get around the enemy troops," Bonham began.

"I figured it was something like that. Did they slow Fannin down too?" Crockett asked.

"Fannin isn't coming, and as far as I know, neither is anybody else."

Crockett gritted his teeth and his optimism vanished.

"We had better tell Travis."

"What about Bowie?"

"Doc said he collapsed last night and he's still unconscious. Doc said he isn't sure if Jim will wake up this time. I'm trying to keep Travis from finding out."

Soon the command staff was gathered in Travis room and Bonham reiterated his statement to Crockett.

"Explain yourself, sir," Travis demanded.

"Fannin said that Houston was still at Washington-on-the-Brazos, trying to raise an army and waiting for Congress to give him authority over the volunteer militias."

"What about Fannin's men?"

"Fannin said he got your letter, and five days ago he marched from Goliad with three hundred men, four cannons, and plenty of ammunition."

"I told you my letters would work," Travis said.

"But after the first two hundred yards, a wagon broke down, and they spent the balance of the day trying to pull the remaining wagons and cannons across the San Antonio River without enough oxen to do the job. When they camped that night, they forgot to tether the oxen, so by morning, the animals couldn't be found."

"That sounds like Fannin," Travis added. "He never bothers with the details."

"Then they learned that General Urrea had crossed the Rio Bravo at Matamoros with nine hundred infantry and one hundred cavalry. With a crossing that far south, they figured Urrea was on his way to Goliad, so they decided to stay and defend their own position."

Carey quickly did the math. "So, unless men are on their way from somewhere else we haven't thought of, there will only be one hundred eighty-nine of us here to fight Santa Anna."

Just then, Private Jackson J. Rusk began shouting outside the door of Travis's quarters. "Colonel, a new line of Mexican troops is marching into Military Plaza from the west, and it looks like they have at least five cannons in tow. We also saw some of their cavalry coming back in on the Goliad road."

Without opening the door, Travis shouted back. "Thank you for the report, Private."

"Well, Kimbell, it looks like you have gotten us into one hell of mess here. No Fannin. No Houston. Just plenty of enemy soldiers to block a retreat in any direction," Travis said.

Kimbell did not respond.

Crockett knew it was not Kimbell's fault that they were trapped and he believed everyone else did too.

"I got back by staying on the west side of the river then coming in from the north around San Pedro Creek," Bonham concluded. "We might be able to get out that way and head for Goliad."

"Yes, but what if we run into Urrea's force?"

Carey shook his head. "I'm afraid we had better get ready for a fight. If their troops are the ones that Seguin's men reported, then Santa Anna will have two thousand men and eight cannons here by the end of today. That's over ten men for every one of ours."

"Maybe we should move everyone to the chapel to start with and not even try to defend the walls," Baker said.

"That's no good, they know where the powder magazine is. They could fire into it and kill us all at once," Evans said.

"So how will they come at us?" Jameson asked.

"If it was me, I would attack in the dark at the palisade and the main gate. I'd sneak my men up close and BAM; I'd hit that wood fence. Once they get inside, we're done for," Baker said.

"I agree about the palisade, but I think I would spread my men out more, maybe hit the north wall at the same time to divide us between the two ends of the plaza" Carey said.

Crockett could only think about the futility of their comments. As he had explained to Sam, the Alamo was not designed to be defended, especially by less than two hundred men.

"So when will they come?" Evans said anxiously, peering out the window.

"I'd say as soon as all their troops get back from the Goliad road. Maybe as soon as Friday," Baker said.

Travis rubbed his hands together. "If it is going to be that soon, I'd better get started on a letter."

"Yes, Colonel Travis, that sounds like a good idea," Crockett said. "I think the rest of us had better make some plans about where to place the men and what orders to issue," he added, trying to overcome his own feelings of frustration and anger.

"As you say, Private Crockett."

Baker held up a cautioning hand. "Colonel Crockett, I think we should ask Captain Harrison to station your Tennessee boys at the palisade right away, and we should tell the other men to retreat toward that position if the Mexicans get inside the walls."

Every man nodded his agreement except Travis who, without a word, turned his chair to a small desk and began writing.

* * *

When Crockett stepped into the plaza from Travis's room, he found Sam waiting for him.

"Mister Jim say give you this ifn he get real sick."

Sam handed him a folded leaf of parchment. It was not sealed, so Crockett opened it. Then he read it aloud.

"The Alamo, March 3, 1836, Dear General Sam, We are stuck here in the Alamo now because I thought that I could convince Santa Anna to avoid a costly war, and that I could convince you and the others to keep Texas with Mexico. But I never got the chance to do either one. The only real issue between us and the Mexican government is slavery, and I think I have proved that Texas can do better without it. After you win the fight I know that you will hold a high political position, and I hope you will consider what I say. Yours truly, James Bowie P.S. Do not allow Juan Seguin to return here. He is a good man, and you will need him."

Crockett looked at Sam.

"Mister Jim say his horse the fastest and to give it to Mister Juan to ride."

"How sick is Mister Jim?"

"Doc say he real sick."

"Yes, but what do you think?"

Water was coming into Sam's eyes as he replied. "I think he be near dyin' Mister Crockett. He coughin' blood and stuff. He sleep talkin to Miss Ursula an don't never wake up."

Sam wiped his eyes with his sleeves.

"Ifn Mister Jim die I's feared Mister Travis gonna claim me an Bettie is his."

The mention of Travis sparked a rare feeling of rage in Crockett. But why was he angry? He wondered. Was it resentment at being trapped in the Alamo by Travis's obsessive preoccupation with himself, or guilt for not seizing command when it became clear that Bowie was incapable and Travis was incompetent.

Mentally he damned the people in Tennessee for turning him out and Travis for sucking him in. Then he regained control of his emotions.

"I promise I won't let that happen Sam. We'll show everybody your freedom document and it will be alright."

"Can't you just take us to General Houston?"

"It's too late for us to get out."

"But Mister Juan fixin' to."

"That's because he's Mexican and they don't know he is with us."

Sam looked down. "What gonna happen to us?"

"I don't know. Right now all you can do is go back and see if Doc Pollard needs any help with Mister Jim. All any of us can do is wait."

* * *

For the next two days, Crockett observed a steady stream of Mexican troops marching back into Bexar from the Goliad road, but there was yet no sign of preparation for an infantry attack.

As the cannons roared ever closer to the Alamo, Juan Seguin rode out the main gate, headed for Gonzales with the letters to General Houston from Travis and Bowie and other letters, written by the other men to their loved ones while they waited.

No man in the Alamo left his post on the wall any longer than it took him to visit the latrine. The women and slaves delivered their food and water. Some of the men could sleep a little, but most could only cat-nap or doze semi-conscious.

Men with a solitary nature seemed to pass the time quietly. Gregarious men, including Crockett and Pollard, talked.

"You know these men better than anybody, Doc. Why are they still here? Don't they know we haven't got a chance?"

"I have thought about that a lot, David. In fact, I have made a study of it. Forgive me for sounding like a philosopher but I think these are not the kind of men who would spend time thinking about the end of something. I think they are still here by choice, and I'll bet you money, they believe that happy times are just ahead. They were lured to Texas by the vision of a new beginning in the same way that their fathers were lured to America. I think they have two things in common that keep them here: they are not afraid to risk everything to gain more, and they have become fiercely dedicated to each other."

Chapter 21

At five o'clock, in the afternoon on Saturday, March 5, 1836, David Crockett called on William Travis in the Alamo commander's quarters.

"The cannon fire has stopped and there is no sign of an attack. This might be a good time to call the men together and tell them the truth," Crockett said.

Travis looked down to his left, then back up at Crockett. "You're right, ask the commanders to bring all the men down from the walls and roofs and assembled them beside the palisade."

Soon every defender except Travis was standing with his back to the chapel. Crockett noticed that Bowie's men stood as a group around their unconscious leader, who lay on the cot they had carried into the plaza from his room in the Low Barracks.

"I am expecting a major attack at any time," Travis began. "As you know, Santa Anna has moved his artillery closer every night, and it has opened at least one major breach, in the north wall. He has over two thousand troops in Bexar, and he knows how vulnerable we are. The time has come for each man to decide what he is going to do." The men began to murmur, then grumble, and finally, thirty-four-year-old Patrick Henry Herndon from Virginia spoke up. "With respects, Colonel, up to now, you officers have decided things by yourself without asking any of us what we thought. Why are you asking us now?"

"You're right, Private. I was hoping that more men would come to help us, so I thought I was doing the right thing."

"So you're saying there are no more men coming?"

Travis did not respond. Crockett could see that he was looking around and decided that he was having trouble mustering the courage to answer truthfully. Crockett was not surprised. Travis had lied to the men so many times, and presented an idealistic assessment so often, he seemed to have a problem doing otherwise.

Travis looked at Crockett. Crockett gave a slow nod and Travis continued. "Yes, that's what I'm saying. We know Fannin is not coming, and Sam Houston is probably not sending any troops because he didn't want us to fight here in the first place. I'm sorry."

Reality had finally given Travis the slap he had coming, Crockett thought, as more and louder grumbling filled the air. When the men became quiet, Travis spoke again.

"As I see it, each of us has three choices. We can surrender and hope that Santa Anna was just bluffing with his red flag. We can try to escape through their lines tonight, even though they have us surrounded. Or we can face their attack."

"What are you going to do, Colonel?"

"I'm going to stay in the Alamo and fight. I think Santa Anna is probably expecting us to try to escape, and he means to kill us all if we try that, or even if we just surrender. So I want every man who is willing to fight with me to walk over and stand behind me."

The men looked around at each other. Nobody moved. Then Travis pulled his sword and walked over to the first man on his left. He put the dull edge point of his sword down into the dirt in front of the man and walked backward until he reached the last man on his right.

"Now, any man who does not wish to surrender or try to escape, cross over this line."

Again, the men looked at each other, and nobody moved. Then twenty-six-year-old artilleryman Tapley Holland walked across the line. He was followed by Bowie and the men who carried his cot, then David Crockett. Soon all the men had crossed except one.

That man had been standing with Bowie's men. Now when Crockett saw him standing alone, his eyes queried Pollard, who was beside him.

"His name is Louis Moses Rose; he is fifty years old. He was an NCO in Napoleon's army," the doctor whispered.

Crockett looked around. Nobody else moved and he concluded that none of the others would allow himself to follow Rose's example, or, at least, none of them wanted to be the first.

"Thank you men, return to your posts" Travis said.

* * *

Soon the Mexican cannon fire began again. All the defenders had returned to their posts, except those tending Bowie. At their request Crockett and Pollard followed as they carried Bowie's cot into the chapel. Inside the chapel, the only Tejano in their group, Carlos Espalier, turned to address them.

"I have found a place to hide Colonel Bowie where he will be safe."

Espalier looked down at Bowie, still unconscious on the cot.

"My family have lived in Bexar for over a hundred years. When I was a boy my grandfather told me that the water in the Alamo well comes from an aquifer that runs under it. He said the aquifer also cools a small room that the priests carved out of the limestone and used as a spring house and refuge from marauding Indians."

Crockett thought the face of the seventeen year old showed understandable pride as he spoke.

"I didn't really believe the story about the room until yesterday, when I found it."

The mouths of several onlookers dropped open.

"It is under a trap door about nine inches down in the middle room on the left. I think it is large enough to hold Colonel Bowie on a pallet, if we lay it diagonally."

Accompanied by Crockett and Doctor Pollard, the men wasted no time ensconcing Bowie in the small room below ground. Two men, Bonham and William Mills, dropped through the thirty-inch square shaft into the six-foot square room, arranged a straw mattress and blankets on the floor, and awaited Bowie.

When the doctor checked his pulse and respiration Bowie awoke. "Give me my knife," he said.

The knife was fetched and given to him. Pollard dosed him with laudanum. Then he was lowered through the shaft by Charles Heiskell, William Lewis, and Robert McKinney. The dusty air made everybody cough.

After closing the ventilated trap door and replacing the covering rocks, they laid a thin rug over it. They brought in the furnishings from Bowie's room in the Low Barracks and arranged things to look as if he had just stepped out. Then everyone left the chapel except Crockett, Pollard and Sam.

Crockett motioned for Sam to sit in the chair by the small desk. "Sam, here is a pistol to protect yourself. I want you to stay in this room, no matter what you hear or what happens outside. If anybody asks you where Mister Jim is, you tell them he went out to fight. They won't harm you if you tell them you are a slave, and when they are gone, you take Mister Jim out of here."

Then Pollard added, "Twice a day, you make him take some water and some of this laudanum. However, don't do it when anyone is around. Do you understand?"

"Yes, sir. I is to stay here and dose him twice a day. If anyone ask where he is, I say he went out to fight. When they leave, I is to take him out. They won't hurt me because I is a slave."

"That's right, Sam. I'll come back as often as I can."

Pollard walked out, but Crockett remained. "You know, when I was a boy Sam, I had a pet raccoon. Most of the time, he played stupid, but every time I put food out for my dog, that coon would trick that dog into chasing him, then circle back and steal his food. There is something about you, Sam, that reminds me of that raccoon. You have the same alert look in your eyes."

Sam looked down.

"This may be the last time we talk, so you don't have to play the stupid darkie with me anymore."

Sam looked directly at him and Crockett continued.

"I know how smart you are, Sam. That is why I know you will understand this. The man that General Santa Anna most wants to kill here is Jim Bowie because he thinks that Jim double-crossed him. Now, if you want to get back at Jim because he was your master, this is your chance. But if you love him like he loves you, you will keep Santa Anna from finding him and, when it is safe, you will take him to the Veramendi Palace. They will hide him and get him a doctor."

Still silent, Sam leaned back in his chair and hooked his thumbs under his arm-pits.

"I hope you get to New Orleans and find a way to go north, Sam. Good luck and God bless you."

Before Sam looked away again, enough of a smile bloomed in his eyes to tell Crockett that he was right, and Sam understood.

As Crockett walked out he turned and saw Sam lean over and put his face in his enormous hands.

* * *

At the Alamo in the pre-dawn of Sunday, March 6, 1836, Crockett was dozing against the chapel wall beside a fire near the palisade. The skies were clear and the temperature had fallen to the upper forties.

The women had kept the fires burning in the plaza, but all the men were at their posts, spread along the hundreds of feet of walls and perimeter rooftops, most of them away from any warmth.

The plaza smelled of burning oak, body odor, cigars, and gun-powder. Since the Mexican artillery had gone silent at ten the night before, few men in the Alamo were awake to notice the smells.

Just after five o'clock, Crockett heard a Mexican bugle to the southeast give the order to charge. Before he could stand, the same southern breeze blew in the sound of a band playing a Moorish fire and death call he knew as "El Deguello". Then the cannon fire started from all directions.

Crockett had no time to prepare his mind for what was happening, roused from his sleep, he began to fight instinctively.

Everywhere he looked he saw Mexican soldiers gathered around the walls, shooting up at the men. Soon he saw Mexican soldiers inside the Alamo and the Texans who were still alive falling back toward his position.

* * *

By six-thirty the sun was coming up quietly. No living Texan or Tejano soldier could be seen as Sam was pushed along by a Mexican soldier with a bayonet. Then Sam saw a familiar face.

From that first Veramendi dinner party five years before, and from Jim Bowie's wedding, he recognized Juan Almonte. From the expression on the face of the Mexican officer, Sam could tell that Almonte recognized him too.

"Where are you taking this man?" Almonte asked.

"I have orders to shoot him," the young corporal replied.

"Corporal, you know we don't execute negro slaves."

"Yes, sir, but we found him with a gun."

"That's alright, leave him with me. I'll take the responsibility."

"Yes, sir, Colonel."

"I believe your name is Sam," Almonte asked.

Sam dipped his forehead.

"I am looking for the bodies of Travis, Crockett, and your master for General Santa Anna to inspect, and you will help me find them."

Sam nodded again. "Yes Master."

"Where is Bowie?" Almonte asked as he began turning over bodies and looking at faces.

"He go out to fight," Sam replied.

They found Travis first, lying beside the breech in the north wall with a bullet hole in the middle of his forehead, and his sword lying near his right hand. His eyes were open, and his face revealed his surprise.

"Travis?"

Sam nodded.

With Sam beside him, still searching for Crockett and Bowie, Almonte looked at the face of every defender on every wall, in every room, and on every square foot of open ground.

Then he walked around the outside of the walls and found seven defenders who had fallen there. As he viewed the bodies Sam saw him making marks on a piece of parchment.

Approaching the front door of the chapel he found more bodies to the right of the open doorway. After adding them to his written tally, he looked into the still dark corner to the left of the doorway and noticed yet another body, face down, this one dressed in buckskin. Using his right foot, he rolled the corpse over, revealing the face.

"Crockett?"

"Yes Master."

"Where was Bowie the last time you saw him?" Almonte asked.

"I ain't seed him soon. Last was over there," Sam pointed toward the southwest corner.

Almonte grasped Sam's wrist and led him inside. "Stand here," he said to Sam.

There was a body on the floor, and three more visible on the cannon platform at the east end of the chapel. He studied the face of the man on the floor first and noticed an extinguished torch a few inches from the man's hand. Near the torch, he saw the beginning of a line of black powder that trailed toward the first room on the left, the powder magazine. Someone had swept away the part of the powder line that entered the room.

Next, Sam watched Almonte climb to the cannon platform, examine the other three bodies, walk back down, and step into the last side room on the left. He felt a little nervous knowing that his sister Bettie was in that room.

Emerging from the room Almonte stepped back and motioned to a private, standing at attention beside the entrance.

"I believe your name is Esparza. Is that correct, Private?"

"Yes, sir."

"Alright, Private, I want you to go tell Captain Castaneda there are women and children here."

"Yes, sir."

"Then I want you to report back."

"Yes, sir."

"I believe I heard your battalion commander say that you had a brother fighting for the enemy."

"Yes, sir," Esparza said, looking down. Sam thought he looked a little sheepish and was probably not accustomed to talking with a colonel.

"Private, I think your brother is one of the men up there on the platform. When you come back, you may want to bury him before they burn his body with the others."

"I'm grateful to you, sir. I will do that."

Sam was impressed with the compassion Almonte had shown for this lowly soldier, hoping he and the other slaves would receive the same kind of consideration, as Crockett had said they would.

Almonte walked back to Sam. "The women in there know you, don't they?"

"Yes, Master," Sam responded submissively again, taking no chances.

"I want you to tell them to not be afraid and to come out here."

"Yes, master."

Sam walked into the sacristy room and, in a moment, he walked out, leading Bettie and a line that included nine women, ten children, and Charlie.

"Now I want them to follow this soldier and wait outside. They will not be harmed."

After these survivors walked away, Almonte took Sam by the wrist again and led him into Bowie's new room. He sat on the chair by the small desk and motioned for Sam to sit on the cot.

"Do you remember me?"

Sam feigned a confused expression. "Yes, sir."

"My general hates your master. If I cannot show him your master's body, he will make it very hard on me and I will make it very hard on you. Is this your master's room, Sam?"

Sam nodded.

"Where is your master?"

His mind was racing. He understood that, for the Mexican general, Bowie personified the rebellion and he was sure that the Mexicans knew that Bowie had been in the Alamo. Did he dare tell Almonte that Jim had escaped or gone for help? He thought not.

"He went out to fight."

Almonte stood, walked over and put his nose an inch from Sam's. "DO NOT LIE TO ME, SAM."

Sam shuddered.

"IF YOU LIE TO ME AGAIN, YOU WILL BE SHOT."

"I'm a slave. You ain't supposed to hurt me."

"YOU HAD A GUN, SAM; YOU ARE A SOLDIER. WE KILL SOLDIERS. NOW, WHERE IS YOUR MASTER?"

For the first time in his thirty-nine years, Sam was faced with making a life-and-death choice for and about himself. There was no one to help him make it, no master, no paw, no maw, no sweetheart, nobody.

Conflicting memories of Bowie, the inconsiderate master, the caring friend, converged in Sam's mind. He felt tormented. Crockett said Bowie loved him. Did he? Did he love Bowie? How close to freedom was he?

Was Bowie conscious? Was he even alive down in that hole? If he was alive and Sam was shot, could he survive until somebody found him? If he was going to die anyhow, was it better to give him up or leave him down there? What would Bowie want him to do? A month before, Jim had told him to save himself. Would he say that now?

Sam felt angry, wishing he had found the courage to reveal himself to Bowie so the two men could have shared their thoughts and feelings as equals. Sam thought that such an exchange might have given him a basis for deciding their fate now. He yearned for guidance one way or the other.

"They is others like me, the other slaves, you gonna shoot them too?"

"Not if you tell me where your master is. If you tell me, I'll see that you, and the other slaves, get away safe."

"Will you see that we all get to New Orleans by boat? It will not be safe for us to travel overland."

Almonte nodded. However, his face reflected sudden surprise.

Sam took a deep breath, fearing that his grammatically correct sentence had revealed too much.

"Will you be safe there?"

"I have a freedom document, and Bowie put money in a bank there for us." Sam felt strange saying his former master's name without his title, master or mister.

"I think Ursula would take great pleasure in knowing that Senior Bowie not only set you free but also provided for your future welfare."

Sam was not sure why Almonte would make such a positive comment about the man he was trying to convince him to sacrifice. Perhaps he was speaking truthfully and could be trusted.

"Where is Bowie, Sam?"

"If I tell you, will you give him medical attention and spare his life?"

"Why, is he sick?"

"He needs a doctor."

"Was he wounded?"

"No."

"I can get him a doctor, but only the General can spare his life."

"He told me that the General was coming here to kill him."

"I don't know."

Sam hung his head and put his face in his hands for what seemed like an eternity, then he raised his head, rose from the cot, walked over to the rug and pulled it away. Lifting the covering rocks he revealed the trap door. Then he sat on the floor in a corner and put his face in his hands again.

Almonte spoke to a soldier in the chapel. "Bring the bodies of Travis and Crockett inside the chapel and lay them on the nave floor, then summon the regimental surgeon. Send a man to notify General Santa Anna that I have two bodies ready for his inspection, and that Bowie may still be alive."

While he waited for the general, Almonte asked Sam the names of the other slaves. Then he wrote out a document and handed it to Sam, who scanned it quickly.

"Give this to the first officer you see. It says to transport you, Bettie, Joe, and Charlie to El Copano, then by boat to New Orleans."

Sam glared. "I know what is says, Colonel. I read and write Spanish too."

"Very well, you may leave as soon as the general sees Bowie."

Sam walked back to the corner and sat with his face in his hands.

* * *

A group of Mexican soldiers brought Bowie up gently from the priest's refuge and laid him on his cot. Awake, he kept his eyes closed while he listened to learn what was happening around him. His blanket was covered with blood that trailed from the corners of his mouth, but he was still breathing normally.

By the time Santa Anna arrived, the Mexican army doctor had Bowie sitting up. He opened his eyes but kept his arms and hands under his blanket.

Through the doorway, Bowie saw Santa Anna pause briefly and look at the bodies of Crockett and Travis, then enter his room. Concentrating on the Mexican dictator, Bowie did not notice Sam, sitting in the corner.

"I hear you have killed every fighting man on our side, General," Bowie said weakly and coughed.

"Every man but you, Senor Bowie," Santa Anna replied with a smile.

Bowie sensed that Santa Anna now expected him to bargain for his life, so he counter-punched. "I know you are going to kill me too, General, but I want to tell you something before you do."

Santa Anna scowled. "I am not interested in what you have to say. I am only interested in knowing where the other rebel dogs are. There were only one hundred eighty-nine of you here, and I know there are many more, somewhere. Where are they, and why did they not come here to help you?"

"I don't think you will want to find them, General," Bowie said, taunting the egomaniacal Mexican leader and feeling satisfied by the defensive expression his taunt produced on the tyrant's face.

"And why is that?"

Before Bowie spoke again, he coughed deeply, and more blood trickled from the right corner of his mouth, following the dried maroon path already there. "

"You made a big mistake, killing all these men. Now their friends will be angry about what you have done here, and they will never stop fighting you."

Bowie coughed again and continued to provoke his avowed enemy. "You will lose the fight because you think you are smarter than everybody else, and you are not. You have planted the seeds of your own defeat."

The Other Rose of Texas

Gritting his teeth, El Presidente responded, "You are gambling with your life, Senor."

"Hell man, I'm dead already."

Suddenly, Bowie flung off the blanket that covered him, revealing his knife with the dull edge in his right palm, and with his last bit of strength, he threw it. The knife flew straight and true, turning twice in the air. Had Santa Anna not dodged it, the point would have stuck in his right eye, but he moved aside, and it only nicked his right ear lobe.

"Almonte, matarlo y quemar su cuerpo con el resto," he instructed, touched his ear and turned away.

As Santa Anna exited the room, Almonte nodded to the two soldiers standing on either side of Bowie's cot. They stepped forward and raised their rifles preparing to plunge their bayonets into Bowie's heart.

But Sam was quicker, even from his corner. He covered Bowie's body with his own and when their blades came down they drove through his back and deep into his own heart.

"Sam, my brother," Bowie cried.

"Los guardias," Almonte shouted.

Two more Mexican soldiers rushed in. It took all four to roll Sam's massive dead hulk off of Bowie and onto the floor.

"Matarlo y quemar su cuerpo con el resto, Almonte said, borrowing Santa Anna's words.

The same two soldados stepped forward and completed their assigned task.

However, Jim Bowie felt no pain as his mind mercifully raised him to a place high above the tortured body on his cot, where Ursula, a red rose in her hair, was waiting to take his hand.

The End

Coda

The practice of slavery in Texas did not stop until the end of the American civil war in 1865, twenty-nine years after the fall of the Alamo. During this period, as an independent republic, as one of the United States of America, and as one of the Confederate States of America, Texas remained in turmoil.

Little evidence exists that Jim Bowie ever tried to prevent or abolish slavery anywhere, or of any tangible results, if he did try. Yet it is true that, after he moved to Texas in 1830, he never again earned his living buying and selling slaves as he had in Louisiana before he came to Texas.

However, much evidence does exist that his well-documented decision to stand at the Alamo, rather than destroy it as he had been ordered, was one of the three key factors that brought about the birth of Texas as an independent republic.

The other two key factors were Sam Houston's leadership in delaying battle against the Mexican army until he could face them successfully, and the fierce dedication of the fighters who avenged the Alamo heroes, both at San Jacinto.

Why did Bowie decide to wait at the Alamo for the Mexican army? As our story suggests, did he think he could negotiate with Santa Anna to keep Texas as a possession of Mexico and free of slaves, and did he believe he could convince his fellow Texans to free their slaves and pay them wages if it meant a war with Mexico could be avoided? The known facts support these possibilities.

But why would Bowie have reversed his early position on slavery in this way? No proof exists that his wife, Ursula, was a devout abolitionist, or that she influenced his views on slavery. However, her father was a well-known liberal, and she was raised in a country that fought a ten-year war for independence from Spain and prohibited slavery in its first constitution.

Regardless of his reasons for making the fateful decision, Bowie's choice to stand at the Alamo gave Sam Houston extra time to raise an army, and the soldiers of that army fought like demons against the Mexican army to avenge their brother Texans who died at Goliad and in the Alamo.

If Ursula's memory or the events and circumstances of her life influenced Jim Bowie to make the stand, then her role in gaining Texas independence was at least as significant as Emily (West) Morgan's, who is called *The Yellow Rose of Texas*. Does Ursula Bowie deserve to be called *The Other Rose of Texas*? Yes.

* * *

Our story is based on reports of actual events in the lives of our characters, when and where published facts could be found. The following provides information about the main facts used in each chapter of *The Other Rose of Texas*.

Throughout the Story (from The Handbook of Texas)
When grown, Bowie was described by his brother John J. as "a stout, rather raw-boned man, of six feet height, weighed 180 pounds." He had light-colored hair, keen grey eyes "rather deep set in his head," a fair complexion, and high cheek-bones. Bowie had an "open, frank disposition," but when aroused by an insult, his anger was terrible.

During his lifetime, he had been described by his old friend Caiaphas K. Ham as "a clever, polite gentleman . . . attentive to the ladies on all occasions . . . a true, constant, and generous friend . . . a foe no one dared to undervalue and many feared." Slave trader, gambler, land speculator, dreamer, and hero, James Bowie in death became immortal in the annals of Texas history.

Chapter 1: Jim Bowie was born on April 10, 1796. In 1812, when he was fifteen years old, he lived on a cotton plantation near Opelousas, Louisiana, with his parents, three brothers and three sisters, whose names are given correctly in the story. A forth brother died young.

Chapter 2: In January 1815, Jim and his older brother, Rezin P., left home to join Andrew Jackson's forces at war with the British in New Orleans. After the war, they traded in slaves, stolen from ships in the Caribbean and Gulf of Mexico by pirate Jean Laffite, and sold at a slave market on Galveston Island (a.k.a. Snake Island).

Chapter 3: In the late 1820s, Bowie speculated in land in southern Louisiana; he lived in New Orleans, enjoying its many pleasures.

Chapter 4: James Bowie's father died in 1821. James and Rezin P. also made money in land speculation, working with local planters. Always ambitious, Jim Bowie gambled for money, and was always deep in debt. In 1826, Bowie met Rapides parish sheriff and local banker, Norris Wright, in Alexandria. Wright refused to make a loan that Bowie requested. There was a fight, and Wright fired point-blank at Bowie, wounding him. After the fight, Rezin P. gave his brother Jim a large butcher knife to carry.

Chapter 5: On September 19, 1827, near Natchez, Mississippi, Jim Bowie was part of the Sandbar Fight. The details of the fight are as given in the story. James was engaged to Cecelia Wells when she died on September 7, 1829, in Alexandria, two weeks before their wedding.

Chapter 6: On February 20, 1830, Bowie took the oath of allegiance to Mexico at Nacogdoches. He was thirty-four years old and in his prime. Jim Bowie carried letters of introduction to Juan Martin de Veramendi and Juan N. Seguin, two rich and powerful Mexicans in the state of Coahuila y Tejas.

Chapter 7: In San Antonio, Bowie posed as a rich man and was baptized into the Catholic Church, through the sponsorship of the Veramendi family.

Chapter 8: Jim Bowie traveled to the state capital in Saltillo with William H. Wharton and Mrs. Wharton, Isaac Donoho, Caiaphas K. Ham, and several slaves. He left Saltillo with fifteen or sixteen large land grants. Jim Bowie's "land grab" infuriated Stephen F. Austin.

Chapter 9: James and his brothers established the Arcadia sugar plantation near Thibodaux, Louisiana. They sold the Arcadia land and slaves for $90,000. Through his friend, Angus McNeill of Natchez, Jim Bowie purchased a textile mill for $20,000.00 and had it shipped to Saltillo, Mexico, and re-assembled. Jim Bowie borrowed $1,879 from Ursula de Veramendi's father and $750 from her grandmother for a honeymoon trip to New Orleans and Natchez.

Chapter 10: On April 25, 1831, in San Antonio, Jim Bowie married nineteen year old Ursula de Veramendi. He had declared his age as thirty-two (he was actually thirty-five). As a boy, Jim Bowie liked to hunt, fish, ride wild horses and alligators, and trap bears.

Chapter 11: After he was married, Jim Bowie spent very little time at home. Jim Bowie became interested in the "lost" Los Almagres Mine. Accurate details of his search for it and his encounter with Indians are given in the story. Elected colonel of a group of citizen rangers Bowie subsequently left Gonzales with twenty-six men to search for the hostile Indians he previously encountered.

Chapter 12: In 1833, Jim Bowie's wife, his two children, and her parents traveled to Monclova, Mexico.

Chapter 13: In September, 1833, Ursula Bowie and her parents died of cholera at Monclova. Bowie was in Natchez, ill with yellow fever.

Chapter 14: On March 9, 1833, Monclova became the state capital of Coahuila y Tejas.

Chapter 15: New Mexican laws passed in 1834 and 1835 removed the barriers to speculation in Texas land. On September 1, 1835, Stephen Austin arrived home from prison in Mexico City. After being elected to command the volunteer Texican army, Austin called for open rebellion against Mexico. On October 3, 1835, Santa Anna abolished all state governments in Mexico. At dawn on October 28, 1835, Jim Bowie led a victorious battle against the Mexican army at Mission Concepcion. Noah Smithwick called him a born leader. On November 18, 1835, Jim Bowie's men captured a pack-train loaded with bales of grass for Mexican army livestock during what was later called the "Grass Fight."

Chapter 16: On January 19, 1836, Bowie rode into the Alamo from Goliad with thirty men and orders from General Houston to destroy the fortifications there. On January 20, 1836, Colonel James C. Neill commanded seventy-eight men in the Alamo. He reported that Texas volunteers had taken most of the munitions and supplies for the Matamoros expedition led by Colonel James Fannin. On

February 2, 1836, Jim Bowie wrote Governor Smith stating that he planned to hold the Alamo. David Crockett rode into the Alamo with twelve men on February 8, 1836, raising garrison strength to 150 men.

Chapter 17: Lieutenant-Colonel Travis arrived in Bexar with thirty men on February 3, 1836. Jim Bowie's father had a brother named David. On February 11, 1836, Neill passed Alamo command to Travis and left. The volunteers elected Jim Bowie as their commander.

Chapter 18: On February 23, 1836, the Mexican army arrived in San Antonio de Bexar and William Travis sent a dispatch to Goliad asking Fannin for help. On February 24, 1836, Jim Bowie collapsed from illness.

Chapter 19: On February 25, 1836, couriers were sent out, including John W. Baylor to Goliad, Charles Despallier to Gonzales, and Robert Brown. A force of approximately three hundred Mexican troops crossed the San Antonio River at the Old Mill Ford and tried to attack the Alamo main gate from La Villita with a single cannon. The naming of the San Antonio River was as described in our story. Alamo sharpshooters were highly effective as described in our story and prevented the Mexican army from using the Commerce Street footbridge. Supplies of food, water, wood, and ammunition in the Alamo were as described in our story. On February 26, 1836, Alamo defenders burned many houses in La Villita so they could not be used for cover by the Mexican army. On February 27, 1836, James Butler Bonham rode to Goliad seeking reinforcements.

Chapter 20: On March 2, 1836, around one in the morning, a group of thirty-two men arrived from Gonzales bringing Alamo strength to one hundred eighty-nine men. Despite the fact that he was a slave-owner, Sam Houston's strong Unionism and opposition to the extension of slavery alienated the Texas Legislature and other southern States.

Chapter 21: On March 5, 1836, according to Louis Moses Rose, William Travis drew a line in the dirt and asked the men in the Alamo to cross it and stay and fight. On March 6, 1836, the Mexicans attacked before dawn, and killed all 189 defenders in the Alamo. The battle is described accurately in our story. Santa Anna asked to see the corpses of Bowie, Travis, and Crockett.

Dean Kirkpatrick

The Other Rose of Texas

Dean Kirkpatrick